THE

PATH

OF A

LOGICAL

LIAR

a novel

FIRST U.S. EDITION

Designed by Ebook Launch

Library of Congress Control Number: 2021922192

ISBN: 978-0-578-25741-9

To my sisters. I love all three of you to The Grove and back.

AVA

I was properly ecstatic when I received my NYU admissions folder in the mail my senior year of high school. After months of anxiously waiting and checking the steel mailbox on our front lawn too many times, it finally came. Tucked away in the thick envelope addressed to Ava Ruth Campbell was a letter that I was accepted. Almost like all of the nights I spent studying at home instead of staying out late with the local kids had finally paid off. It had led to *this* moment.

It was a literal dream come true when I held that purple packet in my hand, so when everything happened the summer before my first year of college, I unwillingly deferred my admission. It was the hardest phone call I ever had to make. I had put it off for so long, dreading the finality of it, that when the nasal-sounding woman at the NYU admissions office called to get an update, I knew that this was it. As much as I dreaded having to do this, and as much as I didn't want to accept my fate, I had told them I was unable to join.

I spent my freshman and sophomore years back home using all that downtime to get strong and healthy again, but that NYU dream was still big and bright in my heart. I can almost describe it as a yearning, pressure-like sensation in my chest. It made me angry every time I thought about where I was supposed to be instead of at home in Arcata, California. I had waited months for the day that I would receive the all-clear from my team of doctors. When that day finally came and they concluded I was healthy and stable enough to attend school across the country, I was bursting at the seams like a too-tight sweater. My mother watched from the door post of my bedroom as I happy danced, listening to my favorited Spotify playlist at full blast. I'm positive her eyes were wet with tears.

I was so lost in the joy of it all that when I eagerly picked up the phone and called the NYU office, it was already after hours; I forgot about the time difference. Nevertheless, first thing the next morning at the literal crack of dawn, I was officially enrolled for the upcoming fall semester and had earned a spot in one of the many sponsorships I had applied to. It was surreal.

— ⁓ —

The bustling JFK airport's intercom ignites as a little chime goes off. A female staff member makes a loud announcement through the speakers.

"All passengers from Flight 091 coming in from San Luis Obispo, your baggage will be at carousel five. I repeat, Flight 091, your baggage is at carousel five."

I am damp from the wet heat that comes with a New York summer, making my way to carousel five to pick up what is pretty much everything I own. I spot my blue luggage and use all my strength to lift the two bags. My heart flutters when, for the first time ever, I hail a classic yellow New York City taxi cab. After a forty-five-minute drive, where I pathetically poke my head out of the passenger window like an excited puppy, we pull up to a small apartment building in Tribeca. This sponsorship is no joke. I hurriedly empty my luggage from the trunk and turn toward the driver. I'm displeasingly shocked at my total.

"Sixty dollars?!" I exclaim.

He takes my money and mumbles an unwelcoming "Welcome to New York, kid."

Gee, thanks.

I lug my baggage up the echoed granite stairwell to the third floor, and make my way to apartment 303. When I slip the key into the top lock and open the door to a small studio apartment, my jaw drops. This place is ridiculous. Holy shit. After unpacking the essentials I'll need for the next few days, I put on my NYU sweatshirt like a giant dork before FaceTiming my family. When they hugged me goodbye at the airport this morning, I got a list of stern instructions from both my parents and my brothers. Mom answers the call on the second ring.

"*Mija*, we were worried about you! Why didn't you call sooner!" my sweet, overbearing mother yells, as if I'm across the house. I tell her that she doesn't have to scream into the phone for me to hear her and apologize for not calling as soon as I landed.

"Do you like my sweatshirt, Mama?" I grin widely and fill the iPhone frame with the purple sweatshirt I'll be living in this year. It wasn't an easy road getting myself to this place, so if I want to wear my pride on my chest, I'll do as I damn well please.

"You look beautiful in purple, baby," she says with a melancholy smile on her face.

I'm sure Mama's struggling with me being gone, the last one of us to move out. I'm her baby, as she's always said, but my parents know what NYU means to me, so to compensate for my absence, I'm sure to receive countless phone calls. It'll relieve the homesickness I'm sure to experience because my family is my life.

After hanging up the FaceTime call, I jump in the shower to wash off the grime from the seven-hour flight and, naturally, spend the duration of my scrubbing crowding my head with thoughts of starting at a new school in two days. Not just any school. N-Y-freaking-U. I'm so nervous, it hurts. But this is going to be good. I need this year, a year away from all the mistakes I've made. A year away from constant reminders of what a disgrace I was, still am. Not that I can escape them if I tried.

AVA

A sliver of sunlight peeks through the white eyelet curtains, and squinting the brightness away, I groggily wake up in my new apartment for the first time and grin. This new life hits me like a bore.

I don't know the first thing about living in New York City, nor what it's like being a real university student, so that's what I set out to do today. It's my last free day before I'm consumed with an overload of reading and late nights spent yawning into a textbook, so let's get the show on the road. After brushing my teeth, taking my medication, and pocketing some cash for a metro card, I Google search the subway schedule while locking the front door of my apartment and head into the humid air. It's so unfamiliar, I'm forced to take a step back. Beads of sweat immediately form on my forehead and upper lip.

I buy a few towels, some groceries, and last-minute school supplies before calling Bridget on the way up the apartment stairs when I get home. Home! Ah!

"HELLO, AUDREY HEPBURN!"

I pull the phone away from my ear, roll my eyes, and groan.

"Hey, Bridge. *Don't* call me that. What's up?" I laugh at my best friend's unmatched lunacy.

"How's NYC, my little college chica?" She spells out the letters. There's no doubt in my mind that the natives of New

York don't say N-Y-C, so I make a mental note to just not. Like, ever.

"It's hot, busy, and confusing. I took a train to Target today." I tell Bridget all about the apartment and my tiring day running errands. "I wish I had Connor here. I wouldn't be sweating carrying all this stuff upstairs if he was." Connor is the youngest of my three older brothers; he's twenty-four, four years my senior. I overhear Bridget's babies yelling for her in the background before she tells me she has to go.

"Ugh, they're screaming. Let's talk tomorrow? I miss you, babe. OKAY, I'M COMING!" I chuckle when she hangs up, already missing my best friend more than words can describe. It'll be hard not having her in New York with me, but I know she's only a call away, because she always has been.

GRANT

The day I can truly admit I hit rock bottom, I am startled awake by a rush of cold air and notice Dina's shadow hovering over me. I am fully in the nude.

"What do you think you're doing?" I hear her voice in the distance, a mad hangover causing the sounds of a pounding construction site to go off in my head. *Just one* is never that when I go out with Louis and the rest of the group. I knew that and still went.

"What do you me——"

Dina and I both turn our heads at the noise interrupting this awfully awkward conversation, Hannah's long legs strutting out of my bathroom, her hair wet and a towel covering her naked body. I vaguely remember that she came over last night, but I was piss drunk, high too, so I couldn't tell you if I called her or vice versa. Whatever. I turn back to Dina when she speaks.

"Seriously, Grant?" Dina exclaims disapprovingly. Her tone of voice feels shitty. I think she may be the only one whose opinion actually matters to me at this point in my meager life. How sad is that? I lay my head back when Dina takes matters into her own very capable hands once Hannah is dressed.

"You. Out. Now. Lenny downstairs will drive you home."

Hannah rolls her eyes but grabs her phone and purse, heading for the penthouse door.

"Call me, Grant! Good morning, Dina!" she calls out in a singsong voice before slamming the door shut. I swear I could keep it in my pants from her annoying Barbie voice itself.

"Now, answer my question," Dina hisses, turning back to me. "What the hell do you think you're doing on this fine morning, Grant Wilder?" With eyebrows raised, she challenges me for a reply.

"Dina, I'm lying ass naked in my bed with a ginormous hangover and the most beautiful secretary in the world hovering above me. I clearly don't know what you're talking about. What's going on?"

She rolls her eyes at my attempt at sweet-talking her because Dina is the only one it never works on. "When are you going to finally start taking responsibility, Grant?" she mutters, putting an opened palm on her forehead in frustration. "I don't get paid enough for this."

I rack my brain for possibilities as to why she's so damn angry with me but come up with nothing. "You're gonna have to tell me what I did wrong this time. Also, can I please get that blanket back?" I ask, nodding toward the white duvet clenched in her hand.

"You had a meeting today," she states crossly, throwing the covers back over me. "Your father and his associates waited at Gianni's for you for over an hour."

I jolt upright and squeeze my eyes shut. "*Fuck.*" I totally forgot about that. Damn it.

"Yeah, fuck is right."

I'd been asking Dad for weeks to set up a meeting with potential partners for a company I'm interested in starting. I graduated from UPenn with a bachelor's in engineering before grad school but haven't done much with it. I figured I'd put it to use and found interest in the metal restoration world. It's a billion-dollar industry. Up my alley, I suppose.

Apparently, that meeting I asked for was today at Gianni's, the Italian restaurant near Dad's office. On any weekday in New York City, that is where you'll find *the* people. Politicians, millionaires, billionaires. From Wall Street to the entertainment industry to the mayor's office, anyone who is anyone could be there signing contracts; talking business; making deals. I royally screwed this up.

"Your father expects you at the house in ninety minutes," Dina says sternly. "And go shower! You reek like sex!"

The two aspirins that Dina hands me before clicking her black patent leather heels to the door are a godsend. After twenty, I'm showered and sitting in the back of Lenny's black sedan, a hot coffee in the cup holder to my left, when he hands me a brown lunch bag of Mom's famous blueberry muffins. Are these laced? Because nothing is allowed to taste this good.

"Good morning, son," Lenny gloats jokingly when I lean back into the plush leather seat. "Long night?"

"I'm fucked, aren't I?"

"Something like that. Hey, I thought you were done with her," he inquires about Hannah. Lenny has been the one to drive her home from my place more often than I'd like to admit.

"I thought so too, but she passes the time."

He shakes his head and wishes me luck when we reach my parents' Scarsdale home an hour later.

I'm sitting in Dad's office being lectured for acting juvenile, for not having my life together, being told to "grow up!" I can't say he's wrong because I tell that to myself every morning in the very big and egotistic mirror in my master bathroom.

"You're almost twenty-eight years old, Grant! You wasted the last few years of your life. This is ridiculous!" I admit and acknowledge to my father that I fucked up. I promise that I'll show up next time. "Next tam? There isn't always gon be a next tam, Grant! For Chrast sake!" His Texan accent is thicker when he yells. I look back at my father in shame because he's right—what am I doing with my life?

"We gave you a good laf, Grant, but you can't live off the trust forever. You have to start earning things for yourself. What did you go to school for? Your mother and I didn't raise you to act privileged and spoiled, son. You know that." *Unlike your classmates*, I assume he holds back from saying. I look at my father and nod respectfully.

"You're right, Dad. I'm really sorry. I didn't mean to embarrass you today." I can only imagine his obvious angst and the awkward excuse he gave his colleagues for me. It must have been humiliating. His voice finally calms.

"Grant, you have the potential to start something big. Your idea is good, son. They were interested when I explained a small portion of it to them, but it's time you start taking accountability and make better choices. I cannot bail you out again." When Dad realizes that I'm not going to come at him with a rebuttal, that I agree when he tells me I'm being an idiot in his own kinder way, he gives me a tight hug and a slap on the back. I think he feels bad for yelling at me, so I slap his back too. I thank my father at his office door before we walk together toward the patio to eat a delicious lunch with the chef herself, my elegant and classy mother. I kiss her cheek after lunch before heading home to the city in the back of Lenny's car.

My father is right. I need to do something with my life. It's been years since I held down a job; since I went a couple of days without partying and getting high or hooking up with some girl I don't know. I make a promise to my father, but more so to myself, to follow through with the idea and to execute it soundly.

Within weeks after cashing in my last favor with Dad, my partners and I sign contracts, buy office space, and hire

employees to get the business up from the ground. Dad is re-
tiring soon, and I'm stealing Dina from his office. That woman
can't go a single day in her life without working, so she joins
me as we venture into this new world. Only a few short months
later, we're up and running. Safe to say that with Dina by my
side, everything will stay on schedule, and I know she'll whoop
my ass into shape when I need it.

—〰—

I slip into the back of Fisher's firetruck-red sports car after
work, though I'm not exactly sure why a private investigator
insists on driving something so flashy. Isn't the point to be in-
conspicuous? When I jokingly asked him about it, he told me
to mind my own damn business. Fair enough.

It's the first and last time I plan on meeting Fisher in person—all of our other correspondence has been via phone call
and fax. Yeah, I had to buy a fax machine because the guy is
so old school, it's bizarre. But what he's doing isn't exactly legal, so . . . Fisher carelessly plops a thick manila envelope into
my lap.

"This is everything on her," he grumbles. "Now get out."
Sheesh.

I tuck the envelope into my suit jacket and ride the elevator up forty-seven floors. Once I'm in the private confines of
my penthouse, I open the envelope to study Fisher's detailed
notes on the girl. In only one week, she's attended Rocco's
Café in Washington Square Park four times and gone to Target once but otherwise has been in and out of NYU campus
buildings. I plan to meet her soon enough. The curiosity is
pressing.

AVA

I t was a Friday morning when I discovered Rocco's, a coffee shop around the corner from my main campus building. I first took a peek into a nearby Starbucks, but when I saw how many other students had the same idea, I sought something quieter. It's become my safe haven from campus in the last week.

I've been sitting here all weekend, working on two written assignments and studying for a pop quiz that's scheduled for 10:00 this morning. It's already 9:45 and I haven't gotten my drink yet. I quickly load my backpack and unplug my laptop when I finally hear my name being called. At the pick-up counter, I look down at two hot cups in front of me but have no clue which one is mine. I seriously don't have time for this.

I take a wild guess and pick up one of the two hot cups, hoping it's the jasmine tea that I ordered because I'm part of the five percent of New York residents (*New York residents!*) who don't drink coffee. (I made that stat up but we'll go along with it.) I hurry toward the exit after taking the cup on the right, and I'm spitting out hot bean water by the time I reach the glass door. *This cannot be happening right now.*

I rush over to the pick-up counter yet again.

"Hi. Good morning. Look, I took the wrong drink. This is a coffee but I ordered a tea and I'm in a really big rush," I explain to the redheaded, freckled barista in a panic. He looks up and behind me as a man reaches around me and grabs the presumed tea from the counter. All I see are his hands.

This guy has really nice hands.

When I turn to explain why he has a tea, I stutter, feeling blood rushing to my cheeks in sheer embarrassment. I don't remember applying ten layers of blush this morning, but I'm sure it looks like I rubbed my face on a Sephora display. I finally come to and explain what's happening.

"Hey, I'm really sorry but I think I stole your coffee. That's tea." I nod my head toward the hot cup in his hands. His nice hands.

"No need to apologize. Here's your tea." As he hands me the cup, I awkwardly take it from him, avoiding eye contact because he's . . . Well, yeah, he's hot as hell. Peering down into my wallet, I see that the smallest change I have is a ten. Add "going broke for a coffee" to my list of college experiences. Love that for me.

I reach out to hand him the folded bill. He doesn't budge.

"Would you take this?" I slur anxiously. "I drank from your cup. I *really* gotta rush to class."

He gives me a look. "I'm not taking your money." He says it like it's the most bizarre thing he's ever heard. While attempting to hold in my nervous laughter, I scan back and forth between him and the door. After both of us insisting for a very hourlong minute, he finally reaches his hand out.

"Fine. You win. Now go to class," he agrees with a smile, plucking the cash from my trembling fingers.

"Thank you! I'm so sorry," I reply in a hurry.

"Not a problem. Have a great day. Enjoy your tea." The pearly white smile he gives me twists a knot in my belly, but it's not a good kind because how many times did Pat charmingly smile at me? Either way, I smile back to be polite and thank him again before bolting out of the coffee shop. From the corner of my eye, I watch as he drops the crinkled money into the glass tip jar. When I turn to glance at him one last time, I find him watching me intently. Our eyes meet and I'm stuck in place for a good ten seconds. He smirks at me and raises a hand to wave goodbye.

I sprint to my 10:00 psychology class and luckily make it in time with a couple of minutes to spare. A portion of that time is spent with my mind on Coffee Shop Man because safe to say, I've been celibate for two years now and he's freaking gorgeous. When I say I've been at Rocco's all weekend, I'm not kidding. Today is the fifth morning I've spent there, so why haven't I seen him until now? *Is he from here? Does he live close by? Why do I even care?*

GRANT

The first thing I notice when I step behind her is her hair, a golden tone to a head of brown locks, the clean scent wafting before me.

A golden tone to a head of brown locks? The fuck is this poetry type shit?

She frantically turns to me, telling me that we've taken each other's drinks, but I hardly hear what she's saying. I am completely and utterly taken aback by her beauty. When I begin to notice a small freckle by her earlobe, I know it's time to come to. My thoughts are interrupted by her hurried words.

"Please take the money, I'm going to be late to class," she babbles anxiously, tucking a strand of long hair behind her ear. When she catches me staring, there's a fearful look in her eyes and she bolts so damn quickly out of the coffee shop. *I'm intrigued.*

"I just found my soul mate," I say to Lenny when I open the passenger door before my ass hits the leather seat of his car.

He chuckles. "I'm here for it, son."

The next day cannot come soon enough. I have to see her again. I'm a ball of nerves when I spot her seated at the back of the café with a pair of headphones that swallow her soft features. I inhale a shaky breath before walking to the edge of her table. With clammy hands, I place down the tea that I've ordered for her and softly cough to catch her attention. When she notices me, her eyes widen and she slips the blue headphones off her head.

"Oh. Hello," she stammers, her voice hoarse and timid. She clears her throat.

"Hi! I'm Grant Wilder," I state, reaching for a handshake. I notice how smooth the inside of her palm is when she reciprocates. Teasingly, I tell her that I brought a tea over so she wouldn't have to steal my drink at the pick-up counter again. She looks up at me with bright eyes, blushing and saying, "Oh. I'm so sorry about that. Thank you so much."

"I'm only kidding. So, how you been . . .?" I ask, waiting for her to fill in the blank. She seems perplexed that I'm asking her name as if this rarely happens.

"Um . . . oh, okay. I'm Ava." *But I already knew that.*

"Nice to meet you, Ava. May I?" I ask, motioning to the tucked-in wooden chair across from hers. I place my clasped hands on the small table and face her. "So, how are you liking New York?"

"Is it that obvious?" She chuckles. *Yeah, it's obvious. Girls like you don't exist here, Ava.* I laugh along with her. "I'm from California," Ava says.

I know that the right thing to do would be to back the hell away from her—to stand up and say goodbye—but I can't bring myself to get out of this chair. Instead, I proceed to ask Ava about school, what it's like living in New York, and about which classes she's taking at NYU. Finally, I muster up the courage to ask her out, knowing it's a terrible idea yet still choosing the wrong route because I have to see her again. Every part of my brain is yelling at me not to do this, but I feel an obligation to this woman even if it means that I'm putting myself in a dangerous position. After looking at me questioningly for about a minute, my having to confirm that *yes*, I'm asking *you* out, she stutters quietly.

AVA

After mystery hot hands man, who I've now discovered is named Grant Wilder, shows up at Rocco's and generously buys me a cup of tea, he pulls out a chair and asks if he can sit.

"Uh yeah, sure. Go ahead," I say with an unsteady voice. I wonder if he can hear how nervous I am. Probably. When he shakes my hand, I notice the roughness of his large palm. I hate that it feels nice. I watch as he bends to sit across from me and scoots forward. That's when I see it. Designer suit. *Pat.* Expensive watch. *Pat.* Fancy tie. *Pat.* It's like the pain from that era of my life is somehow rushing back in, and all of a sudden, I'm slightly terrified of the guy at my table.

"Wow, cross-country. You're brave," he says when I tell him I'm from California. My heart squeezes at that last word and I'm unexpectedly anxious to leave this café because no, Grant. I'm not brave. I'm a coward. I reply with a small smile and take another sip of my tea. After I vaguely answer several questions about myself, Grant stands up to leave and I'm surprised at how much I don't want that even after feeling scared about his resemblance to Pat. I kind of want him to stay. *What the hell?*

"I don't want to waste your time, so I'll head out of here, but do you think I could maybe see you again?" His voice is so deep. Sexy deep.

"Me?" I eye him suspiciously, cross-examining what on earth he's doing standing at my table. I've learned the hard way that guys like him and Pat don't date girls like me. I raise a single eyebrow, hoping to indicate how unlikely this is. I laugh when he scans the café, slips on a pair of glasses, looking hot as hell, and scans the room again before his eyes land on mine. It's then when I realize how green they are. Freakishly green.

"No, my bad. I was talking to someone else," he responds teasingly. "Yes, Ava. You." I spend the next few seconds pep talking myself into how bad of an idea that would be. I'm clueless and naïve when it comes to guys. My parents, my brothers, and Bridget can attest to that. I also know that dating this year is completely out of the question. And am I forgetting that I landed in this city only a week ago?

"I . . . Uh . . ." My voice sounds quiet and raspy, like I haven't spoken for days because I've been distracted by my mental pep talk. I cough to get the silence out of my throat. Grant peeks at me with his eyebrows raised waiting for my reply. He seems hopeful that I'll say yes.

"I don't date." It comes out of my mouth sounding almost rehearsed, but it isn't a lie, so there.

"Who said I was asking you out on a date?"

My face feels hot, ears undoubtedly red because why did I automatically assume he was trying to go out with me like that?

He interrupts my awkward stuttering when I prepare myself to answer. "I'm kidding. I was definitely asking you out on a date, but since that's not your thing . . . a non-date then." He chuckles, challenging me for a reply. I laugh along with him. That was . . . cute.

"What's a non-date?" All I can think about right now is the ass whooping I'll get from my mother if she finds out about this and how amateur my excuse will sound when she does. *But he was being so cute, Mama! Bitch, grow up.*

"I don't know!" Grant exclaims. "I'm kind of making shit up. I just wanna hang out with you." He shrugs and I laugh, agreeing to this non-date but with images of my mom with a flip-flop in hand flashing vibrantly in my mind. He grins too widely, like I've somehow made him the happiest man on Earth by letting him see me again. *What is going on right now?*

Grant asks for my phone, so I pull it out of my bag and reach forward to hand it to him. "There," he says after a few seconds of typing. "I texted myself. Now you have my number." He grabs his coffee from beside the sugar packet holder and lets me know that he'll give me a call.

"It was really great meeting you, Ava. Thanks for not stealing my coffee this time," he jokes, winking at me with his beautiful eyes. "I look forward to our non-date."

Standing beside him at the table, I have to crane my neck to face him properly. How did I not realize how tall he is yesterday? Maybe because I was being awkward as hell and stared at my shoes the entire time.

"You're welcome," I say sarcastically. "Me too." Before walking out the door, he turns back one last time to peer at me with an adorable expression. I smile back and we wave each other goodbye.

Then naturally the avalanche happens. My mind overthinks, running a mile a minute as I replay that exchange in my head. *Why does he want to see me again? Why did he come over to my table in the first place?* I'm not self-deprecating, not really, but I'm realistic because I've lived through this. Because it *killed* me. Wealthy, beautiful guys date wealthy, beautiful girls, and I'm a far cry from that. I only wish I had known it back then. I'm torn between believing that Grant's genuinely interested in being friends or if he's expecting something else like Pat did because I have reason to be; a real concrete excuse to my skepticism.

GRANT

L ove at first sight is not real. LOVE AT FIRST SIGHT IS NOT REAL. *Fuck!* I know how embarrassing this is, but as soon as the door to Rocco's closes behind me and I'm out of Ava's sight, I literally punch the air and grunt a mumbled "yes!" because the fact that I have her number now makes me giddy. She's sarcastic and smart and I love how she rolled her pretty, innocent eyes at me. I smile when she scrunches her little nose in concentration or the cute expression she makes when she's confused. There's also something about the way she carries herself that's kind of sad but also beautiful—like she consciously tries and succeeds in triumphing despite her pain. I like that about her. It's admirable. *Shut up, Wilder. Love at first sight is not real!*

It's the innocence. It's the natural beauty and the tininess and the hair. Holy shit, the hair. I sound so ridiculous, I know, but I want her to want me so bad. The true me. Not the Grant every girl before her wanted; wants. Not for my money or my looks or my reputation in this godforsaken city. I want Ava to want the me that everyone else doesn't seem to notice or care to get to know.

As dumb and irresponsible as it would be to start this, I'd regret ignoring these feelings. I'm not going to let myself walk away from an opportunity to get to know this bombshell of a girl. It's the worst decision I can probably make by pursuing this, but I'm not letting it go and so I tell no one. Because I'm not the kind of guy who *meets someone*. I'm the guy who meets someone and once I fuck them, I forget they ever existed without bothering to find out their names. The people in my life know that, and the moment I'd utter something remotely along the lines of "I met a girl who I really like," everyone will hound me. Knowing Mom, she'd probably celebrate. Yeah, she would *definitely* celebrate.

As much as I'm trying to keep my hopes at bay, it's not going very well. The *at bay* part. The desperation is scary because of how unfamiliar it is. This is unchartered territory for me and I'm afraid of the fact that I want her this bad because I've never felt like this before. Not with Hannah, not with anyone. Nobody.

I'm also incredibly afraid of the truth, of Ava finding out the truth, and of having to hide the truth. When she knows what I know, she'll never want to see my face again. I'm cautious when I say the word *when* because it's inevitable. Somewhere in the back of my mind, I know that this will never last, that I'm starting something I can't finish, but she is too intriguing to pass up. So, I'm being selfish; the potential chaos this can cause is trivial compared to my curiosity in getting to know her. That's huge. Too huge.

I get that I'm reaching a little too far when I say this, but if things with Ava *do* progress, I'm automatically posed with a Hannah problem. Hannah has been in my life for over eighteen years now. I've known the Butches since I was nine years old when my family moved to New York City from Houston, Texas. We went to private school together for ten years, and our families have remained close for nearly twenty. Hannah was never my girlfriend, but she's the one person with whom I have always had a bounce-back relationship, or rather situationship. However, she is *not* my long term.

The first time we slept together was senior year of high school. Then it happened often enough until we agreed to make it a regular occurrence. After all, being with her is easy and impassive. Our lives are similar, she knows my family, and we share the same group of friends, so everything about it is uncomplicated. It was exactly what I wanted—a seamless hookup that required zero effort—until now. Because when I think of Ava, I don't want it to be easy or detached. It's the first time in my life where I feel like I want to work for a relationship, to earn her commitment by showing her who I am; by impressing her and letting her want me organically. Even knowing that this could be a bumpy ride doesn't deter me from her, so I take it as an indication to grow a second pair of balls and call.

AVA

N ow, I won't lie and say that I haven't thought about Grant Wilder much in the last few days, but when I first did this—the whole "dating" thing—I couldn't get Pat out of my head for a second. The thinking then was constant, but now that I'm busy with school, spending all my time on homework and attending classes, it's been a lot easier to focus on something other than a boy.

Tonight is the first one in a while that I'm off, having had back-to-back classes the last couple of days and finishing my assignments early. I take this rare opportunity to settle at home, putting away the clothes that are on *the* chair—you know the one that becomes a black hole of your shit until the pile is so high, you cringe? I then shower and make myself a box of Kraft mac and cheese because it's delicious, that's why, and as I'm clearing off dinner, I feel my phone vibrate. I get a text stating that it's from Grant.

Grant: Hey Ava. It's Grant Wilder from Rocco's. Can I call you?

I wait a couple of minutes before I reply because, *etiquette*.

Me: Sure. The phone rings instantly.

"Hello?" I hesitate a little when answering because I still can't figure out what this guy's game is. I'm so *random*.

"Hi Ava!" Grant exclaims. "I have two very important questions to ask you." I can hear the mischief in his voice.

"Okay . . .?" *Getting straight to it, aren't we?*

"Where are you right now and do you like ice cream?" The determination in his voice is charming. I laugh and smile massively.

"I'm home and who doesn't?" I reply curtly, mimicking the serious tone of his question. He chuckles.

"Fair enough. Where is home? Can I come get you?"

"Uh . . ."

After hearing my delayed response, he interjects. "Don't worry. I'm not a serial killer. I'm just a guy who likes a girl and wants to take her out for some dessert."

I'm still smiling. This is dangerous.

"That's what a serial killer would say," I joke and he laughs with me. "Uh . . . I live in Tribeca. I can text you the address." I straighten myself out and change into a black sweater and Converse, pulling my jeans back on from today. There is no time to fix my hair before the doorbell rings, so disheveled ponytail, welcome! I'm not here to impress anyway. I am what I am. I is what I is.

My hand is kind of, possibly shaking as I open the door for Grant and I'm greeted with a ginormous bouquet of flowers and a delicious grin.

"Hello, hello. These are for you." He jolts the bouquet in my face.

"Wow. That's a lot of flowers. Thank you." *Fitting.* Rich people things. Unreasonably large, expensive bouquets. I almost want to roll my eyes, but I'm not going to hide how good this makes me feel. Am I being stupid? Probably. I take the floral arrangement to the kitchen and motion for him to come inside.

"I'm gonna put these in a vase real quick and then we can go."

He nods and puts his hands in his pockets as he canvasses the layout of my apartment. It's taking me extra time to cut the stems, watching as he seems amused, turning to give me a huge, toothy smile.

"I love what they've done with the place. It looks great."

I tilt my head in pure entertainment, maybe a bit of suspicion, trying to decipher where this is coming from. Displaced charm? Genuine interest? He *loves* my lousy apartment, and his watch can cover my parents' mortgage. Is this a ruse of some sort?

A *ruse? God,* I'll stay single forever. Grant really does seem like a genuinely good guy.

I didn't make buying a vase a priority when I got to New York, so I use my Brita pitcher as a makeshift one. He laughs and calls me creative.

"Thanks." I chuckle. "You ready to head out?"

We descend the three flights of stairs in silence, but it somehow feels comfortable instead of awkward. Pat never stopped talking when we hung out. Pretty sure he loved the sound of his own voice.

Grant finally breaks the silence as we start walking. "So, I have two ideas for this ice cream plan," he begins, holding up two extremely long fingers. "We can either walk to a Ben and Jerry's or we can pick some pints up at a market. It's your choice."

"I choose option two."

Grant leans into me and mumbles, "That was my first choice too." The feel of his warm breath on my neck magnifies the chills I already have from the cold fall evening. I rub my shoulder to my ear in response.

We finally reach a wall of freezers at a grocery store near campus. Yup, an entire fully stocked wall. The best part about NYU is that it's in the heart of the city that never sleeps. The location of this college is even better than I'd originally expected. Grant tells me to get anything I want, so I pick my favorite: cookie dough. A minute later he's walking toward me, juggling four pints of ice cream with a wide-set, adorably child-like smile. He has an unlined, youthful face and I'm curious how old he is, but fuck it. Why bother asking? This is meaningless anyway.

"I *really* like ice cream," he tells me. I laugh and he smirks. Eyeing my hand, he appears to be bewildered as he shakes his head in disappointment.

"I did *not* take you out on this date for you to choose *one* pint of ice cream. We're having an ice cream feast and we'll need a lot of it. Follow me," he says, with a tip of his head. I can't help but notice that he said "date," but I don't correct him. He pulls open the foggy freezer door and adds two more pints to the small plastic basket in his hand. This mundane hangout is turning out to be quite fun. *Like it or not, Ava, but Grant is a cutie.*

"I see you take your ice cream game very seriously," I mock.

"It's a very serious matter, Ava."

I can't tell if he's totally kidding when he glares into my eyes, but his throaty laugh indicates the latter. I've never met someone so carefree and full of life. I miss the days when I used to be that way.

I add another pint to the basket and walk toward the register, which is when I start to notice the stares. Grant doesn't see it, but he has the whole room's attention. I can't say I blame them, but it gives me an uneasy feeling about how ridiculous I must look beside him. He's also enormously tall and I'm only five foot five, but I like the uniformity of it, the two fives.

At the checkout line, Grant turns to me and shakes his head, clicking his tongue three times. As he watches the pints slide down the black rubber conveyer belt, he says, "We're gonna have to work on your ice cream palate, Ava." Once we've checked out, Grant walks us over to a small bench outside the market and excitedly shuffles through the bags.

"Brace yourself. I'm about to change your world." I'm laughing joyfully while Grant observes me and smirks, acting pleased with himself. "So. Let's get down to business," he declares, rubbing his hands together. "These are all ice cream flavors I know and love. The mission is for you to taste every single one, then rate them one through ten."

I peer at him and raise my eyebrows.

"Are you serious?"

"Do I look like I'm kidding?" he sasses, *looking like he's kidding*. I don't think I've laughed more in the last year than I have since meeting Grant. It feels so damn *nice*.

"I can't say no to that."

Looking satisfied, he lays out the flavors like a beer flight on the metal space between us and hands me a plastic spoon, motioning for me to dig in. After eyeing me through every bite, he scans my face once I've tasted all eight flavors.

"So? Was it everything you imagined and more?"

I snicker and shake my head. "Do you want one hundred percent honesty?" He nods. "I didn't love this one, but it wasn't terrible, so I'd give it a six out of ten. I liked these three, so eight out of ten, and these three were meh, so . . . three out of ten?" I point at said flavors as I rate them. "And then cookie dough obviously gets a ten out of ten."

"These two were meh?! How can you do this to me?" he exclaims, tilting his head upward, jokingly distraught. We make light conversation as we pick at this mini ice cream parlor.

"Hey, you're aware that ice cream melts, yes?" Our eyes meet and he stares for a moment before he nods at my question, seeming slightly serious this time. I wonder what he's thinking during those few extra seconds of his observation of me. I wonder what anyone thinks when they meet me.

"They're all yours, babe. We'll put them in the freezer. You'll be stocked up for months."

Um, he just called me babe. Grant Wilder just called me *babe. Don't think too hard about it, Campbell.* I tell him that I can't take home eight pints of ice cream, and he explains that they'll melt if he waits until he gets home to freeze them.

"But, Grant . . ." I say, eyeing him seriously. "Are you asking me to babysit the meh flavors too?"

I can't decipher if my chills are from the ice cream, the weather, or his throaty laughter. Maybe all three, but damn, that manly voice though. I feel it downward.

"Of course," he begins. "What else are you gonna feed me when I come over?"

"You sound so sure of yourself. What makes you think you'll be coming over?"

He pauses before replying, "You're right. How could you *possibly* want to go out with me again? I just fed you three out of ten ice cream."

The walk back is just as fun. We laugh, we chat, and it's just . . . *easy.*

"One second," I say to Grant, spotting a sleek black sports car parked down the street from my building. I pull out my phone to snap a photo for my car fanatic brothers. They are going to love this.

"Are you into cars?" Grant asks.

"Me? Nah, not at all. My brothers on the other hand . . ."

He chuckles and follows me through the front walkway. When we reach my apartment, I unlock the door and turn toward him. This time the silence is awkward.

"Can I help you put these in the freezer?" he offers from the doorway, bags in tow.

"Uh . . . yeah, sure. Thank you." He follows me to the kitchen and we load up the freezer quietly.

I clear my throat to speak. "Tonight was cool. Thanks." We head toward the door together.

"It *was* cool. I want to see you again," he admits. At Rocco's I told him I don't date, and he claimed that this isn't one, but who am I kidding? There was definitely that first-date connection tonight. The spark of something new. Knowing that I want to see him too, I sigh. However much I like him doesn't compare to the sanity I can't afford to lose. Not again, not after last time. It's non-negotiable.

I begin to protest but Grant interrupts me. "Please? I had a great time tonight."

I want to say no, I *need* to say no, but I take a deep breath and nod in his direction. I also had a great time tonight. "Okay."

"I'm excited." Grant smiles and tells me that he'll call. I did tell him I don't date, right?

GRANT

I t's the God honest truth that I got a little panicky when Ava began to protest me seeing her again; I am not willing to let this thing between us end before it has a chance to start. I also don't want to go back to the Hannah days, and without Ava, I undoubtedly will because she's second nature to me. Or my dick, rather.

When Dad held that little intervention in his office a couple of months ago, he told me that it was finally time to start growing up and taking responsibility. So, although the company is running smoothly and doing quite well, I can't help interpreting Dad's lecturing words to mean more than with my career. The thing with Hannah is never going to last anyway, and now that Ava's in the picture, I take it as a sign . . . If after a decade I'm going to be boyfriend material, she's the one I'd do it for. I'm sure Dad would consider that an indication that I've grown up, and my desire for Ava is all the motivation I need.

Aside from my arrangement with Hannah, I've had my fair share of casual hookups, so this thing with Ava is wildly different from anything I've done. Girls like her don't come around often, at least not for assholes like me, and I know in all my twenty-seven-plus years, I've never met a girl so different. A good different. She's the person I want to change for, and it's not *only* because I know what she went through. I mean, she's gorgeous and funny and plain cute. She makes me want to be different than my past and her past, and I want her to want me just the same.

Throughout my privileged life, I haven't had to work too hard for the things that I wanted. I can acknowledge that it's an absolutely pretentious thing to say but it's the truth. Have I grown up incredibly fortunate and wealthy? Yes. Am I denying that? No. But being that Ava isn't jumping at the opportunity to be with me makes things a challenge that I'm looking forward to pursuing. I had this instant change of heart when I saw her the second time at Rocco's, admitting to myself that I can't stay the same guy I've been the last decade if I want any chance to be with her. I want to be different so she'll like me. We've gone on *one* date—and she refused to call it that—but I couldn't wait to see her again seconds after I left her apartment. It almost feels like the change is already happening.

I don't fully notice it though until Louis texts me on Friday night to go out, just as confused as I am when I decline the chance to get trashed and fuck around. The reason isn't exhaustion from work like I tell him. No, the reason is Ava because I'm almost certain she isn't the type of girl who would join me on a night out snorting coke in the back room of a wild club in Hell's Kitchen or getting invited to some random house party and going. Neither would she stumble around the city with a handlebar bottle in hand. But me? That was me just a couple of months ago, and I want Ava nowhere near the people of my past.

If Hannah gets wind of my budding relationship with Ava, she'll set out to sabotage it. I am determined not to let that happen. The late-night hookup texts haven't slowed down, but I've managed to come up with a different excuse the last few times she's asked. It'd probably be best to sit Hannah down and explain that it's indefinitely over between us but I have to be face-to-face with her, and knowing Hannah, there will be blood. Boy, is she persistent. I mean, can I blame her? She's never heard the word no in her entire life. That's why I've been diverting with lame excuses instead of being upfront; the one thing I can't do is tell Hannah that I'm ending this meaningless thing between us because of a girl I've only just met.

AVA

I greet college after a restful weekend to a huge workload. Apparently, every teacher has the same idea in torturing their students, so it's officially essay season. All I've spent my time on this week is schoolwork and research, downing caffeine by the gallon from the exhaustion of sleepless nights spent anxiously studying. Red Bull has been a good college companion to me.

I view my move to New York as a chance to heal and recover from the disaster that was once my life. I promised myself and my parents that I would utilize my time here to grow and come out stronger on the other end. I spent a good portion of the last week thinking about Grant and if he even fits in my life. I can't say that getting ice cream together was ordinary because it wasn't—I had an absolute blast. Pat was the only guy I'd ever been with before, and from one date alone, Grant showed me how fun dating can be and all we did was go to a grocery store. My meager stint with Pat was incomparable in the worst possible way. In retrospect, I realize how inferior Pat made me feel, almost like he was doing me a favor by entertaining the idea of us being together. I've developed this insecurity about myself that I never had before him. That's why the thought of Grant liking me is so bizarre.

As much as I want to convince myself that Grant isn't anything like Pat was, it's hard not to notice that they come from the same superficially perfect world. I noticed it on that very first day. It had always felt weird for me to be with Pat because of how fundamentally different we were externally, and look how that turned out. I would do anything I could to erase what happened with Pat from memory, but sadly, I'm taking this one to my grave. I'll never escape the heart-sinking memories that flood my brain reminding me of what he did to me. What *I* did to me.

Aside from my own irrevocable blame, Pat ruined me. If I wasn't so damn self-aware, I'd even put all the blame on him. It's daunting to think that *one* out of seven billion human beings can take your life and stomp on it to the point where you just don't recognize yourself anymore, because that was what he did. He stole me from me.

I took a month-long internship down in LA, where I met the infamous Patrick McCall the summer before I was to attend my freshman year of college at NYU. I was given the opportunity to work and learn alongside a team of business-men, Pat's father being the boss, to teach me what "the real world" was like. I was going to pursue a business major at NYU, so I was ecstatic when I had gotten hired.

The thing with Pat started off like any new relationship does. We texted, we flirted, we hung out, and I was having a lot of fun. Pat was the first guy who I considered my boyfriend, but I was naïve to think so. He was nice when he wanted to be, and only in private, but otherwise he was vile. Naturally, I only realized this looking back because I was young and stupid and so dang prudish. After a couple weeks of the texting and the flirting, Pat implied that unless I slept with him, things between us would be over. It was this *unnecessary* internal battle that I had with myself that summer whether or not I would lose my virginity to this boy. But Pat was the greatest actor and I was starstruck by him. It was simple. I was going to have sex with a boy who loves me! What could be so bad?

I hadn't thought anything of it when I didn't get my pe-riod for six weeks. It was when I started feeling nauseous that the thought crossed my mind. *Could I be pregnant?* Bridget was the first person I told; she brought over a pregnancy test, because I wouldn't have been caught dead buying one myself, and I nearly fainted when those two lines appeared. It was clear as day.

Bridget had been my savior throughout that ordeal. Not only did she stay with me, hand in hand, while I waited for the imminent lines to show up on that dreadful magenta stick, but she also joined me in telling my mother what was going on. I had expected a bout of screaming and yelling, but all my Catholic mother did was hold me and cry. I had never before felt like such a shameful daughter.

The conversation I had with Pat about the pregnancy, where he demanded that I terminate it immediately, was such a blow to my heart. He blocked my number, and a few days later, I received an unsigned affidavit from the McCalls stating that I would null Pat as the father on the birth certificate should I choose to keep the baby. It also stated that I wasn't to receive nor ask for any child support, and I was expected to sign on the dotted line. I was portrayed as a sneaky gold digger as if I wanted this to happen. As if I planned it.

I was utterly shaken and I was torn. They constructed a false story; made it seem like I had intended to get pregnant with Pat's child with the intention of extorting them out of large sums of money, but I genuinely did not care about any of that. I just wanted support from the boy I thought cared about me. Even loved me. Because once upon a time, he told me he did.

We hired a lawyer of our own. In the beginning, I had assumed that the baby was going to be this new addition to our family, but Mr. Ellison was no match for Pat's expensive and prestigious legal team. It was obvious that we were going to lose if we fought the affidavit, but we still tried. And then the threatening happened. They were persistent. They didn't stop. They were Pat's friends. I was bullied and gaslighted day in and day out. It was voicemail after phone call after text message of his posse demanding that I get an abortion, calling me a gold digger, a whore. The harassment continued even when I changed my number. I was defenseless, I was slut shamed, and I was miserable. So, I decided to just do it. Despite my religious beliefs, I was ready to have an abortion from the mere fact that the baby growing inside of me was Pat's and he had been so awful. I was forced to do the unthinkable.

As a child of Jesus, my family devout Catholics, I was so ashamed by the choice I ultimately made. I knew my parents weren't happy about it, but they knew what was at stake for me, so they stood by my side along with my brothers and kept their opinions to themselves. Every doctor within a ten-mile radius of Arcata knew at least one of us Campbells, so to keep the local whispers from happening, all three of my brothers joined my parents and me in San Francisco for this sinful abortion I was about to have. I was so emotional, thankful, and overwhelmed that they stopped their lives to support me. It is by far one of my favorite memories despite how ugly it came to be.

With the decision in play, I entered the women's center at one of the hospital's many buildings with a heaviness, my feet dragging on the dirty tile, my mind empty. Everything after they prepped me for the abortion happened quickly. Suddenly I was being wheeled into an elevator, toward an operating room, while nurses stripped me of my clothes as they pushed me down the fluorescent lit hallway. Lights flashing, alarms wailing. It was a real live nightmare.

I woke up in the Intensive Care Unit a few days later to a nurse carefully checking my vitals, my mother's calloused palm in my needled hand. When she saw my eyes flutter open, she cried out and prayed so hard that I was beyond confused. When I finally came to, they explained to me what happened. "An ectopic pregnancy," they said. "The baby was lodged in your right fallopian tube. We tried for a safe abortion, but you were losing a lot of blood. Your body went into septic shock."

An abortion gone wrong. They don't call it a C-section because C-sections are for living babies and this wasn't that. They had to remove the pregnancy via surgery, the scar I bear on my lower stomach still shiny and textured and proof of what I underwent in that hospital room. It'll be a forever reminder every time I change my shirt or take a shower that the surgeons had to remove not only one but both of my tubes that day because of an abortion that *I* chose to have. I did this to myself.

"You won't be able to get pregnant naturally, Ava," my doctor said from the foot of my hospital bed. But at that point, all I heard were echoes, my mind shutting off from the pain of what that meant. Mom's weeping is the background noise of every single one of those conversations. I was admitted to the hospital's recovery unit for three weeks because of the sepsis. My life had become ultrasounds, IVs, and a shit ton of needles; they pumped me up with heavy doses of antibiotics and pain medication. And with that, I became a ghost; a shell of a person. I'll never forget how weak I felt throughout the recovery process. I had lost so much weight that I had to be fed and showered, couldn't hold a pen or a TV remote because they felt too heavy for me. It was extremely debilitating.

For those three weeks, sitting in a sterile and lonely hospital room, all I had were my thoughts, too drained to text or read or even call my family. Lying there in my pain was the only thing I had energy for. Every time I thought about what I did, what *I* decided to do despite the pressure from Pat, I would throw up and I would tremble. The crippling anxiety and depression that developed from my time at the hospital from the shame and reality of what I had done caused these chronic panic attacks, numbing suicidal thoughts. When I thought things couldn't get worse, I was admitted to a mental hospital only weeks after coming home from the ICU where I was put on suicide watch because I almost tried to kill myself. I didn't want to live anymore.

My life had gone from pain medication to heavy doses of antidepressants and mandatory talk therapy. Three days of intense psychiatric assessment. The first few sessions, I remember repeating the words *I killed a baby* every time I was asked a question. Any question.

It felt like I had died on that operating table because of how bad I wished I had. My life would never be the same. This experience flipped my life around, turned me into someone so angry and so bitter. I began to truly understand why there were people who felt so sad to the point of ending their lives because I identified with them. They were me.

AVA

As if I'm not stressed enough being nose deep in textbooks all afternoon, I sense something off about her voice when Mom calls to check in on me.

"What's wrong, Mama? You sound off."

"Nothing, mija. I just miss you, *mi amor*," she sighs, busying herself with something in the kitchen. I'm not convinced, so I probe a little.

"Please tell me, Mama. I can handle whatever it is."

"The . . ." She hesitates but I egg her on. "The hospital bills, mija. They keep coming. Your father took extra hours at the factory, but there is interest now." I conceal the sounds of cries from my mother as shameful tears wash down my face, but I act strong because I have to.

"Mama, I'm going to fix this. I'm sorry. I'm so sorry."

"Ava, if I hear you apologize one more time, I'm going to fly over there and hit you with my *chanclas!*" Mom's threatening to whack me with a pair of flip-flops. How Spanish of her. I chuckle when she laughs. "I mean it, baby. This is not your fight. But tell me this—you've been taking your pills, yes? And did you meet with the doctor we found?"

"Yes, Mama. Medications every morning. And I met with Dr. Helstad on Friday. He's very nice. I'm in good hands out here. You don't need to hover." I get blood work and ultrasounds done at an OB-GYN office once a month to rule out any potential flare-ups from the sepsis; to make sure it's easy breezy beautiful down there. Hah!

"Ava, I'm your mother. Don't tell me not to hover! You got sick. You're my baby. It's my job to take care of you, and I cannot do that from California! Are you sure this was a good idea? What if you're so busy with school that you forget to take the medicine? What if . . ."

She's on a worry bender. I used to get those all the time. *Looks like it runs in the family.*

"Hey! Mom! I'm fine. Everything is okay. Please stop worrying. I miss you. I love you. I swear I'm good. Hug Dad for me, okay?" We hang up once I've consoled her, explaining that between FaceTime, phone calls, and constant texting, she'll feel like I never even left, like I'm in my upstairs bedroom.

It's not easy seeing your parents act so ordinarily human—watching them worry and fret and panic just like you do. Your whole life, you grow up with these role models, these flawless people who seem like they live this perfect life, but it wasn't until after my trauma that I started to realize how ordinary and average they were. It was hard for me to watch that transition happen within myself. I wanted to go back to that naïve girl who believed everything was perfect.

But now? Now Mom's dread is warranted. Our government health insurance covered the bare minimum, if anything at all. We're talking hundreds of thousands of dollars in medical bills after the surgery, the recovery, and the in-patient stay at the mental hospital. My parents don't have that kind of money. They never have. We have been living paycheck to paycheck my entire life, so they couldn't ever afford fancy health insurance. The state didn't cover much at all.

Mom's stress eats at me, so I have a thought, a dangerous but possible idea, a road that I wouldn't ever entertain taking if it wasn't for my hardworking parents.

"Ellison and Gomez, this is Kayla." A chirpy young woman answers on the first ring.

"Mr. Ellison please. This is Ava Campbell calling."

"One moment please," she says before patching me in to our lawyer's phone line.

"Hello, Miss Campbell, what can I do for you?" Imagine Mr. Magoo but with more hair. I tell him about my idea, ask him if there's a plausible case here, but he informs me that medical cases are near impossible to win. We can't prove that the physical trauma I suffered had anything to do with the abortion that I was pressured into having because my body produced an ectopic pregnancy on its own. Pat didn't do that part. But Ellison has an alternative idea.

"We can probably stick them with emotional distress if you're up for it. But Miss Campbell, you have to be willing to take the heat." Damn it. I thought I was one and done with this Pat shit. The only consolation is the fact that I'm wiser now. I've been through enough the last two years that nothing scares me anymore. I'll kick this case's ass.

"I can take the heat, Mr. Ellison. What do you need me to do?"

"I'm going to give you a shopping list. Send everything to my email. You ready?" *Here it goes.*

Text messages from that summer? *Check.*

A record of the psychiatric evaluation from the mental hospital? *Check.*

A list of medications that I'm *still* on? *Check.* Mr. Ellison needs receipts? Well, I have it all.

"I'll be the one to share the news with my mother. Thank you. I appreciate all your help."

Mom's furious with me when I tell her that I just got off the phone with the lawyer.

"Ava, what are you doing? We don't need you to fix our problems. You need to stop it, mija! You have enough on your plate!"

But I *do* need to fix this because it *isn't* my parents' problem. Those hospital bills have my name written at the top of them. This is my fight, both then and now. Dad grabs the phone from my panicked mother.

"Ava, darling, they are going to exploit you. We're not letting you do this," he says, his voice tough and serious.

"Dad, I'm over eighteen. I'm suing Pat because those bills are addressed to me. Whether you want to meet with Mr. Ellison or not is your choice. I'm sure I can take care of it from New York. I'm asking you to help me with this case because I'm not backing down, and school is really busy."

Then Mom grabs the phone. I can't help but smile, feeling a little homesick at this typical Campbell conversation. "Mija, no. Stop this nonsense, baby!"

I tell her that I won't hear it, that this is my way of helping and they can't exactly stop me. I need to do my part. I tell my parents to call Mr. Ellison when they have a chance, and I bite my inner cheek to keep my emotions in check when Dad calls me with the good news an hour later. They're calling it *McCall vs. Campbell II*. After feeling so shameful and guilty about everything that happened, I vowed to never speak of two things to anyone other than my family and Bridget: my suicide attempt and my infertility. That list turns to three as I shamefully open a case because of money, the one thing I promised Patrick that summer I had no intention of taking.

AVA

About three minutes after I seat myself at a corner table at Rocco's this morning, Grant Wilder texts me. With all the unwanted stress about the new case, I almost forgot he existed. I had a really great time with him that other night, but I know that starting this thing with Grant is a bad idea. School is a priority, that's a no-brainer, but the moment I picked up the phone to call the offices of Ellison and Gomez, that surpassed school and topped the list. My family and this fight are too important—college is too important—to be distracted over a guy. I can't juggle all three, and I think I've known that for a few days now. Maybe I've been subconsciously trying to forget about Grant to make it a little easier on myself. I tap my phone screen and read his text.

Grant: Hey you! Any chance you're at Rocco's this morning?

Do I lie? Do I pretend to Grant that everything is fine and dandy when I've been incredibly anxious all week? I haven't acquired much of a poker face, so if I'm stressed out, he'll know right away. And I've never been a good liar. I look terrible because I feel terrible, and I genuinely don't want to see him right now, but on the off chance that he'll end up here anyway, I let him know that I am, in fact, at Rocco's this morning.

Me: Yeah, I am.

Grant: See you in ten. :)

Ten minutes is all I have to formulate a backhanded excuse in case he asks me why I look so uneasy, but it isn't nearly enough time. Then, he walks in. I check the time to see that it only took him eight minutes when he said he'd get here in ten. I laugh bitterly. Grant struts over to my table, plants a soft kiss on my head, and leans over to feel my lukewarm cup of tea. He tells me that he'll be right back and rushes toward the cashier. After setting down a large pink pastry box and a new, hotter tea, Grant takes a seat at my table and smiles at me. I'm so flustered and speechless by this man. It's like, why do you have to be so nice? Why do you have to seem like Pat but *actually* be nice? God is playing mind games with me. I don't like this.

Before Grant can say anything, I blurt out, "Are you rich?" and when I realize what the hell I just said, my face turns crimson. He cocks his head, eyeing me quizzically, probably thinking to himself that I am insane. I attempt to come out of this unscathed, so then I start to rant like a crazy person as if that's going to help. I'm spewing a vocal stream of consciousness, here and now. "I'm not a gold digger, *I swear*. I don't want your money. I was just contemplating some stuff, and I don't really know much about you besides the fact that you have amazing arms and gorgeous eyes, and *I swear I'm not a gold digger.* I don't even know why I asked—"

Grant reaches for my hand across the table, likely to shut me up, and tells me to calm down. I breathe a sigh of relief that he's not sprinting out the café door right now and I aim to collect myself. Out of all the questions I could've asked him, why did that one have to come out? I am mortified.

"Are you okay?" Grant asks with genuine concern, still gripping my hand across the table. I nod to assure him, but he doesn't buy it. "What's going on? Talk to me."

"Just stressed out about school," I reply hoarsely. "And some family stuff." *And now you. Get out of my head, buddy.*

"Look at me," Grant says, his eyebrows pinched. "Breathe."

I follow his direction and take a moment to regain the stability I've clearly lost.

"I'm really sorry. I'm stressed out. That was totally out of line." I'm frantic and he knows it. He brings my hand up to his mouth and plants a soft kiss on the inside of my palm. *Damn.* Grant's been sweeter to me in the last few weeks than Pat had our entire time together. That tea thing earlier killed me. They have to be different. I say it again. *They have to be different.*

"Do you want to talk about it?" he asks, green eyes scanning mine.

"There's just a lot of schoolwork, and I've been staying up studying all night, every night, and I'm so beyond exhausted," I say, gasping.

He has a knowing expression on his face.

"Junior year is really hard. I get it. What can I do to help?" The genuine concerned look on his face makes me want to pounce across the table and hug him. *They're different. Pat and Grant are different.*

"I think you already did."

"Baby." Am I his *baby*? This is getting tougher by the minute. We're not at a stage where he can nonchalantly call me that, but right now that word feels like a hug and I really need it. "Define rich." I eye him questioningly. "Well, you asked if I'm rich. So, define rich."

"Can we forget that ever happened please? I don't know why I even asked you that."

"Humor me."

"If you need me to define rich for you, you're rich."

Grant chuckles but seems almost . . . ashamed.

"Hmm . . . fair enough, I guess."

"Don't take anything I said personally. I swear, I'm just stressed out." He nods and gives me a small smile. That small smile widens into a foolish grin when Grant asks, "So I shouldn't take it personally when you told me that I have amazing arms?" I laugh and grab my hand back from his hold to fold my arms on the table, laying down my forehead in pure embarrassment. He tells me to look at him, but I shake my head no.

"Please look at me, Ava." I rest my chin on my folded arms, still unable to catch his eye. "There's nothing wrong with what you said. It was cute and funny and I'm flattered. Please don't be shy." I surrender to his piercing green eyes. "Next topic. Have you eaten lately? Probably not. You look pale. Eat," Grant demands. He motions to the box on the table. "You need to eat." There are at least twelve pastries in here.

"What is all this?" I ask, my mouth watering at the lot of croissants, rainbow cake, cannoli . . .

He shrugs. "I forgot to ask what you wanted."

"You're crazy," I say as I shake my head in disbelief.

"What?" The guy is genuinely confused. He's *so* rich but I don't say that out loud. I demand that he stay and split a chocolate croissant with me. "You can't leave until I leave. I'm not eating all this alone."

"Who said I wanna leave? I'm not going anywhere," Grant replies as he reaches for his chocolatey half. Eventually he helps me pack my bag, puts a few pastries in a smaller to-go box for me to take to school, and walks with me to the College of Arts and Science building. There are bystanders watching us. My eyes dart to the influx of students staring, but Grant doesn't notice any of them. His eyes are focused on nothing but me. Pat always hid our relationship. He wouldn't so much as hold my hand in public. He was embarrassed of me. *See? They're different.*

"Everyone is staring at you," I whisper.

He scouts the area and shakes his head. "Me? Nah, I'm pretty sure they're staring at you." I roll my eyes at him. "When are you free?" Grant asks.

"I turn in my last essay tomorrow."

He looks excited for me. *For* me. "Nice," he offers, high-fiving me. "Can I call you after work?" I canvass up his tall, fit body and nod when I land on his face. He kisses the top of my head before I walk through the doors.

After a morning like that? I mean, that's it. I want this so much. I want *him* so much. I want to try to juggle the shit out of this because Grant is too good, too nice, too perfect to walk away from. And the best part? He *likes* me, *actually* likes me. I feel it. I'm not vying for his attention or begging him to notice me. Grant is taking every initiative required to be with me because he *wants* to. That's ought to count for something.

AVA

I feel like a literal weight has been lifted off my shoulder when I extend my arm and plop the plastic folder on my psychology professor's wooden desk. I'm looking forward to seeing Grant tonight, but that excitement slowly forms into worry *because* of how excited I feel. Which Ava am I right now? Am I the Ava who's gonna take a leap, trust my gut that Grant is good, and see where this can go? Or am I the cautious Ava, the one who is going to let her past determine her future? I have been battling this Yes Grant, No Grant war within me for the last twenty-four hours, and it's nonstop. I want to take this leap of faith but *how*?

I call my lord and savior, Bridget Christ, to discuss. She's screaming into the phone when I say, "So, I kind of met some-one . . ." Although Bridget doesn't have much dating experience—she's married to her high school sweetheart—she's a smart girl who knows me inside out. Hence why she's my lord and savior Bridget Christ.

"Don't get too excited, crackhead. I'm literally calling for advice on whether or not I should keep seeing him." I hear her firing up her computer, fingers smacking the keyboard, ready to play FBI agent and Google the shit out of him.

"Name please," she says in a robotic voice.

I holler. "No way."

"Name please," she repeats.

"No."

"Name please. Name please. Name please."

"You are out of your mind," I shout, laughing at my crazy best friend.

"You're so right. The baby was up at five this morning. I'm exhausted. But whyyyyyyyy won't you let me Google him!" Bridget has three kids under the age of four. She's perpetually holding a cup of coffee.

"'Cause even I haven't gotten that far!"

"So, what's the problem? Talk to me, sista."

I explain it all. The resemblance to Pat, the new case, NYU and my academic overachiever personality. The fact that dating again despite Grant's resemblance to Pat is frightening in and of itself. I didn't exactly have the best experience last time.

"I just feel like it doesn't make sense right now, you know? And it's scary to try this dating thing again! I think I'm gonna end things before they get too good." But even as I say it, I know that I'm lying. I think . . .

"*That* doesn't make sense. You don't get to choose who you'll meet and when. And you're literally admitting to me that so far, it's been good. If you like him, date him. If it goes well, *keep* dating him. And if it goes wrong, I'll bring pliers and a chainsaw." She yawns, like what she said was ordinary. I hate when she's right, but she doesn't know how it feels to be me right now because her husband is a gem. Bridget also never went to college. I know that I'm being a little too cautious, but maybe Grant and I can do this later? I don't know. I really don't know.

"Go. Take. A. Nap," I demand.

I shower once we hang up and give myself an encouraging pep talk in the bathroom mirror. Between the way I'm feeling and the conversation with Bridget, I decide to go with full transparency. I'll tell Grant where I'm holding and that my life is crazy right now. Honesty is the easiest way to go about this. *You can do this, Ava!* My phone buzzes soon after.

Grant: Come outside. I hope you like burgers. :)

Me: Are there French fries?

Grant: What kind of question is that?

Me: LOL. Coming. Dang it, he's cute.

I walk toward Grant's car but come to a halting stop before opening the door.

"Wait, this is *your* car?!" It's the same black sports car from the other night. He watched me take pictures of it. How embarrassing.

"Oops," he says, shrugging. "Hey, pretty. Get in here!" Grant bends his head to call out through the open passenger window. I slide in beside him, and my butt feels warm when I take a seat.

"Seat warmers?!" I am way too excited about this. I laugh at myself.

"Shit, are you cold?" he asks, concerned, fumbling with the middle console buttons.

"Your car has *seat warmers*?!" I shimmy my butt on the brown leather and watch as Grant eyes me in amazement. I spot two large paper bags in his lap, grease stains darkening each bag in random splotches. He fishes through them and hands me a burger.

"Your burger, m'lady." I laugh. He hands me a cup of French fries. "Your French fries, m'lady." *Damn it.* I take a giant bite and he howls with laughter at my chipmunk cheeks. How am I not embarrassed to grub food in front of him?

"Yum, this is so good. Thanks for dinner. How was your day?" We make light conversation, talk about our days, eating French fries out of the cup holder while holding our burgers, and I wouldn't have it any other way. Stupid, stupid girl.

"What's your full name?" he asks.

"Ava Ruth Campbell."

His eyes widen in surprise. "Ruth? Are you religious?"

THE PATH OF A LOGICAL LIAR

I nod. "Yeah, my mom's Spanish. Catholic. Rosary beads and everything." I chuckle, feeling a bout of homesickness. "What's *your* full name?"

"Callum Grant Wilder," he replies. *Solid dude, solid name.* "I go by my middle name. My dad is Callum and his dad is too. Grandpa Cal."

"So, you're Callum Wilder the *Third.*" He turns to chuckle at me. "Sorry, I'm a smartass sometimes."

"No, I've actually never thought of it like that. I guess I am." He glows when he talks to me. Glows! We wrap up our takeout trash after hours of talking and head up the pathway to my building.

"I want to see you again." Grant smiles when we reach the door of my apartment. It's become routine. I take a deep breath. *You can do this.*

"Grant, listen . . . I have a lot going on in my life right now, so I can't be full time with you. I think it might be in your best interest to stop seeing me. I want to see you again too because I enjoy hanging out, but there is so much on my plate. I think it's best if we put a stop to whatever's happening here," I say, pointing between us. It's written all over his face that he didn't see this coming.

"You don't have time for a relationship, is what you're saying?"

"You saw me yesterday. I was acting like a lunatic because of how stressful school is. I just don't think it would make sense if we dated now. I like you but I'm trying to be responsible." *And safe.* He puts a hand on each side of the doorframe and lets his head hang low. Sighing, he stands for a couple of minutes, paralyzing me with his confused expression.

"You couldn't do this before we spent the last few hours together?" He's totally right but I had to. Like a goodbye party, if you will. "Can we talk about this? Am I allowed a proper conversation?" Grant frowns at me, but he's not upset; he does seem genuinely disappointed, and his green-eyed stare makes me vulnerable. "Please. Just give me a conversation." I feel cherished that Grant isn't shrugging and saying sayonara too quickly, so I give in and nod. He follows me into the apartment, taking a seat on the small sofa near my bed. I sit on top of the duvet cover and face him.

"Tell me why you're *really* ending this. We've only spent a few hours together, and it's clear that we have something. You can't deny that." He speaks with such firmness, and every word hurts to hear because he's right. I *do* know it. We *do* have something. We clicked at that café; it was almost automatic. I rub up the length of my face.

"I'm just being realistic, Grant. I have a lot going on right now, and I don't have time for a relationship. It'd be better to end it now than further down the line once we're already invested."

He examines me and laughs disbelievingly. He *laughs*.

"What!" I'm raising my voice now.

"Ava, we already *are* invested. At least *I* am. Maybe things are different for you, but I really want this." Especially with those sad eyes, he's so gorgeous.

If I dismiss the demanding schoolwork and the emotionally draining case, I know that it's wrong to deprive him of the option to prove my preconceived notions wrong when it comes to his resemblance to Pat. But three months down the line when we both realize how different we are, it'll be that much harder to say goodbye. And how can I commit to dating Grant when I have a *list* of secrets that are off-limits, no matter who he becomes to me? I can hardly believe that's a great foundation to any potential relationship. I don't really have a response for him, so I mumble, "Can we just leave it?" I'm a coward.

He shakes his head. "Can you at least give me a chance? You're robbing me of being able to show you that we *could* be together. I don't plan on taking you away from your priorities. I want you to do well in school. But I also want you to make time to see where this can go." When I don't reply, he speaks again. "What's the real reason, Ava?"

I want so badly to tell him the truth, to show him where I'm coming from. So, I settle on a small sliver of it. "I had a bad experience. The last time I dated someone this different than me, well, let's just say it ended badly." *Badly* doesn't cover even a snippet of what happened two summers ago. Thinking about it makes me nauseous. Grant takes a deep breath.

"I'm really sorry that happened to you and maybe one day you can tell me about it, but don't judge a book by its cover, Ava. Let me show you who I am." He's glaring again and every moment that passes, another wall falls down. His argument is convincing. I know that the right thing to do would be to offer him a chance, but giving him a clear-cut answer right now isn't smart for me to do. I'm a planner.

"Can I think about it?" I ask. He doesn't appear as relieved and content as I thought he would be.

"Of course you can. But Ava . . ." He's shaking his head. "Tell me that you don't want to be with me and I'll go. I'm not trying to convince you to date me. I just think your excuse for ending this is bullshit. If you don't like me or if you don't see a future with me, then *fine*. But if you know there's potential, forget all that other stuff and allow me to prove myself to you."

Where the hell is this coming from? Why is he pushing so hard for this? I'm so weak from his words that I can't find my voice to answer him. I internalize everything he says, take it all into account, and nod, hoping he's right. Hoping that he *will* prove me wrong. Hoping that he isn't the guy I'm so afraid he'll turn out to be.

Grant breathes a sigh of relief from the anguish of the last twenty minutes, stands up, and walks toward me on the bed. Taking my hand, he stands me up and wraps my arms on either side of him so we're hugging. His hugs are like butter and I'm slightly concerned at how warm and safe I feel in his embrace. Actually, I'm not concerned, but I'm telling myself that I should be. He pulls back to face me, gently tucking a loose strand of hair behind my ear, and pierces me with those green daggers I've come to love so much.

"Think about it? Let me know where you're at in a few days, but just know that I'll be good to you. I promise." I briefly forget all my doubts and hug him again. Grant breaks the hug soon after and respectfully walks toward the door, holding my hand and dragging me along. I admire that he doesn't expect to stay nor does he ask to. We've hung out four times and he hasn't even tried to kiss me yet, although I wouldn't have minded if he did. But Pat expected sex right off the bat. *How could I have been so dumb back then?*

I shut the white painted door behind Grant and crawl into bed. I know that denying him a chance without trying to get to know him first, the real him, isn't fair. And I can't help but smile at his obvious crush on me.

GRANT

M y attention shifts to my office door, and I'm shocked at who is standing at my desk. I sprint out of my chair and take a giant step back.

"What are you doing here?" I ask.

"You," she replies flirtatiously. She's got this mischievous smirk thing going on, and she's wiggling her eyebrows. When Hannah reaches her hand toward me, I take another step back. "Why have you been ignoring me?" she whines, plopping herself into the leather chair across from mine. When I notice how normal it feels to have Hannah sitting by my desk—hell, coming to my office—I'm immediately anxious for her to leave. I'm with Ava now. Even if she hasn't answered about whether we're going to continue seeing each other, one thing I know for sure is that I'm no longer Hannah's. I never really was either.

"Hannah, this isn't the time. You need to leave." My voice sounds harsh and I wince a little.

"What the hell?" she scoffs in her perfected high-pitched tone, her jaw open and unmoving. I pause to assess her, disregarding everything else around me, and come to notice how *average* Hannah is. There is literally nothing interesting about her. Clearly Ava has changed all hopes of me finding anyone else attractive ever again. My next move determines my choice between my old world and Ava's.

"Listen, I wanted to talk to you. What we did—it was fun while it lasted, Hannah, but I'm not in that place anymore," I explain. "We gotta end this."

She gawks at me, dumbfounded. Hannah's never not gotten what she wanted, and boy, do I know how bad she wants me. She hasn't been subtle about it.

"Are you rejecting me right now?" Again, with that whiny voice.

"I wouldn't call it that." My teeth are gritted. I'm feeling impatient. I shouldn't have to explain myself to the girl I hooked up with. This isn't a breakup. Hannah notices my obvious angst and figures it out pretty perfectly.

"Who is she?" Is it that obvious I'm smitten? I haven't said anything to anyone besides Lenny, and I know he's kept his mouth shut. "Do I know her?" Hannah probes not so subtly.

This line of questioning is pissing me off, as if I owe her an explanation.

"Hannah, we fucked. That's it. I don't have to explain myself to you. I don't want to do this anymore. Can you accept that?"

"Fuck you, Wilder," she huffs before leaving my glass corner office. I look up at the ceiling and mouth, "Thank you." Although it wasn't necessarily a civil discussion, at least it's over. I've been dreading this inevitable conversation once I started declining Hannah's advances via text; once I started hanging out with Ava. I'm glad it's done with. I can still hear the faint clicking of her heels as she sees herself off my floor.

Even if my Hannah problem has been mostly solved, I can't say the same when I think about my relationship with Ava and her clear hesitation the other night. I felt this wave of guilt when she brought up her past, and I sat there nodding like a coward, pretending I'm clueless, apologizing about what she went through as if I was hearing it for the first time. But Fisher did his due diligence. I know everything about Ava Ruth Campbell, but she won't ever know that, as long as I can help it. Well, for now, anyway.

My chest is tight and unsettled when Ava texts to ask me out on a formal coffee date later on in the week. I've respected her space the last few days, but God knows how bad I wanted to text, call, see her. If she's asking to meet, one of two things will happen. I've either been given a chance to prove to her how good this can be or she's decided that being together right now is too distracting. In her defense, I get it. There's no denying that I have quite a reputation in New York City. I regret it looking back. Having that man-whore past is dangerous because it puts me in a position where I'd have to explain myself to a girl like Ava, who doesn't have that past, nothing like it. I know that I don't deserve her. I'll never deserve her. What I do deserve isn't anything more than a girl who's done just the same. What I deserve is a Hannah. Because Ava's a saint, and I'm a sinner.

AVA

I know that I told him I would think about it, and I have, but maybe it was a shitty idea to put that on my conscience, to put pressure on myself to make a decision. I should have listened to Bridget and surrendered because I've been on a "what if" bender, driving myself absolutely insane even though I know how badly I want to be with Grant or at least try to see if we fit. I popped a Xanax for crying out loud. The paralyzing thoughts of my time at the hospital in San Francisco are damning and the Grant situation only leads to overanalyzing that period in my life. Those are the memories that vividly flash in my mind when I think about Pat. No matter what I try to do to move forward, it's impossible. I'm sick and tired of feeling like I can't escape something so traumatic. I can't get away from what happened to me, and it's been two years. Sometimes I wake up and can still smell that sterile hospital room.

I know that I'm doing this to myself—that meeting someone and dating them should be easy and fun, not stressful and scary. I'm torturing myself and for what? It sure isn't Grant's idea. He just wants to know when the next time we can hang out is. I'm the one making this dramatic. Frankly, I'm surprised he's still interested after watching me make such a debacle over a relationship that hasn't yet started. It's immature, I know that, but how else am I supposed to protect my heart? Shouldn't it be this thought-out, meticulous process before choosing to move forward with someone new? Isn't that what everyone who's been heartbroken does?

Bridget calls to check in on me a few days later, not knowing that I've been having a really tough time alone with my thoughts and memories.

"To what do I owe this call?"

"Ugh! Jeremy took the kids to the park, and the baby is sleeping. I missed you. What's up? How's the new dude?" I can almost see her curling up in the corner of the couch with a sugary iced coffee in hand, extra ice. I miss home. I miss her fuzzy couch pillows.

"I've actually been having a really bad week, so thanks for calling, friend." I take a deep breath before giving her more context. "Bridget, I feel like I'll never be able to move on from what happened, and it's been years. I'm really struggling," I croak quietly. I have this ridiculous lump wedged in my throat, and I really don't want to cry right now. I swallow hard. "I've been so gaslighted by Pat that I feel unmotivated to try again."

"Babe, before we talk about this . . . are you still taking the medication?" She seems genuinely concerned and worried about me, and I love her for it, I do, but why does it always go back to the medication? With Mom too. They make me out to be a crazy person, dependent on meds to be a functioning member of society, and it's freaking annoying.

"I'm taking them," I assure her. "But it's not like I can erase what happened from memory. I'm not suicidal anymore, Bridget, but I don't know how to be a new person."

"You're never going to be a new person, babe. You're always going to have that past because it happened to *you*. It's a part of you now, and moving on just means embracing what you went through and being strong enough to live your life despite it. You can do this, Ava. I promise."

"What about the parts of my life that I can't tell anyone about? If things get serious . . ."

"If things get serious, you might change your mind about telling him."

I shake my head, tell her that I'll never change my mind, that they're just too bad, too incriminating.

"Never say never, darling."

I dismiss her because she's not the one living with the guilt of her painful past. And then I get to the big piece of the struggle I've been keeping quiet until now.

"Bridget, he's just like Pat," I whisper into the receiver, hiding the words from the walls of my apartment.

"What do you mean, *he's just like Pat?*"

"No, not like that. This guy is so kind, Bridget, but . . . Expensive *everything.* Car, watch, suit . . ."

She laughs at me. "That doesn't mean anything." But it does mean something. It means we're totally different people from totally different worlds.

"How does it not mean anything?! Pat was an ass to me because I didn't look the part!"

She scoffs. "Ummm, Ava. Not all rich people are assholes. You met *one.* He was a royal dickwad, but part of dating again after heartbreak is taking a chance. Now, I don't even know who this guy is, and you won't let me Google him, but if he only resembles Pat externally, *take the leap. Jump.* You can't plant yourself in quicksand for the rest of your life because of one guy, two years ago. Don't give Pat that power." As soon as she says that last bit, about me giving Pat power over my relationship with Grant, I hang up immediately and text him, asking if he wants to meet me at Rocco's.

He smiles and hugs me when I walk through the door. "Ava. Hi. Shall we?"

I try to decipher what his tone of voice could mean but there's nothing. It's just kind Grant. He motions toward the back tables, the ones I always sit at, so I follow him through the café. I notice his clothes are different than what he typically wears because it's Sunday. It looks like he ran here. He's in sportswear, and the gray sweatshirt he's wearing slightly mutes the harshness of his green eyes.

"Thank you for meeting me," I say once seated.

"You don't have to thank me." He laughs. "How are you? How you been?" We exchange formalities until its apparent I'm to speak.

"I wanted to tell you that I'm sorry about the other night. I'm young and I have a tough time trusting new people. I'm not ready to talk about it yet, but it's nothing you did; it's simply the way I am. This is hard for me, you and I." He's calm, nodding in understanding. "I shouldn't have let you leave the other night without giving you an answer. I didn't mean to string you along or anything, I just needed time and space to come to a decision."

He raises an eyebrow and asks, "And what decision is that?"

"I want to see if this can work. If you still want to . . ." I whisper, my face turning pink.

"Nahhhhh, I'm good," he teases and smirks. It makes me giggle. Grant reaches his long arm across the table and holds my hand.

"It would be my honor, Ava. Thank you for being honest with me. I think it's my turn to do the same?" he says, squirming in his seat. I nod for him to continue. "It's a bit of a disclaimer, but you deserve to hear it. I have a past and it's not pretty. But that isn't me anymore. You might hear things about me, but I just ask that you judge me based on the guy that I am right here, right now, with you." Flashes of guilt cross his face, but then he gives me a sincere, shy smile. If I have a past as nasty as mine, it's only fair to give Grant a chance with a clean slate, just like I expect him to with me. I squeeze his hand and smile across the table.

"Of course, Grant. I can do that."

AVA

I praise Hallelujah after class on Friday when my 2:00 lecture is over. This week was a nightmare, and I am so ready for the weekend. When I reach the stairwell of my apartment after the exhausting day I had, I quicken my steps when I notice something pasted on my door. It's a sticky note. I peel it off and read the messy, boyish handwriting. It says *I miss you* with a really ugly sketch of a heart. I can't stop smiling, so I pull out my phone to text him.

Me: I got your note. I'm crushing real hard right now.

It's nice that I can finally let myself enjoy this thing between us instead of pining over our differences. I have Bridget to thank for that.

Grant: LOL. Cutie. I missed you this week.

Me: Me too

And I did. It really sucked that I was nose deep in school-work all week because I would've loved to hang out with Grant. We haven't been able to do any of that since we agreed to finally do this thing.

Grant: How are you? Any plans tonight?

Me: None.

Grant: I was hoping I could take you out. Dinner?

Me: Sure. What should I wear?

Grant: It's a nice place if that helps but you're gorgeous always. I'll pick you up at six.

This man.

I run a quick load of laundry and gorge a bowl of cocoa puffs before getting ready for tonight's date. Yeah, I said it. *Date.* After taking a quick shower and blow-drying my hair, I split it down the middle and curl a few pieces to give it a little spice. He *did* say it was a nice place. I whisk on some mascara and lipstick before slipping into a pretty black dress, one of the only formal items I brought with me to college. I shuffle into a pair of comfortable boots, and walk to my coatrack when I hear a soft knock. My heart rate picks up, and I have to beg it to stop. *Get. It. Together.*

I open the door and Grant greets me with the widest grin, his eye creases more pronounced. I can't help but chuckle and smile back. The suit he's wearing is crisp and gorgeous, and I'm going to salivate.

"Wow. Hi."

I flush when he bites his lip.

"Hi back. Let me grab my coat." He follows my movements with his eyes, a fiery intensity to them, and I feel it. Like, *feel it* feel it. We walk toward Grant's beautiful car, and he jogs ahead to open the passenger door for me. The car slows as we pull up to a luxurious New York City steakhouse a short drive away. There is a block-long line out front, and that can only mean one thing. *Is he serious?*

I turn to him, wide eyed. "I can't let you take me here, Grant," I exclaim nervously.

"What? Why not?" he asks with his hand already on the door handle. I tell him that this is way too much, too fancy.

"Ava, we're on a date and the food here is amazing. Besides, we already have reservations. Can't back out now," he nudges with a wink. I'm still hesitant when he puts his arm around me and walks us toward the entrance, dismissing the line and being escorted into the restaurant with just the mention of his name. *Of course he does.*

We sit at a table for two in a quaint corner and browse our leather menus. I can feel Grant watching my every move, and after a couple of minutes go by, I put down my menu to glance up at him.

"What?"

"*What?*" he asks with feigned confusion.

"Don't play dumb! You're staring at me!" I laugh.

"You look breathtaking tonight, Ava." He smiles shyly. "Tell me everything about you." *Everything but three, Grant.*

"Okay . . . ask me something."

"Rapid-fire questions?"

I'm giggling when I nod, soon turning hot. Is the heat on in here or am I just nervous? "As long as I go next," I say, placing my folded arms on the table to face him head-on. Is this proper NYC steakhouse etiquette? Screw it. I don't belong here anyway, might as well be comfortable. Grant agrees.

"Deal. All right, Ava. Let's start with . . . your favorite color."

"Green."

"Favorite book."

"I plead the fifth."

He throws his head back in laughter at my reply. "You are so cute. Wow. Okay . . . If you were an animal, which animal would you be?" This question is hilarious. How old is he again?

"A horse or a baby tiger."

He's biting his bottom lip like he did at my door and giving me sexy eyes and *kiss me, damnit.* Why hasn't he kissed me yet! He continues.

"Superpower?"

"Teleportation," I reply. There's instant relief over how much I'm enjoying this stupid bit. It requires more effort to deny this than to just *be*.

"Favorite movie?" Grant asks.

"I plead the fifth again. These rapid-fire questions are harder to answer than I thought." He's shaking his head and chuckling. *Tell me what you're thinking, Grant Wilder.*

"Okay, top *three* favorite movies."

"Um . . . *Ocean's Eleven, Twelve* and *Thirteen*," I reply. Growing up with three brothers who hogged the remote, I became accustomed to thrillers and action movies. I've never watched *Titanic*.

"Wow! NERD ALERT!" Grant exclaims.

I put a finger to my lips and try to shush him while also cracking up. "You're *so* mean," I pout. He gazes at me, reaching across the table to squeeze my hand. Before firing his next question, an accent-stricken waiter approaches our table, telling Grant that it's nice to see him again. Grant orders us a bottle of wine with dinner. I'm not twenty-one yet but we won't mention that on the off chance that Grant doesn't realize how young I am and might be the one to question this when he does.

"Where were we . . . all right, what do you like to do in your spare time?"

"That's a good question. I like listening to music? Reading?" I did a lot of that in my two years of recovery. Mom would go to the library and bring me a week's worth of books to the hospital so I wasn't too bored.

"A bookworm too?" he mocks with a wide grin. I laugh. "I think I'm running out of questions."

"My turn! Favorite color?"

"White," he offers, his voice assured and deep.

"White is the absence of color. It's not its own color," I inform him.

"Great, I'm already screwing up on the first question," he jokes. "And also . . . NERD ALERT!"

I burst out laughing and shrug. "You know what? I'll take it. I'm a nerd and that's fine with me." I mean, he isn't wrong. I wasn't exactly the popular kid in high school. I've been focused on mostly school for the last six years of my life.

"That's *more* than fine with me too, Ava," he says, winking. *You're killing me, man.*

"Let's resume. You're not getting off that fast. Superpower?"

"Hm . . . can I steal teleportation?"

"Well, I stole your coffee, so *yes*. But now we're even."

I make Grant laugh again, and my heart leaps when I hear his deep chuckle. I can't get over how gorgeous he is as he sits across from me. *Me.* My thoughts are interrupted by the waiter bringing our steak dinner, setting down a plate for each of us and pouring two tall glasses of wine. I take a bite out of the food, and it is absolutely divine. I don't want to know how much he's spending on this dinner.

"Good, right?"

I nod. "*So* good. Thank you for this."

"Thanks for not running away at the door. I told you it was delicious," he teases with another wink. No one's ever provoked naughty thoughts in me, but damn, I'd be lying if I said I wasn't attracted to him. I waste no time delving back into the interrogation.

"When is your birthday, Grant?"

"December 16, 1989. What's yours?"

Okay, so we're doing month, day, *and* year. Here goes it. "May 22, 1997."

He nearly chokes on a piece of steak and sets down his fork and knife. Gawking at me wide-eyed, he asks, "Did you just say 1997?" I nod. "Wait, how old *are* you?" Right, so when

I said that Grant doesn't realize how young I am? Yeah, he does now.

"I'm twenty," I reply as casually as I can, wanting to divert from this epically embarrassing conversation now that it's starting to make sense why the thought of Grant liking me this much was so unexpected. *I knew it. I knew there was a catch here somewhere.*

"Wait, wait, hold on. *You're twenty?*" He does the mental math, rocking his head and blinking in concentration. "Well, yeah, I guess you are twenty."

"I'm not lying." I chuckle. "How old are you?"

"I'll be twenty-eight in December."

"Wow," I whisper, peering down into my plate. Now I'm doing the math. "We're almost eight years apart."

"Yeah, I know. I hope that doesn't change anything," he replies wearily. It warms something in me, but I'm still incredibly mortified.

"No, no." I wave him off nonchalantly. "I mean it doesn't for me. Does it for you?"

"Hell no." That vote of confidence is so sexy. "I just hope I don't seem like a pedo," he mumbles.

I sip on my glass of wine as a distraction. but when I'm all twitchy, I excuse myself to go to the restroom. I grip the black granite sink and focus on my breathing. It's sinking in—this is going to end badly, and I already let it get too far. There's no way Grant will want to continue seeing me after finding out how young I am, even if he said things don't change. How can they not? I'm a *baby*.

I am so self-conscious right now. I make my way back to the table before he thinks something is wrong.

"Hey, babe, look at me. Nothing changes here, I swear. I was surprised, that's all."

I sigh. "It's okay, I understand." I slowly pick up my fork and continue eating.

After a few moments, he interrupts the silence. "Ask me something."

I give him a small smile and nod. I regain a bit of the confidence I lost from our age revelation and proceed with the questions.

"Uh . . . let's see," I quietly say as I gather my thoughts. "Any pets?"

"We have a family dog named Ginger, but I don't have any of my own. How about you?"

I shake my head. "No, I wish. I think I'd be a good dog mom." I've wanted one ever since I was a little girl, but we couldn't afford the extra expenses what with vaccinations, vet bills, dog food . . .

"The *best* dog mom." Grant smiles.

"I don't have any questions left." I'm still a bit put out by this *I'll be twenty-eight in December* thing.

"Tell me about your parents. You mentioned that your mom is Spanish. Is your dad Spanish too?"

I shake my head. "No, my dad's American. Grew up in a town outside of Cincinnati. His name is David and my mom's name is Evelyn. My father's parents were really racist, so when he brought my mom home and they didn't approve, he whisked her away to Northern California. He's worked in a factory my whole life, even more. Like thirty-five years, I think. My mom is from Madrid. I'm super close with both of them." I haven't thought about Dad's parents in years. Dad tried fixing that relationship many times, but they never came around to his love for my mother. And that love is ginormous. My parents' relationship is the one I've always hoped to have one day.

"Do you have any siblings?" Grant asks, taking a bite of his steak. He sips his wine, watching me intently as I tell him what makes me, me.

"I do. I'm the youngest of four. I have three older brothers. Devon, Cooper, and Connor. In that order." Grant is so surprised when I tell him about those clowns. Man, I miss them.

"No way! *Really?*"

I laugh at his reaction. "Really. Why?"

"I was not expecting that. Do I have anything to worry about?" He's amused. And yes. They've always been incredibly overprotective with me. They were murderous over what happened with Pat. "What's your hometown like?"

Here we go, Grant . . .. This is where you're about to find out just how different we really are.

"It's a really small town in Arcata, California. I've pretty much been surrounded by the same people my entire life. Everyone knows each other there; it's like we're all one big happy family. One school, one church. I really do love it, but I was ready to see more." *Ready is an understatement.* And it wasn't about seeing the outside world as much as it was getting away from what had become mine.

"Oh, wow. So you're a small-town girl," he jokes. "That's a big step to take. I'm proud of you."

Would you still be proud if you knew the real reason I came here?

"Your turn to divulge, Grant. It's only fair. Tell me about yourself."

He squirms in his chair. I give him an encouraging smile and wait for him to speak.

"Uhh . . . well, my family moved here from Texas when I was nine. Houston. We're four siblings too. I have two sisters and a brother. Annie is the oldest, then me, then Ben and Layla. My parents are Callum, which you know, and my mom's name is Julia. They're such great people, and I can't wait for you to meet them," he sneaks in casually. "I graduated with an engineering degree from UPenn."

I ogle at him. "You went to UPenn?! Well, check you out!" He blushes and I laugh cheekily. Ivy freaking League. I feel lucky to be sitting across from this beautiful, successful man who is so out of my league, it's laughable. I notice the sudden silence around us and scope out the restaurant to find that we're the last ones here.

"Hey, look! Everyone's gone. I didn't realize that we've been here that long!" I whisper across the table, quietly laughing with him. We were so caught up in each other, it's like the world around us stopped. That's the best kind of date. I'm really enjoying tonight with him. *Gah, I'm so lucky.*

"Let me pay and we'll go. Wanna grab your coat?" He greets me a couple of minutes later at the coat check; I hand him his coat and he helps me into mine. A gesture like that? Pat could never. *This* is what I need. Grant is *exactly* what I need.

"The food and wine were incredible, Grant. Thank you."

"Thank *you* for agreeing to try this with me," he says, lowering himself to kiss my cheek.

The ride back to my apartment is comfortably quiet. A minute before we reach my apartment, Grant takes my hand and kisses it, holding it against his lips for the rest of the drive. I can hear the whoosh of my heart beating in my chest. I don't know why I'm so shaky. A simple touch, a simple kiss, a simple compliment. They get me. They get me so bad and now I'm wondering if it's too much too soon.

The silence follows us from the car ride, and the only sound heard is our footsteps on the pavement. As soon as we reach the lobby door, I turn my head but not before Grant's lips are on mine and he's kissing me. I'm winded as I kiss him back, unable to breathe. He's holding my head in his hand and kisses me with passion and conviction, and man oh man, I'm done for. *This* is a kiss.

"I'm sorry. I just—I've wanted to do that all night," he breathes. I smile up at him because, I mean, look at the guy! And he's wanted to do that all night? *Him?* Mr. Ivy League, tall, gorgeousness wanted to kiss *me?*

"You have such a crush on me, Grant Wilder." I laugh.

"I really do." He cups my cheeks and lifts my face up to look at him. "I'm gonna kiss you again, okay?"

I nod and let him, so he kisses me, softer than before. I glance at the door.

"Do you want to come inside?"

Grant raises an eyebrow at my question, curious that I've asked. "Are you sure about that?"

"Yes."

We sit together on the sofa, Grant's arm around me, and the length of our thighs pressed together. I lay my head on his shoulder, and he cuddles me into him.

"I had a great time tonight," he whispers into my hair, his thumb like a fireball stroking my shoulder and making it hard to concentrate because of how attracted I am to him. The anticipation of tonight—the wine plus the kiss plus inviting him over—is probably why he has to say, "Earth to Ava."

I lift my head up to look at him. "What?"

"I was asking if you wanted to walk me out." He chuckles. "You good?"

"No, I don't want to walk you out," I reply without looking at him, feeling my face warm at what I'm implying. Nevertheless, he requests confirmation.

"And why is that, Ava?" Something in his voice sounds playful but also serious, like he knows that this is a big deal for me. I also know that I probably come off as inexperienced, but I still don't want him to leave.

"I want you to stay here tonight. Is that okay?"

He nods and bends to stand from his position on the couch. As soon as he begins shrugging off his suit jacket, that's the moment everything gets much too real and I feel myself chickening out. Am I supposed to have sex with him tonight? Do I want to?

Obviously I want to.

"Are we about to have sex?" It comes out of my mouth before I have the chance to hold back my blunt question, and my eyes widen in surprise. Why do I seem to do that with Grant?

"That's entirely up to you, Ava," he responds, gazing at me in concentration, his thick black eyebrows pinched and serious.

"I mean, I want to. But I don't really know how . . . I mean, I know what it is. I'm not a virgin or anything, but maybe a little bit? I'm not sure if I'm considered one." I've said way too much, and I purse my lips in an attempt to shut my stupid mouth up.

Grant squeezes my shoulder and smiles sweetly. "You're ranting again."

I remember that hectic morning at Rocco's. Clearly, he does too.

"I am. I do that when I'm nervous."

His eyes soften and he takes my hands in his. "There is *zero* expectation here, Ava. I hope you know that. Zero."

Of course I know that, and the fact that I have no doubts that Grant is good and kind and patient is the moment my anxiety turns into resolve. I will no longer compare Grant to Pat, because although I claim that they come from the same world, they are in fact worlds apart. It's good versus bad. Kind versus evil. Right versus wrong.

Grant watches as I mentally set this bounding goal for myself. For him, actually.

"Do you want to have a conversation about this? I think we should get it out of the way, yes?"

I hesitantly nod, gulping. I'll be as vague as possible; the layers on this story are onion-like, and I'm not ready to divulge anything personal to Grant yet. "I slept with someone only one time. That's it. I'm not experienced or anything. But I . . ." I step forward and I'm timid when I say, "I want that with you. Maybe not tonight but soon." I feel chills when he puts his finger under my chin and tilts my head up to look at him.

"Me too, babe. Soon sounds great."

He's so big and tall and strong, and I wonder how making love to Grant will compare to what I did with Pat, but I know that it is hugely incomparable. It would be an insult to Grant if I think about it for one more second, so I don't.

GRANT

I wake up beside Ava on Saturday morning with this fullness I can't quite pinpoint but know that I have never felt before. All I know is that it's because we *didn't* sleep together last night, which sounds utterly bizarre coming from me, but it's true. Asking me to sleep over simply because she wanted me there for companionship was so different and unusual than anything I've done in the past with any girl and in the best way possible. It made me feel like a man, like a *taken* man.

I lie next to Ava and watch her body move up and down in slow motion as she inhales, exhales. Her delicate hands are clasped together acting as a pillow under her head, and she's almost literally curled up into a ball, her thighs resting against her belly. Gently, I tuck a loose strand of hair behind her ear before quietly tiptoeing to the bathroom. I hope to find a spare toothbrush, so I browse through her bathroom's drawers and cabinets. That's when I discover three orange plastic bottles that make my heart stop.

Ava Ruth Campbell. Take one tablet by mouth every morning with food.

Ava Ruth Campbell. Take half a pill as needed for anxiety.

Ava Ruth Campbell. Take one tablet by mouth every morning for depression.

My hand shakes holding these pill bottles, reading and re-reading the labels over and over again. I have to force myself to still my arm to stop Ava from hearing the pills rattle against the hard plastic, but it's pointless because I hear her faint voice call out my name and pause in the doorway when she sees what my hands are full with. With her eyes wide, her cheeks flushed, she rushes over to grab them from my hand. She looks around the bathroom at the open cabinets and drawers, and I instantly know how this looks.

"What're you doing?" Her voice breaks, like she's willing herself not to cry. I close my eyes and inhale deeply.

"Ava . . ." I have no words because from her stance, I look bad. I look like a monster.

"Were you snooping around or something? Trying to find things out about me?" Her voice is laced with anger, but more importantly, it's laced with hurt. Pain. Betrayal, even. After last night's conversation and the way that this looks, I can understand how she feels.

"I swear I was just looking for a toothbrush," I beg.

"I don't believe that," she sneers.

"You think I wanted to find those?"

She uses the back of her hand to swipe the tears that are rolling down her cheeks, and as I hear the words exiting my mouth, I wish I could fucking backtrack. That was bad. I should not have said that. All I meant was that I don't want her to be in enough pain that she has to be medicated. To her, it looks like I don't want to date someone who is.

"I certainly didn't want you to." When I walk toward her, she takes a jolted step back. "Please don't touch me," she whispers. I motion for her to follow me to the couch, but she stays under the bathroom doorframe with her arms crossed.

"I'm fine right here," she croaks quietly, fiddling with her feet, eyes down and embarrassed.

"Were you planning on telling me?" I ask, watching as she jerks her head up to face me.

"Tell you what? That I'm fucked up? Yeah, probably not." She's breathless and embarrassed and ashamed, and I wish I could strip her of every insecure feeling right now. I know that what she went through wasn't easy. I know that it was hell. I tell her not to say that about herself, ask her to please talk to me. She shakes her head and remains silent, looking at the floor. I remember the conversation that we had at Rocco's earlier this week when Ava said that she's not ready to talk about her shit. But then she said she wanted to do this with me, and we went on a date last night, and she asked me to sleep over, so I'm a little confused. Does she want this or not? And in what way?

"You don't really tell me much. I don't understand."

"I'm a private person," she replies in conclusion, like this conversation is one and done.

"Okay . . . But you and me are trying to start something here, are we not? If you're going to discuss private matters with someone, shouldn't I be on that list?"

"Not necessarily." She shrugs. The casualness of her response itches my skin, and I have to focus on remaining calm. I'm the bad guy here, so I don't get to be mad.

"Ava, if you don't tell me private things, then what are we doing here?" God, it feels good to say that. "I understand that you've been through a lot, but you're not really giving me any hope that I'm worthy of this private, exclusive side of you."

"I'm not unfaithful to you or anything," she interjects. *Huh?*

"I know that. I'm just asking that you stop being so secretive to the point where you refuse to tell me anything about your past." I sound angry but I'm not. Not really. I feel despondency more than anything because I know that there's a story to tell.

"I barely have a past!" Ava interjects. "And forgive me for wanting some privacy. It's been two months at best, Grant. I don't owe you my life."

My deception is bad, I know that, but the mere fact that I know all about her past has me dying to hear it from her end. I shake my head.

"I'm not asking for your life. I'm not asking for anything other than the bare minimum, but you won't even give me that. There's something you're not telling me. Are you denying that?" Timidly, she shakes her head out of sheer defeat. I don't want to win but I want her to trust me. "Do you want to tell me? Do you even want to be with me?"

She whispers to the ground, objecting. "You know I do."

"Do I know that? Because I'm literally standing here explaining that I'm not sure what I am to you."

"I'm . . ." She walks toward me. "I'm sorry. I just have a hard time opening up because I never really did it. I mean, I was never in something serious before. Well, maybe I was. I thought it was serious. But what you and me are . . . it's different. It's new and I just . . . I don't really know what I'm doing. I don't want to hurt you. I promise. But talking about my past is something that I don't really know how to do. I've never done it before, so I'm clueless. Do I just approach you one day and tell you how depressed I once was?" Ava's eyes are sullen and she pants. I grit my teeth. *Fucking McCall.*

I watch the insecurity pouring out of Ava, the shame and hesitation, and I immediately regret saying anything at all. She's right, she doesn't owe me anything. We've only hung out a handful of times, but somehow, I already feel so close to her. I look at her with so much sympathy.

"See? I don't know how to do this."

"Ava . . ."

She grabs my hand, takes a deep breath. "I'm sorry. I am. I know you weren't snooping. I know I haven't been transparent with you and I'm sorry."

Guilt claws at my chest. She has nothing to be sorry for, and I do, but I need her. I want her to be all in like I've been since our second encounter. I'm feeling really desperate right now, and it's probably such a turnoff.

"I need all of you to do this. You know that, right?" I ask.

"Are you saying that . . . that if I don't tell you, you're going to break up with me?"

My heart sinks into my belly, and I'm frantic that she can think this of me. McCall really ruined her perception of relationships. I grab Ava's face.

"No way. No. I'm not ending this. Please believe me. I just want you to know that I'm here and I'm yours, and it would mean a lot to me to have you at your fullest. Whether it's tomorrow or in a year. It's something that would make me happy."

She nods understandingly. "Okay. I get that, but I don't feel ready yet," she whispers finally before walking over to casually make her bed. It's awfully silent, and after ten, twenty minutes, I coax her to look at me.

"Ava." She looks up but doesn't speak. "I'm sorry I found the bottles before you were ready to tell me, and I'm sorry for coming on too strong. I guess I have a hard time accepting that it hasn't been too long and you don't have any obligation to me. When you're ready, you'll let me know. Until then, let's move forward as best we can."

"Thank you." She smiles. "I like that plan."

GRANT

A va and I have developed this sort of routine the last couple of weeks. Work for me, school for her, lots of making out and hanging out whenever she's free. Then there's this awkward elephant in the room every time we're together since I found those pill bottles in her bathroom cabinet. I can sense that she's retreated, like she's protecting herself against potential heartbreak even though we planned to move forward that day, because she doesn't know that her story won't come as a surprise to me. However, the more I think about it, the more I realize that it will. Reading about her life on paper, about some girl I didn't know yet, won't come anywhere close to the emotional conversation face-to-face; to hearing about Ava's painful past after developing these monumental feelings, so big and bold and foreign.

I pick up the phone as an incoming call lights up the screen, and I close my office door when I see that it's Ava. No one needs to overhear our conversation. No one needs to ask me questions. Even Dina.

I make a mental note to give Ava a designated ringtone. "Hey, babe."

"Hey, hey. Uh . . . are you busy right now?" I can hear lively chatter and traffic in the background. She must've just finished class. I start to load my pockets with my wallet and keys, clasp my Rolex on, and grab my suit jacket from the back of the black leather office chair.

"Not at all," I tell her. "Why, what's up?" I'm already power walking toward the elevator because of this palpable excitement I feel that I'm about to see Ava. I am such a joke, but sorry not sorry.

"Can I see you? I wanted to talk to you," she calls out, the New York City commotion obnoxiously loud in the background.

"Of course. Wanna come over to my place?" I ask hopefully. She's never been over, and I want to share it with her, to watch her in my space and feel the comfort I know I will when she's hanging out at my apartment. It'll feel more like home than it ever has, simply with Ava there, and I'm excited when she tells me that yes, she'll come over, that she's going to take a train and I should send her the address.

"You sure, babe? I can come get you." I don't want her taking the subway. There are creeps there, and she is too precious for that. Like I said, I am a joke.

"I'm totally sure." She chuckles.

"Okay. Just mention your name to the doorman. His name is Bobby. He'll let you in."

As soon as I exit the elevator at the penthouse floor, Ava jumps up from her position on the floor by my front door and grins at me.

"Hi!" she calls out, then quickly covers her mouth when she realizes how loud that came out. "Hi," she tries again in a whisper. Every man on this planet should experience a greeting like that when he comes home from work at least once in his lifetime. She walks toward me down the quiet hallway and gives me a tight hug. "I missed you."

I chuckle. "Yeah?" I feel her head nod against my body. She then looks puzzlingly at my chest.

"I think you're getting a phone call." I hurriedly unlock the door and tell her that I'll be just a couple of minutes. I watch as she hangs her coat on the coatrack and settles her JanSport backpack on the ground near it. What a throwback.

I observe every inch of Ava from my home office door, curious what she's thinking as she surveys her surroundings at my apartment in the heart of the city. I let her do her thing because for now, I'm going to take her in, and I'm forced to turn my head to hide the enormous grin that's taken over my face. Ava is wearing a long-sleeved pink T-shirt that peeks out from under a pair of denim overalls. They're rolled up to her ankles, making room for a pair of black high-top Converse. The black beanie that sits loose on her head makes me smile. I have never met anyone like this girl. I'm not sure they exist.

I watch as Ava walks around my kitchen with her hands in her pockets, lifting her head to study the walls, the fridge, the cabinets. Eventually she makes it to the living room, then dining room, still fixated on observing every detail of my house that she can get her eye on. The way she walks slowly with her head tilted; her eyes squinted—it's as if she's at an art gallery. I find it so authentic and beautiful.

"You like it?" I call out as soon as I hit the end call button.

"Of course I like it. It's so . . . *luxurious*. So fancy!" she exclaims in a terrible British accent. I howl.

"To what do I owe this awesome surprise?" I ask when I reach her. She's standing at the wide black leather sectional placed squarely in the middle of my living room and places her hands on my shoulders, taking a deep breath.

"I've been thinking about this awkward tension between us the last couple of weeks. I know you feel it because I do too, and Bridget gave me some sage advice," she admits. I bend to kiss her, and she smiles against my lips.

"What's that?" I place my hands on top of hers on my shoulders and study her expression.

"That the only way to move forward is to let go of my past. I think I need to tell you what happened to me. You think that too, right?" Her eyes are honey, looking up at me so innocently and hopeful, and it makes me feel hopeful too because she's finally ready.

"I think it's a good start," I reply cautiously.

She takes a deep breath and plops herself down on the couch. "Okay, cool," she says.

I sit beside her and smile. I'm always smiling with Ava. "Cool," I mimic.

"Well, once upon a time . . ." she begins but stops to giggles uncontrollably. I laugh with her. *I'm obsessed.* "No, it's definitely not that kind of story. Okay, let me start over. So, the summer before I was supposed to come to NYU for freshman year, I got this internship at a real estate office in LA because I was a business major back then. And there was this boy . . ."

"There's always a boy."

"Yes. Well, not for me. I never dated or partied or anything like that. I had just turned eighteen, and he was my first proper crush. His name was Pat, and his dad was the boss." She studies my eyes for any hint of judgment, but it won't come. *It won't come, Ava.*

"Oof. The boss's son," I say.

"Yeah. So anyway, he liked me back and we started hanging out a little and everything felt normal, but then after a few weeks, he was putting a lot of pressure on me to like, sleep with him, and the worst part is that I started considering it even though I'd never done that before." She blinks down to her lap, scratching the fabric of her overalls in a nervous tic.

"That's messed up, Ava," I whisper, angered and wildly defensive of her. I want to rip his throat out.

"I know it is. We ended up . . . I don't want to make you uncomfortable, Grant," she stops herself to say. How is she thinking about *me* right now? The kindness on this girl, I swear.

"You're not, babe. Don't worry about me."

She nods. "Okay. Um, so we ended up doing it because I was stupid and I would've done anything he told me to at that point." She winces before saying, "This next part is kind of really bad, okay?" I bend to kiss her, assure her that there's no judgment here. That I want her to feel comfortable with me.

"I got pregnant and by the time I found out . . . wait, why aren't you reacting?" she questions. "And like, kicking me out or something."

Scanning my face like she did my apartment, she searches for a reaction, but I don't give her the one she expects. I already knew this. I look at her like she's speaking gibberish.

"You're serious," I state. "You were expecting me to kick you out of my apartment."

"Kind of? Well, not kick me out but maybe get a little mad?" she admits.

I kiss her again. "You think I scare that easy?"

"I don't know but—"

"Why don't you finish? I want you to get it all out. Does that work for you?"

She nods. "Yeah, okay. So, I got pregnant and by the time I found out, I was already back home up north. When I called Pat to tell him, he kind of ghosted me and then I was sent an affidavit. Do you know what that is?"

"I am familiar with an affidavit, yes. What did they want?"

"They wanted me to disappear. They claimed that I planned the pregnancy to have leverage over them so I could ask for money." She's got these doe eyes when she talks to me, innocent and real and genuinely confused, like the thought of what they were implying still doesn't sit right with her. After meeting her, I realize the same.

"Let me get this straight. They thought you went down there for an internship to seduce the rich boss's son into getting you pregnant so you could extract money from them." I say it out loud to let her know that I understand what they were doing; the story they were using.

"Isn't that crazy?"

I kiss her. Again. "It is crazy. It's absurd. Tell me more." So, she does. She tells me about the decision to abort the baby because of the pressure from Pat and his friends. That her family was supportive despite their religious beliefs. That she had to travel away from Arcata for fear of damaging her spotless reputation.

"When I got to the hospital, they found that I was having a really dangerous ectopic pregnancy. It's basically when the baby doesn't make it to the uterus and it tries to grow in one of the tubes. They couldn't abort the baby safely and I was losing a ton of blood, so I had an emergency surgery and my body went into septic shock."

I close my eyes, cover my mouth, and breathe. Holy shit. What they did to this poor girl. I hug Ava fiercely, tightly, and whisper that I'm so sorry in more ways than one.

I hold her face, look her deep in the eyes. "You are so incredibly strong, Ava. I need you to know that. You have to know that." She darts her eyes away from mine, and I notice her fingers fidgeting on her thighs.

"Do you really think that?" she whispers. She seems shocked, like she doesn't hear it enough. Ava has to know how strong she is for overcoming this; she needs to be told that something of this magnitude requires resilience, and she absolutely has that. I vow to tell her myself.

"Really, Ava."

She shakes her head disbelievingly. I hate it.

"Well, I'm not finished. You might think differently."

I place my hand on her thigh and gently rub my thumb across the denim. "After you tell me what happened to you?" I ask to confirm.

"Yeah."

I shake my head. "Ava, I guarantee that I won't. I've already made up my mind about you, Miss Campbell," I smile.

She chuckles and looks adoringly at my face. I think she's finally just as hooked as I am.

"Yeah? What's that?"

"That you are totally and utterly perfect," I claim.

"No." Her voice wavers. She shakes her head hurriedly. "I'm not perfect, Grant. Let me finish."

Nothing changes on my end, I mean it. Ava is so good and pure and her strength makes me appreciate her even more. This conversation changed things for me. She continues with her story.

"I was sick for a long time, and it made me really anxious and depressed. I had—*have*—a lot of guilt because of what I did, and sometimes it's hard to live with it. That's what the meds are for. It's just so I can live my life somewhat normally," she whispers, her voice shaky and pained. "I can't believe I just told you that."

My heart constricts and I feel like flying to LA and beating Pat up myself. I'm angry for her. I'm angry because it's been two years and he still has somewhat of a hold on her. She's still recovering, and that's Pat's fault.

"It doesn't faze me that you're on medication, Ava. I only care that you're happy. I wish you believed me when I say that nothing changes. I'm in this, I'm committed. You know that, right?"

"Yeah," she purrs, leaning over to give me a hug. With a light kiss to my neck, she buries her head and tightens her grip. "I do know that."

"Is there anything else you want to tell me?" I whisper into her hair.

"No. That's the whole story."

AVA

I told Grant everything. Well, not everything. I didn't mention the suicide attempt or the mental hospital or the fact that the doctors removed my tubes. And here's the kicker—I also didn't tell him that it's not an entirely crazy thought that Pat and his dad believed that I got pregnant for money because look where I am now. I am suing him for money, proving to the McCalls that they weren't too wrong about me.

However, what I did tell Grant felt liberating to say out loud. I've never had the opportunity to tell my story to someone. Bridget and my family were the only people who knew what happened before Grant, and now that he does, it feels right. The transparency between us feels comforting, and I can honestly say that opening up to him has drastically changed our relationship. I would never say it out loud, but I feel like a girlfriend now, a proper girlfriend to *the* Grant Wilder. Fancy schmancy.

When I found Grant standing in the center of my small, tiled bathroom, those pill bottles so vibrant in his hands, I was shaken to my core. I hadn't thought of the possibility that he'd stumble upon them innocently, so I automatically assumed he was out to get me. Out to get me like Pat was. I couldn't bring myself to assume he wouldn't snoop or spy or whatever I accused him of doing. In that moment, I was terrified, but time and time again, Grant proves to me that he's unfazed. By everything he knows and everything I share with him. My past and my present and my everything. He's still here.

We spend the next few weeks chained at the hips, spending as much time together as possible considering both our work and school schedules are demanding. But we've figured out how to make it work. I rarely have a chance to miss him, and when I can't get away from my ridiculous pile of schoolwork, he comes to hang out at my apartment just so we can see each other. It's annoyingly cute and I love it. Just the other night, he surprised me with a pizza and a board game. We played Monopoly until one in the morning; I was such a mess the next day, but it was worth it. Grant profusely apologized for my exhaustion, had felt that he took me away from my priorities, but I assured him that it was fine. It was sweet that he was so cautious, though. I really liked that.

I've been updating Bridget on all things related to Grant and me, and she's been adorably proud at how I've been handling it. She also knows not to mention anything about him to my parents or my brothers. It hasn't got anything to do with Grant, of course, but I want to give it more time. I know that they'll worry when they find out I'm across the country with a boyfriend. If I'm even that. Is calling someone an official girlfriend or boyfriend a thing or is it an assumption? Like, is he going to ask me or should I assume that's what I am to him? I have to ask Bridget how that works.

We're almost off for Thanksgiving break in a few days, so school's been quite the whirlwind since all the professors have been a little cruel about it, but I finally get a night off, so I call Grant immediately.

"Hey, babe, how's the essay going?" he asks. I can literally hear a smile in his voice, and it gives me the heart flutters. Did you know that they're a real thing? Oh, yeah. I'd read about them in books, the butterflies and all that jazz, but assumed it was an exaggeration because I didn't feel any of it with Pat. It is not an exaggeration. I groan.

"Ugh, I finally finished it. Who knows if it's any good though."

"I'm sure it's perfect, you smartass." He chuckles. Grant knows I'm a bit of an overachiever when it comes to school. "So, if you finished the essay, does that mean that you're free tonight?"

"It does! Can I come over?" I have an appointment with Dr. Helstad tomorrow morning, so I can't stay the night, if that's even an option. I make a mental note to ask Bridget if "staying the night" is a thing too. *So many questions!*

"Of course. You don't have to ask me that, babe. I'll come get you." He hates when I take the subway, insists on picking me up and dropping me off, and it's not the worst thing in the world. It saves me money and creepy glances from subway station weirdos, so I'll take it.

"Come show me your gallery wall," I say when we enter the foyer of Grant's apartment. Yes, a foyer. It's a fancy rich person thing, I've learned. I take his hand and drag him toward the dining room.

The gallery wall consists of wall-to-wall, corner-to-corner, floor-to-ceiling picture frames of . . . well, everyone in his life, I presume.

"This is amazing, by the way," I tell him. "Okay, tell me everything."

"These are my parents, Julia and Callum. There's my big sister Annie, her husband Jackson, and their three little ones. That's my little brother Ben and my little sister Layla. They're twins."

"What! Your family has twins!" I exclaim excitedly, swatting his arm. "Why didn't you tell me that before? That's so cool! What are Annie's kids' names?" His voice is deep when he chuckles. It's so hot.

"This one is Madison. She has my whole heart. I was actually the first one to hold her in the hospital aside from her parents. She was wailing, as babies do, but the moment I held her, she stopped crying, and that's when I knew I was a claimed man." He snickers lightly, turning to tell me more. "This little dude is attached to Annie. His name is Jackson Junior but we call him Jack. And then there's Baby Joshua. He calls me Gat because he can't pronounce my name." The way Grant talks about his family, the pure joy and light in his face, breaks me apart because I watch as this man goes on about his love for his niece and nephews and I know that I'll never have a clan of children myself. And he'll be a father one day, and those children will never be mine. But I laugh and act like nothing's haunting me.

"That is so adorable. They're beautiful, all of them. You have great genes," I say, smiling over at him. He puts my arms around his waist.

"Even me?"

I roll my eyes. "Especially you."

"Yeah?"

"Oh, please. Have you seen yourself? You're like a . . . I don't know, sculpture or something."

"A sculpture." He chuckles. "That's definitely a first. Come, let me feed you." He kisses me strongly, winks, and drags me to the kitchen.

As I keep Grant company while he cooks, I notice pictures of his niece and nephews decorate the refrigerator door and a kindergarten project framed on the side table beside the black leather couch. It warms my freaking core.

"Do you like kids, Grant?" Why am I doing this to myself, exactly? Do I want to break my own heart tonight?

"I love kids. They're just little assholes that are cute as shit." He laughs, turning to the stove and then back at me to watch as I howl in laughter. When I compose myself, I walk over to him and lift myself onto the counter. He kisses me quickly and brings his attention to the pot and pan on the stovetop. He's making pasta primavera, and it smells absolutely divine. Fancy schmancy.

"Look at you, being all swanky. How did you learn to cook?" I'm beaming at him and he's beaming back, and his eyes are dilating and man oh man. I get to kiss this man? How! So, I do. Before Grant has a chance to answer my question, I interrupt him.

"Kiss me," I demand. "Wait, no. I'm going to kiss you." I shimmy my butt on the counter across the three feet of space between us and courageously grab his perfectly chiseled face.

"Mmm," he hums against my lips. "I like kissing you. You taste good." Instant flutters. The horny kind this time.

"You may now answer the question."

He shrugs. "My mom cooks a lot, so we all picked up on it. Tell me about the essay." Before Grant knew about the medication, I intentionally hid my major from him. I felt like it was too cliché and had a hidden meaning, which I guess it does, but now he knows that I'm majoring in psychology.

"I actually learned something really cool when I was doing research that I wanted to share with you. Did you know that when someone cries tears of joy, it starts in the right eye, but tears of sadness start in the left? I thought that was fascinating. Our bodies physically feel a difference when we're happy or sad."

Grant starts plating the food, grabbing utensils and a pitcher of water from his fridge. He turns to smile at me. "What're you feeling right now? In this moment?"

"Hungry." I laugh. He rolls his eyes and I get that I can be annoying, but I don't know, I'm too scared to admit aloud how happy I am. I feel like if I acknowledge it, it won't stay that way. I'd rather just feel it than say it, and I totally feel happy with Grant. There's no denying that whatsoever.

We sit across from each other at the kitchen island to eat, and I tell him more of what I've discovered while doing research for my essay. He tells me about his day, his week. It's comfortable conversation with zero expectations, and I love how natural it feels.

"Wanna come to a party with me next week?" His invitation is spoken nonchalantly, while he's clearing off dinner and pouring us a couple of glasses of wine. Oh yeah, I'm a wine person now. Fancy schmancy.

"A party? Together? Like, as your date?"

"No. Not as my date." My face flushes as I quickly look away. What does *that* mean? Grant rushes over and bends to be at eye level with me. "Not as my date. As my girlfriend. That's what I was trying to say."

"Oh. Oh," I say, chuckling at myself. "Girlfriend? I didn't know we were there."

"Ava . . ." He seems put out, tired. He shakes his head.

"What?" *What did I say wrong?*

"I don't get you sometimes," he exhales heavily.

No one gets me. I'm a closed book. I don't even get me half the time. I spent the last few months killing myself over whether I would be Grant's girlfriend at all. Now that he's said it, I feel insecure and reluctant because of the level of attachment that implies.

"Yeah, sorry. I'm not very easy," I admit. "I'm sorry."

"No, Ava. That's not my point. It's like, you told me your story, you see that I'm unfazed by your past, and I'm practically begging to be with you. I am trying to prove to you how committed and loyal I want to be to this relationship, but you're rejecting it at every opportunity, and I'm thoroughly confused. Do you want this or not? You seem to be happy with me. Are you not happy?"

So, that thing I said earlier? About not wanting to acknowledge my happiness? Well, here it is, biting me in the ass.

"Of course I am!" I interject hurriedly. I want to say more but I hesitate. I want to tell him that I've never felt this happy in my entire life. I want to tell him that I'm scared that this is too good to be true. I want to explain to him that I learned the hard way that good things don't happen to me and the fact that he stumbled into my life feels almost unrealistic. I want to tell him that I'm protecting myself by not being hopeful but I don't. I just look at him, and almost try telepathically explaining why I'm not saying more. He looks at me with pity and I hate it. I hate that look so much.

"Don't look at me like that, Grant," I snap. I don't want his pity. All I want is to finally have a chance at feeling normal, and being with Grant as is doesn't give me that feeling because of how peculiar our relationship is. Look at him and then look at me. It's plain as day that this thing between us is abnormal. Sometimes I feel like he's with me because he's doing me a favor. Knowing that he thinks I'm pitiful destroys me.

"Like what?" he asks, clueless. His thick eyebrows are pinched together, his eyes appear dejected, and me? I feel depleted and raw.

"Like you pity me. Like I'm damaged. Don't make it obvious that you think that about me." At this point I'm insulted but, more so, embarrassed. Maybe I shouldn't have told him what happened between Pat and me because he's learned how to read between the lines. Or rather I gave him every tool in the whole dang shed to piece together how broken I was. Am? How the scars of my past run so deep that I'm here and I'm a girlfriend, but I can hardly say it out loud. I watch him listening to me, but I can't quite read the expression on his face.

"What?" I feel myself panicking, getting defensive about who I am now and anxious about who I was then. Grant knows all about my past I'm so desperately trying to leave behind, but the way he looks at me makes me feel like I'm that same girl I was two years ago, and I know that I'm not. I know I grew. I know I changed. I'm not really broken anymore. This conversation is bringing back awful memories. I close my eyes and count to ten to calm myself down before this escalates into a full-blown panic attack. I open my eyes and look straight at him.

"What!" I ask again, raising my voice. Grant winces.

"He really did a number on you."

Ouch. I feel tears coming on. I really don't want Grant to see me cry right now, so I swallow the lump in my throat and jump off one of the three acrylic barstools tucked under the marble island. He stops me when I head for the door.

"Ava, wait. I'm—"

"Don't say that stuff to me. Don't bring him up. I didn't tell you about my past so you can remind me of it when we're together. You have no right to do that. I'm going home." I'm panting in rage as I make my way down the elevator and toward the subway stairs.

When I slide into bed, after mopily washing up, I focus on the white painted ceiling, replaying what happened tonight. How it went from one hundred to zero. I don't know why Grant said what he did because it hurt. I'm not an expert on relationships, but I know this much: bringing up an ex is crossing a boundary; it's completely disrespectful. I just really don't want to be mad at him.

I want to give Grant the benefit of the doubt. Ever since I was a little girl, if I ever got into a fight with a classmate or a friend, I remember my father sitting me down and explaining that sometimes people can be mean because of their own insecurities, or maybe simply because they had a bad day. I've always tried to think that way, and it suddenly hits me when I recall those memories with my burly, softie father.

Maybe Grant feels insecure that I didn't take on the girlfriend title so naturally, but it was only about protecting myself and not getting too excited about this thing between us. I wasn't trying to reject him, but on his end, I'm sure it felt that way. Do I want to be Grant's girlfriend? Hell yeah, I do. I mean, I am. I am his girlfriend.

GRANT

I think I'm being too persistent, pushing and shoving my way into Ava's life because of how desperate I am to be hers before it's too late. It's embarrassing, might I add, to be the one with expectations of a relationship, but I can't stop myself from being impatient. I want to be with Ava so bad. I'm not familiar with any of these feelings. I have always been on the other end, on Ava's end, having women beg for relationships, calling them needy and running. Not that Ava is necessarily doing that, but I feel like I'm sure those girls did when I denied them something more. I guess the actions of my past are back-firing on me.

I slide into the back of Lenny's limo the next morning and tell him what happened last night. I've been updating him on everything Ava related since I met her, and I'm pretty sure he's liking this new side of me. After all, I haven't called him at 6:00 A.M. from a random girl's house in months. He's probably loving that part of all this.

When I tell him about my fuck-up last night, he seems genuinely concerned.

"I've never felt like this about a girl before, Lenny. And the fact that she's not throwing herself at me like girls have in the past is making me paranoid that she doesn't want to be in this relationship like I do."

He watches me from the rearview mirror and nods. After a couple minutes, he speaks.

"Grant, if Ava was like the women in your past, you wouldn't be feeling this way about her. You like Ava because she *isn't* running to be with you. You like her *because* she's different. You like her because she poses a challenge to you. Now, Grant, don't play games with this poor girl's heart, but I'm sure you can understand her hesitation when you throw yourself at her. How did you feel when Hannah did it time and time again?" I groan and he laughs.

I felt annoyed and uninterested when Hannah came on to me, asked me to be hers, asked to marry me. And every time it happened, it shoved me further away until it became preposterous. I feel nauseous when I think about that stupid pact now.

Instead of showing up at Ava's place before work, which is what I'm dying to do, I send her a simple text message apologizing and letting her know that she can take her time and that I'm here when she's ready. It's apparent that she really does need space; I haven't heard from her since she left my apartment last night. What was going through my head when I looked her dead in the eye and told her that Pat really did a number on her? Only an idiot would do such a thing.

"Hey, Lenny, tell me I'm an idiot," I call out.

"Huh?" He glances at me like I'm nuts.

"Say Grant Wilder, you are an idiot," I demand from the back seat.

"My pleasure, boss. Grant Wilder, you are an idiot."

I chuckle and salute him, before heading into the office.

It's been six hours with no word from Ava, so these days that means six hours that I'm near losing it. I feel desperate enough to call Annie for dating advice since she did things the right way when Jackson came along. They're really great together, and the whole family loves him.

"Hi, Uncle Gat!" Annie calls out on speaker, the kids echoing her words.

"Hi, kiddos! Who's excited for Thanksgiving?"

Madison immediately grabs the phone from Annie's hands and sends me a FaceTime call. She is determined as ever as she walks upstairs to her bedroom and flips the camera to show me her outfit for Thursday.

"Mom bought it specially from Italy. Do you like it?" Her smile is contagious when I rave about how beautiful she is and how all the boys are going to want to kiss her.

"Ew!"

I laugh at her adorable reaction and ask, "Hey, Mads, can I talk to Mommy?"

"Okay. Here, Mommy," she says, handing Annie the phone after racing down the steps. "Uncle Grant wants to talk to you."

"Hey, bro!" Annie shouts to the camera while stirring a pot on the stove. I watch her turn off the flame and bring her attention back to me. "What's up?"

"I thought you'd be thrilled to hear that I met someone. It's pretty serious." I am watching it happen live. We need news coverage. Annie is jumping up and down, screaming, and her big blue eyes are popping out of her face cartoonishly.

"You're insane. I'm not doing this over FaceTime." I end the video chat and call her back. "That's better. You're a different breed, Annie."

"Oh, shut up! Forgive me for being excited that you met someone after TEN FUCKING YEARS!" She catches herself swearing and yells to the kids, "No F bombs! Mommy made a mistake!"

"How lovely, An. Jack is gonna go to school tomorrow and tell his teacher than he's four fucking years old." I laugh when she panics. "I'm kidding."

"Ugh, you're annoying. Okay, so tell me everything. Her name, where she's from, send me a picture this second, aaaaand why'd you call?"

I brought this on myself by calling Annie, so I go ahead and divulge everything to her, front to back, starting with meeting Ava at Rocco's and nothing before.

"Wow! She can do so much better than you!" Annie yells into the phone when the picture I sent of Ava gets delivered.

"Annie!"

She laughs mockingly. "Okay that was mean but she's beautiful." I am giddy that I have Annie's approval. "Tell me all about her!" This is the fun part, where I get to talk about Ava. Like I said, giddy.

"For sure. Okay, she's from Northern California. She has three older brothers. Uh . . . her mom is Spanish and her dad is White, so she got the perfect mixture of both. I know that she looks pretty in pictures, but she's so gorgeous in person, Annie. I can't stop staring at her." And it's true. I want to look at Ava all day. As ridiculous as this sounds, I scroll through the few pictures we've taken together every night before bed. I wouldn't dare tell a soul about that though. That's next-level smitten. *Grant Wilder would never.*

"How old is she? She looks young," Annie asks.

I guess I saw this coming. Here goes nothing. "Oof. She's twenty. She's a junior at NYU."

"No!" Annie gasps.

I wince at her reaction. "Is it that bad? Am I being inappropriate?" Annie assures me that it's fine but I ask her not to tell Mom and Dad how young Ava is before I have a chance to. Besides, Ava only looks young. She's wise beyond her years.

"Okay, but they have to know. And what about Thanksgiving? I hope you're gonna bring her."

"Let's tackle one issue at a time, Annie dear."

"Okay, fine. Tell me why you called. You must be feeling desperate."

I explain my pressing need to label this, to make it real and concrete and official. I tell Annie without ousting Ava that she's been hesitant to jump into something after a bad breakup. Saying anything more is not my place.

"I mean, it sounds like you're doing everything you can. You're giving her space and you texted her earlier today, but maybe shoot her another text, let her know that you haven't forgotten about her and that you miss her. Women like to be fought for. Too much space can sometimes cause damage rather than good."

Without any mention to my family until now about our relationship, knowing that Ava's stance hasn't been as all-in as mine, I'm glad I finally called Annie to talk about such a present and important thing that's been going on in my life. I haven't mentioned anything to anyone, for that matter. I'm trying to be respectful to Ava's hesitation, but I figure that telling one sister is harmless. I listen to Annie's advice and immediately text Ava saying, **I miss you. Hope you're having a good day. XO.** Once I'm home from work and it's been a few hours since I hit send, Ava finally texts back.

Ava: I miss you too. How are you?

Me: Same old. Just got home from work. I owe you a proper apology.

Ava: Yeah, you kind of do.

I'm taken aback by Ava's directness, but seconds later, she sends an emoji of a smiley face sticking out its tongue. I take that as a good sign and snicker.

Me: When can I see you?

Ava: As soon as you open the door. 😊

Quickly jogging toward the front door, I grab Ava for the biggest hug I can muster, holding onto her backpack in an embrace too. She laughs in my arms and hugs me back just as tight.

"I am so glad you're here right now," I tell Ava earnestly. My God, have I missed her. More so now that I have her in front of me. Absence makes the heart grow fonder, eh?

"Me too."

"Yeah?" I ask.

Her eyes lift up to meet mine and she smiles, kissing me softly.

"Very much yes," she whispers, kissing me again.

"Let's do something fun. I want to take you out. Wanna walk to go get dinner?"

Ava and I find ourselves at some random comedy club close to my apartment that serves tapas and drinks, Ava's idea entirely, the flashing dotted lights catching her attention. I have definitely never been here before. After ordering a margarita and a burger for her and an old fashioned for me, we're led to be seated in a quiet, plush booth on the balcony of the small theater. Before the show starts, I lean over to whisper in her ear.

"Ava, look at me." Her pouty lips rest on the black straw in her drink, and her eyes are big and bright when she turns to face me. "I'm sorry about last night. It wasn't fair of me to comment on your past like that. You are not damaged. I don't want you to ever think that about yourself. I don't let you. You're strong and I'm proud of you. It wasn't my place to mention him, and I acted like a dick."

She stretches her face to kiss me and shrugs. "I forgive you, Grant," she says, taking another sip of her margarita.

"That's it? No rebuttal?" I chuckle lightly. If it's that easy, I'll take it. She shakes her head.

"No rebuttal. I missed you so much today and I felt kind of stupid for leaving last night. I wish I would've stayed and we could've talked. I know I have to work on that, but for now, I'm happy to be here with you." Passionately, I grab her face to kiss her and she leans back, eyes wide, cheeks flushed. I love catching her off guard. I love her innocence.

As the small-time comedians perform one after the other, presenting their bits, hoping to get those five minutes of New York City fame, I watch Ava giggle and laugh hysterically. She cheers each one of them on as they walk off stage, clapping, hooting, hollering.

"You look so happy," I whisper into the side of her neck. I have my arm wrapped around her delicate shoulder, and she leans closer into me. She looks up and smirks shyly.

"Because I am." It takes me by surprise, the best kind, when Ava intertwines our fingers, kissing the palm of my hand and then my cheek. "Because I'm your girlfriend." My breath hitches at that word. She hated it only last night.

"Yeah?"

She nods excitedly and it's fucking adorable. "Yup. Yes. Affirmative. I am your girlfriend. I am Grant Wilder's girlfriend. Hey!" she calls out to the waitress. If she wasn't a little tipsy, it'd be a bit rude, and that makes me laugh. I'll tip her well.

A short brunette with pigtail braids comes over to our table. "What can I get for y'all?"

"Can I please have another one of these?" she asks, pointing to her now finished cocktail. "Oh, and guess what? I'm his *girlfriend*," she brags, pointing her thumb at me. "And he's my *boyfriend*."

"Lucky you," the waitress says, winking at Ava.

"I know, right? Isn't he's so hot!"

I am cackling on the outside at this amazing girl who is somehow mine, unbelievably mine, and on the inside? I am falling quickly and deeply, and I don't think I could stop it even if I tried.

—ϡ—

When we arrived at my apartment last night, I kissed and held Ava with completion because that's how I felt. I felt a fullness, whole, that she was now *officially* my girlfriend. That word had always been so foreign to me and avoided as often as possible, but with Ava I wanted to announce it to everyone I knew, much like she did the cocktail waitress. After drunkenly begging me to have sex with her and my having to say no because of the obvious, she moped and whined in her drunken state but passed out in a matter of minutes as soon as we got into bed. I cuddled her small body against me while we slept, and now, she stirs awake beside me and groans, no doubt suffering from that hit-you-like-a-brick hangover. She downed two cocktails in a matter of minutes and this girl is tiny. I slip out of bed to grab Ava a couple of aspirins and a glass of water. I hand them to her and sit to her right.

"Good morning, you. How are you feeling?"

She looks like a mess, a cute, adorable mess, as she brushes the hair out of her face and groans.

"Can I take a shower here?" she croaks sleepily, covering her eyes with her forearm. "I don't feel so good."

"Of course you can. Welcome to your first hangover, Ava."

It takes her a good ten minutes to fully wake up. She groans again as she slips out of bed to grab her backpack from the foyer floor before coming back into the bedroom. When she lifts the bag onto my bed, our eyes shoot to each other's as the echo of pills rattling against hard plastic sounds. She shrugs.

"Yup. There go my crazy pills!" Ava says it with such bitterness, and it hurts to watch her feel this way about herself.

"Don't say that," I snap. "They're not crazy pills, Ava. Stop it." She looks at me in bewilderment.

"Hm," she hums.

99

While Ava takes a shower, I go to the kitchen to brew a pot of coffee for myself and prepare a tea bag in a giant mug for Ava, but hold off until she's out of the shower to add hot water to it. My girl isn't going to drink a lukewarm tea. Ava's tying her long hair into a wet braid as she walks toward me at the stove, smiling cheekily. She's wearing my giant UPenn sweatshirt that I slept in last night and a tiny pair of shorts. Her legs are long and bare and gorgeous, and I have to turn away before I strip her naked and take her on the kitchen island.

When I tell Ava that I'm whipping up some pancakes and smoothies for breakfast and that it'll be ready soon, she does a little shimmy, a happy dance if you will. I'm an omelet kind of a guy, but I'm in a pampering and cooking mood, giddy that I'm here with Ava, that she woke up in my arms, in my bed, that she's only a few feet away and loving how comfortable she seems to be here. Besides, getting dressed up to go to breakfast sounds too unappealing, and those tiny shorts tell me it's the same for her.

"What was that for?" I laugh.

"I love pancakes. You're spoiling me."

When they're nearly done cooking on the griddle, I ask Ava to grab the maple syrup and butter from the fridge and meet me at the island. She swats my hand away when I reach for my breakfast.

"Pancake stacking is an art," she explains, acting especially serious. "Do you trust me?"

"I trust you." I eye her pointedly, trying hard not to laugh.

"Okay. So, you take said pancake. Lay it nicely in the center of the plate. Spread on a little butter and a lot of syrup and then you stack another one on top and do it again. A little butter. A lot of syrup. Stack." Her perfectly shaped eyebrows are pinched as she meticulously prepares our individualized plates of pancakes. I've got my own little private IHOP chef over here. She snickers when she catches me staring at her mouth sucking maple syrup off her thumb with her pouty lips, blushing madly, her face turning a shade darker. I've been dying to be intimate with Ava for a while now, but I can understand that she might be hesitant to jump into it. That doesn't mean it isn't hard as fuck to wait. Sleeping in the same bed last night didn't help. I had to conceal my boner about a hundred times.

She slides my plate of pancakes in front of me and nods toward it.

"Eat," she commands. I try hard to mask my cough after only the third bite because this is way too sweet but she notices.

"What! You don't like it?!" she exclaims. Her plate is nearly finished.

"A little too much syrup for my liking, but the effort was an A-plus, baby." I had a smoothie while she was showering. I'll be fine.

Ava rolls her eyes at me and takes another giant bite. "Okay, Grandpa," she mumbles with chipmunk cheeks. I am howling with laughter and lifting her over my shoulder as soon as she swallows her last bite of syrup with a side of pancakes.

"Take it back!" I call out.

"No way!" She laughs hysterically, smacking my back and my butt. "Put me down! I'm gonna puke!"

"Not until you take it back, Grandma!!" I tickle her feet and she pleads for mercy.

"Fine! Fine! I take it back!" I set her down.

"That'll teach you," I wink, grinning hugely, noticing how Ava's face takes on a sudden seriousness as she glances at me wide-eyed. Taking a jolted step forward, she kisses me hard. Then again, deeper this time. What happens between us next is instant. We're breathless and wild and carnal within a matter of seconds. But as soon as her soft fingers reach for the hem of my T-shirt, I grab her delicate wrists.

"Wait," I whisper between our lips. "What's happening right now?"

"You don't want to do this?" Ava breathes, swallowing thickly as she pants from the unexpectedness of it all. I'm panting pretty hard too.

"Of course I do," I explain. "I just need you to tell me what *this* is."

"I want you to have sex with me," she whispers shyly when she speaks, unable to look me in the eye. But I don't want her to be nervous with me if we're really about to do this right now because now that Ava's said it, I'm hesitant. I ask her if she's totally, one hundred percent sure about this; if she feels ready. She nods.

"Yes, Grant. I am very ready."

I take a step toward her, my girlfriend, kissing her lightly and softer than before.

AVA

"Okay," Grant replies quietly when I tell him that I'm finally ready to do the dirty. "But if at any point you feel uncomfortable, I need you to tell me." I nod hurriedly. Blah, blah, blah. "Promise me, Ava."

"Yeah, okay. I promise. Can I please take your shirt off now?" My boldness comes to me as a surprise, but it's not like I haven't prepared myself to have sex with Grant for a while. I've wanted this for so long that now the desire to be with him is plain painful. My body aches, throbs, as I imagine him naked, us naked together. The prospect of finally learning how to have an intimate relationship, and with Grant in particular, has me desperate and eager to have him already. I mean, have you seen the guy? He looks fake.

"Yeah," he replies gruffly, helping me slip the shirt over his head since my tiptoes don't match to his six feet, five inches. I peeked at his driver's license at the comedy place last night. He's exactly a foot taller than me and I find that kind of cool. Enough of that though.

As soon as the cotton hits the floor and Grant stands shirtless in front of me, I pause to assess my surroundings and okay, yeah, probably to drool too if I'm being honest.

"Wow" is all I have to say when I look at his hard stomach, the dusting of hair across his chest, the hugeness of him and his height and how he towers over me. Grant rolls his eyes and tries pulling me toward him.

"Come here," he mumbles. I take a step back, wanting to observe every inch of his beautiful body before things get wild and I won't have time to just . . . *look*. He's perfect. "Baby, come here."

"Wait! I have to inspect the merchandise!" I giggle because I'm nervous and giddy. He laughs because I'm weird.

"You're too funny, Ava Ruth. Are you really sure about this? If you're not ready—"

I slam my lips to his because he just called me by my full name and also, it's getting annoying to keep assuring him. I'm an adult. I think I know what I'm signing up for. My face feels heated, my body pulsing, when we're kissing like this, but it's not enough. *None* of this is enough. I position myself flush against Grant's body releasing an unexpected guttural moan into his perfect wet mouth.

"I really want you," I breathe into the small space between us, placing my sweaty forehead against his hard shoulder.

"Me too, baby. I just don't want to cross any lines with you." Grant is worried about me, and he has no reason to be. As hard as it is to admit, this isn't my first time. Grant isn't my first, and I think I kind of hate that.

"You won't cross any lines with me, Grant. You're my boyfriend. I trust you. Just . . . *have me*," I beg quietly. "*Please.*" Plump lips meet mine then, and he caresses my sides, my back, my butt with his giant, warm hands. My hair elastic is soon strewn somewhere by my bare feet, and Grant begins unbraiding my hair while his mouth explores mine. He swiftly lifts me up, and I gasp as he wraps my legs around his waist and shoves both of his hands in my undone, messy hair. He walks us toward his bedroom with his face buried in my neck and sits on the giant bed, placing me down in front of him. Between Grant's height and my lack of it, we're nearly at eye level. For the umpteenth time, he asks with his emerald eyes if this is okay. I smile and kiss him.

"Are you always this cautious when you sleep with someone?"

"No. But you're not just someone." He emphasizes it like it's obvious. It's sexy as hell.

"No. I'm your *girlfriend*," I whisper loudly, teasing him. "How fancy of me!"

He chuckles and pulls me by the neck. "You absolutely are my girlfriend. Come here," he demands hoarsely, his deep voice making me feel things in my lower belly. There's a sudden change in the air when he does that, like he's finally telling me how bad he wants this too. I feel a fire on my bare skin when he slips my sweatshirt off, and I have instant goose bumps from his long fingers tightly digging into my bare hips. I catch him paused, staring at my belly, stilled. *Shit.*

"Oh," I say, my voice shaky. "That." Grant is eyeing the scar below my stomach. If we were in a darkened bedroom right now, which is what I expected our first time to be like, I wouldn't have to worry about him seeing the scar because it's not too noticeable. But because it's before noon and there's a decent amount of sunlight seeping in through the curtains in Grant's master bedroom, he spots it right away. When he doesn't say anything for a good minute, still staring at it, I feel a little queasy and grab the sweatshirt from the floor to cover myself. "Sorry. I should've told you——"

"No," he interrupts, shaking his head furiously. He rips the sweatshirt out of my hands and chucks it behind me. "Don't you dare apologize. It just caught me by surprise."

"Okay. Well, yeah, I guess it is kind of weird to have that scar when I'm not a mom, you know? But you're the first person I've been with since it happened, so I guess I forgot to give you a disclaimer. I think it's maybe because the last ten minutes happened really quickly, and I forgot you were going to see it." I talk a lot when I'm nervous.

Grant looks up at me then with a beautiful sweetness in his vibrant green eyes. He shakes his head.

"I stopped to look at it because I love it, Ava, not because I don't."

This man. I kiss him so hard, his head in my shaking hands. I have to will myself not to cry at the sheer emotion I feel when he says that. "Why do you love it?" I whisper.

"It's a homage to your strength, to your resilience. You should own it, babe."

I smile tenderly at him. "You can't say such sweet things to me and not expect me to want you and your hot body."

Grant slides the elastic of my shorts down and unhooks my bra and mutters a soft *fuck* when I'm standing before him in just a pair of lavender lace underwear that I may have picked up at Victoria's Secret days after our steak dinner date and slipped on after my shower earlier in hopes that this would happen today.

"Damn, Ava, you are so gorgeous," Grant mumbles, standing from his seated position on the corner of the bed. I inch forward to shakily pull Grant's gray sweatpants off, and now we both stand here in his master bedroom in nothing but our thin underwear. I keep my focus straight ahead, staring at his abs in front of me. I suddenly feel really shy and nervous as it occurs to me again that this thing between us is so unconventional, and that scares me. Grant's body is beyond perfect, and I'm suddenly insecure about mine when I see us standing almost bare naked together.

"I can't believe this is actually happening right now," I whisper to his chest.

"Which part?"

"That you actually want to do this with me."

He tilts my face up to look at me and lifts his eyebrows. "You're kidding, right?" I shake my head, bite anxiously on my lower lip. "Ava, I'm the one in disbelief that *you* want to do this with *me*."

I scoff self-deprecatingly, and it gives me a sinking feeling because *why?* Why does Grant want this with me? He could have literally anyone in the world. I'm sure women throw themselves at him, but here I am standing almost fully naked in his bedroom and I feel a bit awkward. Grant could fuck a supermodel and no one would blink an eye. I am not a supermodel. I am nowhere near a supermodel. This just doesn't make any sense.

"Oh, please. Have you seen yourself? *Everyone* probably wants to do this with you. I'm nothing special. I feel so . . . *average.*"

He sits back on the bed and sighs. "Baby." Grant rubs his warm hands all over my naked body, feeling every inch of me, and replies with "You're *really* not. Average is when you find a room full of girls who look copy and pasted. You're the most unique person I've ever met. You're different, Ava. You're cool and clever and unlike anyone I've ever known. I want you and I like you and I need you *because* you're different." *Jesus.*

Grant takes my hand and palms his crotch, showing me how hard I make him. "Is that proof enough for you?" I blush and nod, so he finally lays me on the bed and climbs over me.

Grant worships my body beneath him, and it's tender but rough and passionate but sweet, and when he's finally hovering above me and I tell him there's no need for us to use a condom, he pauses and pinches his eyebrows together.

"I don't know about this, Ava. You got pregnant . . ."

"I swear I'm covered, Grant. I'm not going to get pregnant. *Please*," I beg. *Please distract me from thoughts of why I'm never going to get pregnant.* I arch my back so he gets the hint, and he's slow and careful, but as soon as he pushes forward, it stings.

"Ah." I react quickly and his eyes widen as he throws himself backward about five feet away from me. It was only a pinch, but it caught me by surprise.

"Oh my god, I am so sorry." Grant is frantic when he apologizes, guilt blanketing his face as if he intended to hurt me. If only all men were like this. My stark-naked body feels exposed and cold without his heat warming me up or his movements making me sweat in pulsing pleasure.

"Can you come back here?" I laugh, reaching for him. "You're too far." He slowly inches forward and rests on his elbows on either side of my head, leaning back to look at me.

"I didn't know it was going to hurt you. I'm sorry," he says, bending to kiss me.

"It's okay. Me neither." Grant has a look of confusion on his radiant, sweaty face. "What?" I ask.

"It didn't hurt for you the first time?"

I shake my head. "No. It was kind of uncomfortable, but it didn't really hurt."

He tries to hide his smile but eventually snickers and kisses my cheek. "You're so cute, Ava," he mumbles into my neck, kissing the length of my jaw.

I push him off of me, confused.

"I'm cute because it hurt with you?"

"You're cute because you don't realize what you just implied."

"Huh?" I'm sure I give him a look that reads *I have no idea what you're talking about* because he gives me a wide grin and chuckles.

"If it didn't hurt you the first time but that did, I probably have a bigger dick than Pat." My cheeks turn pink and I cringe beneath him. *So, dick measuring contests are a thing. Hmm.*

"Ew, Grant." He howls with those sexy eye creases and I laugh with him because his happiness is contagious and also because he's pretty and fun to look at.

"This is the best news. I gotta go shout it from the window." He cups his crotch with both hands and scurries to the window, sneaking behind the curtain and pushing the glass open until it's just slightly ajar. A rush of freezing cold winter air makes its way into the room, and all I can see from the small sliver of opened curtain is a glimpse of the New York City skyline and Grant's ass.

He has a beautiful ass.

"Hello, New York City!" Grant shouts from his stance by the window. "I have a bigger dick than my girlfriend's ex!" He slams the window shut and rushes toward the bed. "Fuck, it's so cold out. Okay, we're good. Come here." He makes me hold him tightly and rub up his arms for warmth.

"You're crazy." I can feel the vibrations from his husky laugh when I giggle at what he just did. He gently brushes the hair out of my face and smirks.

"Crazy for you, baby. Are you comfortable? Cold? Let me get you a sweatshirt." I grab his arm the moment he attempts to sit up in bed and leave, and I feel myself wetter at the view of his bare, broad back, contoured and perfectly sculpted. It makes the needy throbbing heavier.

"Wait. We're not gonna . . .?"

"I don't want to hurt you again."

I shake my head and pull him on top of me. "I'm going to be fine, Grant. Please? I've wanted to do this with you for weeks."

When I said that sex with Grant was going to be incomparable to the three minutes Pat lasted, I wasn't kidding. As soon as the first bit of pain subsides, it's so erotic, it takes me a while to process what is happening as it's happening, the thrusting, moaning. I'm having sex with Grant Wilder. Grant Wilder is in the nude and on top of me.

I feel more confident than I ever have in my entire life. Grant groans into my neck, and I beg him repeatedly not to stop because holy shit, *I have never*. He intertwines our hands above my head, stares intensely into my eyes, and eventually pauses to consider the scenery.

"You look breathtaking under me, Ava," he chokes raspingly, his voice straining to speak as his eyes flutter closed in immense pleasure. That pleasure is from *me*. *How is this my life right now?!* "You feel so good, Ava. It's so good."

Once it's over, all that is heard for a solid five minutes is our heavy breathing.

"What?" I breathe, looking away shyly when he lifts his head to gaze at me. He pulls my chin to face him and stares into my eyes in awe. "Why are you looking at me like that? Was I too loud?"

"No way."

"Then why?"

"Because you're so beautiful," he whispers, sweeping the sex hair out of my face with both hands, kissing me sweetly. "And that was incredible. *You* are incredible."

Well, what do you know? Grant Wilder had sex with Ava Campbell and *enjoyed* it. Why do I feel like a pretty big deal right now?

"Really? Was it . . . like, good for you?" I ask awkwardly to ensure that I understood him correctly.

He chuckles and shakes his head in amusement. "You're adorable, you know that? Yes, Ava. That was spectacular. We should do it again."

Grant lifts me on top of him in one swift movement and looks up at me, grinning hugely with both his hands tucked behind his head. I cover my very exposed and very small boobs with my arms, but Grant pulls them away, telling me not to cover myself. There's no shyness after what we just did, so I embrace it. I play with his thick, black waves and match his giant, goofy smile.

"Why are you smiling so big?" I laugh.

"Because I feel lucky that I got the girl."

GRANT

Exhausted perfectly describes the way we feel after earlier today but in the best damn way. I don't remember when exactly it happens, but Ava and I fall asleep in my bed together. I think we both lazily collapsed after number three, and I wake up sometime before five with a fully naked Ava snuggled into my side still knocked out, her wild hair sprawled all across my chest. I suppress my laughter when she snores ever so slightly and sighs in her sleep. *This girl.*

Memories of today flash in my mind and it's impossible not to think about every detail that we did today. Three times in two hours. Pretty sure that's my new record.

Everything about the way Ava looked as we were having sex was so gorgeous, and throughout the few hours spent in bed, her expressions varied between pleasure, desire, shock, adoration . . . At one point, she just started laughing. Out of nowhere, she burst into a fit of laughter and I was so confused.

"What? What happened?" I asked. She wrapped her arms around my back and pulled me closer. "What's so funny?"

"No, nothing." She giggled quietly. "It's just . . . you." The way her eyes dilated when she glanced at me was insane.

After today, I can appreciate why people do the whole "till death do us part" thing. I absolutely get the hype of being with the same person for the rest of your life because if that person is *the* person, then who the hell else do you need? Sex felt entirely different with Ava than it ever has with anyone else, and there have been plenty of women in my bed. But as I watched my girlfriend softly moan and pant under me, finding her perfect movements so sexy because of her beautiful innocence, I knew in that moment that I don't ever want to do this with anyone else. There is no one else who can make me feel more whole and complete like she does. Ava is it for me. And did I love the fact that she unintentionally told me that McCall sports a smaller dick? Yes, I did.

Ava slowly stirs awake in my arms and lifts her tired eyes to look at me.

"Oh, hi. Was I snoring?" I shake my head and kiss her hair. "Mmmm," she hums.

"You good, baby?"

She nods, her cheek rubbing against the hair on my chest. "So good," she purrs, hooking her bare leg over mine. My phone has a sudden influx of messages come through and buzzes loudly on my night table. My right arm is hugging Ava, so I reach my left arm over to retrieve it. Ava watches as I scroll through the messages, making a point not to look at the screen. I respect her for it even if I have nothing to hide. Nothing *on this phone* to hide.

"Is everything okay?" she asks worriedly.

"See for yourself." I turn the screen so Ava can read what has my phone blowing up. The title of the message chat reads **Wilder Family** at the top of the screen, and they've gone ham with the text messages. In the first message, there's a picture of Ava and me, the exact one I sent to Annie yesterday. That woman can't keep her mouth shut to save her life. Ava's eyes widen when she sees the photo of us and reads my family's very surprised reaction to it.

Annie: surprise!!!!!

Mom: ????? Who is that

Ben: wait what

Dad: Grant you look very happy. Who is that?

Layla: what Ben said

Annie: Granty finally has a girlfriend!!!!! He isn't gay you guys!!!

Mom: silly Annie. Grant who is she I am calling you

As soon as the word **Mom** flashes on my iPhone screen, I'm all jumpy because my girlfriend and I are ass naked and we just woke up from a postcoital nap. Ava suppresses her laugh and throws a palm over her mouth when she sees the clear panic in my eyes. I ignore the call. *Wrong place, wrong time, Mom. Can't a guy get some privacy?*

As soon as my thumb taps the decline button, Ava erupts into laughter. I watch her cackle in pure enjoyment, my chest tightening at the euphoria I feel when I'm with her. I am so damn possessed by this woman. Reopening the chat, I text my family back, this time making sure that Ava has a clear view of the screen.

Me: Never been gay. Yes, I have a girlfriend. Her name is Ava and I am very happy.

She scrunches her nose and beams up at me. I kiss her forehead.

Dad: Hope you are bringing her on Thursday. So lovely. Looking forward.

Annie: you BETTER bring her tomorrow

Mom: I will be very angry if you do not bring her for Thanksgiving dinner. Does she have any allergies? Grant no ignoring

I wanted to mention bringing Ava to my parents' Thanksgiving dinner weeks ago, but I figured she'd freak at the prospect of meeting my family so soon after *officially* starting to date. But now that she has seen how *angry* my parents will be . . .

"What were your Thanksgiving plans? Wanna come to my parents' house and you can meet everyone?" I speak to her head because she has her eyes trained to my phone. She clears her throat.

"Uh . . . I was going to go to one of the dorms. This girl named Chloe invited me for a Friendsgiving dinner there. She's the RA."

"Change your plans? Come with me," I insist hesitantly, gesturing for her to look at me. She bites her lip, a little nervous. It's outrageously sweet. "Are you ready for that, babe?"

"Are you sure you want me there? I don't want to—"

I laugh. How could I want her anywhere other than at my side at all times? If I could shut down NYU I would, just to have her near me 24/7. "Of course I'm sure. You're my girlfriend. You're coming. Do you have any allergies?"

"Yup. Penicillin. Can't make it."

I laugh and she chuckles at her own joke when she sees that I liked it. I shoot a quick text to my family to let them know we'll be there and tap her shoulder.

"Come shower with me," I say as soon as I hit send and put my phone back on the nightstand. She sits up from her snuggled position against my skin, our bodies unsticking themselves when she moves away from mine.

"Like both of us together?" she asks. I tell her yes and she shrugs. "Okay." It feels fucking great knowing that I'm giving Ava so many of her firsts. We really just shower since I think we're both pretty spent after what we did today and yes, she sprays me with the water jet and yes, she attacks me with soap suds and yes, it's the most cliché and sappy thing in the entire world, but you know what? I love that I have a chance to do these things with her, so I embrace every bit of it and continue to torment Ava with the showerhead, spraying her face over and over until she's choking from water and laughter.

—⚭—

Ava insists on wearing my clothes once we get out of the shower, and after throwing on some briefs and a hoodie myself, I meet her by the bathroom sink, kissing her temple and smiling at her beautiful face in the mirror. I watch in awe as she brushes her long, light brown hair. She's wearing a pair of my socks, tiny underwear, and yet another one of my sweatshirts that hits her mid-thigh. *Utter fucking perfection.*

"You look so pretty. Wanna hear a fun fact?" I ask, walking over to my sink a couple of feet away. I've only ever used the one on the right, and I'm grateful that I can finally share the double sink with someone who is wholly mine. I love that Ava can claim something as simple as a bathroom sink at my home now that we're together because her standing to the left of me seems like the most natural thing in the world. Everything with her feels authentic and real. I love this place we're finally in.

The toothbrush I gave her this morning leans next to mine in the black marble holder on the bathroom counter, and I pause to glance at them contentedly before taking both out and walk to hand over hers. She officially has a toothbrush here. Shoutout to Colgate. This is some big relationship level stuff.

"Well, thanks for telling me that I have bad breath." She chuckles. *Women.* "What's the fun fact?"

"Your hair is the first thing I noticed about you." Signature nose scrunch. Obviously.

"Well, do *you* want to hear a fun fact? Your hands are the first thing I noticed about you. When you reached around me and took my tea." She begins to brush her teeth in the mirror and I stand behind Ava, wrapping my arms around her shoulders and kissing her temple hard. I love that memory. I love how we met, even if it was premeditated. It was so cinematic and that part, I hadn't expected. Guy meets girl at coffee shop. Guy asks girl out. Guy falls for girl. Guy gives girl toothbrush to keep at his house.

"I only took your tea because you *stole* my coffee, you thief!"

She laughs and places her toothbrush back in the holder alongside mine. I reach for her tiny body and she snuggles into my chest, wrapping both her arms tightly around my waist. She places her chin in the middle of my abdomen and looks up at me.

"I'm happy I met you." I bend to kiss her full lips.

"I'm more happy I met you," I say.

"Today was . . ."

"Yes?" I ask, teasing.

"You know," she whispers shyly, swallowing. "So, are you gonna feed me or what?"

Oh, shit. We haven't eaten since this morning. Plus, add in a couple of hours of intense sexual cardio—Ava must be famished. My mind's been elsewhere. I've been a little distracted.

"Shit, sorry. What do you want to order?" I would've loved to cook dinner, but I didn't bother placing a big grocery order for this week because of Thanksgiving tomorrow. Mom always sends us home with heaping piles of leftovers.

"Ooooh, I get to choose!" Ava exclaims. "Uh . . . how about we get some pizza? Is that good? And maybe we can watch a movie while we eat?"

Ask and you shall receive, my girl.

When the pizza arrives twenty minutes later, I hand Ava a couple of water bottles and two wineglasses to put by the pizza box in the living room. She leaves one of the wineglasses on the kitchen island and places a single glass along with the water on the coffee table by the couch opposite the giant TV.

"No wine tonight? Are you traumatized from this morning's hangover?" I chuckle. I can't believe we were at the comedy club only last night. It feels like a lifetime ago when I called Annie fretting about my relationship with Ava. Shit, am I glad she told me to text her a second time because everything seems to be falling into place so perfectly. Today might be the longest but best day of my entire life.

"I wanna feel good for tomorrow. It's a big day."

Oh, that's right. The meeting of the parents. The bringing home of the girl. Yeah—*the* girl. I strut with determination over to Ava by the sofa and grab her for a kiss, deepening it before leaning back and smiling.

"They are going to love you. I promise."

Ava sits curled into my chest on the sofa, holding a slice and watching the TV screen, but I only have eyes for her. Every time I take a good, hard look at her, I feel lucky that she's really mine. Those pouty lips, the small nose, the almond-shaped kind eyes that hold every hardship she's endured but also all the strength she's had to fight it. Her hair, *my God*, her hair and the way it falls down her back, thick and shiny and perfect. I tell myself every day not to get too attached to Ava knowing that this isn't long term, but I can't help it. Every time I'm with her, it's never enough. I crave more, I yearn to see her when she's not with me, and I am terrified of how threatening that is for my own heart.

GRANT

When Ava turns around once I've zipped up her red velvet mini dress for Thanksgiving dinner this evening, I can't help the enormous grin that appears on my face when I take in the view. There's something about her youthful face that glows so beautifully but especially now. Maybe it's the deep red against her tanned skin or the gorgeous hair styled in a long braid down her back. Maybe it's the delicate collarbone exposed through her low neckline, or maybe it's that I'm so infatuated with her that I hold her at the highest regard, and how excited I am about introducing her to my family tonight.

"Do I look okay?" she asks, straightening out her short sleeves, yanking at her dress. She tucks the few strands of hair that have come undone behind her ears and looks up.

"More than okay. You look stunning, babe. Also, I have something for you." When I bought it, I wasn't sure if Ava would scare from the gift or appreciate it, but I felt I had to get her something to celebrate us and Thanksgiving. It seemed perfect at the time. Now, I take the Tiffany blue box out of my suit jacket pocket and hand it to her.

"Wait, what! Is this what I think it is!" she exclaims. "Is this from *the* Tiffany's!"

"Happy Thanksgiving, Ava baby." I smack a massive kiss to her lips.

"Are you sure about this, Grant?" she asks before opening it. "I didn't know we were doing gifts. I didn't get you anything."

I chuckle and nod toward the box, telling her to open it already. As soon as she spots the bracelet, she can't seem to hide her smirk, wrinkling her delicate nose and looking up at me.

"You got me a bracelet?"

"Do you like it?"

She carefully removes the jewelry from the box and looks at it in the light. "Of course I like it. I love it. It's so pretty, Grant. Will you put it on me?"

I take the thin silver chain from her fingers, and clasp it on, turning it so that the diamond heart stone is visible at the top of her arm. It shines beautifully against her skin and the red velvet dress and her delicate, clean wrists.

"It looks perfect on you. Exactly how I expected." Ava steps toward me, hugs me tightly, and sighs. She doesn't let go for a while. "You good?" I ask.

"Remember how scared I was in the beginning?" she whispers. I nod, my chin resting at the top of her head. "I never had to be. Not with you. You're good for me."

My chest tightens, scared and so damn guilty at what she's saying because of how much I know that I'm not.

"Do you really believe that?"

"Yeah. I think I did for a long time, but you know me . . . I'm just a big old scaredy cat, and I don't really know what I'm doing most of the time. But you make things easy because you do know what you're doing. I feel like figuring out this new place with you has been exactly what I needed after what happened." She tilts her head, scans my eyes, hesitant to say more, but as soon as I open my mouth to speak, she interrupts me. "Thanks for taking a chance on me. I didn't really think anyone would, not for a long time."

My heart constricts at that sentence. *Why am I doing this to her? Why am I letting her fall for me?* But I know exactly why. It's because I'm falling right back.

"That's not what's happening here, Ava baby. I feel like you're the one taking a chance on me, letting me prove to you that I can be a decent boyfriend despite my lack of experience. You make it easy because you're you. Maybe we're just perfect for each other, hey?"

She nods and chuckles, beaming up at me and scrunching her nose. She shrugs before saying, "Yeah, maybe."

I kiss her cheek before taking her hand, intertwining our fingers, and walking to the door.

"Shall we?"

We take the Porsche out to Scarsdale because Lenny is obviously off today, but I'm not sure I want Ava to meet him just yet. I have a driver. She takes the subway. It might give her another reason to question this, even after the conversation we had minutes ago. No bueno.

"You wanna take care of the music?" I ask, handing her my phone. I feel at peace driving through quiet city streets heading toward the suburbs with Ava beside me. It's blissful. She doesn't let the first song she chooses finish playing and browses through a bunch of different playlists, toying with the volume dial, her diamond bracelet, the passenger window . . .

"You nervous?" I ask. I reach over to clasp my hand over hers to stop the fidgeting.

"You know I am. Isn't meeting the parents like a really big deal? I haven't even told my family about you."

I don't love the sound of that, but she's always been cautious. I do wonder why though.

"Yeah, it's a significant step, I would say. Do you want to tell your family?"

She nods immediately. "Of course I do and I will, eventually but . . . Grant? Do you think this is moving too fast? We had sex for the first time only yesterday." She speaks quietly, like there's a pastor sitting in the back seat, like she's sitting on a pew at church.

"*When* we have sex doesn't mean anything." I laugh. "Ava, we did it . . ." I do the math in my head ". . . five times in twenty-four hours. I'm not sure that it matters."

"Don't make me sound naughty!" she whines, shoving my shoulder.

"Do *you* think it's moving too fast? Because I'm happy where this is going. I meant it when I said you're it for me." I've told this to Ava before and have truly believed it since we met, but when I say it right now, after we've had sex, once she labeled herself as my girlfriend it feels liberating. She's right that we only first slept together yesterday, but it really did happen all at once. We didn't stop for hours this morning. It was ridiculous.

"Well, I was actually hoping to ask you what that meant. You said it when I told you about my abortion too." As soon as she utters the word abortion, her head turns to watch the road and the lights blinking on the bridge above us. I knew what it meant for me then and I know now. But Ava entered this thing between us expecting it to never work. I came in trying my damn hardest to make her mine, and now that I have, I don't want to give her any reason to withdraw. I can't really afford it right now.

"I want to tell you, babe, but you scare off too easy. Let's not go there tonight." I chuckle and squeeze her hand in my palm.

"No, not anymore. I'm not scared anymore. I told you at your house. I even said I was your girlfriend." Her eyes plead with me to tell her how I feel, to give her that sense of security she so badly needs, and even *that* breaks my heart.

"Okay," I exhale. "You're it for me means that I've done the dating and the hooking up and I've met other women, but once I found you, it was settled. You're it for me. That's it. You." *Like a weight off my damn shoulder. Fuck, Wilder.*

"You mean . . ."

I nod and kiss her hand again.

"Yeah. That." Marriage. Wife. Babies. The whole nine yards, which has always been frightening and far out in the future but not when it comes to Ava. I could marry her tomorrow, and as crazy as that sounds, because I know it does, it's true. What was once an unrealistic plan is now the most motivating thing I have going on in my life. Too bad the chances of that happening are way too fucking slim.

"Okay," she mutters to the fogged-up passenger window.

Is it fear that I sense in her voice or have I simply brought out the nerves after admitting something so bold and big? Ava is clearly not ready to have this conversation, and I know it's too soon in our relationship to go there, so for now, I'll take her meek "okay" as a win.

Once kissing Ava before heading inside, we walk side by side up the driveway of my parents' home, and I knock and open the door to the brick Scarsdale property an hour outside the city. I call out into the foyer that we're here, Ava in tow, her hand clammy and tight in my grasp. It's the most foreign thing for me to walk into this familiar place with a girl beside me; it's never been done before. Every holiday party, birthday, or event that my parents have hosted here, I was always one to walk in alone, and I had also always been perfectly fine with that. But the way Ava's hand feels so comfortable in mine, delicate and bony, makes it feel like I've done this dozens of times. And now, thinking of doing it any other way after today is simply out of the question.

Madison runs toward us first decked out in a black tulle dress, and I release Ava's hand to lift her up and squeeze her tiny little body with love. I can see Ava observing this exchange and I'm hoping I'm making a good impression, knowing that

I'll probably try to silently impress her for the rest of my life. Madison glances to my left.

"Hello, my name is Madison," she proclaims, extending her small hand toward Ava.

Ava reaches her hand up toward Madison in my arms and gives her a light handshake.

"Hello, Madison. My name is Ava. I'm a friend of your uncle Grant's." Her voice is soft and delicate and, fuck, I need her under me this second. Again. It's been *hours*.

"Don't you mean girlfriend?" Madison asks, one eyebrow raised like she means business. She is all Annie. This kid is going to give her parents a run for their money. Ava turns to me and laughs, tilting her head lovingly.

"Yeah. Girlfriend."

My heart warms, my body is thrilled, and I grab her hand as soon as I put Madison down.

"Come, babe. I want to show you off." We walk hand in hand into the gilded living room. My parents and siblings are seated on the velvet sofas and chairs placed strategically in front of the wood fireplace. Ben and Jackson are pouring cocktails by the bar cart, and as soon as the whole family spots Ava and me, the room quiets significantly. Ava shyly steps a few inches behind me, still holding my hand but now with both of hers, tightly. I feel the fast strumming of her heartbeat on the inside of her wrist. It's sweet how nervous she is but I'm not. Not at all. I've been dying to show her off for weeks.

"Happy Thanksgiving, everybody. This is Ava." I tug Ava out from behind me and watch as her face blooms pink. I turn to look at her and smile proudly, grateful and so damn happy that this woman is really mine. "My girlfriend."

"Hel—" Her voice comes out hoarse and her cheeks redden deeper. She clears her throat and tries again. "Hello. Happy Thanksgiving. Thank you for having me." She waves to no one in particular. That's when Annie crashes into Ava and grabs her in a giant bear hug.

"Ava! Hello! I'm Annie, Grant's big sister. *God*, I've been *dying* to meet you! You are so freaking pretty. Grant, she's so pretty. Happy Thanksgiving! How *are* you?"

Holy shit, I love this. This isn't a bit. Annie has genuinely been anxious to meet Ava, nudging me all day about when we were going to get to the house.

"Nice to meet you, Annie," Ava replies shyly. "Thank you. I'm doing good. Madison is really cute. I love her outfit."

"Thank you! Oh, that girl has her uncle wrapped around her tiny little finger. Doesn't she, Grant?" Annie chuckles, rolling her eyes. She ain't wrong. That kid owns me.

I ask Jackson how much Annie has had to drink, and he holds up two fingers.

"Pfft. Are you sure she had *only* two?"

"We got here ten minutes ago."

There it is. I watch from behind Ava as she's dragged around the room by Annie, introducing herself to Jackson and Layla, hugging my mom, Ben, my dad. I don't know why she was so nervous. Despite how shy she is with everyone, she's a natural. Or maybe that's just her personality, her kindness, her strength that make her so easy to talk to, so likeable.

Mom's been trying to catch my eye for the last twenty minutes to undoubtedly give me her seal of approval on Ava, so I finally look at her and she gives me a serious nod. An elegant and graceful Mom nod. I lift my eyebrows in question and she nods again but quicker, like she's stamping an approving seal with fresh hot wax on the first girl I finally brought home as mine. I spot Ava sitting on the beige rug in the center of the living room giving Annie's Jack a high-five and playing peek-a-boo with Baby Josh. I snag her attention and she's truly glowing.

"You look so beautiful," I mouth to Ava across the room, smiling widely.

"Come sit with me," she mouths back. I join Ava and Jack as they build a Lego sculpture, loving her genuine excitement for him when he explains the towers and trains he can build. Like I said, my girlfriend is a natural.

"Where's Ginger?" Ava leans into me and whispers moments later. I laugh that she remembers his name from the one time I mentioned him at dinner and lead her to the back porch, where our red-haired Newfoundland loves to hang out despite the freezing cold weather that is a New York winter. I open the porch door slightly and call for him to come inside. Ava's jaw drops and she immediately falls to her knees in front of him when he skips toward us. She scratches behind his ears and lets him take his time smelling his way around her.

"Holy shit, are you cute. Hello, cutie doggo!" she exclaims in a high-pitched voice, cracking up when he licks her entire face. Her eyes and nose scrunch as she gets devoured by this mutt. I cannot handle the sweetness on this girl.

"Ey, buddy. Off," I demand.

"No, it's okay. I don't mind. Ugh, he is so precious, Grant," she says, looking behind and up at me. "I am so jealous of you right now."

Ava nods excitedly when I tell her, "I can bring him home sometime if you want." Dad might have separation anxiety, but I think he can handle it for a couple of nights. It'll also give Martha a break from frequently cleaning after Ginger's constant shedding. And since when did I start calling my apartment home to Ava? I do wonder if she considers it home. Sometimes home can mean a person, and I wonder if she considers *me* home.

I kneel to sit beside her and scruff Ginger's fur. "Hey, babe. You wanna see my bedroom?" I turn to ask.

"Umm, *yes*, I want to see your bedroom!" She swiftly jumps up from her seated position on the floor and takes my hand when I reach it out for her. We ascend the rounded stairwell, and I open the door to my bedroom down the left hallway, letting Ava in before me.

"This is it."

She wastes no time observing every inch of my childhood bedroom, the desk, the bookshelf, the posters. All of it. The way she seems genuinely interested feels really important and flattering, like she wants to know who I am as a person, how I grew up. It's almost as if she's trying to absorb as much information about me as possible just from the contents of my bedroom. She lightly traces one of the many trophies on the bookshelf and squints to read the engraving.

"I didn't know you played basketball." She crooks her head to gaze at the wall of trophies and memorabilia, all engraved with my full name, all gold.

"Yup. All throughout high school and a couple of years in college." I lean against the mahogany dresser watching her, my legs crossed at the ankles.

She glances at me. "Why'd you stop?"

Have I ever answered this question? It takes me a moment to formulate a reply.

"Hmm . . . I'm not sure I ever loved it, actually. There was pressure on me to try out for the varsity team in high school because I was well over six feet by the time I was a sophomore, and I guess it stuck. It was a great way to blow off steam as a teenager, but it was never going to be a career for me. I quit when I realized that I had to focus on other things that I wanted more."

Nodding at the right time and listening intently, Ava gives me her utmost attention, and I feel like the luckiest guy that she cares. Ava cares to know me, every part of me, and no woman has ever asked about me like she does. I don't even think I've brought a girl up to this room since high school. She walks across the floor to stand before me, wrapping her arms around my waist, squeezing tightly. She beams when she glances up at me.

"You look like your mom." She grins. "The hair. And the eyes."

"Yeah. That's the consensus." I nod with a smirk. I've heard that one before. She bites her lip nervously when she confesses that she likes my family, and I bend to kiss her.

"They like you too," I say into her mouth.

Her eyes are full of hope and excitement when she asks, "Really?"

"I'm positive that they love you already. My mom gave me her seal of approval with just her eyes and a nod, my dad slapped my back three times and gave me a tipsy thumbs-up, and Annie gave me the eyebrows when she saw you playing with the kids." My recollections make Ava laugh out loud for a few seconds. Then it's quiet because suddenly the air in the room shifts to something serious and significant, like there's a stage and we're expected to announce something monumental. I know what I want to say, but I also know that we're not there yet. Ava looks me in the eyes, then changes her focus to my neck when she feels that air too. She toys with a button on my shirt, her other palm pressed flat on my stomach, and I'm convinced she's read my mind when she timidly says, "I want to tell you how I feel right now, but I can't find the words."

It's surreal; I feel like I'm on top of the damn world, and for the first time I can declare that I truly have Ava's entire heart. And it scares the shit out of me—the responsibility that comes with that knowledge is unquestionably the biggest form of pressure I've ever felt. This incredible woman deserves so much, the absolute world, and who am I to claim that role? I'm not enough for her, and I ask myself if knowing that but still dating her is selfish of me. I know it is.

"Try," I tell her, needing to hear it. It's not at all for my ego but rather for a sense of security knowing that I am Ava's and Ava is mine. And yes, I realize that it absolutely does make me selfish knowing that this is likely temporary, but I also sometimes feel that maybe it'll get so good between Ava and me that even when the unescapable happens, she'll somehow see past it and stay. It's sort of this ongoing battle within me.

Ava takes a deep breath. "I feel like you gave me a place to be me. I don't ever have to pretend with you. I don't have to be anyone other than myself, and that scares me because I have so many issues and a really shitty past, but you see through all of that. You see me and no one has ever done that before. Granted, I haven't been in plenty of positions like this one, but Pat was ashamed of me and you're not. You flaunt me and you take me places and you're proud to be with me, and that makes me . . ."

The fact that Pat had her and didn't gallop around town screaming that he did baffles me. He didn't know how good he had it, and for that, I'm glad, because his misfortune led to my fortune. Ava is my fucking treasure.

"It makes you what, Ava baby?"

"It makes me want nobody else. Ever." She looks up at me, her eyes glossy, and she shrugs one shoulder. I kiss her so deeply, we inhale each other's air, and I have to pull away only when it's hard to take a breath.

"Me neither. Like I said, Ava. You're it for me."

All throughout dinner, I replay what happened between Ava and me upstairs, and the guilt becomes this giant pressing thing on my brain; it's almost physically painful. I am in way too deep now, and the deceit is getting worse and worse as Ava falls harder and harder for me. The longer this relationship lasts, the worse it'll be at the end, and there truly is this inevitable collapse, a demise of our relationship that no one can stop, despite how good this gets. Not me, not her, not anyone. It's happening and she is completely oblivious to it.

"So, tell us about yourself, Ava." Mom motions across the table to Ava sitting beside me, our plates full, our glasses filled. Ava was right earlier when she said that I look like my mom. The twins are a mix between both of our parents, and Annie is totally Dad's blue-eyed daughter, but I'm undoubtedly Mom's younger male clone. I get my thick, dark hair from her, the piercing green eyes that Ava can't look into for more than a minute, the deep eye creases. Mom smiles warmly at the both of us sitting side by side.

Ava quickly peeks at me, sets down her knife and fork with a clink, then gently clears her throat. I grab her small thigh under the table and give it a light squeeze, reminding her that I'm here and I'm hers and she has nothing to be nervous about.

"Um . . . Okay. My last name is Campbell." She speaks softly, looking up as she thinks of what to say next. "I grew up in Northern California. Uh . . . I'm twenty years old." Ben and Layla simultaneously choke on their food, and I can't help being in awe every time they do something twin-ish, even after twenty-three years, but right now I want to slap them. Ava doesn't miss a thing. "Yeah . . . I know I'm young but we didn't know." She chuckles. "I mean, Grant didn't know how old I was."

"Age is just a number, darling," Annie assures Ava across the table, winking her bright blue eyes.

Ava chuckles, then turns to Mom again. "This food is delicious, Mrs. Wilder. Thank you so much for having me. All of you."

Ava's right to praise Mom's exceptional cooking. I've grown up eating gourmet food for breakfast, lunch, and dinner, but unlike my friends who had private chefs cook for them, I have a mom who went to culinary school so she could learn how to cook for my dad and, eventually, her four children. Mom's food is insane.

"Oh, please, sweetheart. Call me Julia! Mrs. Wilder is this old bloke's mother," she calls out, pointing to Dad and rolling her eyes for Ava's amusement. I love how comfortable Ava seems to feel here.

Thanksgiving dinner proceeds with natural chatter, Annie talking nonstop with Ava about girl things, I suppose, and Layla asking her about the classes she's taking at NYU because between the four of us, Layla will probably win a Nobel Peace Prize one day. I feel super grateful to my sisters for making Ava feel so welcome and comfortable and remind myself to thank them later before leaving. Ava's eyes shine when she speaks, her body loose, and I can tell she's having a genuinely good time. I pour her a glass of wine and she giggles quietly.

"Don't get me drunk in front of them. I'm gonna act crazy," she whispers into my ear, my head bent to listen to her quiet confession.

"I'll share the glass with you," I mumble into her ear. And while we're here . . . "I can't wait to get you naked later. You look so beautiful right now. I can't stop thinking about this morning." I kiss the soft skin below her ear, and she blushes, bringing her attention back to the slice of pumpkin pie on her plate. Annie catches my eye and grins hugely.

"What?" I mouth, eyes wide to make her stop. Annie is a loose cannon when she's drunk.

"I've never seen you like this," she mouths back. She raises an eyebrow, telling me something with that look; trying to make a point that Ava being here is a really big deal, and I couldn't agree more. I tell my sister the truth.

"I've never felt like this." Annie and I are as close as siblings can be, but this is uncharted territory for us. The last time I spoke to her about girls was probably back in high school, over a decade ago. There wasn't ever a need for that conversation because I've never been the relationship guy before. This feels good though. Honest and pure.

"I love her. She's so cute," Annie mouths back. She does a little shimmy in her seat, and I roll my eyes but also match her grin because of how excited I am about tonight and how successful bringing home a girl, *the* girl, has been.

"I know."

—⚏—

"Hey, babe? You okay over there?" I ask Ava on the drive home from dinner since she's been quiet ever since we got into the car ten minutes ago. She kisses my hand in hers, nods, but doesn't turn to look at me, resting her head on the window. On our way out of my parents' home, she was all smiles, giving tight hugs to my parents and siblings, profusely stating that she had an amazing time and that it was great meeting everyone. Mom insisted I bring her back as soon as possible and suggested we do dinner in the city one night soon.

But now, my beautiful girlfriend seems so down and uneasy, and my chest tightens. "What is it?"

In a small voice, she says, "They're so nice. Everyone. Your whole family."

"You say it like it's a bad thing." I chuckle awkwardly.

She shakes her head. "No, of course not. Obviously. I just wasn't expecting that," she says, finally turning to me. "Is that wrong of me to say? I'm not trying to be rude."

I reach over to grab her hand and tightly squeeze it.

"I know, babe. You're never rude. Why weren't you expecting that?" She shrugs, then blinks forward to the windshield, loosening her grip on my hand. "Baby?"

"I don't want to talk about it," she mumbles, fidgeting with her fingers in her lap, her red mini dress riding up and causing me to shift in my seat. "But thank you for encouraging me to come tonight. I had a really good time."

"We've got about an hour left to the drive, and I don't want you to be sad. Talk to me, babe. Let's figure this out together." Has anyone ever expected Grant Wilder to say that to a girl? No. No, they wouldn't have, but it just happened and I mean every single word. I want Ava to feel comfortable coming to me with whatever's bothering her, and right now it seems she'd rather brush it off than talk about it. "Ava baby," I push.

"It's about Pat and I don't want to offend you because it's like obvious that I'm comparing you guys but I don't want to, it's just automatic, I can't stop it and I think you do it too sometimes but more so me and I don't know why and I'm sorry and I don't really think you're anything alike but—"

"Whoa, whoa. Babe, slow down. You're ranting. What's up?"

She scrunches her eyebrows when she finally looks at me. "I just told you what's up," she says, confused.

"Okay . . . let's start at the beginning. Why do you compare me to Pat?" This is so fucking comical, it's ridiculous. This deception is killing me. Sometimes I want to yell the truth in her face so she can stop being naïve. Sometimes I get angry that she's still so clueless.

"I don't want to say."

It's the money, it's gotta be. On her end, we're alike because of the nice clothes and cars and watches. The materialistic stuff; the things she can see with her own eyes. Financially, we're nothing alike.

"Why are you so uncomfortable around money, Ava?" I squeeze her neck, stroke her cheek with my thumb to ease the awkwardness I'm sure she's feeling right now.

"Blech," she groans, shaking her head. "Ew. I don't want to talk about this."

I chuckle softly at her reaction because of how *Ava* it is. I'm so obsessed with her.

"Let me just say one thing. There's a good and a bad side to everything. I know that you saw the bad side of money with Pat and his family, but my family are really great people. They're far better than I am."

"Do you guys give charity? Is that bad to ask? Yeah, probably. Okay, don't answer." I laugh at her, poke her arm until she smiles. "What?"

"You're a clown sometimes."

"I'm just annoying." She giggles, swatting my hand away. "But your crush is too big to realize it."

I reach over to kiss her temple quickly before focusing on the road again. "Yes. We do. A lot of it."

"Good," she whispers. "That's really, really good." And the simple fact that Ava needed assurance that my family *gives charity* proves that this girl is way too good for me; I am way too out of her league.

—⁓—

When we quietly walk into my bedroom an hour later and slip each other's clothes off in the dark, my mind floods with reasons why this is so wrong, and I feel a deep desperation when we make love. I imprint every part of Ava naked in my mind so when this all ends, I can remember it forever. The way her neck blooms pink, her tight grip on my arms, her soft sounds. The way she catches my eye when I'm above her and smiles shyly, her slim, naked body against my tall, muscular one. The disproportionate size of us and how perfect we fit despite it. The way she hugs me as soon as it's over, tightly against her, and doesn't let me move for minutes, not even to clean her up.

"Don't move. Just stay here with me," she orders, panting and shaking in my arms. I feel the up and down of her breathing, her chest touching mine, not touching mine, touching, not touching. I kiss her cheek, down her torso, and stop at that shiny scar. The scar that brought her here, to me. I stare at it for a while and finally kiss it lightly. When I meet Ava's face again, she's wiping tears away from her face.

"You scare me sometimes," she whispers. "You're too perfect."

"You're the perfect one here. I'm just trying to keep up."

GRANT

Thanksgiving weekend was intense, not only because Ava and I slept together for the first time or because she met my family, but it was mainly the conversations that we had in my bedroom and on the drive home. I know that Ava saw something different, this degree of change that I couldn't have suspected but at the same time did. Once she's met my family, everything becomes this big deal, like "Grant has a girlfriend!" and suddenly, with everything out in the open, things between Ava and me are so solid.

The mood of our relationship somehow feels calmer, more relaxed, like now that people saw our dynamic together and support us being a couple, it's some sort of validation that we're good together. Not that I ever needed it, but I think Ava did since she was hesitant to jump into this thing with me because of our very obvious differences. I'm glad she finally does have that validation, though, because her overall hesitation from day one has been my biggest insecurity about our relationship. However, I would say that things are really good now. She's been on cloud nine with me since Thanksgiving weekend, and it feels good knowing I can provide that level of happiness for her.

Between Thanksgiving ending and Christmas/New Year's break coming up, Ava has been swamped with schoolwork. I haven't seen her since Sunday, and it is already Friday. I've convinced her to sleep over for tonight, so when she texts that she's finally done with class, I tell her to meet me in the office lobby instead of at my apartment. I have a couple more work things to wrap up and a few contracts to look over and sign before the weekend, and I don't want her waiting at my place alone.

Dina's certainly noticed how antsy I've been all day, so naturally, she questions why in a very Dina-esque way, flaunt and all. No one brushes Dina off; when I try, I'm met with raised eyebrows and a judging look. She puts a hand on her hip for a little *oomph*.

"Okay, fine. I'll tell you," I surrender. "So . . . I kind of have a girlfriend."

Dina looks pointedly at me and puts her hand to her heart in mock offense. I guess it is kind of weird that I haven't told her yet, but Dina would figure *it* out instantly and I can't risk anyone knowing.

"And you didn't think to tell *me*, your favorite person in the world, huh?" she sasses. I chuckle.

"Sorry. She'll be downstairs soon. Let me see if she wants to come up," I tell Dina, before rushing to the elevator.

Stretching on her tiptoes in the lobby of my office building, I find Ava reading the list of occupants to the right of the elevator in the glass encasing. I don't immediately say anything for a minute of quiet observation, but she feels me staring.

"What does that stand for?" she asks, pointing at my office line.

"My name," I explain. Thinking for a minute, she finally puts it together.

"Wait, you *own* the company?" she asks, her eyes wide.

"Yeah," I mutter.

"What! You didn't tell me that! That's impressive, Grant."

I hug her to me and lift her beanie just slightly to kiss her forehead despite the people around us who are somewhat staring. I know how this looks. Ava is wearing a silver puffer coat, loose denim jeans, and her trusty Converse sneakers. I'm in a two-thousand-dollar suit and a Gucci tie. Ava is short, I'm tall. She's young, I'm not. But fuck it, right? Appearances don't mean anything.

"You want to maybe come up for a couple minutes? I'll introduce you to some people?" I offer Ava hesitantly. But now that things are out in the open with my family knowing, I expect her to say yes and she does. Easily. She smiles, nods, and drags me back to the elevator. I unstrap her backpack and hold it under my arm. It's just the two of us when the elevator doors shut, and I immediately grab her face to kiss her hard. She giggles.

"What?"

"That was hot," she loud whispers, kissing me again. "Like in a movie."

"You're hot," I murmur into her neck. "You're my movie star. I missed you."

She pushes me away when the elevator stops on my office floor, the 34th. "So, who are you introducing me to?"

I wrap my arm around Ava's shoulder and walk her through the floor, saying hello to all the employees as we pass by the receptionist and cubicles toward Dina's desk across from my office. We halt in front of her.

"Dina, Ava. Ava, Dina. Girlfriend. Secretary. Second mom. Confidant."

Dina laughs at that last bit and stands to shake Ava's hand and give her a warm hug. "Hello, honey. Well, aren't you a pretty little thing!"

Ava looks back at me and smiles. "Thanks, Dina." She speaks softly. "It's nice to meet you. Thanks for taking care of Grant." She turns to the side and pats my stomach three times. "You sure are keeping him busy."

"Oh, that we are! How are you liking New York?" Dina asks, making light conversation and giving me *the eyes* whenever she can. The wide ones, the approving ones, that are combined with a smirk. I'm grateful for it because Dina's opinion has always mattered to me. Next, I introduce Ava to Adam, the CFO of my company, and finally, we make it to my corner office. I close the door behind us and grab her hand to pull her close.

"I really missed you," I mutter, leaning back to look at her and smile at how shy she is. That nose scrunch gets me every time.

"You're sappy, Grant Wilder." She giggles. "Who knew!"

"With you, I'm the sappiest of all the saps." She bursts into a fit of laughter, puts both her hands on my cheeks, and squeezes.

"I like you, weirdo." She observes every corner, knick-knack, and frame in my office as she does; slowly, meticulously, closely. I fucking love how she does it and I'll never tire of seeing her in her element like she is now. Finally, she makes it to my desk and plops down in my office chair. I've made sure to remove all files and documents that can screw this relationship up for me and tucked them away in a cabinet across the hall. Ava settles her arms on the armrests of the black leather office chair and swivels around in circles. She cackles when she catches me leaning against the wall with my hands in my pockets, watching her every move. Lifting her Converse-clad feet, she crosses her legs at the ankles and rests them on my desk. It's fucking sexy.

"Do you ever do that? I would do that all day if I worked here." She laughs, looking around at the view I see from my desk every day.

God, I like her. It doesn't stop. Every day is something different. Every time we're together she does something so minute and insignificant but it somehow makes me fall for her harder than I could imagine. It's not the sex, it's not the fancy dates, it's just being with her. Hanging out and grabbing a bite and taking a walk. Everything with Ava is so magical, as sappy as that sounds. She's a complete dork and I love it so much. It doesn't remind me of how young she is; rather it brings out the fun side in me, and I feel myself changing day by day as Ava's boyfriend. I'm an entirely different guy from the person I was before she happened.

"Not really but now every time I swivel, I'll think of you."
I wink at her before taking a picture of my stunning girlfriend.
"Wanna go home? I want to change before we do dinner. I'm
starving."

She nods, jumping up from the chair and hooking her giant puffer coated arm in mine. "Let's go, fatty."

I laugh, shake my head at Ava's unexpectedness, and exit
the building with her arm to my side the entire way down.

We quickly make the run to my apartment several blocks
away because it's cold and we don't want to wait outside for a
cab. We let out a heavy breath once we've arrived. I don't
think I've said the word hi to her yet.

"It's so bloody cold out!" she exclaims. "Why do I live
here?!"

I point to myself and say, "This guy. Hi, baby."

"Hi, you," she replies. "Long time no see!" The cold has
turned her nose red, and her hair is a staticky mess, but she's
glowing. I don't know, she just looks . . . perfect. Gorgeous.

"You look pretty," I say. "I like your beanie."

With yet another signature scrunch of her nose, she replies, "Thanks."

I tell her that we'll leave for dinner as soon as I change. I
know that Ava can get a bit intimidated when we're out in
public and I'm in a suit, so I dress casually, hoping to make
things easier on her. She jumps from the couch when I exit the
bedroom.

"Daaaaaaaaamn," she calls out, wiggling her eyebrows.
"Someone's looking all kinds of sexy."

"Yeah, you're right. You are. Let's go." I laugh.

"'Kay, but let me first pee." She throws her coat and hat
on the couch and skitters off. My eyes nearly bulge out of my
head when I see her walk toward me a minute later.

"Is that a Coldplay sweatshirt?" I ask.

She looks down at her chest. "Yeah, its Connor's. Why?"

That's it, I'm done for. Sprinting, I put my head between her legs from behind to lift her up on my shoulders. In between her shrieking and laughing, she attempts to tell me to put her down. I try leaving the high-ceiling living room and she bumps her head.

"Ow," she groans, palming the wall by her face.

"Oh, fuck," I mutter. I hurriedly set her down on the kitchen island and grab an ice pack to place on her forehead.

"I'm so sorry. I wasn't thinking." I'm frantically apologizing when she brings a soft hand to my shoulder and gives it a light squeeze, smiling sweetly.

"It's fine, Grant. Relax. It's just a little bump."

"I'm tall," I explain, stating the obvious.

"Good job," she says sarcastically. Ava gives a sad attempt at a wink. I smother her with kisses and laugh at how adorable her half wink is. "You're weird. You get excited about the most random things that I do."

"No, I think I just get excited about *everything* that you do."

She shrugs. "Yeah, probably."

I rub up the length of her thighs and bring my mouth to her neck while she ices her head. When I nibble on her ear, her breath hitches.

"Grant," she breathlessly whispers, setting the ice pack beside her and grabbing my waist resting between her legs. I kiss my way across her cheek and take her mouth, heavy and wet and plump. I slide my hands under the sweatshirt that got us here, and she softly moans into my mouth.

"I need to have you right now. Let's go to bed," I mumble, lifting her from the marble island.

She nods hurriedly. "Please," she pleads with me, breathless. "Wait, no."

"No?" I ask.

She nods toward the living room. "Couch." I grin hugely and take her bottle lip between my teeth. "Is that okay?" she mumbles.

"Fuck yeah, it's okay." I walk us over to the couch, sit back, and groan when Ava straddles me with her thin, long legs. Seconds later, she feels my hardness beneath her and grinds against me, fabric on fabric, but it's not enough, we both know that. She jumps off of me and strips her pants, underwear, and shoes in less than ten seconds. I am seated on my sofa in this ginormous living room, staring at my stunning, naked girlfriend in nothing but a pair of purple socks and a Coldplay sweatshirt. I am a lucky, lucky man.

Ava glances at my crotch, then back at me. I nod and stand, tugging at my waistband.

"Lay down," I demand. She shakes her head and pushes me back down. *Is she . . .?*

Yup. She is. Ava climbs on top of me and stares, shell-shocked. She looks down then looks back up, down, up.

"I don't know what I'm doing," she whispers, her voice tight.

"I think you know exactly what you're doing."

"Do it. Help me," she breathes.

It feels like I black out from the pleasure. It's almost too much. Ava has me stammering, and when it's over, our heavy breathing forms a cloud of carbon dioxide, and everything feels right in the world. Euphoric.

"You are another level of beautiful, Miss Campbell."

"I'm hungry," she hums into my now sweaty neck.

I laugh, turn my head, and I kiss her over and over and refuse to move when she tries pushing me away. She quietly chuckles against my lips.

"You wanna stop kissing me for five seconds so we can go eat?" she whispers softly, her head on my shoulder.

"That sounds awful," I reply.

"Well, starvation sounds awful." I slowly lift her off me, and when she stands and looks down between her legs, she glances up at me wide-eyed and utters, "Oh."

"Sorry about that."

She shakes her head. "No, no, I just never . . . you know," she says, shrugging. "I didn't mean to make you uncomfortable. Sorry." Her cheeks are pink when she looks up at me again.

"You didn't, baby. I'm good. I'll be right back." I retrieve a towel, wet it a little, and clean Ava up. She redresses, I tuck my dick back into my pants, and we sit side by side tying our sneakers in unison. We retrieve our coats and head to eat, and the entire elevator ride down, I can't stop thinking of how I lived before this girl but quickly realize that I didn't. I was barely getting by, and she came and changed everything.

On our walk toward the restaurant with Ava's hand in mine, she turns and nervously looks up at me.

"So . . . I have to tell you something. And I also have a question." She's got that sex afterglow, and her hair is a little tangled, and I can't help but snicker.

"What?" she whines.

"You look like you just had sex."

"I wonder why." She mimics my deep voice. I laugh because with this one, I'm always laughing. "Okay, for real. I have to tell you something."

"Me too," I say. I've been avoiding mentioning the birthday party next week because it's so un-Ava, but it's happening and I want her there. "You first," I tell her.

"My brother Devon is in town for a day," she begins awkwardly. "I was wondering if you wanted to come for drinks with us later? I was gonna go alone, but I thought maybe you'd want to meet him?"

There's no way I can say no to that, but my heart is pumping hard and suddenly I feel nervous. The intimacy that I'm meeting her brother pulls me even tighter to wanting something long term with Ava. I know it's impossible, but I still want to be the guy she brings home proudly.

"Yeah, sure. We'll head over there after dinner. My turn?" I explain the birthday party, the extravagance of it, the fact that my parents have gone all out since I was nine, my first birthday in New York after moving here from Houston. When she senses my hesitation and the fact that I'm trying to sell this party as no big deal, she interrupts me.

"It's *your* birthday. It's *your* party. I'm *your* girlfriend. I'll be there, Grant." It's exactly what I need to hear.

Over dinner, Ava confirms that she finally told her family about me, and I'm worried that this could be the beginning of the end; it might be impossible to hide things when it's not just Ava in the picture.

"What'd you tell them?" I probe, bending to take a bite of my lemon branzino. Ava ordered a fettuccini dish, and she's currently sitting opposite me, scarfing it down. That sex really did make her hungry. She swallows a big bite and shrugs.

"That I met a guy who I like. Don't make me say more just to boost your ego," she jokes.

I look at her in feigned shock. "Ava . . . you—you *like* me?!"

She spits out the water she's just sipped from her glass and starts laughing uncontrollably, covering her mouth when other patrons eating beside us glance at the ruckus we're making. Grabbing a napkin, she brings it to her face and whisper-shouts, "It's coming out of my nose!"

"Ewwwww," I tease.

She throws the napkin at me and rolls her eyes. "You're the worst."

"I'm the *best*," I correct.

"Yeah," she smirks, looking straight at me. Her eyes are shining and her cheeks are red from the few sips of wine she's had with dinner and she looks perfect. "You really are."

—ɰ—

The plan is to meet Devon at a cocktail bar near Ava's place in Tribeca, so we hail a cab over there after dinner, arriving a few minutes early. Ava drags me along by the hand as she observes her surroundings and people-watches. Again, like an art gallery. Scanning the room on her tiptoes, she scouts out the space for Devon. As soon as Ava spots her brother, she runs over to him and hugs him so tightly, with a huge smile on her face. Earlier I was nervous but I'm so glad I agreed to come. Watching that made it worth the probable anxiety I'll have when Devon gives me The Talk. There might be a bit of inebriation exhibiting Ava's reaction right now because the wine from dinner was kind of strong, but that's what makes it even cuter. *God, I love her.*

Shit. Hold on a second.

Did I just admit that I love her?

Yeah, I totally did.

Wow, okay. I love Ava.

Holy shit, I love her and all it took was Ava giving Devon a giant bear hug. Do I tell her? No, I don't tell her. Ava will run. It's way too early. But yeah, it's official. I am so in love with Ava Campbell.

I watch as Ava turns her head, scanning the room for me, and grinning like a goofball once she sees that I'm still standing where she left me.

"This is Grant," she shouts over the loud music, pulling me by my wrist. Devon and I shake hands and exchange formalities. We find some seats at the crowded bar, then order two beers and the cocktail Ava asks for. We both gawk at her when she calmly downs it in three gulps.

"Whoa, there, cowgirl!" Devon exclaims.

She rolls her eyes in response. "Oh, yeah! I'm a drinker now," she jokes.

I raise both hands in innocence. "You good?" I quietly ask Ava.

She looks up at me with bright eyes and nods. "*So* good."

"What do you do, Grant?" Devon asks, turning to face me.

"Oh! I know this one!" Ava calls out. *Burp*. She laughs at herself. "Manufacturing! Scrap metal! Technology!" Holy shit, she's drunk and I'm falling even harder. I chuckle and agree.

"Yeah, she pretty much got it. You?"

"I'm an accountant out in Chicago," he replies, explaining that he lives with his girlfriend but they are thinking of moving. "I'm in town for an interview I had earlier today hoping to land a job out in Brooklyn. Tell me more about your manufacturing scrap metal technology business." He chuckles, nodding at Ava.

"Blah, blah, blah!" Ava perks up. "Y'all are boring. I'm going to pee."

"You okay going alone?" I ask.

She grabs my face with both hands and smacks her lips to mine. In front of Devon.

"Always worrying about me, aren't you? I am mucho bueno."

Ava is unlike anyone I have ever met in my entire life but *how? How* is she like this? How did she experience an abortion gone wrong, a sickness, anxiety and depression, but come out stronger, tougher on the other end and so incredible? It's like Pat sat there trying to beat her down, and instead, she raised up her middle finger, healing and growing into the beautiful, vibrant woman that she is. I'm in awe of her. I would've never been able to bounce back and be happy again after something so traumatic happened to me. Not many people could, but Ava is the strongest person I know. I am so damn proud of her.

While explaining the ins and outs of my business to Devon, he cuts me off short. "So how long have you been dating my sister?" he asks, taking a big gulp of his beer.

"About four months, now," I reply wearily, clearly surprising him by the look of his expression.

"Damn, she's good. We had no idea." I explain to him that she wanted to keep it private for a while until it became real. To me, it was always real. From the moment she took eight bites of ice cream. "Does she still do that . . . ya know, the walking around thing," he wonders, turning his finger airborne.

"Yes!" I shout, laughing with him. "Literally *every time* she sees something new. She did it earlier today at my office. I'm like, it's not *that* interesting."

"Indiana Jones. We'd call her that as a kid because she was always exploring, doesn't matter what. She still does it, huh. Man, I've missed that kid." He chuckles, lifting his beer glass.

"Yeah, Ava's pretty damn great," I add, nodding in agreement. Great doesn't begin to cover a quarter of it, but it's not like I'm gonna profess my love for his sister to him. Yeah, *love*. It happened. Grant Wilder fell in love.

"Hey, man, listen . . ." Devon starts, turning in his seat so we're face-to-face.

Well, the nerves about meeting Devon boils down to this point. Here comes the older brother warning speech.

"Ava has been through so much, more than you could possibly imagine. I'm not sure what she's told you, but we both know that this relationship is a bit . . . unconventional. Be careful with her. I don't know you, man, but I have to look out for my sister." Devon emphasizes the word "unconventional," and I feel this weird pit in my stomach. I guess he's right, but I'm not even wearing a suit tonight. I wonder what part of my dynamic with Ava makes him question the normalcy of our relationship.

I nod before replying, "As you should. I appreciate it, Devon. Ava is safe with me, I swear."

"Do you love her?" He challenges me with an intimidating stare, and it's weird for me because I'm usually the one doing that. Green eyes as an advantage, of course. *Well, Devon, I just admitted to myself about thirty minutes ago that I'm in love with your sister, so yeah.*

"I do love her, yes," I reply, loving how comfortable I am hearing those words exit my mouth.

He nods curtly. "Does she know that you love her?"

"I haven't said it to her yet."

"You should say it to her. If you mean it, you should tell her. She needs it."

I nod in affirmation, understanding what he's implying here. Devon knows how bad Ava needs someone to protect her, and I'm so fucking privileged and glad that I'm that guy; that I now officially have her oldest brother's blessing to *be* that guy. There is no greater feeling in the world.

AVA

My mind is hazy, my legs fairly wobbly as I leave the bathroom in search for my brother and my boyfriend. I think I drank that cocktail a little too quickly, and the wine earlier brought me to this bar already tipsy. I blink my eyes a few times before scanning the room to find them. When I spot them easily, because naturally Grant is the tallest guy in the room, I notice that they're in the middle of an intense discussion. I have no doubt that Devon is warning Grant or at least something along those lines. I wiggle my way in between two of my most favorite guys ever and wrap my arms around their necks to collect them from the bar. The alcohol has made me tired and I'm a little too drunk right now, so I tell Grant that I want to go home and head toward the exit. While Grant hails two cabs outside, one for us and one for my brother, I sit beside Devon on the metal bench outside the bar.

"You good? How you feeling?"

I'm laughing internally because Devon has never seen me like this before, and it's probably the fifth time so far that I've gotten drunk this year. Part of the college experience, I guess, but not really since it's with my boyfriend and not at a frat party or whatever. I like it better this way. So much better.

"I'm fine, Dev," I mutter, leaning my head on his shoulder. "You're being such a big brother."

"Whoa, weird! I wonder why!"

I laugh and swat his arm. Didn't I say that same thing to Grant earlier? I chuckle to myself. We Campbells are all the same, aren't we? Grant catches my eye from a few feet ahead and with a thumbs-up asks the silent "You good?" I nod.

"What do you think of him?" I ask my brother, slightly gouging for some information on their talk earlier. They were pretty huddled up. It's obvious they were discussing me.

"I like him. Seems like a good guy. He's friendly and outgoing," Devon replies, nodding in concentration.

"You can say that again."

"Be careful," he begins to lecture, turning to face me. With his eyebrows close together, he appears pretty serious, so I sit up straight and face him. "I don't want to see you get hurt again. Especially after that other asshole."

I put my hand on his shoulder to ease his angst. "Grant is really good to me, Devon. I'm super careful, I swear, but I don't have to be. Not with him," I assure him, realizing it more myself as I speak the words aloud. It's true. I'm not sure I've ever actually verbalized that. Who exactly would I have said it to? But I'm one hundred percent confident that I'm safe with Grant, that he cares about me unconditionally. He's unfazed by anything I tell him, and that's how I know that he is mine no matter what. I give my brother a tight hug and tell him goodbye before he heads to the airport for an early morning flight.

"See you Christmas?" he asks, kissing me on the cheek.

I nod and smile at him. "Of course."

Devon shakes Grant's hand, Grant hits his back like guys do, and then my oldest brother slides into the back of the cab and waves goodbye before driving away. We slip into our own cab then, and the driver drops us off down the block from Grant's place. When we exit the car, Grant puts his arm around my shoulder and starts us in the direction of his apartment.

"How you feeling, drunkard?" he teases me, kissing my temple softly. I unintentionally burp in reply, coaxing a husky laugh from my ridiculously handsome boyfriend. I'm genuinely embarrassed to be standing next to this hot piece of meat. Oh, yeah, I'm big-time drunk.

"You're so hot," I say, clearly out of my mind. Amusement fills his every feature as he waits patiently for me to say more. *Burp.* "I kind of like you."

"That's great, babe, because I like you too. More than you know."

—m—

When we're back in the comfort and warmth of Grant's place, I slip into his bed and clutch the blanket until he crawls in beside me. While cuddling tightly and whispering nonsense—he refuses to have sex with me while I'm drunk even if I consent to it—he receives a text. He reaches his long arm to grab the phone from his nightstand and taps the screen. Quickly reading the message, he places it facedown on his chest. I'm a little put off by his reaction toward the message, so I ask if everything is okay.

"Uh . . . yeah, all's good," he mumbles quickly. As drunk as I am, I can recognize how off he's acting, so I ask him what's up. He takes a deep breath and flashes the screen to me.

Hannah: Hey you. The gang is getting together at Freddy's next week. I better see you there. ;)

"That sounds like fun. Who's Hannah?" I notice Grant wince when I say her name, and I think I might be a little too drunk for this discussion right now, but I probe anyway. He takes a deep breath and turns to face me, his pretty eyes on mine. Grant seems worried.

"Hannah is . . ." He stops, racking his brain for an answer.

"Yeeeees?" I ask when he doesn't finish his sentence for a good minute.

"She's the . . . Fuck," he mutters, frustrated, closing his eyes and rubbing up the length of his face. "I don't want to make you uncomfortable."

"You won't." *He might.* But at this point, I am way too curious and drunk.

"Hannah's the uh . . . the girl I used to, you know . . ."

"Hook up with?" I fill in. He gives me a reluctant nod. "Oh. Okay . . . Are you guys, like, still friends or whatever?" What do I expect to gain from this conversation? Do I think Grant is cheating on me? Would it be considered cheating if he slept with someone else right now? I mean, *it would, right?* We *are* together.

"Not like that, obviously, but we're all part of a big group," Grant explains. He looks like he's hating this conversation so much.

"Oh. Cool," I say, my voice small. He notices and swiftly turns to face me head-on.

"Ava," he states strongly.

"Hmm?"

"This is probably the worst conversation for me to have with you." Grant seems genuinely uncomfortable right now. It looks like he'd rather be talking about anything else. If I asked him how to change a tire, I'm sure he'd explain the hell out of it, animated and everything, just to get out of talking about *Hannah.*

"Why's that?" I ask, kissing him quickly. "It's just me."

"Because I'm not that same person anymore, and it's hard talking to you about who I once was." Why is Grant so convinced that he's an entirely different person from before he met me? He acts like his past is years away. It's only been months, he told me. I ask him that. He scoffs. "Trust me, Ava. I'm loads different."

"Tell me how," I beg. It's only fair. I told Grant so much about my past. I don't think he's told me even an iota of what his looks like. "Tell me who you were."

"I really don't want to do that." Grant darts his eyes from mine like he's guilty for something. I ask him if he's still that person, and he profusely states that he isn't.

"Then tell me. I'm curious. And I'm a little tipsy still."

He chuckles and taps the tip of my nose. Grant takes a big breath and turns on his side to face me.

"Okay. I was . . . I was extremely irresponsible. I don't think I held a proper job for more than a few months at a time. I partied a lot. I gambled . . ."

I mean, I could've guessed all of this, but it's a lot to take in. Not that anything changed between us—I still adore him remarkably—but this stuff fascinates me. I've never met or spoken to anyone who's dabbled in all the nefarious things, and I guess this also makes me feel a little insecure to be his girlfriend.

"I don't really want to be telling you this." Grant is the one who seems to be incredibly insecure and awkward though. And I get it, I do. I mean, I'm young and clueless. Maybe he feels like he's tainting me a bit, being a bad influence by telling me, but I want to hear more. It's interesting and I'm curious and like I said, I'm drunk.

"It's just me, Grant! I'm not going anywhere. Tell me more. Did you do drugs?" He winces, nodding slowly. "That's cool. What kind?"

"Ava." He laughs this time. "No."

"What!" I whine.

"We are not talking about drugs right now," he says, shaking his head at me. I beg him to tell me but he refuses.

"Please! Just tell me!" I continue to whine. "Did you do heroin?"

Grant howls in laughter. Genuine laughter. It makes me smile.

"No, Ava, I did not do heroin. Now can we stop please?"

I feel bad, so I agree. "Fine. I never did drugs, you know."

"I could've guessed that," Grant says, looking pointedly at me. It makes me giggle.

"It would probably make me have a panic attack." He looks at me longingly, his eyes softening, and plants a light kiss on my lips.

"You've never had a panic attack with me," he utters quietly, caressing my hair, moving it from my eyes. And he's right. Now that I think about it, I realize that I haven't had a panic attack since I landed in New York. Not one and that freaks me out. Is it Grant? *Holy shit.*

"Whoa, you're actually right. That's pretty telling, isn't it?"

"You tell me," he mumbles into my mouth. I swallow thickly and bring my eyes to face him. Grant looks so hopeful. By now, the alcohol has worn off, so I'm not as much of a chatterbox. I know that whatever I'm about to say is going to make Grant happy, so I go ahead and say it since I also feel this in my heart. Although part of me is a little frightened, I'll take what I can get because those panic attacks were the worst.

"Me not having a panic attack with you in four months? It's a pretty big deal, Grant. I used to get them really bad. They were chronic." I remember sitting in my sterile hospital room, pressing the red emergency button by my bed to call for a nurse because I felt paralyzed in my own body and couldn't communicate from the sheer panic I felt in my chest. My limbs would lock up, and I'd hold my breath but not intentionally. It was a coping mechanism; otherwise, I'd hyperventilate until I was breathing hundreds of breaths per minute and then I'd black out. That's happened more times than I can count, and the fact that I haven't had to deal with even one panic attack in the last four months is huge for me.

"What were they like?" he asks, tracing my eyebrows and my lips softly.

"Like I couldn't breathe. Sometimes it felt like I was drowning in a swimming pool. Sometimes my arms and legs would lock up, and I'd feel paralyzed. Sometimes I'd vomit from all the shuddering." His face falls and I casually shrug my shoulders; it's my reality at this point. It's harder for him to hear it than for me to experience it because of how used to it I am. If I had a panic attack in this moment, I wouldn't blink twice. I'd let it pass and move on with my night. Grant, however, lets it break him a little bit.

"Oh no. Baby . . ."

"Am I too fucked up for you?" I mumble, unable to make eye contact with Grant because of the pity I just witnessed pass through his face. I never wanted to feel broken or damaged with him; I just *am* broken and damaged. Or I was. I can't ever differentiate between whether my trauma defines me or if my trauma has simply guided me to where I am today. It's a fine line.

"Did you not just hear what I told you about myself?"

I shake my head at his "explanation."

"That's different, Grant. That's just you having dumb fun. That's the kind of fucked up you get from drinking or drugs, not from depression."

He grabs my face to steal a wildly carnal kiss. When he breaks away from me, he stares into my eyes, coaxing me to listen to what he's about to tell me. "You are not *too* anything for me. You're perfect for me, Ava. You're my girl."

I wrinkle my nose and giggle. "Okay, Casanova." I laugh, rolling my eyes. He lifts his phone from beside his pillow and extends his arm to put it down. I nod toward it when he looks back at me.

"We should go," I tell him.

"Huh?"

"To the party. We should go." Grant quickly declines. "Why not? It'll be fun."

"I don't want you around those people," he states strongly, almost like he's concluding the conversation here.

"Those people," I say with air quotes, "are your friends. Don't you want me to meet them?" Who *wouldn't* want to introduce their girlfriend to their friends? Isn't that the first thing people do when they're proud of the relationship they're in?

"Ava, trust me. You don't want to be at this thing," he argues, becoming a little frustrated at my persistence. I don't think his concern is about my comfort, rather his fear of bringing me around his friends, but I can handle it. Besides, it'll give me a glimpse into Grant's life, and I'm finally ready for that. He's been so honest with me tonight, and it's obvious that he's changed or has every intention to. I don't fear that Grant will be that person again, so what's the harm?

"It's not a big deal, babe. We're just going to a party together," I push convincingly.

Finally, he smiles and raises his eyebrows at me. "Did . . . did you just call me babe?" he asks teasingly, nudging my side with his elbow.

I roll my eyes at him and push his arm away. "I'm drunk! It doesn't count!" I say, laughing. I'm not really all that drunk anymore. It totally counts.

Climbing above me, he buries his head in my neck. "What're you doing to me, Ava?" Grant whispers against my hot skin.

"You tell me," I reply, tightening my arms around him.

He takes a deep breath. "You're changing me. For the first time in my life, I finally like who I am."

AVA

I'm sprawled out on Grant's leather sofa waiting while he changes out of his work suit before the party at his friend Freddy's house tonight. Within the last hour that I've been at his house, I've noticed how anxious and tense Grant has been, and it seems odd to me that he'd be so nervous to spend time with people he's known since high school. I mean, could his friends be *that* bad? Is it *me*? Or can this unease coming from Grant be from something entirely different, unrelated to the party we're on our way to?

Jumping up from the sofa when Grant exits his bedroom, I immediately pause to assess his new ensemble and blink down at my outfit to find that I hate what I see. My face must look like I've smelled something sour.

"What?" he asks, confused by my weird reaction. "You don't like it? Should I change?" I shake my head and head toward the door, but he doesn't let me off the hook that fast. "Hey. Ava. Look at me. What's wrong?"

I point between us. "This," I mumble. Look at how I'm dressed compared to him! I'm in a purple NYU sweatshirt and my trusty denim overalls. Grant is wearing a cashmere sweater, suit pants, and fucking designer loafers. This is the first time I've felt truly insecure about how I'm dressed, and I hate that this is happening because I love my style. I love my clothes.

"What do you mean, *this*," he asks, annoyed, frustrated, almost *mad*. His green eyes are doing this glaring thing.

"You know what."

"No, I really don't. You're going to have to explain it to me, Ava," he replies curtly.

"It's just . . . us. We're so different."

"Ava . . ." He sighs, looking away, seeming aggravated with me. "Don't do this again. Come on. We're way past that." I nod and move past him, but he stops me again. "Babe, don't just walk away. Talk to me."

"Look at us, Grant. We're so incredibly different that we look stupid together. I look so damn stupid standing next to you," I say before taking my arm back and finally twisting the doorknob, exiting the apartment. The keys jingle as he locks the front door and meets me by the elevator. He slams his finger on the down button and turns to face me.

"This *really* pisses me off, Ava," he stresses strongly. I cock an eyebrow at him. "Why do you care so much about how we look on the outside? It's just clothing! Nobody knows our dynamic and how happy we are behind closed doors. It's no one's business anyway."

"I don't want to look like I don't belong with you. Especially tonight. I don't want to change myself either," I say. I'm reminded of all my time spent in therapy, discovering self-love, recognizing that Pat's opinion of me didn't matter; that I don't have to look any part, fit any mold, that I have to be authentic to myself and find people who love that person. It makes me uncomfortable that I look so wildly different than Grant but not enough to change myself. Never enough to change myself. He curls his arm around my hips and pulls me close to him when we step onto the elevator.

"I don't want you to change yourself either. In fact, I won't allow it. The first time I saw you in those overalls? My heart leapt like four miles. I was in awe."

"Really?" I chuckle. "When was that?"

"I swear on it. It was the first time you came over to my place. You were wearing a pink shirt under these, and I had to hide my giant smile from you because I looked ridiculous," he admits, hooking his finger in my right shoulder strap. I chuckle and hug him tightly, thankful for his reassurance. As long as he loves them and as long as I love them, who cares, right? Fuck it.

"Sorry. Maybe I'm just nervous for tonight. Thank you," I whisper into his neck.

"You don't have to thank me, Ava baby. The only place you have to fit in is here," he says, putting a palm to his chest. "All that other stuff doesn't matter. No one else matters." I lean back to look at him, stifling my laughter at how cliché and cheesy that was. He rolls his eyes when I can't take it anymore and burst into a mocking laugh.

"Oh, shut up!"

—⟋⟋⟋—

Grant underestimated how lovely his friends are, so naturally I'm wondering why he didn't want to bring me tonight. Freddy's fiancé Elizabeth introduces me to all the friends and explains the rules of beer pong before pairing up with me to start a game. I catch Grant smiling cheekily halfway through our second round, knowing that he's had a bunch to drink and is feeling pretty jolly about it. Since when did we become party people? Hell, this is *fun*.

Grant comes to stand beside me, throws his arm around my shoulder, and smothers my head to his chest. He kisses my forehead hard. I laugh and ask him what he's doing.

"Keeping you close," he murmurs. His hand grazes my back throughout the rest of the game, and he high-fives Elizabeth and me when we win the second round. My face flushes beet red when he tries kissing me in front of everyone, and it makes him laugh when I don't let him. We stand close to each other throughout the night as Grant introduces me to all of his high school friends as his *girlfriend*, and hands me his red Solo cup when I ask to try some of his beer. He howls when my face wrinkles in disgust.

"Aww, Granty, you've stooped pretty low, haven't you? Your next contender wears overalls? You ended things with *me* for *her*?" I swiftly turn around when I hear a female voice ask from behind me, laughing amongst her friends. I find a hot blonde assessing me from head to toe. She then smirks at Grant beside me.

"Hannah, don't you fucking dare!" Grant booms, silencing the room. I'm dumbfounded at his ability to claim an entire room of people but also at this fight unfolding before me. "I'm not taking your shit with her. Not this one. Over my dead body."

So, *this* is Hannah. Grant used to sleep with *that?* And now he's sleeping with *me?* Is the guy blind? The challenge in Hannah's eyes scares me. This could be straight out of the *Mean Girls* movie, it's ridiculous. *It's 2017, Hannah. We don't make fun of people's clothing.*

"When will you ever learn, Granty? I never lose." She winks with her pretty blue eyes and blows Grant a kiss before strutting away in giant heels. Grant is fuming, taking a step toward her, the veins in his arms bursting out in rage.

"Hannah—"

I put my hand to his chest to calm him, to keep him from doing something stupid or saying something mean. I make him look at me. "It's okay," I say into his eyes. "I'm fine."

"No, Ava, it's not okay," he insists, sparkly white teeth clenched tight, his sharp jaw flexing in hot fury. "She can't talk about you like that."

"Damn, Wilder. You're whipped as fuck. You sure this one is worth it?" a male voice calls out from the sofa, chuckling, a tumbler of amber liquid in his hand. Grant whips his head around and glares at him.

"What did you just say to me?" There's a venom in Grant's eyes so foreign; so wicked.

"Hey, man. Relax." Whiskey guy looks scared, and I would be too if the look Grant was giving him was directed at me. The cat-like green color of his eyes can be so intimidating sometimes. I can barely look at them for more than a minute. Grant holds his stare for more. Finally, he speaks, his demeanor hostile and vicious.

"Did you just ask me if my girlfriend is worth it, Louis?"

"Grant," I whisper, grabbing and tightening my grip on his thick wrist. "Don't do this. Let's just go home."

He rips his arm out of my grasp and heads for Louis' position on the sofa. I run after him and the moment Grant's arm lifts to hit him, I slither between these two hot heads, Grant's elbow bumping my head. I wince in pain and his eyes widen a moment later; frozen like snow, he doesn't waver but stares at me terrified. The look in his eyes shocks me because of how scared *he* looks. Gritting his teeth, he turns to face Louis again.

"If you don't treat my girlfriend with the utmost respect, I'll have your fucking head."

"Oooookay!" I yell, intervening. "The end! Show's over!" I put my palms on Grant's stomach and push him toward the front door.

When we're out from among the crowd, he speaks low so only I can hear him.

"Don't leave me. I'm sorry," he whispers desperately. "But please don't go."

Does Grant really assume I'm going to *leave him* over this? He didn't do anything to me. His frightened expression pains me, and I quickly reassure him that's not what's happening here.

"That's insane, Grant. You're drunk. Don't say that. I'm not leaving you, but I think you should go outside, okay?"

160

"Okay," he murmurs solemnly, heading for the door. With a small voice, he asks, "Are you . . . are you coming home with me?" *My heart.*

"Of course I am. I'm just gonna go pee. I'll call us an Uber." I kiss his cheek and scurry to the bathroom. I'm washing my hands at the kitchen sink when Elizabeth walks in, smiling. It's obvious that she witnessed that whole ridiculous ordeal.

"Hey," she says. I say it back. She turns to face me and gives me another sincere smile. "I was pretty surprised when Grant Wilder brought a girl here tonight. And held her hand. And tried to kiss her. And introduced her to his friends. And couldn't stop smiling." Elizabeth speaks carefully, as if I can comprehend all her words and their meaning just by her tone of voice. She's acting as if it's the first time he's done this, and I find it hard to believe. As awkward as it is for me to acknowledge it, Grant was a total womanizer.

"You were surprised? Is that . . . unusual?" I ask, taken aback by her genuine disbelief at the fact that Grant brought me to this party on his arm. She cocks a perfectly tweezed eyebrow.

"I've known Grant for ten years, and he's never brought a girl to any of these get-togethers." Her facial expression reads *Need I say more?*

"Oh," I mutter softly.

"He looks at you like you're the only person in the room. I've never seen Grant like this before. Not once in the last decade. He's totally in love with you, Ava." When she says those seven words, my heart beats fast, faster.

"I wouldn't say that," I reply, chuckling. But inside, I'm freaking out. Isn't this what I wanted to hear all this time? That he *is* different, that he's changed? So why is it that the only thing running through my head is the fear that once I divulge my full story, the three parts that I intentionally left out, he won't want me anymore? It'll be too much; too intense; too much liability. But I stand by the promise to myself that those are the only three things that I will never tell him despite what happens between us. I have too much pride to lay myself completely bare, even to Grant. Between the suicide attempt, the case, and the fact that I can't ever have children, even someone like Grant couldn't handle the drama and responsibility that comes with that.

However, with Elizabeth's words comes this realization that I can't let Grant fall in love with me *unless* he knows the real me; the *whole* me; every part, good and bad and ugly and tainted. Whether he says it to me now or in a year, I know good and well that he needs to know the full truth about me before he can make that giant declaration, and I have to question whether or not I want him enough to one day be obligated to let him in on the truth.

Elizabeth interrupts my thoughts. "I don't doubt it for a second, Ava. Just know that Hannah will never stop," she says, placing a supportive hand on my shoulder. She proceeds with explaining that Hannah has made it tough on any girl Grant has tried to be with.

"Why hasn't he said anything to her?" I ask. Is he that submissive with Hannah that it's affected his entire dating life until I came along? That's ridiculous. *I mean, you're almost twenty-eight. Stand up for yourself.*

"I guess he never found anyone who was worth the fight until he met you. I mean, Hannah is a monster. She always finds a way to sneak back into Grant's life, and it's been like that for ten years. Be careful? I'd hate for Hannah to destroy what you two have. You're good for him, Ava."

After insisting that I accompany Grant to her and Freddy's wedding in February and hugging me tightly, I thank Elizabeth before leaving toward Grant downstairs.

AVA

I t's like a boxing glove jabs me in the face when I'm reminded of this ongoing McCall case days after Freddy's party. Mom calls to update me on the progress with Mr. Ellison, and it's either because of school or being with Grant that I haven't come to terms with the fact that it's really happening. Up until now it's been mostly background noise. We've had the most incredible last few weeks together, and tomorrow is supposed to be perfect because it's Grant's birthday and birthday party, that this is the unavoidable buzzkill I've been expecting because I know all too well that things are usually too good to be true.

I'm told that the McCalls recruited a team of world-renowned psychologists to examine my situation as part of the discovery phase. The lengths these people will go for money that is pocket change to them! I can't even comprehend the cruelty of their persistence. Mr. Ellison thinks they're stalling for time. Apparently rich people do that in cases like these. Pat's family knows good and well that we could never afford to pay Mr. Ellison for months of work, and they'd rather spend their money on lawyers than on me. Bastards.

Releasing my frustration over the phone to Mom isn't going to help with anything. I know she'll feel terrible about what they're putting me through, so I lie and tell her that I'm okay before hanging up and going to study. But when I spend the whole late Friday at the campus library trying to concentrate on a few upcoming exams, Mom's words replay in my head until I'm a mess of panic and sweat, unable to concentrate. It isn't only the conversation from this morning that's put me in this anxious position. After talking to Elizabeth the other night, I'm in a deep panic over this hidden part of me that I'm afraid Grant will find unattractive once he knows. And the guilt and stress over knowing that I *must* come clean eats at me the whole day to the point where I can't study more than a paragraph at a time before feeling like I'm going to vomit. I won't feel better until I tell Grant *something*. I think I'm going to tell him about the case. At least I can divulge one of the three things from my list in hopes that I'll feel less guilty for what I'm hiding. I'm just praying he doesn't judge me and understands why it's necessary for my family to do this.

Why did I keep it from him to begin with? This case against the McCalls is an ongoing thing in my life, present and real, so why do I feel this anxiety over Grant knowing about it? I mean, I haven't been involved much before this morning—my parents and Mr. Ellison have been sorting everything out in person—but did I feel it wasn't important enough for him to be aware?

No, that can't be it. I've thought about the case constantly since I called Ellison's office months ago. It's the humiliation; I didn't tell Grant because I'm embarrassed about it. I'm going through a mental roller coaster. It's the anticipation, the speculation, this limbo where I don't know what's going to happen until it does, and when it does? I'm to be the center of attention. My mind and heart and health are going to be the center of attention. How is any of this fair?

I hate how weak I am. Then and now. Then because I'm still feeling the repercussions every single morning when I swallow an antidepressant; if I don't, I might want to kill myself again. I'm not okay. I need to get out of this building. I don't have the energy or strength to make the trek home, and Grant is at work right now. But desperate times call for desperate measures. He answers on the first ring.

"Hi, baby!" Grant exclaims. I can hear him smiling. It hurts my heart.

"Hi. Um . . ." My voice wavers. It's shaky and throaty and weak.

"Where are you? I'm coming to get you," he states immediately. He knows. He hears the way I sound and he knows.

"Are you sure? You're working. I don't want you to—"

"Ava, where are you?"

Twenty minutes later, he's strutting through the library to the table where I'm seated, the near soundless room becoming significantly quieter. And everyone is staring at him. When they follow Grant's path toward me, I feel all eyes on *me*, everyone wondering how *I* landed *him*. When he reaches my table, Grant crouches down next to my chair and takes my face in his hands, kissing me deeply and publicly. *Publicly.* Everyone is staring.

"What was that all about?" I whisper to Grant. "What're you doing?"

"You're my girlfriend and I wanted to kiss you," he whispers back. I give him a skeptical look. "Because I know you're wondering what they're thinking, and yes, you're worthy of me and I'm not afraid to show it. Oh, and hi," he says, smiling and stroking my cheek. I'm blown away by him, by his words and who he is. This trusting him with my life thing is not going to be easy.

"Hi," I croak.

"You okay, Ava baby?" I bite my lip to keep from crying and shake my head no, afraid that if I utter even one word, I'll be a sobbing mess. "Let me take you home. Come on." He stands from his crouched position beside me and reaches his hand out. When I lean forward to get my bag from the floor, Grant pulls me back slightly and bends over to grab it. He pulls me out the library exit toward his car. I get in when he opens the door for me.

"Talk to me," Grant says on our way to my apartment, squeezing my knee in support. I put my hand over his and tell him that I will. When we arrive at my apartment, he places my bag at the foot of the door and faces me. He tells me that I look pale, asks if I've eaten. I shake my head.

"Let me grab something quickly, I'll——"

"We could go eat, Grant, but I need to get this off my chest before I chicken out."

He nods, takes my hand, and walks me to the bed, sitting on his knees opposite me so we're face-to-face.

"What's going on?" His eyes are filled with worry, and it breaks my heart at how deceptive I've been with this man who has only wanted the full me, since day one, because of how much I mean to him. Because of how much he likes me.

"I lied to you." There, I said it. *Way to be blunt, Ava.*

"You lied to me," he repeats slowly. He doesn't look disappointed, just curious. I nod. "Okay . . . about what?"

"The night that I explained the pills and the abortion and what happened with Pat—I told you that was all of it when you asked me if there was anything else to tell. It wasn't all of it."

It's not as cathartic as I thought it would be. There are two more unchecked items on that list. I don't think I'll feel that emotional and mental freedom with Grant until I tell him about the suicide and the infertility, but I know in the depths of my heart that I could never bring myself to. They're both just too bad. I continue explaining.

"I know that it's your birthday tomorrow, and I'm really sorry to put this on you, but my mom called me this morning, and it's been on my mind all day."

Grant rubs my thighs up and down, and coaxes me to look at him. He shakes his head.

"Never mind my birthday. What didn't you tell me?" he asks softly and I'm so thankful that he isn't mad. I know I would be if my significant other told me that they've been lying to me for the duration of our relationship.

"My family is suing Pat for money. I didn't want to tell you because . . . I don't really know why. Because it's embarrassing that we need the money, especially since you're—"

Grant hastily interrupts me. "Ava, no. You can't—*no.*" He looks pained, wounded, and as shitty as it is, I feel comforted by that.

"No, what?" There's this intense hardened look in his eyes, guilt and shame, and I feel terrible. "I'm sorry. Pat made me out to be a gold digger. I didn't want to ever seem that way with you. I think that's why it was so hard for me to accept that you were wealthy like him."

"*Ava.*" His voice breaks. It's hard for him to get my name out. "I would never, ever think that about you. You know that."

"Now I do but when we first started seeing each other, I didn't know you very well. You didn't know me either. It was a reasonable insecurity."

It's only come to me now, funny enough. It wasn't that I hated the glitz and glamour of Pat's world. It wasn't that the people were different, but it was the way that *I* was made to feel about myself with Pat. I was in shock when I got the affidavit. I didn't care about the money. I never had. I didn't ask for a dime. Their baseless claim is the reason why I've had such a hard time being happy and content with Grant despite our differences, and that makes me livid. He is all that is good in this world, and I lost precious time with him because of *them.* My hesitation to be with Grant because he's rich is undoubtedly Pat's fault and it enrages me.

I watch as Grant scans my face, worried and scared, before grabbing and hugging me tightly.

"I'm sorry that you're going through this, baby," he says into my neck. "I'm here for you. Whatever you need, okay? I'm so sorry."

I shrug. "It is what it is."

—⁓—

Grant has his eyes trained on me, staring, when I wake up the next morning naked in his arms, tightly intertwined under my thin duvet. I smile hugely at him.

"Happy birthday, babe." He continues to watch me but doesn't answer. I poke him then. "Happy birthday, Grant." It's this unblinking stare that he gives me, and all I can do is stare back. But his eyes are so green and bright, I have to look away. It's too much.

"Don't look at me like that," I whisper into his shoulder. I hate the pitiful look from him. From anyone, but especially him. I don't want his pity. I just want him to stay despite what I tell him about me and my life and my past. Not these weird stares, like he's thinking about how broken his girlfriend is. "I didn't tell you about the case so you'll pity me, Grant. Please stop it."

"It's not pity," he murmurs. "It's just . . . I'm so sorry."

When Grant leaves to run a few errands for tonight, I spend my morning in a bit of a daze, aimlessly walking around my apartment thinking about and hating the way he made me feel this morning. There are other ways to be supportive instead of this brooding, glum vibe he was putting out as soon as we woke up. His reaction makes me feel somehow worse than I did yesterday. I have no energy to feel excited about tonight's party, but I know that I have to fake it and deal with all the serious shit afterward. When I get back home from a tiny grocery run, Grant is waiting for me on the steps of the walkway. I muster up a smile and wave.

"Hey!" I call out, walking up the concrete path. I drop my bag, hold his face, and kiss him hard. "Hi, birthday boy."

"Let's go inside, yeah?" He lifts my bag off the ground and leads the way toward my unit. I'm not sure why this is the reaction that I have, but suddenly, I feel angry. Grant hasn't smiled *once* since last night even though it's his birthday today.

"Why are you acting like this, Grant? You're making things really depressing," I scold loudly as soon as the door shuts behind him.

His eyes widen, eyebrows pinched. "I'm trying to figure that out about you!"

"Figure *what* out?" I ask.

He exhales heavily. "Ava. You're going through this case with your family, and all you can think about today is my birthday, and it's a little ridiculous. It's just a birthday! Who gives a fuck!" Grant turns guiltily away from me the moment he shouts.

Did he just call me ridiculous for being excited about his birthday? Even though I feel irate, I don't give him the reaction that he expects from me after yelling; I'm not doing a table tennis fight right now. No way. Not on his birthday.

"Your party starts in a couple of hours, Grant. You should go get ready." I say it calmly, steadily, but inside I'm fuming.

"Enough about my birthday, Ava. I swear to God," he utters, teeth gritted. This anger is completely irrational. He's being mental. My eyes widen.

"Why am I the bad guy here? Why are you being so mean?" I ask, my voice laced with fury. He looks enraged with me and throws his long arms in the air.

"Why do you care so much about my birthday, huh? Riddle me that, Ava."

My jaw drops when he says this. I'm dumbfounded. "What answer can you possibly think I'll give you other than I care about your birthday because I care about you. You're my boyfriend. It's your birthday. It's not the hardest equation to solve," I *unnecessarily* defend myself, spitting words at him.

"You're just . . ." He rubs his forehead, frustrated.

"I'm what?" I challenge.

"Stop being so strong all the time. Cry. Throw something. Be angry. You're going through hell. Why aren't you acting like it?"

If this conversation wasn't so infuriating, I could laugh. The truth? I learned to bottle up my emotions and bury them deep in the crevices of my chest because thinking about that abortion day in and day out is the reason I almost slit myself to death. If I let myself dwell on the case and continue to think about the history behind it, I'd become the old Ava, and I'm not looking to do that. That isn't me anymore.

"What good will that do me?"

"Maybe release all that pent-up anger you have? That seems to me like the normal thing to do for someone in your situation."

"To throw something?"

"You know what I mean, Ava. Don't mock me."

"What answer are you looking for here, Grant? Sure, why don't you hand me a plate to break? What's your problem with how I'm coping with my shit? Why do you even get to have an opinion?!" I shout. *This is what I do.* I deal with things internally. It's what works for me. How dare he question that.

"When you called me to pick you up from school yesterday, you looked like you were about to lose it. You looked broken and scared, Ava, but when you told me about the case, you were too calm. Too collected. Now today, you're all chipper about my birthday. That seems really weird, Ava."

Grant doesn't understand why I'm coping this way. I don't understand why he's being a royal dick to me. I indulge in his absurdity because I'm not going to sit here and defend myself. I shouldn't have to.

"Okay. So I'm *weird*," I retort.

"That's not the point!" he shouts back. "Like, maybe if you didn't keep everything bottled up, you wouldn't have to be medicated."

My breath hitches. I feel my stomach churn and my chest tighten. I feel my body run cold with chills. There's a lump growing in my throat. I am so speechless right now. I want to smack him across his pretty little face, but it's his birthday, as much as he wishes I didn't acknowledge it, so I save the fight for another time and deflect.

"That's really . . . you should go. I think it would be best if you went home, Grant."

He sucks his teeth and nods curtly.

"Yup. Noted." And then he leaves.

GRANT

A s I stand on the wooden platform set up in front of my living room mirror, a grumpy and plump Italian woman fits me in my tux for the party tonight. When I look at my reflection, I despise the person looking back at me. I don't expect her to come tonight, not after what I did earlier, and it'll feel pretty shitty to walk into that party alone without her on my arm. This is the first year that I finally have a girlfriend and I want to show her off. I want to walk into that party with Ava beside me, but only I am to blame for the reason why that won't happen.

It came out of nowhere. It was so cruel and so unexpected; I can't explain what compelled me to say those awful things to her. Maybe it's because I'm upset that Ava only told me about the case now when I've known all along. Maybe she doesn't trust me to be wholly herself and that bothers me. Maybe she doesn't feel like she can be vulnerable with me and *that* bothers me. But the person who acted with apathy toward Ava wasn't the same me that I've been since August. It wasn't the Ava Grant. It was the old me and now I'm wondering if maybe that person will always stay. Maybe this new guy I've been trying to be for Ava is simply a mask concealing my true colors so I can be worthy of her goodness. Maybe I'm permanently an asshole, unable to be changed.

The side gate of my parents' house leads to a wide, outstretched backyard, where my party is set up and beautifully. Mom is quite the party planner, so every year I show up, get drunk, and pass out upstairs. As soon as Louis sees that I've arrived, he calls out that the "birthday boy" is here, and everyone cheers, claps, hollers. This fucker thinks I forgot what he said to me about Ava at the party the other week.

I wave and smile to my guests and head straight for the bar to drown these shit feelings I've suffered since leaving Ava's apartment. I don't feel like socializing or explaining why my girlfriend isn't here so—*to the alcohol!* Seconds later, Annie follows close behind and grabs my arm with a perfectly manicured hand. She studies my face, shaking her head disapprovingly. Annie has this sixth sense where she can read people all too well. Now, she can instantly tell why I'm acting so broody, so she asks, "What did you do?"

"Acted like a dick," I answer gruffly, telling her the truth. Although dick doesn't begin to cover it. I was plain cruel. She laughs bitterly and rolls her eyes, but I can't blame her.

"You are so stupid sometimes, Grant." Annie's disappointment in me somehow makes this worse. Does my sister think I don't know this? When it comes to Ava, I'm an idiot because of the love and the deception, and it's making me crazy.

"Yup," I reply with feigned indifference, taking a long chug of my old fashioned. I look away but she forces me to face her and raises her eyebrows.

"So, that's it? It's over? No more Ava?"

My stomach sinks at this possibility being verbalized, and now I'm mad at my sister. She's being way too honest, and I'm clearly trying to escape what I said to Ava earlier with my nicely decorated glass of bourbon.

"Shut up, Annie," I spit angrily and turn away.

I avoid everyone at my party who knows about Ava and me, and I snap at Dina when she innocently asks where the girlfriend is. I don't want to be answering questions of where she is right now because it's a shitty reflection of who I am, and I'm not prepared to face it until I can face her and apologize. Annie said that I'm acting like the Hannah Grant, and that's exactly the guy I've been trying to escape for months. I drink a little too much and obnoxiously mope at my own party. Then the speeches happen.

Dad gushes about me like I'm a saint, and it pisses me the fuck off. Mom does too and Louis pretends like he didn't treat my girlfriend like shit last week. I undo my tux button when walking toward the stage, hug both of my parents, slap Louis on the back, and head to the makeshift bar for another but halt mid-step at the sound of her quiet, shy voice.

"Hey," she utters softly, tapping the mic. "Hi everyone. Um, I'm Ava. Grant's . . . girlfriend."

I gawk at her, stumped and so unworthy of what she's doing right now that I want to kick her out and tell her to stop because of how undeserving I am of her and of this. When she finds me standing by the bar, her eyes soften, her shoulders relax, and she lifts a hand up to wave. She turns her kind, amber eyes toward the crowd and continues speaking.

"If you know me, which most of you don't—well, all of you don't actually—uhh . . . you'd know that I'm not one for speeches. And yeah, there are a lot of you here tonight, so I'm kinda nervous."

My chest aches, my stomach twists, and I'm a giant self-hating mess as I watch this beautiful girl of mine standing up on stage at my birthday party. I grip the back of my neck tightly as I watch Ava talk about me, the boyfriend she's so proud to be with not five hours after I likely broke her heart.

"But Grant taught me a lot in the last four months that we've been together, and one of those things is to take chances, so that's what I'm doing here because I'm kind of shaking right now. Maybe it's just really cold out tonight." She shrugs and chuckles with the crowd. "Umm . . . but I wanted to take this chance to say a few words about the birthday boy."

Ava takes a deep breath, pulls out her phone, but shakes her head and puts it back in her pocket. "I wrote some notes, but I don't think I need them. Grant . . . he's more amazing than you all know. He's got the biggest heart and he's not made of steel, although he'd probably prefer that you think so." She laughs. "But sometimes it feels like Grant brought me back to life. I have never before felt happiness like I do when I'm with him because of how incredible and kind he is. I feel so, so blessed to know him and . . . I hope you guys do too. I'm so lucky that he chose to be with me. He's the best person I've ever met. So, Grant. Happy twenty-eighth birthday. You make me really happy."

I run. No—*sprint* toward Ava by the stage. I hold her head and put my lips to her ear.

"You shouldn't have done that. Not after what I said earlier. I didn't deserve that." I'm frantic, gripping onto her like she's my lifeline because she's become exactly that.

"Not here," she begs. "Please not here." I kiss her forehead, let the crowd get excited that Grant Wilder finally has a girlfriend, and whisk her off to my old bedroom.

"I'm so sorry," I blurt as soon as I close the door behind us. *I love you so much,* I want to say. She stares at her feet, nodding.

"You really hurt me," she says to the ground, unable to look me in the eye. "And I don't know why you did it. But I needed to let you know that I appreciate you. I know that person earlier isn't you."

"It is me. It's been me for years," I admit.

She shakes her head. "It's not you. You made a mistake. Here," she says, handing me a box. "I got you a birthday gift."

"Ava . . . You deserve to be angry. I don't deserve what you did out there. Don't let me get away with this." I'm begging her to act accordingly, but she won't budge. She shakes her head and in a small voice says, "I know that you're sorry. What else do you want me to do? Just let me be. *Please.*"

I turn the gift in my hand and begin to open it. From my peripheral vision, I can see that she's watching me unwrap the pearlescent wrapping paper, wiping tears away with the sleeve of her white fuzzy sweater. I stop unwrapping the box.

"Ava, come here." I pull her against me, and she sniffles into my chest.

"You hurt me," she whispers.

"I don't know why I said that. I'm sorry, Ava. I swear I'm sorry."

She rubs her face clean and takes a step back, breathing in and out before nodding toward the gift. "Open it."

I do. I unwrap the thin, rectangular box and remove a silver pen from its perfectly outlined felt. I turn it in my hand, noticing small words etched into its side. Squinting my eyes, I look closely to read the engraving.

I'm happy I met you. Happy birthday, Grant. Love, Ava baby.

I don't love this gift but rather I feel mad that Ava is being a complete pushover like she undoubtedly was with Pat. With me, I want her to be strong. I want to make her strong.

"Why are you happy that you met me? You can't let me treat you like shit and give me a gift, Ava." I want her to be angry. I want her to shove me and throw something at me and scream.

"I'm not measuring our relationship to what happened earlier. There is so much more to us than that." She takes my hand, kissing it hard. "I'm gonna head out, okay?"

I panic at the thought of her leaving, afraid that she'll come to her senses between now and whenever I see her next and leave me.

"Wait, no," I slur frantically. "Stay. We'll dance and drink and have fun. I'll take your mind off things."

She shakes her head profusely. "I didn't want to be here. I'm hurt. But it's your birthday and I felt like I had to do something meaningful, so I did"—she motions to the backyard window—"that. And then this," she says to the gift. "But I can't pretend that everything is okay because it's not."

As hard as this pill is to swallow, no pun intended, I know that she has every right to leave right now even if it is my stupid birthday. I don't deserve anything more than a goodbye from her at this point.

"When can I see you?" The alcohol from earlier is making me jumpy.

"Before my flight," she replies. "Devon got me a ticket. I'm leaving on Saturday." Ava is heading back to Arcata for Christmas and New Year's break and then I won't see her for over a week. Why the hell did I open my stupid mouth? I'm an idiot. She's going to have all that time at home to ponder this relationship, and she'll do the right thing and leave. I won't be able to handle it. I love her too much.

"Okay. I'll see you, Ava."

She stands on her tiptoes and kisses my cheek. "Happy birthday."

I watch her huddle into herself and walk away.

GRANT

I lay in my empty bed on Saturday night when I got home from the birthday party, but I couldn't fall asleep, thinking long and hard about what I said to Ava. It didn't help that the space beside me felt hollow and bare. I felt each memory of that conversation with her sink deeper within me until I wanted to pull my hair out. I was and am so incredibly angry with myself. What was I thinking? It doesn't bother me that she's on medication. It *really* doesn't and for the last six days I've been trying to figure out why I said that.

Maybe it's because I didn't know she was medicated before that morning in her bathroom. Maybe it's the fact that I couldn't have prepared myself for finding those orange plastic bottles in her medicine cabinet. Fisher never added that information to his full report on Ava. Maybe I felt ambushed by those rattling pills because they were an indicator that there was so much about Ava that Fisher didn't deem important enough to add to her file, and I felt a little scared going in without the full story. *I don't know.* The point is, I hurt her and badly. She seemed so shattered after the speech and that killed me.

Aside from a few sporadic texts since my birthday party, I've gotten radio silence from Ava and for good reason. But now it's Friday and Ava's flying home tomorrow, and I'm in a little bit of a panic. I can't let us spend weeks apart without fixing or properly apologizing for what I did. When I ask Annie for unprecedented advice on what to do, she suggests that I call

THE PATH OF A LOGICAL LIAR

Ava. What other choice do I have? So, I listen to my big sister's advice once again, bobbing my knee up and down in anticipation as I wait for Ava to answer the phone. I hear a click on the fourth ring.

"Hey." Her voice wavers and I can't stop scolding myself for how big of an idiot I am for ruining the one real good thing I had going for me.

"Hi, Ava . . ." I swallow apprehensively. I clear my throat. "How are you?"

"I'm okay. I've been packing all day," she answers. I can hear a zipper being closed on the other end of the line, hangers clinking together. She grunts and I find it sexy. Six days of celibacy isn't easy.

"Are you excited to go home?" I ask, making light conversation to avoid the elephant in the room, knowing that someone's going to have to bring it up, and it's obviously going to be me.

"Yeah, very," she replies.

The line is quiet then, so I take a deep breath and ask if she's ready to see me.

"I know that I have no right to ask you this, but you told me that you're going home tomorrow, and if you're open to it, I was hoping to see you before your break." I release the breath I've been holding when she replies.

"Yeah, sure. I wanted to see you before break too." Ava's voice is soft and quiet and holy shit, do I hate myself. I was the one who did a number on her this time, her own boyfriend. How could I? She is the love of my life.

"Thank you so much. Let me know when's a good time?"

"Now is fine. I mean, whenever. I'm not busy."

I'm scared of the Ava I'll see when she opens the door for me. I don't want to see that I've broken her. I want the strong Ava. If that means that she'll hate me, I don't care. But she's had too much progress from the past to retract into a shell over my dumb comment. I took something that she hates about herself and I exploited it. I want her to hate me because I had no right going there. It didn't even make any sense. The whole fight appeared out of thin air. I had no solid point or reason; I was just fighting to fight, and I can't actually pinpoint why.

"I'm gonna come over now. Is that cool?"

"It's cool. I'll see you soon."

I won't show up empty-handed, but I'm hoping Ava lets me drive her to the airport tomorrow so I can give her the Christmas gifts then. I pick up Thai takeout on the way over assuming she hasn't eaten dinner yet. It's only 4:00 P.M. I close my eyes and take a deep breath before finding the courage to knock on Ava's door. She's wearing my UPenn sweatshirt when she opens it and I smile. I nod toward it.

"At least you're wearing my sweatshirt. That's a good sign, right?"

Ava glances down to her chest and then up at me, shrugging. "I missed you." She gulps, moving to the side to make room for me. "Thanks for bringing food. I haven't eaten all day." With that, I head straight for her small kitchenette, grabbing plates and forks, the hot sauce, and a couple of cans of seltzer. She plugs her phone in to charge by her bedside and meets me at the small table where I've prepared ginormous plates of food for each of us.

"Yum," she says, sitting on her knees in the chair across from me, digging in. "What is this?"

"Thai. There's a great hole-in-the-wall place by my apartment."

"It's yummy," she repeats, taking another hefty bite. We eat together and it's awkward and no one's talking because the food is great, but I hate what's happening here. Ava doesn't seem to despise me, which is good. And the sweatshirt thing is good. And the "I missed you" thing is excellent.

"What time is your flight tomorrow?" A meek dinner at her small kitchen table before she leaves for break doesn't do it for me. I need more Ava Time before she travels across the country and I don't see her for ten days.

"Like noon-ish?" she ponders after swallowing a forkful of noodles. "I have to check."

"Can I drive you? Would that be okay?"

"Really? I was gonna take the subway and then a shuttle to the terminal."

Over my dead body. Luggage on a subway? Fuck that.

"I'd really like to take you if you'll let me." I sound desperate and hey, it's because I absolutely am. I deserve this desperation, this fear of losing Ava; what I said warranted any and every excuse for her to end things. I'm quite literally sitting at the edge of my seat waiting for her to tell me that we're over.

"I'll let you. I'd much prefer it. Thank you." She smiles. After polishing off our plates, we stand up to clear off and she washes the few dirty dishes, placing them on a drying rack. The silence when she shuts off the sink is bloody painful.

"Please say something," I tell her once she's faced me. "I don't want to overstep. I need you to be the one to start this conversation."

Ava leans her back against the kitchen sink and crosses her arms.

"I've been trying to figure out what to say to you for the last six days," she admits. We make eye contact and stare at each other for a while. I'm not sure I've ever seen Ava in a bun, but it sits messy at the top of her head, and she looks adorable. I love the way my sweatshirt sits on her small frame, baggy and long, that she has to roll the sleeves up to her elbow for them to stay there. I love the tight black leggings painting her slim legs. I love the pair of hot pink Tweety Bird socks that she's sporting on her small feet. But most importantly, I love *her*.

"To be blunt, Grant, you fucked up," she says finally.

"I did fuck up," I agree.

"What were you trying to accomplish that night? I don't get it."

You and I both, Ava. "I don't know. Nothing."

"Does it bother you that I'm on medication, Grant, because—"

I interrupt her immediately. She can't go there. She can't think that.

"Ava, no. I swear. I don't care. I mean, I care because I want you to be healthy and happy, but I don't think you're less than because you're medicated. It came out of nowhere. I was mad that you were being strong because you didn't have to be, but I promise it has nothing to do with that." Huh. I hadn't realized that could be the reason until it slips out. "I wanted you to be vulnerable with me because you're my girlfriend. I wanted you to cry and let me hold you while you did. I wanted the opportunity to be a boyfriend and comfort you, but you spoke monosyllabically, just stating facts. I get that you were being strong, but that bothered me."

"Why would that bother you? I thought you liked that I was strong. You've said that to me before," she recounts. "And newsflash, Grant, but telling you what was going on *was me being vulnerable.*"

"You're right. I think I was frustrated because I was there to console you and you didn't seem to need consoling. Maybe I snapped because I couldn't relate to you or the way you were reacting. I don't know, Ava."

"You can't relate to me because you've never been through something traumatic before, Grant. You have a picture-perfect life." She seems put-off, pissed, resentful that I've had it good and she hasn't. "I've been through more in eighteen years than you have in twenty-eight." I had no authority telling her how to cope with her situation when I've never been in her shoes, nor have I experienced such a trauma like she has.

"Does that make you mad?" I ask.

Ava shakes her head. "No. I'm mad at the Universe and I'm mad at God for what happened to me, but I'm not mad at you because that's life. We all have different paths, but you stood there judging me for not reacting the way you would have, assuming things about me, giving me unsolicited medical advice, and I realized that you didn't understand my reaction because you've never had to react to anything like that in your entire life." She's panting, her voice raised, and as she speaks with passion and conviction, the bun at the top of her head wobbles and everything about her in this moment is perfect. It's real because she's real, and I can't help myself from falling deeper in love with her.

"You need to understand something. When your life is filled with so much hardship, you learn to keep every reaction at bay. If I didn't, Grant, I'd be a sobbing mess 24/7. I wouldn't be a functional person, and obviously that's not an option anymore. I got better for a reason. I'm at NYU for a reason. I cope with my shit the way that I do because I don't have any other choice."

My heart is breaking with every word that exits Ava's mouth. It hurts to listen to this because of how much she has come to mean to me.

"Ava, I'm so sorry. I snapped out of my own insecurities, and it was wrong. I didn't mean a single word I said about you or your medication. You're perfect to me."

She looks spent as she closes her eyes and slumps her shoulders, shaking her head.

"You had no right, Grant. You had no right."

I walk forward and thankfully, Ava doesn't flinch, allowing me to come close to her, to put my hands on her face. I am dying to tell her that I love her but stop myself. She places her forehead in the middle of my chest.

"You hurt me so bad." Her voice breaks. "It hurt more than anything Pat ever said or did to me, and I don't know how but it's true."

I know, though. Because when someone you love deep in your soul betrays you, you feel it everywhere, in your gut and in your bones and in the pores on your skin. When it's anybody else, it's as simple as a blow. Ava just admitted to me, without saying the words, that she might be falling in love with me.

"Because I have a responsibility to you that he never did. You're my girlfriend and you deserve to be treated with the utmost respect, and that's not how I treated you last week." I grab her face and tilt her head to look at me so I can say this to her eyes, to her soul. "I can't express how sorry I am. I was wrong and I acted like a complete asshole and you don't ever need to forgive me for this, but I need you to know that I am very, truly sorry."

"I don't want to break up," she says hurriedly, scanning my face with her longing eyes.

I smile. "Good because I *really* don't want to break up." I bend to kiss her soft lips. She kisses me back.

"I'm sorry about leaving your party," she mutters, her cheeks reddening.

"I'm just glad that you showed up in the first place. I was *not* expecting you to come and that speech? It ruined me in the best way possible." I graze my thumb on her shoulder and tuck a piece of hair behind her ear. "Thank you so much for everything you said up there."

She shrugs. "Everything I said was true."

"Was?" I tease.

She smirks. "Is. Whatever."

"I'm gonna kiss you again." Ava leans her body against me as soon as my lips touch hers, pants, pulls at my hair, and it's rough and eager like we can't get enough, like we're trying to fit in as much now to compensate for the last week and the next two. I have always been cautious in bed with Ava, but right now, we're both animalistic, ravaging and pulling and tugging, and I feel a desire like no other. She unzips my sweatshirt, tugs off my T-shirt, and huffs against my bare chest.

"I want you so badly," she whispers, her breath hot against my bare skin. "This was the hardest week ever." *Say no more, baby.* "I'm gonna give you everything. I promise."

—⟩⟩—

We eat cold Thai leftovers for dinner on Ava's undressed bed when we wake up at eight. The exhaustion of exploding sexual pleasure begged for a proper nap, sweat and hair and fluids dirtying the sheets and in need of a wash with hot water and bleach. I spot a red and green striped gift bag in her hand when she walks toward me from the closet, her naked body wrapped in the blue throw blanket that lives on her sofa. Her smile is shy when she hands me the bag and sits beside me.

I grin and kiss her forehead long and hard when she cozies up into my side.

"What's this?" It's bizarre, the feeling of fearing you've lost someone and then somehow getting them back within a matter of hours. Ava had every right to leave me after what I said to her considering how fragile she is about her past, but she's here and she's smiling back at me and handing me a gift, and I am thanking my lucky stars—there might be a whole damn galaxy up there that's on my side.

"It's your Christmas gift, silly. Duh," she replies, rolling those big, beautiful honey eyes at me. I chuckle and begin unwrapping the small gift box. Sitting atop the cotton cushioning, there's a lone key.

"Is this what I think it is?" I ask, pleased at her shy expression.

She nods, climbs on top of me, and buries her face in my neck. "Yeah," she rasps. "I may have done something really embarrassing." I reach over to the bedside table to place the box down and wrap my arms around Ava's body. I ask her what she did, ready to embrace it, already chuckling to myself.

185

"I looked up big gestures to do for your boyfriend for Christmas online, and that was on the list."

I hold her head and bring her to face me. Her cheeks are flushed and it's the cutest thing in the world. I throw my head back and howl.

"Stop," Ava whines, her lips in an endearing pout. "I already prefaced that I was embarrassed! You're so mean!" I kiss her so hard, again and again and again. "Does this mean you like it?" She giggles, pushing me away.

"I *love* it, Ava baby."

A key. A key means a future, means that I'm a part of her life indefinitely. And I realize how I have to savor every single second I have left with Ava before it's all over. Before she realizes that for us, there's no such thing as forever.

AVA

I spend the last few days before my flight home studying for midterms, taking exams, and packing my summer clothes that have been tucked away since September for Christmas break back in California. I am so damn excited to see my family, I feel queasy. And nervous, even. I don't feel like the same person who left Arcata four months ago. I wonder how it'll feel being back. I wonder what my mom will say when she sees me.

It should have been impossible, but I don't know how I kept my cool during the hours leading up to Grant's birthday party because he didn't deserve it. I should've reacted the way he wanted me to, but toward him, not the case. I should've yelled out of pure anger, but I couldn't bring myself to do it, not on his birthday. I felt weak and at a disadvantage, so when I asked him to leave my apartment and chose not to join him in getting ready for the party, I felt ashamed. It was his birthday after all, and it's not like we broke up or anything. It was a couple's quarrel, if you will.

The speech I gave at the party was unexpected. I stood on the sidelines of his parents' backyard and watched Grant's mother, father, and friends speak so highly of him, and I felt this pressing need to do something as his girlfriend; it wasn't enough that the people who were expected to speak did. I felt an obligation to give him that same validation but from me. It was frightening to stand in front of a billion-dollar crowd, but I shook the stage fright and focused on Grant because I knew what it'd mean to him. I think it went well.

I was being honest when I said that I didn't believe it was him who said something cruel to me. I was truthful when I told him that I believed it was just a mistake on his part. I think I surprised him, judging by the sheer confusion on his face. He wanted me to hate him. I didn't have it in me. Because I don't know . . . he's just Grant. He's my Grant and it wasn't hard to forgive him. I'm pretty sure I did immediately.

As soon as Grant lifts my suitcase onto the baggage scale and I've been handed my boarding pass by the sweet ticket agent, he turns to me and smiles sadly. I'm going to miss him so much.

"You got a minute to sit with me before security?"

"Of course. I have like two hours until takeoff."

When Grant called yesterday after giving me almost a week of space, I wasn't sure if it was going to be the finality of our relationship or an apology or what. I knew that he had been in the wrong, that I was owed the apology, but the basis of his mean comment was because I hadn't given him a chance to console me like a boyfriend should. He told me I was speaking monosyllabically, and it reminded me of those days, the days at the mental hospital and the therapy sessions upstairs in my bedroom in Arcata. It was and is my way of shutting out the pain, speaking factually, like saying "I killed a baby" or in this case, "I'm suing Pat."

I hadn't wanted to sob to him, to seem weak and damaged, more than I already am. This was my way of letting Grant in on one of the three things I had been keeping to myself without making a big deal about it. I felt like I was giving him the opportunity to console me by calling him from the NYU library bathroom, but he needed more. Grant needed me to cry into him while he held my convulsing body. I couldn't be that girl to him. I can't ever be her.

We sit together on the rickety metal chairs by the airport entrance, the bustle of New York City streets making its way into JFK, families and couples and businessmen lugging their bags and rushing amongst each other. Grant takes my backpack and places it between his legs, then bends to zip it open, rustling through it. I look at him suspiciously.

"There's some underwear, my book, deodorant... What're you looking for exactly?" I laugh, but stop when he pulls out a black, modern labeled box.

"This. Merry Christmas, baby," Grant says, kissing me when I take the box from him. He must've snuck it in my bag when we were loading the trunk of his car. I carefully peel the plastic coating off the box and open the magnetic flap. Sleek matte black headphones sit folded uniformly in the black and red interior of the box, and on the inside cover, it reads *Beats by Dre Noise Cancelling Wireless Headphones*. My jaw nearly hits the ground.

"This is insane," I state, eyes wide, staring into the box, too afraid to remove the fragile and undoubtedly expensive headphones from their spongey outline. Grant shrugs.

"I know you like to listen to music when you study. Figured these would be useful so you could focus better when you're at Rocco's and walk around your apartment since they're wireless." I wrap my arm around his neck and squeeze.

"They're perfect. I'm gonna use them on my flight. Thank you so much, Grant." I smile and shyly lean in for a kiss, hoping we're not being stared at, that I'm not being judged. *Religious guilt, baby.*

"I have another gift for you," he murmurs against my lips. I back away and look at him, shaking my head. He shrugs. "It's Christmas. Two isn't nearly enough, but that's what I got for now." He kisses me and winks. Before I begin to protest, he reaches into my backpack again and pulls out a Tiffany blue box like the one he handed me at Thanksgiving. My eyes widen in disbelief.

"No, Grant. This is crazy!"

He's not having it, chuckling at my outburst. "The only thing that's crazy is me. Crazy for you. Open it," he demands, nodding toward the blue box. I can't believe this.

"No way," I breathe as soon as I lift the lid of the small, square box.

"Yes way," he mimics with a grin, kissing my forehead.

"Grant . . ." In the box lies a diamond necklace in the shape of a heart to match the bracelet he gave me on Thanksgiving. "This is way too much. My gift to you cost like five dollars. This is probably like five thousand. I can't take this." $4.30 to be exact. All I did was replicate a key and got a little spunky with the design.

Grant shakes his head. "Stop that. You know it's not about the money, babe. Now, can I please put it on you?" He immediately snaps a photo of me wearing the shining necklace, then flips the camera and cuddles me into him. I pout my bottom lip for the selfie, and he turns to me, looking apologetic.

"Awww, you're killing me with that face. I'll see you so soon, baby!" he exclaims.

"I'm gonna miss you," I whisper, swallowing down the lump in my throat. It'll be hard being away from him for so long.

"We'll FaceTime every day, Ava baby." Grant lifts my backpack and holds my hand until we reach the security line. He cups my cheeks and kisses me. "Same time next week?" he asks.

I nod. "Yeah, I'll send you my flight info." We hug tightly for a while. "Merry Christmas," I sigh.

"Christmas Merry," he replies. When I laugh, he pinches my cheek. "There's the smile I love. Now, go, babe. You don't want to miss your flight."

I wave and enter the security line, and when I look back several minutes later, he's standing at the entrance to the airport with his hands in his pockets, watching me, waving when he sees I've caught him. I blow him a kiss and he blows one back, winking before leaving through the automatic glass doors.

—⁊⁊—

After the best flight of my life, these noise cancelling head-phones making it an absolute breeze to relax, I run toward my parents and Cooper standing at the revolving baggage belt. Mom and I hug for a full five minutes, and I'm pretty sure Dad wipes a tear from his undereye when he takes me from Mom. *My dad, the softie.*

I text Grant once I get settled at home to let him know that I've landed safely and promise to introduce him to every-one via FaceTime later this week. I've met his entire family. Aside from Devon, no one really knows much about him, but I'm confident he'll hit it off with everyone—he's just that kind of guy.

Mom and I spend the day in the kitchen, preparing our very famous and delicious "All Around the World" Christmas Eve dinner. Since Mom is Spanish and Dad's American, there is always an unusual variety of foods at our Christmas table, but that's what makes us who we are, and I wouldn't have it any other way. When we say grace before digging in, I close my eyes. The memories of Grant from the last four months flash in my mind. I am so incredibly grateful that I found him this year. That *he* found *me* this year.

While my brothers and I are unwrapping our presents on Christmas morning in matching Santa pajamas of course—Mom won't let that tradition go no matter how old we get—the doorbell rings and Connor stands up to check who it is.

"It's for you, Indiana Jones!" he calls out from the front door. The boys still call me that from time to time. I pretend to be annoyed about it, but I secretly love that it's still a thing. There's a ginormous box sitting on our front step, and Connor and I lift it together and carry it into the living room. I grab a key ring and use the jagged edge of the house key to open the box. Inside, there's the biggest bouquet of roses I have ever seen, the white ones in the middle forming the shape of a heart.

My brothers tease at how lovestruck I look as I hurriedly run up the stairs two at a time and close my bedroom door before pulling out my phone to FaceTime Grant.

"You're crazy, you know that?!" I exclaim immediately.

He laughs. "Well, Merry Christmas to you too. I'm glad you like them." He lifts himself off the couch at what looks to be his parents' house and walks down the hallway, stopping to lean against the wall. "You look so gorgeous. I miss you. How are you, babe?"

Ugh, can he be any sweeter?

"I'm really good. I've missed my family. It's good to be home. Are you all at your parents' house?"

He verifies, walking over to the living room, where everyone passes his phone around to wish me a Merry Christmas. Madison takes the liberty of letting me know that Grant bought her an American Girl doll *and* a pink, glittery scooter, and Callum insists that I join them for Christmas next year. I feel so flattered at how excited they are to talk to me and even more so when I hear Annie's son Jack shout in the background, "Also me want to say hi to Uncle Gat's goolfend!" I chuckle and compliment his awesome reindeer pajamas.

"Wanna meet my family?" I ask Grant excitedly when his face reenters the screen. "They're all downstairs." I flip the camera so everyone can wave to him; Devon tells Grant that it's nice to see him again, and Connor and Cooper egg him on about the black sports car that I sent them a photo of all those months ago. It seems like a lifetime ago when Grant and I had that ice cream date. We've come so far, and I'm itching to get back to him, to kiss him and hug him and pounce.

"We heard so much about you!" Mom exclaims in her Spanish accent. "When are you going to come to Arcata so we can meet you! Ava tells us you are very tall."

Grant chuckles shyly. His eye creases are so damn sexy when he does.

"Soon, I hope. Nice to meet you, Mrs. Campbell. Hope you all have a very Merry Christmas. Is Ava's father around?" I turn the camera on me and tell him that I'll go grab Dad from the kitchen.

"Merry Christmas, sir. My name is Grant Wilder. I wanted to formally introduce myself and tell you that your daughter makes me very happy."

Dad winks at me, giving his approval, and I'm surprised at how instant that was, but I shouldn't be. Grant is the perfect gentleman, and I know my parents are loving that about him, even if they're meeting him on a screen. It's an all-around good time. I feel so relaxed and relieved at how proud I feel having a boyfriend who I want to show off.

Mom knocks softly on my bedroom door later that night after a delicious and boozy meal filled with snorting laughter and shared memories. I'm pretty sure I hissed at Devon a few times throughout the meal, especially when he mentions that cocktail incident at the bar where we met.

"Come in!" I call out from under my blanket. Grant and I have been texting nonstop today. It may have gotten heated at one point, and not in a bad way. In a very sexty way.

Mom peeks her head through the door. "Hi, mija. You have a minute to talk, yes?" I nod and scoot over on the bed to make room for Mom to slip in beside me. "I cannot help but notice the diamonds you are wearing," she says straightaway. I was afraid this would happen, but what did I expect? They're pretty noticeable. I couldn't exactly hide them under my clothes.

"Grant bought me this one for Thanksgiving and this for Christmas. Do you like them?"

She pauses before replying. "They are beautiful, mija," she sighs.

"Are you mad? Is it too much?" I look worriedly at her. Mom always knows best.

"It is not too much but it is much. What is this guy like, Ava? It seems he is very *rico*, like the other one."

Rich. Like Pat. I could laugh at her comment. If she only knew the internal roller coaster of hesitation I went through when I first met Grant because of how expensive he looks. I clarify to ease her suspicions.

"He is rico but he is *nothing* like the other one, Mama. I would never do that to myself again." I explain the history of my relationship with Grant, the reluctance to start something with him, the conversations with Bridget, and the fact that I've come to realize that not all rich people act the same, that Grant is proof of that; that he's decent and kind and careful with me.

"He's a good person, Mama," I tell her, squeezing her bony hand in reassurance. "You trust me, right?"

"Of course, *mi amor* . . ." She hesitates to speak but then asks, "Did you tell him about what happened?"

I take a deep breath before replying. "I didn't tell him everything, but I told him a lot. He knows about the abortion and the medication and the case." Mom's surprised when I tell her this, that he knows about how traumatic and dramatic my life is, that I trust Grant enough to tell him about my past. I explain that it's a big deal for me that with all that knowledge, he's still here, he's still with me, that it doesn't scare him.

"Nothing scares him." I laugh. "He thinks he's made of steel."

GRANT

They've been watching the ball drop as a family since Ava insisted as an eight-year-old girl, fascinated with observing every colorful inch of the TV screen and trying her hardest to stay up until 9:00 P.M. for the fireworks show. And I'm the one fascinated with observing her, learning how there are things about Ava that haven't changed in over a decade. It's comforting, in a way, knowing that no matter what this woman goes through, she pulls through stronger than before and only grows in her own skin. I have so much admiration for my perfect girlfriend. I could never come out as resilient as Ava has if I had endured the same trauma. Not many people can say they would.

It wasn't like I was going to spend New Year's with Louis, Hannah, and the gang as I have for the last ten years, so I decided that I'd surprise Ava and come to Arcata to celebrate it with her and her family. I remembered that Devon mentioned he does accounting in Chicago, so after a bit of research, I found his number and called him. He was shocked to hear from me, but when I told him I wanted to surprise Ava for New Year's Eve, he was totally on board with the idea and super excited for his sister. It was sweet.

All the Campbells were in on it. Ava's father, David, and Devon insisted they would pick me up from the airport even after I told them ten times that I could take an Uber, and Ava's mom helped get her out of the house, taking her for an impromptu lunch so I could sneak up into her bedroom. It would be impossible to explain her excitement and how that made me feel when Ava casually strode into her bedroom and shrieked when she saw me standing there.

"What the . . ." she muttered, confused, but when it registered that I was in her bedroom, she dashed into my arms and I laughed, lifting her and holding her almost as tight as she was squeezing me. It was euphoric. Ava's family has welcomed me so genuinely that I can't help but have hope that this can one day be permanent. I know it's wishful thinking, and that breaks me a little bit.

The Campbells and I sit together with the wine and champagne I brought to celebrate, sprawled out on the couches, recliners, and carpeted living room floor, chatting about the likely frozen reporters at the annual scene on live TV. As much as I love the city I live in, I'm not complaining about the weather here in California tonight. New Year's hasn't been this warm since I've lived in Houston.

I wrap my arm around Ava's shoulders, curling her into me, holding a glass of pinot noir in my other hand. Every few minutes, she takes it from me and sips just a tiny bit. An unamused reaction blankets her face and I chuckle.

"I wanna like it so bad but it's too bitter!"

I lean forward to the coffee table and grab a champagne flute and the bottle, handing over the bubbly beverage once I've poured her a hefty glass.

"Here," I say. "Try this instead." After tasting a small sip, Ava lifts her head and nods at my questioning face. "Better?" I ask.

"Much." Ten minutes later I find that her glass is empty, and when she looks up at me in awe and bewilderment, I can't help but smirk at the way her eyes flicker open and shut, the glassiness indicating that this tiny one is undoubtedly drunk. When I call her out on it, all she can do it giggle loudly, burp, and then giggle some more. I kiss her forehead.

"You're cute," I whisper into her messy head of hair. Ava's brothers tease and joke, and it's even cuter when she argues back, too drunk to form proper words, telling them that she's "burping because of the bubbles" and "why are there so many bubbles?!" *I'm done for.*

"Happy New Year's, Ava. You're the best thing that's ever happened to me," I mumble so only she can hear me. I bury my lips into her hair, taking a deep breath, memorizing the feel of Ava's body against mine, her soft hair on my lips. I won't have this with Ava forever, and I feel an anxiousness, a need to cherish every second together so I can remember it when all I have left of Ava are the memories.

"Happy New Year's, Grant. You've become everything to me," she mumbles back.

The depth of what that means is too much. The liability I have over Ava now is enormous, and I know how dangerous the progression of this relationship has become. We are in too deep. I am in too deep because Ava has become the love of my life. I am so in love with her, and I ask myself if it's possible to rid a piece of your soul from your system should you have to. In this case, I know that I will.

Eventually, the champagne tires Ava and she curls into my side, resting her arm over my abdomen and laying her head in the crook of my arm. I keep my lips on her forehead and play with her hair, paying no mind to the screen in front of me. She snores lightly and I smile, softly scratching her back as she sleeps quite literally on top of me. I've had this girl naked in my bed, in my mouth, yet something about this scene feels more intimate than anything we've ever done.

When I notice that it's been quiet without the hum of New Year's chatter, I turn toward the rest of Ava's family to find them all watching us. When they see that I've caught them staring, they awkwardly blink away.

Were they staring because they hated what they saw or was it something else? Shock? Confusion? I'm starting to feel a bit uncomfortable.

Ava steals my attention away from the middle of the room when she stirs awake in my arms twenty minutes later and groggily looks up. "Hey you. Was I snoring again?"

"No," I lie, kissing her forehead for the umpteenth time. "Tired?" She nods against my chest. "Let me take you to bed." With another nod from her, I lift both of us from the couch in one swift motion and literally carry her up the steps into bed. After a kiss and a tight hug, I quietly close her bedroom door and walk downstairs. As soon as my foot hits the landing, all ten Campbell eyes are on me, and it immediately feels like I'm on display. When their eyes don't leave my face, I awkwardly shove one hand in my pocket to steady the slight shaking and point my thumb behind me.

"She's asleep."

"Does that happen often?" Cooper asks forwardly. "Do you put her into bed often?"

I look at him, confused. "What?"

"Well, do you?"

I hate the way it sounds coming from him, and since he's her overprotective brother, this can't possibly be a good sign.

"I'm not sure I understand your question, Cooper. Was there something wrong with what I did? Evelyn, David," I say, addressing Ava's parents directly. "Have I done something to disrespect you, your family, or your daughter?"

"No. You haven't. I think what Cooper is trying to say is that what we just saw between you two was . . . unusual, at best," David explains, his wife nodding beside him. Ava is a perfect mix of the two.

"Why? Because she fell asleep and I carried her into bed?"

"Not necessarily. I think it's more so that she's very comfortable with you, and for Ava, that's saying something. None of us have ever seen her like this before." David looks at me pointedly when he speaks, like he's trying to explain something more. I don't fully comprehend it though.

"What part have you never seen before?" What are they implying right now? She's twenty years old. They can't possibly suggest that Ava has never been this happy before tonight.

"Smiling and laughing? Getting drunk and excited, beaming with happiness? Some would call that love," Evelyn explains, her accent thick and pronounced.

I know Ava has strong feelings for me that go beyond the emotional levels of a budding relationship but *in love?* Soon, yeah, maybe. I know she's close because of what she said before she left for break, how the pain I caused her was worse than what Pat did, but I shake my head.

"I'd love for you to be right, but I really don't think Ava is quite there yet." The Campbells look amongst themselves, chuckling. I give them a confused look, eyeing them narrowly. I just don't see how this is funny. I clear my throat, rubbing the back of my neck as I say, "Listen, I'm sorry if I did something out of line. That was not my intention whatsoever. Uh . . . I think I'm going to head to bed if that's okay. Happy New Year's."

Immediately, David stands and walks over to me. "Hey, Grant. We're in shock. We don't mean to be rude or make you uncomfortable. I think we're all feeling really grateful that she has you now. Ava is fragile. Strong but fragile. We see you together, Evelyn and I, and I think our hearts are soaring seeing our daughter this happy. She's got a beautiful smile, doesn't she?" His eyes glass over when he speaks about Ava, and my heart jolts, thinking about the shape of her smile, the lighthearted sound of her laugh. It's my favorite thing in the world and what it means? That's even more mind-blowing.

"She does," I agree.

"So, thank you for letting us witness it again. We sent her off to New York a little broken, and she's come back seeming whole again. You're good for her. She's needed you before she met you, and we're glad that you found each other."

I look up to see Evelyn nodding at me, her sons too. But something about David's words doesn't sit right with me. I know about Ava's past. I know what she went through, that it wrecked her and she succumbed to a deep depression because of it, but she had a support system, did she not? Her best friend Bridget, her parents, her brothers. Telling me that Ava needed me before she met me feels like she's been lonely either way—with or without everyone she loves surrounding her. That I was the missing piece because I wasn't there throughout her trauma, but I'm here now. I can't wrap my head around that. It makes no sense.

"Why do you say that? We've only been together, like, four and a half months."

"She tried to kill herself," Connor blurts out, his eyes widening when he realizes what he just told me. It takes me a few long moments to process what he's said, and when it finally hits me, the hairs on my neck stand and I'm quite literally covered in a cold sweat. I sit where I did earlier and run my hands through my hair. Finally, I look at him.

"What did you just say?" This can't possibly be true. She would've told me.

"You heard me, man."

"No," I say, shaking my head hurriedly. "Ava is good. She's fine. She's healthy."

"It's true." Devon perks up. "We found her crying in the bathtub, holding a razor, repeating the words 'I killed a baby' over and over again."

I jump off the armchair and cover my mouth with shaking hands. *Ava tried to commit suicide?* His words hit me right in the gut, in the chest. It feels like I can't breathe.

From my obvious shock, Connor says, "She hasn't told you?" I shake my head.

"About this? Not a word."

"You mean . . . you don't *know*?" Cooper asks.

My head juts to all corners of the room as each one of her brothers speaks. My heart is fucking pounding. I feel like I'm going to vomit or faint or both.

"I know about the abortion and the medication. She told me she was really depressed afterward, but she never told me about the . . . *this*." Because it'll hurt to say suicide out loud. It even hurts to think it. Ava killing herself? I've never been more terrified than I am in this moment about what I've done and who I am.

"What did she tell you about the abortion?" David asks.

"That there were complications and she was in recovery for a while. She told me that her recovery caused her depression because of how weak and helpless she became. I know that she's been on medication and spent a long time trying to get better before coming to New York."

Evelyn interjects. "Let me tell you something that Ava will never accept herself. She would've had to abort the baby either way. The pregnancy wasn't healthy. The baby wasn't growing in the right place. Any doctor would've called for an abortion at the first ultrasound because of how dangerous the pregnancy was. It could've been fatal. But the fact that she made the decision on her own and traveled with all of us to San Francisco with the intention of aborting the baby haunts her."

The wind is knocked out of me. I'm an internal mess. Everything she went through was in vain? This is crazy. Ava is tormenting herself for nothing?

David speaks now. "She hates it when we try to reason with her. Ava is very dead set on the fact that she killed that baby. She won't take any other explanation. She says that it was *her* doing and *her* fault that the pregnancy didn't result in a child." My heart breaks for her. I can't bear this. "There were good days and bad days," David continues. "Sometimes she'd suddenly be content with what happened, but most of the time, she was angry with herself."

Why does Ava do this to herself? Why does she *want* to be sad, at fault, depressed? It resulted in an attempted suicide! And Pat? Oh, don't get me started on Pat. The guy is scum. He's malicious. But I guess I'm not that far off.

"He really tore her apart, didn't he?" I receive solemn nods of affirmation in regard to what Pat did, and with this new revelation, I want to slice my own throat. "I'm not good for her," I say to the ground. "She deserves better. She needs better."

"I don't think so," Evelyn objects.

Something in my blood stirs, and I suddenly feel pissed off. They met me *today*. How can they possibly know what's best for their daughter when they met the man she's dating only a few hours ago?

"Don't judge our relationship based on one exchange while she was drunk. I've done things I'm not proud of. Ava deserves someone as good as she is, and that isn't me." I'm almost angry at this point. I'm probably making a terrible impression, but when you love someone, you want the best for them, even if it isn't you. *Right?*

"Grant—"

"No, I'm serious. I came to Arcata in hopes that you'll approve of me, but after hearing this? Now I'm wishing you didn't. She needs someone better."

"Ava needs someone who's going to care for her. She seems to trust that person is you," Evelyn says slowly. "Our daughter is a smart girl. If she's with you, it's for a good reason."

"But it's not, Evelyn. And hearing this . . . I shouldn't even be here."

"It's okay to bring baggage into relationships, as Ava has. It's jarring to see how one person can make her this happy, but if she can do that for you too, then there's no question here. And I assume she does make you happy?"

Holy shit, is that an understatement.

"She does. So happy but . . . why didn't she tell me? Ava opened up to me about everything else. Clearly there's a reason this was off the table."

Evelyn sighs heavily, followed by a hard swallow. "The guilt of what she thinks she did has consumed her. I'm sure it still does but not like it was when she was home. Her eyes were so dead. She did not ever smile. Ava was barely a person, and that's why we put her on the medication. That she told you about it is quite a big deal, and the fact that her guilt does not consume her when you're together . . . Before you, it was her entire life. Ava lived and breathed that guilt, but it isn't like that anymore. I can guess that the reason she did not tell you about the bathtub incident is because of shame. Maybe embarrassment? Fear? I am not surprised. I don't expect her to ever tell you herself, Grant." Somehow Evelyn's words hold more value and meaning because of her eloquent accent. She holds a crumpled tissue in her small hand, rubs beneath her eyelid.

"She's been through too much. I don't want to hurt her," I whisper, hiding the strain in my voice. It's not easy playing two people. It's not easy being a fraud to someone you love because of all the lies you have to concoct. Of course I never intend to hurt Ava, but if I'm being honest with myself, I know that one day I will. I already have.

"Will you?"

"I'll be honest with you; I don't have the greatest track record when it comes to women."

Cooper speaks angrily, his eyebrows cinched. "Are you serious, man? After all that we told you about Ava finally being happy with you, you can't end things with her because you think she needs someone better than you. She chose you. Be grateful and show her why."

I take a deep breath. "You're right. I just want what is truly best for her." *And that isn't me.*

"Then make her happy as best you can because I swear to you, we have never seen Ava like this."

I nod and promise Ava's parents that I will try to make her as happy as I can. I hug Evelyn and shake David's hand. When I do, I ask, "Would you mind if I went up there? No funny business. You have my word."

"Sure, son. Go for it," David replies with a serious nod.

I solemnly climb up the steps and crawl into Ava's bed beside her. As I lie here, mentally replaying everything I heard downstairs, my heart feels like it's being squeezed tightly in a giant fist, threatening to suffocate me to death at tonight's revelation. I feel physically pained because my girlfriend once tried to kill herself and she was never going to tell me about it.

It's been four and a half months with Ava, and although at the beginning things were uncertain because of Ava's fears and hesitation, as of late, our relationship has felt really promising. God knows the moment I met Ava and asked to see her again, it immediately felt like I was zipping my chest wide open and handing her my entire heart in hopes that she'd be gentle with it. Now I'm realizing that she's trying to be a little too gentle with hers.

I hug Ava's back to my chest tightly and bury my face in her silky hair. I want to whisper that I love her more than anything but I don't.

"Where have you been all my life?" I mumble instead, sure she hasn't heard me. But to my surprise, she mutters a reply in her sleep.

"Waiting for you to find me." With those words, I can't stop my tears from falling down my face and into her hair, thankful that she's drunk enough not to witness my unending turmoil in the wake of her deliberately concealed and heartbreaking secrets.

AVA

S tretching my arms out wide as I stir awake in my bed, I nearly scream when I hit Grant's face beside me. He's here, in my bed, in my bedroom, casually watching me with an intense look in his eyes, his brows scrunched together.

"What're you doing here?" I ask, wide-eyed. "My parents—"

"I asked your dad for permission. Come here." Grant kisses me lightly before pulling me quite literally on top of him, our stomachs kissing. Brushing the hair out of my face so he can look at me better, he leans forward to kiss me again, tracing the line of my jaw with his warm hand. I turn my head to kiss his palm and smile at his perfect morning face, brush my fingers through his sexy bedhead. When I apologize for decking him a second ago, he chuckles quietly and with his big thumbs swipes under my eyes and cleans his fingers on his white T-shirt. Last night's eyeliner.

"I look like a raccoon, don't I?" I pout.

"The cutest raccoon. Morning, baby," he rasps, his morning voice making me feel all the things. I reach for those inviting lips and tell him the same. His eyes are dull, his smile sullen, and it makes me frown.

"You okay?" Something about him seems different than last night. Heavier.

"Yeah, of course," he says, brushing it off as the effect of last night's drinking. "I'm good. You hungry?"

—⁓—

They've been quiet all morning, dancing around me and barely speaking more than a few words, and I know in my gut that something happened when I went to sleep last night. My brothers are a lot of things, but they are not quiet people. I notice Grant and my parents exchange odd looks, and after thirty minutes of this unbearable awkward silence, I can't take it anymore.

"Okay, did something happen last night when I fell asleep?" Instead of replying, they remain silent and still, shifting their attention to Grant. Anger flares within me—I know that whatever happened last night is going to hurt me.

"What did you do?" I ask in a panic. "Coop? Dev? Connor?"

"We're just trying to protect you, Ava." Devon says it calmly, collectedly like he's trying to hold me back from reacting like he knows I will and I do.

"From what!" I snap. "Someone better start talking." When Grant reaches for my flailing arm, I shove him out of sheer frustration and anxiety. He's taken aback. "No. Don't, Grant. What're you guys not telling me?" When they don't answer, I glance over at my parents. "Mama? Dad?"

"Relax, mija. It was only a short conversation," Mom explains. *Only* a conversation? With my boyfriend of less than five months? No, no, no, that isn't fair. I want to know what the fuck transpired when I was drunkenly asleep upstairs, and I want to know now.

"Tell me what happened," I demand loudly, unsure where to put my focus, unsure who let the cat out of the bag. Unsure *which* cat was let out of the bag. Mom tries to speak up, but Grant puts a hand on her shoulder and she stops talking. It's crazy how he towers over her small frame. She's even smaller than I am.

"I'll take care of this," I overhear Grant mumble quietly. Taking long strides to the back door, he opens it and its protective gate and motions his head toward the backyard. "Come," he says to me.

"No. I want to hear it from them. You'll sugarcoat anything you say to me."

"Come outside, Ava." His hard tone is unusually serious, so I follow him outside and sit on the rickety tan lawn chair. I turn to look at him.

"So, what happened last night? You had a unified discussion about me with *my* family? Were you trying to get me drunk so you could talk to them without me there?"

He balks, his eyes nearly flying out of their sockets. I know that's not what he was trying to do. I say it anyway. "What?! No!" he shouts, offended that I can even think that. I don't actually think it, but I'm pissed.

"Then tell me," I demand. "And I want the truth, Grant. Don't fluff it up to make me feel better." I'm waiting for the moment he says something that will kill me, that will make it hard to breathe. I know it's coming. The look in someone's eyes when they know how messed up you are is not lost on me. Grant exudes that right now.

"They told me what happened."

Eyeing Grant narrowly, my heart rate picking up, I'm wondering what on earth he's talking about because of how much has happened and how much I've hidden. The last thing I need is my family divulging my own shit that I don't ever intend to tell him. Could last night's conversation be about . . . *No. They wouldn't.*

"Keep talking." My voice is shaking.

"They told me about your . . ." Grant has trouble saying whatever it is out loud, and the moment he blinks his eyes away from mine in shame, I know. When it's hard for him to even look me in the eye, it becomes so damn obvious to me what he now knows. Nevertheless, I egg him on for confirmation.

"My what, Grant?" I ask impatiently. "Spit it out."

"Your suicide attempt," he whispers, his voice straining and tight.

I momentarily freeze when Grant says it out loud, but hadn't I figured this out already?

"Nothing happened," I blurt immediately, but as soon as it leaves my mouth, he jumps out of his chair. There's this palpable rage that blankets Grant's face; he is absolutely livid right now.

"What?!" he yells.

I wonder how many ears are pressed to the back door. I don't even care. I keep lying; at this point, when it comes to Grant, I'm good at it. "I didn't do anything. Whatever they told you was an overreaction." I lie and he knows it.

"You know, I don't believe you. You're lying to me, Ava. This is your M.O. when you're confronted with anything personal. You brush it aside. You pretend it is moot. But *this*? *This* you don't get to brush aside. This time, you have to talk to me."

I laugh to deflect, as if it's nothing. I am so frustrated and exhausted at the knowledge that it was once my life; suicide attempts, the mental hospital, therapy. That shit was once my *entire* life, and I DON'T WANT TO RELIVE IT ANYMORE.

"Grant," I say softly this time. I look at him pointedly, hoping I can calm his anger with my façade. "It wasn't a big deal. Leave it."

He pulls back when I try to touch him. "Don't, Ava. I'm your *boyfriend*. We've been together for five months. I deserve to know this shit!" His teeth are gritted and I know it's the fact that I'm lying to his face that's killing him. My parents told him. Grant knows what happened. I can't exactly run from that.

The exploitation by my family boils the blood in my veins. This is *my* story.

"Why am I not allowed to have some privacy? Why do you insist I disclose everything that's going on in my life? You don't *own* me!"

Grant's angry flare shows in the way he balls his fists at his sides and clenches his jaw. I can almost spot actual fumes coming out of his nose, his ears.

"*You tried to kill yourself!*"

It hits me like it brick when he says it, hearing it come out of his mouth, in his voice. *Grant knows.* My heart sinks. I feel nauseous.

"Don't say that. *Don't fucking say that.*" I'm shaking at this point, the sheer panic in my chest pounding, making it hard to take a deep inhale. I can only muster shallow breaths, and I know that this is the start of a panic attack. I've had so many of them, and this is how they start. The burning chest, the dry throat, the heaving. But remember when I told Grant it was a big deal that I hadn't had an attack with him? I don't want him to witness this. I can't afford for him to watch me fall apart.

I swallow hard. I close my eyes. I sing the ABCs in my head. Grant interrupts me at *V*.

"Ava, you don't think that's something you should've told me?" he asks, his eyebrows raised, no doubt waiting for my surrender. I refuse.

"In case you haven't noticed, Grant, I'm trying to keep you around. Not push you away. I'm not going to cry wolf so you'll stay with me." I focus on every breath I'm taking, trying to calm myself.

"Wha—are you kidding me? Ava! Jesus Christ!"

I walk toward the door, unwilling to have this conversation, but Grant stalls me, pulling my forearm, and demands that I face him.

"Please." Grant looks up at the sky and rubs his green eyes before facing me again. My body freezes. There are tears in those pretty eyes. "Please tell me."

It breaks me to see him like this, and I can't say no to him anymore. I'll give Grant whatever he wants. I walk over to him and place my hands on his contoured chest. I nod to the ground.

"Okay. I'll tell you anything you want to know." Even if it means this is the end for us, I don't say. I'm down to one thing on that list. That's my threshold. That one is off limits. He grabs my face, searching my eyes with his wet ones.

"I want to be with you; I'm not running away. I've proven that to you over and over again, but I can't be kept in the dark with you anymore. It's been long enough, Ava. You just hide. Do you know how frustrating it is for me to feel like I'm prying because of how unwilling you are to share anything? If you trust me enough to share a bed with me, then why does this have to be so hard?"

"Because I don't want to risk you leaving or thinking differently of me." God, it feels good to say that. Lying is a workout.

"That's bullshit," he barks. "I've proven myself by now. You know that I have."

It doesn't matter if you've proven yourself. I have to feel normal with you.

"Do you think I don't see this relationship for what it is? You're doing me a favor by dating me because you pity me. Poor, small-town, depressed girl meets rich, city, popular guy. In what world, Grant, would someone like you date me if it weren't for pity? Riddle me fucking *that*!"

Grant's chest falls, his face deflates when he looks at me. He shakes his head and takes a breath. "That's you talking. Not me. I shouldn't have to prove my desire to be with you as much as I have. It's been five months, Ava. You think I'm with you for pity, even after five months? You met my family. You met my friends. I'm here, right now, in *your* hometown, meeting *your* family. How great of an actor do you think I am that I can keep up this apparent façade for *five months*?"

Do I? Do I believe that Grant wants to be with me without any other motives? Because since day one, I've felt uneasy about the unconventionality of our relationship. I have *never* felt strong and secure in our differences. Asking if I'm too fucked up for him, saying how stupid I look beside him, *genuine bafflement that he wanted to sleep with me.*

"Why won't you believe me?" he whispers. "What changed? Things were good when you left New York." *You came here. You turned my world off kilter. You made our relationship way too real.* "I just want to be with you, Ava. I want you to stop fighting it. I want you to tell me the truth."

"Fine," I say, my voice flat. I plop myself on the grassy back lawn, Grant awkwardly sitting across from me, his long legs crossed, limbs everywhere. I proceed to tell him the story of how my brothers found me in the bathtub, holding a razor, moments from slicing open my wrists. Vertically. That's what kills you. Horizontally, I was already comfortable with. It was already a part of my daily routine.

"I couldn't live with the guilt anymore. I didn't want to live at all. They called 9-1-1 and grabbed the razor out of my hand. I remember Devon flushing it down the toilet while Cooper and Connor lifted me from the bathtub and wrapped me in a towel, all of them looking away from my naked body. Connor and Cooper were in tears. Devon stood there in shock; his face was so pale. That's the main image I have from that day. His mother is Spanish and his pale face was as white as paper. After the ambulance came, they had me transported to a mental hospital where I lived for a month."

I say this last part to the ground, watching my fingers pulling strands of grass from their roots, feeling like what I'm telling Grant is just like it—pulling the roots out from under this already fragile relationship until *what?* Until he comes to his senses? I can't bear this anymore.

"And after that?" he croaks.

I shrug. "I went home. Got help. Took college classes online. Went on meds . . ." At this precise moment, it dawns on me that not only have I confessed to Grant that I'd been keeping something huge from him, but I just gave him a detailed play-by-play of the events surrounding my suicide attempt. I feel myself numbing, coming to the sheer realization that Grant now knows too much. I'm too transparent to this man. I'm angry. I'm pissed. I feel manipulated. I walk back to the house and scan the kitchen, where my family members stand, a little in shock.

"Who told him?" I shout.

"I did," Connor says.

I stalk over to face him, yelling as my voice cracks. "You had no damn right to tell him that! How could you do this to me? *You're my brother!*" I shove Con as hard as I can, my vision blurred by the huge droplets of tears buried in my eyes. When Grant pulls me away, tightening his grip on me, I try my hardest to pull from his grasp, but he's too strong. Of course he is.

"Ava!" he yells in my face. "Stop it!"

"Why are you even still here?" I cry out to Grant, swiping at the tears that just won't stop. "You were supposed to leave by now! Go! Go back to New York! Go back to your picture-perfect life, Grant! Leave me out of it!"

His nostrils flare. His jaw flexes. His hands fist. He hates that I just said that. "That's enough, Ava."

With the deafening silence in the room, my mom's small sniffles sounding louder, I cough out a sob and then it keeps going.

"Ava—"

I cut him off. I feel my blood boiling, my chest constricting, the sobs tightening my body until I release every last one. Hearing his voice makes me mad.

"No. *No, Grant.* You don't get to come here and invade my life and speak to my family behind my back. You don't belong here. And I don't belong with you."

I turn to face my brothers then, my mom and my dad; I can't watch what my outburst just did to Grant. "You guys betrayed me. I hate you so much," I cry into the palms of my hands, shaking my head. I run upstairs because after all, I do have a flight to catch in a few hours. Besides, I can't just stand there as my family stares at me with a vast number of expressions on their faces, and not happy ones. I can't help feeling like I'm laid naked and bare on display for everyone to watch and judge in disbelief. When did I lose faith in my own family? Grant did that. He took that from me.

As I reorganize my clothing and pack everything back into my suitcase, I think about this feeling of not wanting to leave home because of how safe it is, nor do I want to stay after what happened earlier, and that frightens me. I'm scared but mostly I'm ashamed. At getting mad that Connor told Grant, that I hid a huge part of my past from my boyfriend until now, and that it happened in the first place. Maybe I would've eventually come to the decision to tell Grant about my suicide attempt but not any time soon. I simply wasn't ready. This was *my* story to tell, and Connor took that from me when I still hadn't decided whether Grant would know at all. I hear a soft knock at the door and find Dad leaning on the door post, watching me pack up to go back to New York in a few hours.

"Dad, please. I already feel shitty enough. Just go, okay?" I feel bad saying that because I've never been this kind of daughter. I told them that I hate them and I don't. Not at all. I love them with every bone in my body.

"I'll go, sweetie, but can I first get a little chat with ya?" I solemnly nod and stop folding the Christmas pajamas that Mom bought the six of us. It'll be nice to wear them when I'm back at school and feeling homesick. Dad sighs heavily once he sits beside me. "I want you to know, baby, that we had the best intentions last night. We would never do anything to hurt you. Please believe me."

"I don't care. It wasn't Connor's place, Dad. Or yours or Mom's or anyone's."

"I know. You're right. But will you listen to me for a moment? I want to explain what happened." I stay quiet to let him continue. "Last night after Grant brought you upstairs, we spoke for a bit. He felt a bit insecure when we were all staring at him walking down the stairs after putting you into bed, but after seeing you so happy, we wanted him to know. We were trying to explain to him how good he is for you and that we were a little bit in shock. From our perspective, your enjoyment last night showed us that we've never seen you truly happy until now, and he wanted an explanation. I know that Connor shouldn't have opened his mouth, but I think he felt that Grant deserved to know. We were surprised to hear that you hadn't told him about the . . . the bathtub. After seeing the two of you on the couch together, we figured this was the real deal and that's why we didn't know that we were betraying you."

Dad hugs me when he sees my chin quiver, my eyes glistening on the verge of more tears. I feel so freaking *sad*.

"I've been lying to him, Daddy," I say into his neck. "How can that be considered the real deal when he doesn't know how messed up I am?"

"Sweetie, don't talk like that." He grips my shoulders, faces me, and shakes his head. "You are not messed up. You are beautiful and you are strong and you are perfect."

"Yes, I am. It's true, Dad. I've accepted it by now because I don't have a choice, but I'm not convinced I'll find someone who will love 'me for me,'" I say with air quotes.

"So, you lied?" he asks softly.

"Sort of, yeah. I just didn't tell him the whole truth. But Dad, I told him a whole bunch, and it's only been like five months. I told him what I did because I like him. I like the way he makes me feel, and I mean, yeah, forgive me for wanting just a smidge of happiness in my life again. It's pretty simple, Dad. I lied so he'd stay." I get literal shivers down my spine when I tell Dad the God's honest truth, hearing it out loud for the first time. I feel cold, an ominous air surrounding me.

"It's not like that, honey," Dad objects. "I don't think you have to do anything to make Grant stay."

"You can't say for sure. You don't know how he's feeling or what he's thinking right now knowing his short-term girlfriend has been *admitted*."

"Ava—"

"That's what it was, Dad. And I can't blame him if he wanted to leave at this point, but you can't deny that I'm messed up. I put chemicals in my body every day to make me happy. I know that I'm your daughter and you love me unconditionally, but you have to be honest too. No one wants that responsibility on their hands. Especially a guy like Grant."

I speak with assurance, conviction. I think I'm being logical right now because if I let the emotional side win again, I'll just be a blubbering mess. My sobbing earlier was enough for one day. Do I have more in me? Oh, yeah. Rivers filled. But suppressing how I'm really feeling is easier than letting it out over and over again, so I swallow down the lump in my throat and let the head win over the heart. Dad shakes his head, disagreeing.

"No, baby. You spent two years in your own personal hell, and now you're on a bit of medication to make that pain and anxiety bearable so you can live a normal life again. If Grant wasn't prepared to stick by you through thick and thin, he wouldn't be *here*, in Arcata. He wouldn't insist on knowing you, but he does because he cares. The poor boy is in love with you, Ava. He's just trying to know you. To get to know his girlfriend."

Part of me cringes at that sentence, the other hopeful, the overall feeling I get hearing Dad's words making me nervous. Elizabeth said it too, but I can't think about that right now when it could very well be that Grant is downstairs strategizing how to break up with me.

"Grant is a good man, Ava. Do you think he'd still be here if he wasn't? Do you think your mother and I would let you continue dating him if he wasn't? Your brothers would've had a field day with him had they suspected he wasn't a good fit for you. I understand that you might be hesitant to be honest with him but don't be. No man would work hard for a girl if they weren't in love with them. I think you need to put more trust in him. He is not that other one. I truly believe that Grant is here to take care of you. It's obvious to us and it should be to you."

Oof. I give my father a tight hug and nod. Maybe he's right. Maybe Grant is the unconditional one in my life. Maybe this is all I need for the rest of it. The guilt of my earlier freak-out in the kitchen holds in my chest until it's been an hour since Dad left my bedroom and there's still no word from Grant. Making my way downstairs toward the guest bedroom, I gain the courage to knock on his door.

"Come in," I hear him call out, his deep voice instantly taking the edge off, calming me. There's a half-full suitcase on the floor and a black bag filled with toiletries in Grant's hand when I enter the room. We look into each other's eyes for a long moment before he puts down the cosmetics bag and sits on the bed.

"How you doing? You okay?" he asks gently, concerned.

Damn it, I feel guilty. I should be asking him that. I'm the bad guy here. Standing before him, I nod to the ground, finding it difficult to form a reply.

"Ava." Looking up, I notice his bright green eyes reflect so much sadness. I think my suicide attempt broke him a little bit. I think my spitefulness broke him too. "Please say something," Grant begs.

"I hate that you know. This is really hard for me."

"Why? Tell me why you didn't want me to know." His voice is thick and heavy, and these emotions that his words are laced with are so telling. I know that Dad was right when he said earlier that Grant is in love with me. I don't know why me, I have always wondered why me, but just like I didn't get to choose who I fell for, Grant didn't either. The sad thing is that I don't know if Grant loving me is a good thing. I can't have kids, for God's sake. He'll hate me when he finds out I've kept that from him. I know he will.

"I'm embarrassed. I don't know you that well, Grant. It's only been like five months."

He closes his eyes when he sighs my name. "Ava . . ."

"It's true. I get that because you've already done the dating thing, you're set and happy with me, which boggles my mind as it is, but I haven't. This is new territory for me and if I don't want to tell you my deepest, darkest secrets, I have that right. I wish you understood that." I speak matter-of-factly, but the main reason I didn't want to tell him is because I didn't want him to know how deep these wounds go. That what I told him back in New York was but a dot on the map that is my past. That the meds and the abortion and all that nasty jazz *aren't* the worst of it. Grant tilts his head to the side and looks at me.

"Do you want to do the dating thing, Ava? Am I preventing you from that?" He doesn't ask because he's jealous but because he feels that he might be taking something away from me; the experience of meeting different people and finding out what I want from a relationship. But is there even a point? Isn't finding your person determined on the dynamic you have with them, not the comparison to your past relationships? Because when it comes to Grant and me, I *love* our dynamic. Even though externally we look as opposite as black and white, we have really good fun together.

I shake my head. "I don't think so. I really like what we have together and I don't want to do this with anyone else, but . . ."

"But what, babe?"

"You've been expecting transparency from me since day one. I just need a second to choose what I want to divulge to you and when on my own. You've been pressuring me to open up about my past, and I don't want to. I can't give you the whole story right away. Not yet, at least. I told you about the pills because you found them. I was almost forced to tell you, and that's kind of annoying. I don't regret it because you reacted phenomenally, but coming to you with that story was really hard for me. Bridget was the one who convinced me to do it. I would've ignored it and shoved it under the rug for as long as I could."

Grant's been insisting that I tell him everything about my past that I don't think I ever got to come to that on my own. It feels a little calculated and I don't like it. All I ask is for Grant to be patient with me so when I finally decide to let him in, it's of my own accord and I can feel good about it. Like I did when I told him about the case.

"Okay. I'm so sorry. I totally get it, Ava. I think maybe we're just not on the same page," he says slowly. This sounds awfully like a breakup, so I tell him that. "No! Ava, no. Never. That's not what I'm saying. We just need to find a happy medium, okay? And we will. I'll work on giving you more space when it comes to your past, and maybe you can be more open with me on your own? But no pressure. I promise." I tell him okay, and he mentions that there is one more thing. I ask him what it is. "You need to stop comparing our differences and start focusing on what we have together. We're different. No one is denying that, but so what? Who cares?"

I nod at him. I like this plan.

"Come here," Grant says, pulling me to him. He puts his forehead to my belly, and I close my eyes and play with his hair and let the emotions wash over me for once without suppressing them or pretending they're not there. And I can finally admit to myself that I'm in love with Grant Wilder. That I want forever with Grant Wilder. It doesn't feel scary. It doesn't feel like much at all, to be honest, because I've known it for a while. It's just an emotion that I'm letting myself finally feel.

"Will you tell me what happened last night?" I whisper, asking for his point of view after hearing it from my father.

Grant exhales heavily. "After I brought you upstairs, your family was raving about how you've never been this happy. Your brothers, your parents . . . Your dad even said that you needed me before you met me. They were on this Grant Super Team, and I was confused, Ava. I knew about Pat and the abortion, but that sentence was intense. It was heavy, so I asked what they meant."

I listen quietly, stop myself from walking away, hating this. Hating that what I hear is so true because of how terrifying it is. I need him. I need him and I can't stop myself. I don't want to feel dependent on Grant, yet I feel like my life would be empty without him. Like I'm not my own person without him. That my orientation into adulthood has been Grant Wilder in the flesh; if we're being honest, before I got better, I was a child. And the proof is the fact that I fell for Pat and his pretenses without noticing even one red flag. I was wearing rose-colored glasses, and everything about him seemed great. Normal.

"Connor and Devon told me the story," Grant continues. "I cried a little bit. I still can't believe that happened. I've been willing myself not to fly to LA and kill Pat at the sound of it. You're my girlfriend and I need you, and knowing you were going to take away the chance at me ever meeting you broke my heart. I don't know what to think, Ava." Ouch. What does that mean? "There isn't anything I can do, right?" I back away at the sound of that.

"This is exactly why I didn't want you to know. No, there's nothing you can do, Grant, because it's over. It's in the past. It happened and I've moved on and I got better. I'm better now, Grant. You get that, right? I need you to believe that I'm better. *I don't need your help. I don't want your pity.*"

"Wait. No. That's not . . ." He eyes me frantically, reaching for my hands, bringing me toward him. It takes everything in me not to pull them away. "That came out wrong. I'm not calling you helpless. I just want to make you as happy as I possibly can because you're my girlfriend, Ava, not because I think you're helpless."

"You do," I relent.

"I do what?"

"You think I'm helpless. You have these sad eyes when you look at me all the time."

He shakes his head hurriedly. "I think you're confusing that with plain emotion. You make me *feel*, Ava. That's what you're seeing. I'm not sad. In fact, I'm insanely happy with you. All I want is for you to be happy with me just the same."

"I am. You make me really happy, Grant. I tell you this all the time."

He pulls me into him, tightening his grip around me and finally cupping my cheeks to face him.

"You have no idea how much that means to me." He slurs his words from the rush of them.

"I'm sorry," I say with utmost sincerity. I was acting demonic earlier. I'm so embarrassed. He didn't deserve being put in the middle of a family dispute like that. Grant didn't really do anything wrong. He didn't ask. Connor just told him.

"Don't be sorry, babe. We're gonna be okay. Let me take you home."

Devon drives Grant and me to the airport and helps us unload our suitcases out of his trunk. The goodbyes I gave to my parents and brothers were callous and distant, and I hate leaving them with this bad taste in my mouth after an amazing Christmas together. And as awful as it is, I can't help but put a little bit of the blame on Grant for this outcome. Things would've been so normal if he never showed up. It's ridiculous and I don't harbor any resentment, not really, but I guess I'm just frustrated at the drama of it all, but maybe it's me. Maybe I've become a different person in the last five months, and Grant had nothing to do with it whatsoever. Maybe I'm the problem, that I've been the problem all along, as to why my life is such a dramatic mess. Maybe I'm not as mature and strong and "over it" as I think I am.

When it's just us two at the airline check-in desk, Grant booking us new (first-class) flights back home, I notice myself acting awkward from this personal revelation that makes me cringe. Typically, I'd press myself against his side but I don't. I don't hold his hand as I've done countless times, and I can tell he sees something is off with me. If this revelation is true, that I'm immature, that *I'm* the problem, then this relationship I have with Grant is senseless and not just because he's wealthy and I'm not. Grant is much older than I am, and wiser, and I feel so stupid.

What was I thinking starting something up with a guy who is twenty leagues ahead of me? I'm losing all confidence in our relationship. This mental roller coaster that I'm putting myself through is killing me. The doubt can be so draining sometimes.

"Baby? You look unsettled. Is everything okay?" He puts his arm around my shoulder, kisses my forehead. I shake my head, so he hugs me tighter. "Tell me what's on your mind."

"I feel really young with you," I admit.

He immediately unhooks his arm from my shoulder, grabs my hand, and interlocks our fingers as we walk toward our respective gate.

"Why do you feel really young with me?"

"Because I am?" I reply, evidently.

"And what's the problem with that?" he asks.

"Because I'm so immature," I whisper.

Grant chuckles, shaking his head. "You're a lot of things, Ava, but immature is not one of them. I swear."

"I don't feel very independent when I'm with you." The truths are coming out, aren't they. God, what am I doing? It's like I'm trying to self-sabotage the best relationship I could ask for.

"But you are independent, Ava. Completely. You call the shots here, babe," he says pointedly, his eyebrows raised, a hidden smirk on his perfect lips.

I shake my head. "It's more so how I feel about myself when I'm with you. But I don't want you to do anything differently, so I don't really know what to do here." I speak to the ground because I can't face him, the embarrassment of today making me recoil inside.

"Then maybe embrace it?" he suggests, shrugging his shoulders. "Embrace *us*. Embrace being taken care of, because I sure as hell love it more than anything. Like I said millions of times, Ava. *I want to be with you.*"

"Why?" Is it *because* I'm younger than he is? Is this some weird "Daddy" complex?

Bitch, that's enough!!

"I feel accomplished when I know that I've done something to make you happy. It's not an age thing. It's a you thing."

Gah, my heart.

"Can I ask you something?" Grant nods and assures me that I can ask him anything. "I've made this so complicated, from the beginning. I've never been all in like you are and I haven't exactly made things easy. Why are you still here? Why are you so persistent? I'm not trying to be self-deprecating; I just need to know why this is so important to you. Why *I'm* so important to you."

"I like you a lot, Ava. A lot. You're fun and funny and smart and kind. *You're so kind* and I feel really good about myself when we're together. This relationship is so different than anything I've ever been in, and I like that because *I like who I am when I'm with you.* I don't want easy, Ava. I want you. Easy is why I've been single for ten years. I want you *because* you're not easy."

How did I get so lucky? I kiss his cheek and nod in understanding. "Well done, sweet talker," I tease. I smile sadly when Grant chuckles at my joke.

"Don't be sad. It's a good life, Ava baby."

We enter the boarding line, scan our passes, and walk toward the plane. Once seated, Grant turns to face me. I rest my head back and look at him, smirking.

"I've never sat first class before. This is really cool."

He points to my smile. "You see that? Right there? That's why I do what I do. It makes everything worthwhile. Even your persistent reluctance," he jokes, bending to kiss me. Grant fits a sleep mask on my head and lowers it to cover my exhausted eyes. Crying and yelling and fighting with the people you love is grueling.

"Go to sleep," he says. "You need your rest for tonight."

"What's tonight?"

"We're going to a party."

"We are?" I ask, blinded by the velvety fabric of the first-class exclusive eye mask. I slowly lean my head until it reaches his shoulder. I get another forehead kiss. They're my absolute favorite.

"Yeah. The Wilders' yearly after-New-Year's-Eve New Year's party. That's why I came to Cali. Their party is the day after."

Of course they have an annual family party. They're so damn rich.

I relax in my seat, let sleep engulf me, and wake up six hours later to Grant nudging my shoulder.

"We're home, Ava baby." Those words have a bigger impact on me than he could ever know. I groggily stir awake and smile upward, the mask still covering my eyes.

"Home."

AVA

As soon as our plane landed in New York, Grant ordered an Uber. Once we grabbed our suitcases from baggage claim, we rushed toward the car that drove us over to Scarsdale, where Grant's parents' party was being held. It was probably the best party I've ever been to. Julia and Callum were genuinely ecstatic to see me there, and I was so flattered when Callum hugged me at the front door, saying, "We are so happy to have you in our family now, Ava. Happy New Year's, sweetheart."

It totally did feel like I was a part of their family, especially when Annie made me join her on the dance floor with Layla, Ben, and Grant to yell (not sing) the lyrics of "Mr. Brightside" in a huddle of Wilder kids. Grant and I didn't stop dancing together throughout the night, and at one point, I think the DJ was playing just for us. The waiters handing out glasses of champagne chuckled every time I took them up on their offer and grabbed a glass; I couldn't possibly count how many I had that night. We also may have snuck away from the party to make out wildly, messily, and drunkenly in Grant's childhood bed, but I don't kiss and tell.

We slept there that night, having had our suitcases with us, too drunk to sit for an hour-long car ride back to the city. As Grant and I nakedly slipped into his bed, I genuinely felt content and worry-free for the first time in my life. Spending time with Grant and his family at the party was an incredible end to a shitty fight earlier that day; it helped us to go back to normal, which was key.

It's been a few weeks since the party, and Grant and I have honestly never been better, which is why I feel so deflated when Dad calls to update me on the McCall case. Again, it's like this happy bubble I'm living in can't possibly stay whole. It's gotta burst and it absolutely does when he tells me that Mr. Ellison and Pat's lawyers scheduled a deposition for the end of February, only a month away. A deposition where I'm put under a microscope, with a camera in my face and fancy lawyers asking me questions that are triggering and debilitating to answer. And having to see Pat? My whole body is shaking, and I interrupt him.

"I can't do this, Dad. Find another way. Tell them I said no." My voice is trembling. I know this isn't going to work. I know that the moment we served the McCalls with this case, it meant my small involvement would come to the point where I'd inevitably have to see Pat and his father again.

"Sweetheart, this is the litigation process. You have to be there to answer the questions because the case is about you. But they've agreed to do it in New York so there are minimal disruptions with school. That's good, right? Hey, I know it's scary, but Mom and I will be there with you throughout the whole thing, honey. I will hold your hand and you can squeeze mine as tight as you have to. Bruises and all."

I've always known that this was probable. I *was* forewarned, but now that it's here, I'm thinking there is no way I will survive this. *This,* I'm not strong enough for. I can't be in a room with Pat in a month. I just can't do it.

Pretending as if I didn't hear a word my father said, I say, "Dad . . . you're gonna tell them no, right?" I feel weak when I talk. The other end of the line is silent. "Right, Dad?"

He exhales heavily. "I don't know what to tell you, sweetheart . . ."

I think I'm in shock. Who's *forcing* me to do this? I opened this case for my parents on the premise that I wouldn't be involved. An interview or a deposition or whatever they call it sounds pretty fucking involved to me.

"Why would you let them do that to me?" I waver.

"Honey, I don't mean to upset you," he says calmly. How can he be so nonchalant about this?

"This isn't fair," I shout at the receiver.

"Ava—"

"You know that this isn't fair, Dad. The least you can do is try to get me out of this! I'm doing this for you, Dad! I'm reliving this for you!" I'm a mess of yelling and tears when I hear keys clinking against the metal deadbolt and my door begin to unlock. I momentarily forgot that I was exuberantly happy before this phone call and that my boyfriend and I had planned a date for tonight.

"I have to go," I say to my father. "Bye."

GRANT

"Everything okay in here?" I call out, cautiously opening the door to Ava's apartment with the key she gave me for Christmas. My heart aches when the reason behind the muffled yelling shows on Ava's face as soon as she turns to face me. Her cheeks are streaked with dried tears, and she looks absolutely heartbroken. Big brown eyes look up at me as Ava idles by the doorway, trying hard to stifle her cries. Her voice is shaky when she speaks.

"Hey, um . . . I know we had plans to hang out tonight, but . . . can you please go? Now is really not a good time." She slides the fabric of her sleeve beneath her eyelid and swipes at the tears threatening to stream downward.

I hate that Ava is asking me to leave and I'm desperate when I say, "We don't have to do anything tonight, but please let me be here."

"Grant—"

"Please, Ava. Please." She looks up at me, her eyes pooling with tears as she slowly nods. "Come here," I say, pulling her into a warm, much-needed hug. Ava's body feels tense like she's holding back tears, and I hate that, but not like the day of my party because then, I wanted Ava to cry *for me*. Now, I need her to cry *for herself*.

"You can cry, Ava baby. Let it out. I'm here. You're my girl, okay? I have you." I hold her head against me as she finally surrenders and sobs into my chest, her hands fisting my sweatshirt, dampening the thick cotton with her uncontrolla-ble tears. I walk us deeper into her apartment and lean my back on the kitchen counter, allowing Ava to take solace in my tight grip. I want her to know what a coward I am by being here and holding her, but I can't lose her. I need her so damn bad. *I love her so damn bad.*

I feel Ava's back shudder beneath my palms, her cries vi-brating throughout her small body, and it absolutely ruins me. I'm somehow regretting that fight last month even more; watching Ava in pain right now hurts me more than it did to know she wasn't coming to me for consolation. When her cry-ing subsides and she finally looks up, my chest feels like it's splitting in two at the view in front of me. My beautiful and perfect girlfriend on the brink of destruction. Her innocence and her un-deservingness pulling something tight in my chest, the truth on the tip of my tongue. I bring my thumb down her dampened cheeks and trace her big lips in the stillness.

"It's killing me to see you like this, Ava," I say finally. "Tell me what I can do." I feel her cold hands slip beneath my sweat-shirt as she rubs up my bare back, placing her forehead in the center of my chest. She shakes her head. Finally, she speaks.

"Did you drive here?" she croaks, her voice sounding weak and spent.

My God, Wilder, what are you doing to this poor girl?

"Yeah," I reply.

"Will you let me drive your car?"

"Of course." I chuckle.

"Wait, really?" she asks, surprised but excited despite the tears she just cried.

"Really. Did you think I'd say no?" I pinch my eyebrows, smirk at her.

"Well, yeah," Ava says, shrugging. "I mean that car is worth like two hundred thousand dollars or something."

Two hundred grand? It's pennies to me. Compared to Ava, it's nothing. It's air.

"Baby, your happiness is worth more to me than any car," I tell her. She sweetly smiles and scrunches her nose. I love when she gets shy with me. "You're asking for a little joy ride, aren't you?" A shy grin forms on her face, and she happily nods. I love her so much.

"Yeah, kind of. Is that okay? I'll be safe, I promise."

I dismiss her concern and grab my keys from the kitchen counter.

"No question, baby. Let's do it. Grab your coat." As we descend the echoey stairwell of her building, I turn and ask, "So, where are you taking me?"

"I think I want to surprise you."

Ava's surprise joy ride lands us at Rockaway Beach despite it being dirty and uninhabited, but my little tourist doesn't know that. She tells me that she searched up the nearest beaches, so here we are. It's also a decent thirty degrees out. I notice that watching the water from the windshield of my fairly small sports car isn't what Ava came here for, and when she lowers the windows and leans her head against the headrest, closing her eyes, I can tell how bad she wants to be out there. I exit the car and grab the extra coat I always keep on hand from the trunk.

"What're you doing?" she calls out from the open window.

"Giving you what you want." I open her door and reach out my hand. "Come."

"Really? But it's too cold. I feel bad."

I brush her off, help Ava into the ginormous coat, and lead her toward the water. We sit on cold sand, and I warm Ava's curled body in my lap, my arms encasing her small frame. Her only focus is on the water, and she stares motionlessly ahead, almost like she's not looking at anything at all. When she finally comes to and lays her head back on my shoulder, I whisper in her ear.

"I'm so happy you're mine."

"Mmm," she hums, holding my arms closer, tightening my grip around her body.

"You saved me," I whisper into her hair. "You saved me from myself." With that, she turns in my embrace and straddles my lap, hooking her wrists at the back of my neck. I receive a typical Ava response when she replies to my heavy words with a nose scrunch, a goofy look, and a strong kiss. I get the chills as she rakes her fingers through my hair and kisses my neck, leaving her head on my shoulder.

"You're kinda my hero, Grant," she says, voice low but promising, breath hot against the skin below my ear. I want to throw her off me, scream "NO, I'M NOT!" but her admission does some powerful things to my heart. I'm feeling so much love and admiration for this girl right now. I want to tell her that I am insanely in love with her, but I'm too scared. Ava is unpredictable and I can't lose her, especially with how fragile she is now. Saying something big like *I love you* could potentially cause more harm than good. It's not a risk I'm willing to take. I turn my head to the side and kiss Ava's forehead.

"Your hero, huh?"

I feel her cold nose brush against my neck when she nods in reply. "You mean a lot to me, Granty." This is the first time she's used the nickname my family calls me by, and it creates this bond, this feeling of protectiveness over her because she really is my family. I plan on making it official one day, if by miracle I become a lucky bastard. I ask Ava if she's happy and she says yes.

"I'm happy because of you. You made me feel alive again."

Holy shit. My mission for the past five months has been to change this girl's life, and the fact that she's essentially told me in this moment that I did my job is jaw dropping. I'm in a bit of disbelief.

Ever since August, Fisher, Rocco's—it's the only thing I've strived for when it came to my relationship with Ava. All I've ever wanted was to take this broken girl and put her back together with every laugh and smile and gift. With every kiss and every hug. With every moment we spent together, lying naked in bed, sitting across from each other at a restaurant, partying, drinking.

"Really?" I pull back to look at her, my large hands gripping her small waist. "I make you feel alive, Ava?" *Like I said: disbelief.*

"Yeah," she replies, nodding quickly. "Because you're so fun. You make me have a lot of fun."

That's all I've ever wanted. If only she knew. I tickle her until she cracks up and in one swift movement, lift her and myself to our feet.

"Dance with me, baby," I demand, putting my hand out for hers. Ava smiles skeptically and puts her palm in mine. I bring her flush against my body and dance while humming, the heavy sand making our already awkward movements wobbly. She giggles.

"You're sappy, Grant Wilder," Ava mumbles, her cheek flat against my chest.

"How's that?"

She smiles when she looks up at me. "Because of the song you're singing."

"You know it?" I've been caught. I laugh.

"Do I know the song 'My Girl' by The Temptations? Yes, I do." I snag her in a heated kiss when she rolls her eyes at me, looking up proudly. "Am I?" she breathes. "Your girl?"

You're more than my girl; you're the love of my life.

"No one has ever been my girl more than you have, and no one ever will be. You're it for me, Ava baby."

She shivers at that moment, unintentionally I hope, and her teeth chatter. We make a run for the car and blast the heater to its highest setting, using it as a makeshift fireplace, fighting over the vents and laughing easily together. The car ride is quiet when we head toward Ava's place, but as she lays her head against the window, without looking at me, she hooks her fingers through mine and kisses my hand strongly, keeping her lips on my skin for a good thirty seconds.

"Thank you for tonight, Granty," she whispers to the foggy glass. "You're it for me too."

If only she knew the thank-yous I owed her, for giving me the five months we've had together, knowing that time is ticking and the expiration date of this relationship is coming up sooner than I'd like. Ava and I sleep naked, wrapped up in each other having fallen asleep after making quiet, passionate love. By the time I wake up at 7:30, she's gone.

GRANT

Freddy and Elizabeth are tying the knot today, and with Ava on my arm, I feel a sense of pride walking into this party, being able to introduce her as my girlfriend. It's a beautiful Sunday afternoon in early February, but the weather is warm enough that it feels like a June wedding. The appetizers and cocktails are being served outdoors on the outstretched, grassy plot parallel to the wedding hall before the ceremony begins. Ava follows as I make my rounds outside greeting old friends, and she thinks I don't notice when she stares, captivated by me, mesmerized, but I do. This is my first attendance at a wedding with a girlfriend. It feels momentous. The faces I've been getting when saying *I'd like you to meet Ava, my girlfriend* are humorous. Grant Wilder sure has a reputation.

Ava squeezes my arm and excuses herself to use the restroom, emerging minutes later and walking toward me with a frozen expression. When I see that Hannah is watching us from behind Ava with a vindictive smirk on her face, I know. I know because this has happened countless times. I want to be cheerful for Ava, making her forget whatever meaningless bullying Hannah likely just did that has her so shocked, so I put on a cheerful voice and say, "Hey, baby! What can I get you to drink?"

"Grant, I'd like to go home," she whispers firmly, her voice literally trembling.

"What? We just got here! Let's have some fun!" I exclaim, hoping to coax some excitement from her even though Hannah can be merciless. Denying me with a frantic shake of her head, Ava tells me that she's so sorry but she's leaving, that she'll take a cab, that she wants me to have a good time. There's no chance I'm going to let my girlfriend leave a wedding in a *cab*.

"No, *we're* leaving," I say, grabbing her hand and squeezing it. When we shuffle into the car, I pause before starting the ignition.

"What did she do?" I ask knowingly, because Hannah is as ruthless as they come; always has been the textbook mean girl. She's like a fucking *Gossip Girl* character.

"I don't want to tell you," Ava breathes shakily.

"You don't have a choice." I hate how harsh I sound, but Hannah can't get away with it this time. Every other time I didn't bother doing anything about it because the girls Hannah was shooing away didn't mean much to me anyway. But this time? This time the girl means the world and I'm in love and I'll die before I let Hannah hurt her. This is the reason I didn't want to take Ava to Freddy's party to begin with. I didn't want her exposed to the people from my past because of how wrong my past is.

"I don't want to," she replies, repeating herself. "Please don't make me. Let's just go home." But I am going to make her. I'm not the kind of guy who shrugs it off and moves on when someone hurts my girlfriend.

"Give me a play-by-play right now, Ava. Start talking," I demand.

"Grant—"

"Now."

With a heavy breath, she surrenders. "I was in the bathroom when she walked in, and immediately, I felt like I was under a microscope. From the moment I walked in all through washing my hands at the sink, she wouldn't stop staring at me, looking at my body and my clothes and my face, so I innocently asked, 'Can I help you?' and she's like '*You? Help me?*' and then she laughed, so I said, 'Then stop staring at me' and she—" Ava closes her eyes and takes a breath. She shakes her head no because she *really* doesn't want to tell me.

"Ava, so help me God, finish that sentence," I demand.

"She shoved me into the bathroom sink."

I'm wildly manic as I aggressively unbuckle the seat belt and bolt out of my car toward the wedding hall. I'm going to give that bitch a piece of my mind. Before I have a chance to walk even ten feet, I'm pulled backward, my arm in Ava's weak grasp.

"No, no, no," she begs, tears pooling in her pleading, widened eyes. "Please don't. It's fine, I think she was just drunk. Let's go home, Grant. Please." I keep walking forward, but Ava pulls at my arm tighter, harder. "Please," she begs. "Just leave it."

I want to destroy Hannah piece by piece for what she's done to my girlfriend, but after watching Ava plead so desperately, I respect what she wants and slide back into my front seat. Ava would be furious with me if I started drama in the middle of someone else's wedding, so I don't. However, when I sit back down by the steering wheel, the anger I feel for Hannah is still boiling my blood. I rip out of the parking lot, zooming toward the direction of my apartment. Ava grabs my arm.

"Grant, slow down!" she shouts in a full panic. "You're driving crazy! Slow down!"

"Why are you not livid right now?!" I instantly regret it as soon as I scream at her but too angry at Hannah to be calm.

Ava strengthens her grip on my arm and begs me to stop driving so fast.

"Please slow down. Relax, okay? You're driving recklessly."

"WHY ARE YOU TELLING ME TO RELAX RIGHT NOW?!" I boom, the sound making her jump.

"Shut up! Just shut up for one second!" she yells, paranoid and terrified, like I'm being irrational. When I see how distraught Ava is, I admit my irrationality and put my foot on the brake. The rage is burning in my chest and I'm breathing so hard that my lungs hurt. My mind is confused as I glance at Ava, unable to fathom how she's so much calmer than I am when she's the one who was hurt.

"Why does she own you like this?" Ava questions heatedly. "Look at how you're acting because of her."

"*Own me?* That bitch doesn't own me, Ava. What're you saying?" I spit, irritated at her implication.

"Elizabeth told me that she's like this with everyone you try dating," she says to the passenger window. "I just don't understand why you let her."

"I don't let her. She just does it, and up until you, I never cared to defend anyone."

"But why? What does she have on you? Why doesn't she let you date other people?"

If I expect full transparency from Ava, which I absolutely do, then I owe it back to her. I take a deep breath before saying what I'm about to. Am I thrilled about this? No. But Ava deserves to know the truth if she's being targeted because she's my girlfriend.

"We made a really stupid pact years ago that if we're not married by the time we're both thirty, we'll marry each other. It's dumb, Ava, and it's ten years old and obviously it will never, ever happen, but I think Hannah took it a little too seriously and might be waiting in the wings, weeding out the competition for another two years."

"Oh," Ava mutters.

"But you know she has no chance, right? You know that I'm yours. Tell me that much, Ava."

She turns to look at me and nods. "I do know. But you should've defended anyone she was cruel to, not just me."

How is Ava thinking about my past dates and what Hannah did to them right now after what Hannah did to *her*? She is so incredibly selfless. Calming me down with chills on my leg, Ava's hand never leaving my knee, I have a burning urge. *I love you so much,* I want to say.

But instead, I tell her, "You're the best person I know." Ava's head shakes against the window, where she keeps it for the duration of the drive back home.

As she stares into my sweatshirt drawer, Ava taps her lips in nothing but a towel wrap, deciding which one of my hoodies she's going to steal to wear to bed tonight. After the unnecessary drama of earlier this evening, we took a much-needed, relaxing shower together. It was the only component we needed to relieve the stress of my reaction to Hannah's psychosis. Ava pulls out a tattered gray hoodie from the bottom of the back pile and throws it on the bed. I laugh.

"What?" she asks, pulling out a pair of her underwear from my top dresser drawer and awkwardly hopping into them. I get a little distracted, watching my girlfriend work her way around the bedroom in nothing but a pair of blue underwear, so Ava asks again. "Why'd you laugh?"

"Why'd you choose that one?" I ask back.

She shrugs. "I don't know. I like the gray. Why?" I cross the room and kiss her face until she giggles, cupping her boob, sucking on her neck. "What's your deal with this sweatshirt?" she breathes shakily. Finally, I lean my head back to face her.

"High school basketball."

Ava's eyes widen in pure glee as she turns her head to glance at the sweatshirt on my bedspread.

"No!" I nod, grinning hugely. "This is ten years old? This is high school Grant's?!"

"That, my love, is the sweatshirt of the 2008 Masters School varsity basketball team captain. That's some big deal shit you're about to wear to bed, Ava."

"Ooooooooh, aren't I lucky," she mocks, wiggling her eyebrows and slipping the sweatshirt on quickly before I can snatch it away. "I'm keeping it."

"Ohhh, no you ain't." I jerk forward to playfully tug the sweatshirt back, but she runs across the room, laughing proudly.

"What're you gonna do about it, Wilder? *Pull* it off me?"

It's the cutest fucking thing when she giggles nervously, all giddy, running away from me with challenge in her eyes. I finally catch up to her in the living room—because before I wasn't really trying—and lift her body over my shoulder, smacking her butt in mock disapproval. Instead of smacking my butt or back to get me to put her down like last time, she grabs the elastic of my briefs with two hands and pulls as hard as she can, sodomizing me with Calvin Klein cotton. I will now have permanent wedgie rug burn.

"Holy shit!" I call out, putting her down. "Ow!"

"Don't mess with me, Grant. I am a wedgie champion. Just ask my brothers," she declares before winking and walking toward my bedroom. I click my tongue and shake my head but inside I'm exploding. I haven't had this much *real* fun like I do with Ava since college. All the "fun" I've had since then has been under the influence of either alcohol or coke. Sad, isn't it?

Ava hangs her towel on the back of the bathroom door and chuckles when she sees me enter the bedroom.

"How's your ass crack doing?"

"Permanently damaged, thanks to you. Come here."

She tackles me onto the bed and holds my face, kissing me deeply, the length of her small body pressed against mine. Ava straddles me as I lie beneath her with my hands behind my head, glued to her every expression.

"Tell me about high school," she says.

"I went to Masters. Have you heard of it?" She shakes her head. Of course she hasn't. Masters is a prestigious high school in New York. I tell Ava all about it and watch how she listens intently, hanging on to every word that exits my mouth as I describe the giant campus, my friends who I'm still in touch with today, and the fact that my parents sent me to Masters School to get the best education they could find as close to home as possible.

"What were you like?"

I smile at her and she smiles back, biting her lip. "What do you think I was like?" She raises an eyebrow at me, like she's asking if I *really* want to hear her take. I nod.

"Well, you were captain of the varsity team, so you were obviously athletic. You were probably super popular and hot, *obviously*," she emphasizes, rolling her eyes. I chuckle. "Okay . . . you had a lot of girlfriends? And your teachers loved you? Everyone worshipped you. Straight A's."

"You think so highly of me."

"How did I do?" she asks, smirking.

"Eh. All right, I guess. You get an A minus on your work tonight, Miss Campbell." She throws her head back laughing and bends to kiss me. "You're in a good mood tonight."

"I don't know why I feel so giddy right now." Ava takes a deep breath and changes positions as she's suddenly timid, quietly playing with my thick hair. It's a few minutes of comfortable silence before she speaks again. "You make me so happy, Grant. Let's go to sleep."

In typical Ava fashion, an announcement like that doesn't get any attention. I don't even mind that she's escaping from her very honest words because even telling me that is enough. I don't need a full conversation from her. I do wish I recorded that, though. For later. For when I'll need it.

I spoon Ava's body tightly touching mine and hook my leg around hers. I put my face to her hair and take a deep breath.

"I'm gonna marry you, you know."

She freezes in my arms and holds her breath for a good thirty seconds. "When?" she whimpers quietly, her hot breath hitting my arm that's wound tightly around her.

"As soon as you let," I respond as assured as I'll ever be. *Tomorrow. Next week. Say the word.*

"What if I don't?"

Huh? Is there a possibility that Ava would never want to get married? That seems unlikely given how traditional she is, but I'm exhausted and she probably is too, so I reply with, "I'll wait until you do."

Ava pecks me quickly before turning to fall asleep. I have trouble sleeping, myself, worried that I've said the wrong thing, that I've been too abrupt. By the time I wake up the next morning before 8:00, Ava's side of the bed is empty and she texts that she'll see me later.

GRANT

I've been completely miserable sitting on Ava's bed for the last thirty minutes, waiting for her to come home from wherever the hell she is. When she left this morning without telling me where she went, like she's done countless times in the last six months, I was pretty damn pissed. Last night felt different. It *was* different. I know she felt it too because of how happy she said she was. So when her side of the bed was empty when I woke up, I was plain mad. Standing from the bed when I hear Ava's keys in the lock, I shove my hands in my pockets to keep from reaching out to touch her as soon as she walks in like I always do. She's undoing the bun at the top of her head when she opens the door and smiles massively when she sees that I'm here.

"Hola!" She's super chipper, glowing, and walks with a literal bounce in her step. How could she not? Last night was perfect. I, on the other hand, feel threatened at Ava's lack of communication and honesty about where she disappears to one morning a month. Not once did she tell me; I had to calculate the timing myself. It's like Ava will always have one foot out the door no matter what I do, how I treat her, how good we are together. Now, I know that this relationship hasn't necessarily been smooth sailing from the get-go, but no matter what we're faced with, we seem to prevail through it quite well, so why is Ava still holding out? It's not like she knows or anything. Objectively, this place we're in looks like a perfect, happy relationship. Her perpetual hesitation is confusing at best.

"Where were you?" I question curtly, challenging her with my stare that I know intimidates her.

Ava's face flashes with guilt, and she busies herself with the elastic on her wrist.

"Nowhere." She shrugs, gathering her beautiful light brown hair at the top of her head, configuring a neater bun than the one she walked in with. Ava walks toward me in tight jeans and the Masters sweatshirt she wore to bed last night. I mean, she did warn me that she was going to steal it among the other hundred that she's taken, but I don't mind. I kind of love that she prefers to wear my clothes over hers. To preserve my smell, she doesn't wash them, and I find that adorable.

Her reply infuriates me.

"You weren't nowhere. Where are you coming from?" I ask again, probing her to answer me out of desperation more than anything else.

Her hands pause at the top of her head and when she finally finishes tying up her hair, she presses her skinny arms to her sides. Ava squints her eyes in puzzlement when she looks at me. "What's going on?" She sounds worried, even a little anxious, but she still isn't telling me where she went this morning and I'm only getting more frustrated with her.

"Don't answer my question with a question," I snap. My voice is demanding. "Where were you, Ava?"

"I . . . Why are you doing this?" She looks between both my eyes, shaking her head, her eyebrows pinched and nervous and *terrified*.

"Doing what? I'm asking my girlfriend where she was at eight in the morning because she certainly didn't wake up beside me."

Finally, she surrenders. "I was at a doctor's appointment," she states apathetically, looking straight at me, all business. There is a sudden emptiness in her eyes when she replies like it's not her that's telling me this long-awaited truth.

"That you go to every month," I add. She watches me, bites her lip, and nods. "What kind of doctor?" I press, hoping to get every bit of information out of her. I told her I was going to marry her last night, for God's sake. Why is *she* doing this?

"A gynecologist."

"Why?"

Ava takes a deep breath, looks at the wall behind me, and closes her eyes. "I'm . . . I'm not going to tell you that." And there she goes—Ava shuts down. I can already suspect that this conversation is going to be disastrous unless one of us concedes, and it's not going to be me. We've been together too long for her to continue keeping things from me. I told her about Hannah. I told her about the drug use. I tell her everything. *Well . . .*

"So, I'm just gonna keep finding things out about you, huh."

I sound far angrier than I feel. The truth is that every time I come to realize that Ava is intentionally hiding things from me, I get scared. I'm scared that she isn't giving me her full self because she somehow knows this is going to end, and when it does, it'll end badly. But then again, I could be projecting my own fears onto her.

"You know everything about me," she objects quietly, fidgeting with her fingers, playing with the drawstring of her sweatshirt. Ava breathes deeply, stares at the ground, and if I wasn't so frustrated, I'd run to comfort her. I'm pretty sure I'm scaring my girlfriend right now.

"Clearly I don't. What else are you hiding?" God, I'm the worst kind of person because of what *I'm* hiding, but somehow, I weigh that differently. That's bigger, huge, ginormous. This thing that Ava hid from me is just a stupid doctor's thing. So what's the hesitation?

"Grant—"

I stop her before she can come up with another lame excuse.

"Tell me what I don't know," I interrupt, demanding she spit it out already.

Ava shakes her head in defiance. "Please," she begs quietly, her face paling, her eyes falling. "Don't do this."

My stomach is in knots at her soft voice pleading with me, but right now I'm letting my anger win because I just have to. I have to know. "Start talking."

"There were three things," Ava murmurs, staring at her shoes, the destroyed and dilapidated Converse sneakers that are so her.

I'm not sure I hear her correctly, so I ask, "What? What did you say?"

She clears her throat before trying again. "There were three things," she says, surer now.

"Three things, huh?" I laugh dryly, glancing away from her angelic and pure and beautiful face. I'm making her out to be the bad guy here while all along *I've* been the bad guy. I'm being another level of cruel right now, but what she doesn't know won't hurt her yet. Besides, Ava isn't someone you walk away from no matter how wrong being with her is. I've come to understand that quite well the last five-plus months.

"Yeah," she confirms.

"Three things that you were never going to tell me?" I ask to clarify, confused at how perfectly designed this seems. "What was it, like a list of some sort?"

"Yes." I watch as Ava's shoulders slowly inch forward, as she crosses her arms, huddles into herself, and avoids any and all eye contact with me.

"What are the three?" I push her to continue, at this point becoming completely apathetic to the clear anguish she's experiencing right now because of how badly I need to know the truth.

"Grant—" Her voice is soft, pleading.

I think I'm watching Ava slowly break in front of me, and instead of walking over, holding her, consoling her, I irritably ask, "What are the three, Ava?"

"The case and the suicide attempt," she spits out in a jumble of words and sounds. It makes me even angrier.

"Don't fuck with me. That's two. What's the last one?" I boom and Ava jumps at the sound of my voice.

She shakes her head, her cheeks turning pink, the bun on her head coming undone.

"I'm not telling you."

"Ava—"

"Break up with me, Grant. I don't care. But I'm not telling you." This time, she's tougher when she talks, looking straight at me, and quickly, I'm the one who's intimidated. This is big. If she's implying that she'd rather we *break up* than tell me the truth even after a night like last night, this is big. This is bigger than the case or the suicide attempt. This is the consequential piece of Ava's puzzle that she never intended on sharing with me. Not in the beginning and not now, almost six months later.

"Come on, Ava. What could be so bad that you can't tell your own boyfriend?"

"Something that will make you no longer my boyfriend!" She's terse as she speaks with finality, offering no explanation and essentially giving me no chance to prove her wrong. Ava has already made up her mind about how I'll react to whatever it is that she believes is so terrible, and she did this months ago. When I don't say anything in response out of pure anger, she takes a small step forward. I take a jolted step back, and her demure face flashes in hot pain.

"Can we please go back to normal?" Ava begs, her eyes straining to hold mine in place. "Please, Grant." It's amazing how Ava can go from this curt, no-nonsense woman to a scared, young girl within seconds. If I look at her beautiful face for one more second, I'll cave and she'll win and it'll feel to me like we're back at square one. It'll also give way to Ava keeping secrets from me in the future, and I don't like that idea.

"What's normal, Ava? A relationship where you don't let me in? Where you hide things? What's normal?" I shout back at her and her chin quivers. I quickly look away because like I said, I'll cave.

"I just can't," she whispers, shaking her head. Ava is making a decision. So am I.

"I'm leaving. I have to go," I mutter in pure defeat. Ava has won this one because tomorrow? Tomorrow I'll miss her too damn bad, and I'll call her to let her know that she can *take her time* because I've missed her.

"Please don't," she whispers, begging and petrified. "Grant," she hollers after me. "Please!"

I blatantly ignore her heartbreaking pleas and head for the door, trying hard to turn off the part of myself that loves this woman with my entire being.

"I can't have children," Ava calls out when my hand fists the creaky doorknob.

I freeze in place and slowly turn to look at her.

"*What?*" My voice is choked. It hurts to talk right now. It hurts to breathe.

"I'm infertile. I can't have kids." Ava gulps nervously, never taking her eyes off of mine.

What the fuck is she talking about?

My chest falls. "No," I whisper, shaking my head.

"Yes," she says tersely.

"No, Ava, that can't be." *I would have known.*

"It *can* be. It *is*. That's number three. Are you happy now?" she scoffs.

"*Happy?*" I shout. "You think this makes me *happy?*" Ava's pretty honey eyes widen, and she quickly shakes her head.

"No. Sorry," she mumbles.

Something immediately dawns on me, and I could almost fucking laugh.

"Is that why we've been having unprotected sex this whole time? When you said you were covered . . . You didn't mean birth control, did you?"

"No. I didn't mean birth control." My heart sinks as I watch Ava take on this look, empty and numb, when she stares back at me. She once explained it. *When your life is filled with so much hardship, you learn how to keep every reaction at bay.*

This isn't the reaction of a twenty-year-old, emotional, and fragile girl telling her boyfriend that she can't have children. This is the reaction of a girl who sat in a bathtub and tried to kill herself. This is the reaction of a girl whose life motto is to live with guilt and self-hate over something she didn't have a choice in. I thought the affidavit was bad. I thought Pat was bad. I thought the abortion was bad. The meds. The depression. The suicide attempt, but this? This breaks me. This tears me apart. This makes me love her more than I ever have.

"Tell me what happened. Why can't you have kids, Ava?" She shrugs.

"It wasn't a standard abortion." She motions to where her scar is, the shiny one that runs in a small line across her lower abdomen. "The surgery," she says, shrugging again. I hate how lightly she's taking this. Where's the crying? Where's the *"I'm so sad that I'll never get pregnant"*?

When your life is filled with so much hardship, you learn how to keep every reaction at bay.

"What about the surgery?"

Ava fills her lungs with air and stares into my eyes. "They removed my tubes, Grant."

I turn around, take several deep breaths, and rub my teary eyes before facing Ava again.

"That means you can't have kids? Who told you that?"

"What do you mean, *who*? It's science. My doctors told me that if I ever got pregnant, it would be like point something percent of a chance. They don't have enough data on it because of how rare it is. It's happened like twice in recent history so, yeah. Infertile. No babies for me."

"*Oh my God,*" I whisper then, taking it all in, hoping that maybe at one point she'll tell me that it's a joke, that she's lying, that she's been on the Pill this whole time because of how unemotional she is right now. That isn't happening. Ava learned way too early on in life how to turn off her emotions. How to go unfazed by the worst parts of life because of how used to it she's gotten. Part of that is my fault.

I stare at Ava. Ava stares back at me. It's a game. No one is losing. Finally, I speak.

"When were you gonna tell me?" This is enormous. Ava didn't tell me about this for a reason because . . . Because she knows I love kids, that I want children of my own one day. She saw me with Madison. She saw the kindergarten art on my fridge. There is evidence of my niece and nephews all over my house. It's been in her face all along.

Is Ava's infertility a dealbreaker? I know that I want kids, I've always wanted kids, but I want her more. *Right?* Can I be with Ava for the rest of my life, just the two of us, no children or grandchildren in sight? I can, I tell myself. I have to. I need Ava and she needs me and I have wrongs to right. The longer I stare at her, the more I understand that Ava's future is mine too, and I'm okay with that. We'll adopt or some shit. I'm not letting a doctor determine the rest of my relationship with her.

"I don't know," Ava says finally, shaking her head. "I don't know," she repeats.

"After we got engaged and married and I told you I was ready for a baby?" Because that future with Ava has been on my radar for *months*. She knew that. I said it *last night*. My words are too much for her, and she looks away before replying.

"I hadn't thought that far," she says to her bedroom wall.

"You had to have thought that far. You knew my intentions were to marry you. I said it to you less than twelve hours ago."

Ava looks up then, her attention caught, her face fallen.

"Were?" she croaks, emphasizing that painful word, if it were true. It isn't. I've made up my mind. Ava is it for me.

"No. Ava—"

She takes a step back, swallowing thickly. "That's okay. It's fine. It's okay. I knew this would happen. That's why I've been avoiding it for so long."

I panic then because of how sure she is. Because of how she's clearly lost faith in me, in *us.* "I didn't mean *were,* Ava. I'm not ending this." I speak firmly, coaxing her to look at me, but she doesn't. She fiddles with her feet, staring down at them.

"You said *were,* Grant. And I think you should end this. Maybe I would've if I had the courage to do that, but I don't. I need you to make it official; I don't want this life for you."

I'm in love with you, I want to say. *I'm not going anywhere.*

"This life for me? What life? A life with you? I've wanted that for months, Ava," I protest, my teeth gritted at how *easily* she can walk away from this. From me. "I don't know what you think you're doing, but I'm not ending this. No fucking way."

"I'm saving you, Grant. Just take the opportunity. Say what you need to say and we'll hug it out and then you'll go."

How dare Ava treat me like I'm disposable right now, after everything we've been through! She met my family. She met my friends. She gave me a key. She introduced me to her brother. I met her parents. I met her entire family. I stayed in her house! *Saving me?! Is she for real?*

"Stop it, Ava," I command. My clenched teeth are about to snap.

"No," she says with confidence. "I care too much about you to let you throw away your life for someone who doesn't bring anything to the table. I'm saving you, Grant. I'm saving you."

"STOP SAYING THAT!" I scream piercingly, the rage I feel exuding out of me; it's nearly tangible.

Ava closes her eyes calmly and takes a giant, deep breath. "Are you angry because I can't have kids or are you angry that I hid it from you?"

She opens her eyes, challenging me with a look I can't quite put into words. I can't even tell what she wants from me right now; a part of me feels like she's begging me to give up. Like she wants me to walk away. Like she wants me to use this reason to end things, as if I've been looking for an excuse for a while and finally have one. But I'm not as meticulous and deliberate as she is. She literally planned for all of this to happen. I specifically planned for it to not.

"I'm angry that you had a calculated list, Ava! I'm angry that you're assuming I'm ending this! I'm angry that despite the last six months, you act like you don't know me, like you have *zero* faith in me. Like our entire relationship amounts to nothing. What the fuck!" I yell, hands waving, spit flying.

Her nostrils flare, her jaw flexes. There's fury in her eyes when she yells back at me. "THIS IS YOUR *FUTURE*, GRANT! The next sixty years of your goddamn life! Don't make *me* out to be the bad guy for trying to *protect* you!"

By now she's sobbing, and it's taking everything in me not to hug her and tell her to forget I said anything; to pretend that the last twenty minutes never happened.

"*You* are my future," I explain to her as slowly as I possibly can. "I had made that abundantly clear to you from day one, Ava."

"On day one, you didn't know what you know now!" she cries, truly exasperated and mad at me that I want to stay despite what I now know about her.

The only thought that crosses my mind when I hear Ava say that is *love*. *That I love her*. And that's why I slip up and reply with, "On day one, I didn't love you like I do now."

Ava freezes. She looks away, sobs into her hand.

"You can't say that to me," she sniffs, wiping her eyes, her nose on the sleeve of her sweatshirt. My sweatshirt. "That's not fair." She is absolutely right. This is the worst moment to use the L word for the first time. I didn't mean to say it, it slipped, but I'm not exactly going to take it back. I still mean it. I've been in love with Ava for months.

"Why not? You've known for a while; I know you have. Everything doesn't change once I say it out loud." *Who am I right now? Who does she want me to be!*

Ava shakes her head, scoffs irritably. "Yes, Grant, it does."

"Why?" I snap loudly. "Why do things all of a sudden change?"

She's doing this. Ava is letting everything change because of what *she* thinks is better for *my* future. Am I not allowed to choose her? Is anyone allowed to choose her if she can't have kids? And if the answer is yes, then why isn't it allowed to be me? *Why not me?*

"Because now I'll never be able to forgive myself if you stay with me. I won't allow it."

I'm beyond enraged at her response. "Well, guess what! I'M NOT ASKING FOR YOUR FUCKING PERMISSION!"

My booming voice hits her like a brick, and she looks terrified. It hurts to watch Ava take on this scared look after what I've said, and I know it's wrong when I do it, but I storm out of Ava's apartment, slamming the door behind me.

AVA

I know that he's standing a few feet away from me, watching as I type up my essay, but I pretend he's not there, focusing on the music blasting from the headphones he got me and the word "community" on my computer screen. When I find it silly how the letters merge together and almost laugh at how weird a lowercase M looks, I know I'm officially losing it. I feel him coming over to me, and I start to sweat, a wet film forming on my chest, my armpits, my upper lip. The closer he gets, the angrier my blood feels at the fucking audacity.

I swiftly unplug my laptop from the outlet beneath the wobbly wooden table and pack up my backpack before withering out of the café's front door. I hear him call out after me, but I don't turn around, power-walking down the pavement with determination, having no particular destination in mind because I can barely think straight right now. A strong, firm grip grabs my wrist half a block later, and I hate myself for loving the way it feels; having missed it. I've felt this perpetual gnawing ache without him the last few days.

"Ava. Would you please wait one second?"

"Wait for what?" I ask, looking ahead, refusing to make eye contact with this green-eyed no-show I have come to love burningly. After slamming my apartment door that night, he's ignored every call or text from me, and all I wanted was closure. I knew it was over, that was obvious, but our stint, however short it lasted, couldn't have ended with a yelling match and a door slam. I've been trying to get hold of him to have a civilized conversation to say goodbye, but he ignored me and now he's shown up, three days later. I'm sure he can feel the rapid pulse on the inside of my wrist.

"I . . . I have a lot of explaining to do," he begins, leaning into me, letting go of my arm. "I know I do." And it's the fact that he's admitting that *he knew* it would hurt me but still stayed away for three days that sends me reeling.

"Why are you back?" I turn to face him, gasping when I'm reminded of how gorgeous Grant is, as if I could ever forget, leaning my head back and trying hard not to beg him to kiss me. "You made it very clear that what I told you the other night was a dealbreaker for you, and I get it. I do, I swear. But don't try fixing the hurt that you put me through when you disappeared for a few days by showing up unannounced where I'm studying. That's not fair."

"It wasn't intentionally unannounced. You weren't answering my calls this morning," Grant defends himself.

"You didn't call me," I snap back.

"I did, Ava." I whip out my phone and he's right. Three missed calls. A couple of unread text messages.

"I was studying," I explain.

"I know. That's why I came. I figured you were here. It wasn't to get you off kilter. I was just scared that you were ignoring me for good."

I scoff. This has got to be a practical joke.

"*You* ignored *me*. *Not* the other way around," I whisper-shout, recounting all those unanswered messages I've sent him.

"Ava." Grant glances down the street at the bystanders frustratedly walking around us on this busy New York City sidewalk. "Can we please talk? Come to my house."

"I'm not going to do that," I tell him pointedly.

"Then let's go to yours."

I nod and slide into the plush seat in the back of Lenny's limo. Oh, yeah. Grant has a driver. I was a bit put off by that when he told me. Even more so when he explained why he only told me *now*. Lenny drives him to work every day. He told me after six months. It was a little ridiculous but I let it go. Priorities. He's a sweet man, Lenny. I like him.

Grant's head is bent forward between his legs in shame or something like it two leather seats over. I avoid watching him for more than five seconds and gaze out the window instead. His stress is giving way to my forgiveness, and I know he doesn't deserve it.

"Lovely weather we've been having!" I'm feeling obnoxious. "How's your day going, Lenny?" I call out from the back seat, needing something to busy myself with. Moping with my forehead against the glass window like I'm filming an indie music video is just depressing.

"Can't complain, Miss Campbell. And you?" Lenny responds with a kind smile.

"Oh, don't call me that! We're buds, Lenny, are we not?" I laugh when he does and make him agree to call me Ava. I glance to my right and find Grant watching me, a sweet calmness to his eyes.

"What?" I ask. "What're you looking at me like that for?" Shaking his head, he closes his eyes and turns away.

The apartment windows rattle as the door slams shut behind us but then it's quiet. Pretty dang quiet. Grant puts his hands in his pockets and finally speaks first.

"You're right, what you said earlier. What happened last week was a dealbreaker for me, but not how you think." My heart sinks, I admit. I feel like we were finally getting somewhere. I had missed him in the time spent away. I missed him and it hurt. "I was more surprised at this sudden need to be with you, something way fiercer than ever before, once you told me about your infertility."

"What—"

Grant slips one hand out of his trousers and lifts a large palm up to stop me.

"Just . . . let me finish." Feeling his desperation, I nod. "I know this is going to sound crazy, I *know* it does, but ever since we met, I felt like you were put into my life on purpose. Like, by God or something. There's this finality that I feel with you, and I haven't ever felt this complete with anything ever. Not work or school or my career or a girl, and that feels monumental, Ava, because I'm almost thirty years old."

My heart does this dance. As angry as I am, with the right to be, I feel all the more flattered. Full. I want him to keep going because it feels so amazing to be wanted like this. It has *always* felt so good to be wanted as much as Grant wants me. I'll admit that I always questioned it because of how unusual this is, but knowing how much he was willing to go through so we can be together? Overlooking my past because of his feelings for me? Being that desirable to someone is hard to come by. Grant continues.

"When you kept demanding that I end things with you, I was upset. It felt like the last six months were moot, that what you felt for me wasn't even a fraction of what I was feeling for you. I think I was scared that you were so willing to walk away from what I thought was a perfect relationship. I haven't done this in a long, long time and that's if you can even count high school, but you're different. For me and as a person and in general. When you told me that you couldn't have kids, all I kept thinking was that this was it for me. My life fell into place and it all started to make sense. I felt complete and satisfied with my life and about *you* and *us* and our life together and I couldn't tell you right away because I knew you'd freak out if I said that I wasn't going to have kids either. And you probably will right now because it's only been six months, but you deserve to know why I disappeared the last few days. My mind was racing at how calm and together I felt, how your reality became my reality and the peace that came with that. I've been trying to understand and put a name to this insane desire to make you mine forever, and it sounds crazy that it came at a time where you were so convinced things would end. But that made me want you even more." When I fail to reply to Grant's *ridiculous* declaration, he awkwardly retreats.

"Okay . . ." he pants. "I'm finished."

What the fuck am I supposed to say to that?

"I can't figure out what to say to you," I whisper, the truth on the tip of my tongue, too afraid to say it because of how *insane* it sounds. How do you ask someone you've known for only six months, someone so obviously wrong for you, if they're telling you that they want you forever, indefinitely, despite your flaws and imperfections? Because that's how this sounds.

"Did I cross a line?" Grant asks apprehensively, his expression weary.

"No, no." His insecurity warms my ears, my neck, my shoulders. It feels so right and as bizarre as that is, it's him. With me, he's awkward and silly and sappy and not the Grant who everyone else knows. This is the version of Grant that I get, my little slice of heaven that is only mine, that no one else gets to see or know or meet. I love him. I love my Grant.

"You're right when you say that it doesn't make sense to me because it doesn't. I knew what I was doing when I hid it from you and then when I told you, but that's why you had to pry it out of me. I thought I was breaking my own heart by telling you that I was never going to be a mother, and a part of me was content with that because at least I wasn't lying to you anymore. I'd been preparing myself for this outcome for months."

He shakes his head hurriedly. "When the words first fell out of your mouth, I think *you* broke *my* heart. For that first minute, I was calculating in my head that it would never work because Annie has kids and I always thought I'd have kids so that was that."

"And then?" Because that seems completely reasonable to me. Grant is a family man. For him to give up ever being a father so he can be with me is just plain wrong. It's not okay.

"I looked at you. I took a good look at you and all of that speculation dissolved into this *aha* moment. It was like my life was decided for me, then and there, and I was *thrilled*." Grant looks at my eyes, left to right to left to right, and studies me. He must see the shock written across my face. "Ava, I felt like you were putting together this puzzle right in front of me, and the end result was the rest of my life. You said you couldn't have kids, and I thought, well, if she can't have kids then I won't have kids. It didn't feel wrong or scary or painful. It just felt *right*."

"Grant." I can barely get his name out. The lump wedged in my throat is so swollen and ginormous, it's uncomfortable. "You're scaring me. I think you're too infatuated with this new connection, with me and how different I am to your past and you're letting it cloud your judgment. Isn't this your first serious relationship? I don't want you to wake up in fifteen years from now and resent me because you never became a father."

"If I woke up in fifteen years from now and you were next to me, that would be enough."

"Grant—"

"I love you," he breathes.

My face falls. *Because once you say it, everything changes.* "Stop," I whisper, afraid of what he's saying, afraid of what he's implying.

"I can't stop."

"It's not fair of you to just . . . you can't come here and tell me that you love me after . . ." I don't even know what to say.

"I do, though. It's true. That day at Rocco's, I knew you were going to change my life and every day following, I knew I could never lose you. Last week validated for me that I want you for the rest of my life. I'm in love with you, Ava," he declares straight to me, his green eyes trained on mine with every powerful word that exits his mouth. "Please let me be in love with you."

"It doesn't make sense," I whisper, shaking my head. "This is too much, Grant."

"It's the only thing—Ava," he interrupts himself, grabs my hands in his, and bends to look into my wet, teary eyes. "Hi, Ava baby. You listening? It's the *only* thing in my life that has *ever* made sense."

I nod, I think. I don't really know. I'm discombobulated and my mind is racing. I think Grant hugs me or kisses me or maybe both. I'm not sure. My head is spinning, but he grounds me, envelops me in a blanket of his flesh, my flesh, limbs and hair and sweat. When he breathes into my neck, relaxes his weight on top of me, coming down from immense pleasure, I'm able to think again. My brain works and I feel slightly what he described minutes ago. I feel full and whole and complete.

AVA

"Three more days," I say to Grant sitting across from me at my small kitchen table. "It's going to be hell." The deposition is coming up and I've finally accepted that it's really happening after being in feigned denial since Dad explained to me that I'm going to be asked a series of questions in front of a legal team and a camera. In three days.

When I first called Mr. Ellison and he explained that my mental state is what we can "stick them with," I knew that eventually I'd succumb to this emotional pressure. I've been hoping to come to terms with it and to ready myself for the pain I'll undoubtedly have to go through so that when it's here, I don't die from shock. Grant and I talk about it a lot. He gives the greatest encouragement and support and assures me that everything will work out in the end. *If not one way, then another, baby.*

We eat cereal and milk for breakfast before Grant goes into the office and I go to my morning study group then to an evening math class. What I will never get tired of seeing is my six-foot-five boyfriend sitting across from me in a trillion-dollar suit with a five-hundred-dollar haircut and a hundred-thousand-dollar watch eating a bowl of Fruity Pebbles in my small, meager apartment. Without replying to my mention of the deposition countdown, Grant quickly rinses off his bowl, grabs his briefcase, and scurries to the door.

"No goodbye kiss?" I call out. He comes to a halt and rushes over to me.

"My bad. I love you. Have the best day." He kisses me and I wave him goodbye with a wide smile. It won't ever stop feeling as good as it does when he says it. Not once or twice but Grant says *I love you* so often and freely, it's as if he's making up for so much lost time. I get the flutters when I hear his deep, sultry voice saying those three words to me, honestly and genuinely. It's sexy and sweet and perfect. I love him so much and he deserves to know that.

Grant texts me thirty minutes before math is over.

Grant: Are you busy? I need to see you.

I have some homework, dreading the five-thousand-word essay I have to write, but his urgency has me worried.

Me: Psych essay. Is everything okay?

Grant: Yeah. Miss you. Do the essay here.

I shrug and climb the subway stairs to cross the tracks and head in the opposite direction of my apartment toward Grant's. Before I have a chance to lift my fist to his door, he opens it. And what's weird is that I'm not met with a grin, not a smile. Nothing.

"Hi," he says curtly, unable to meet my eye.

"Hi?" I reply warily, standing in place, watching him. This is weird . . .

"Come in. Does the dining room table work for the essay?" he asks as I walk through the foyer beside him, throwing my coat over the leather couch. I find it odd that Grant is asking me to sit in the dining room, such a formal space, when I've always done homework in his kitchen. I also find it odd that my boyfriend didn't hug or kiss me hello. But I brush off the confusion, nod, and quietly sit myself down, slowly pulling my laptop and psych textbook from my backpack. For thirty straight minutes, I can feel Grant's eyes on my profile from across the room, and when I glance up to confirm that it's me he's looking at, he blinks away like he's been caught. I swiftly save the doc I'm working on and slam my computer shut.

"Is there a reason you asked me to come over?" I ask to the wall behind him because those green eyes bore into me. I become vulnerable under Grant's scrutiny that I can't speak to his face when they're on me. Before he replies, he struts toward the dining room and places himself in the chair opposite me. With pinched eyebrows, pegging me with those daggers, he asks, "Do I have to have a reason?"

"Are you serious right now?" I sneer when he gives me a questioning look. "I was asked to come over even with my having to write this paper, but you barely said a word to me in the last half hour and you're doing that weird staring thing. So why am I even here?" I'm frustrated with him. Grant has quirks that I like, but there are small snippets of him that drive me insane. This being one of them. If he wanted to spend time with me or go out, then I understand asking me to come over. But calling to ask me to sit in his apartment in silence is ridiculous.

"I'm sorry," he says straight into my eyes. It infuriates me.

"Stop doing that! Stop staring at me!" I shout, jumping from my seat. He shakes his head, looking down at the table, and runs his fingers through his hair.

"I'm sorry . . . I'm not trying to make you uncomfortable. Ava . . ." he mutters, rubbing up the length of his face. "Listen, it's just that I had a shit day and I wanted to see you. That's all this is. I'm sorry, okay?"

I slowly sit back down across from him. I've never seen Grant like this, so torn, confused. He intertwines our fingers when I reach to grasp his hand. With a shaky inhale, he asks, "Can you come here? You're so far."

I turn the corner of the table and stand before him, our hands still perfectly knitted together. Grant looks to the ceiling and releases a slow breath, tapping his lap for me to sit. There's this insecurity in his eyes that I swear I've never seen before. Not like this. *What is going on right now?*

"What happened?" Grant immediately shakes his head. "Tell me," I persist. Without answering, he uses the back of his hands to rub . . . are those tears? Is he crying? "What happened, Grant?" I beg, putting my hands on his face.

"It's nothing. Just a bad day. Feeling a lot of pressure. Seeing you is making me emotional." *My heart.* I wrap my arms around his neck and hug him tightly, kissing his five o'clock shadowed jaw. The moment Grant's face hits my neck, he chokes out a sob. *Oh my God.*

"Babe . . ." I whisper. I squeeze Grant against me and rub his hard back, soothing him. "I'm here, okay?" Playing with the hair at the back of his head, I kiss his neck and allow Grant to take solace in me as I've done with him so many times before. Once composed and without looking at me, he stands us up and walks across the floor.

"You must think I'm a pussy for crying to you."

"No, I don't. I don't think . . . *that*," I say to his back. When Grant exits the bathroom, tissues in hand, he finally faces me.

"I don't want to fuck this up. You mean too much to me."

"Why do you think you're going to fuck it up?" Grant has been nothing but incredible to me since day one, even when I made things hard, when I was rude or hesitant or when I hid . . . everything. Grant reacted to every single incident in the last six months flawlessly. He is the perfect gentleman and the best boyfriend I could ever ask for.

Avoiding the question, he says, "I'm scared, Ava. This is all brand-new to me. I've never felt . . . I've never wanted someone so bad. I've never been in love before. There's just something about you."

I swear I just felt my heart skip a beat. On one hand, Grant and I are so different but on another, we share that in common: this is both of our first relationships. Without realizing it, I've expected him to know how to perfectly navigate this new place at any given moment in the last six months, and maybe I've put too much pressure on Grant that now he's afraid of making any mistakes. The moment this dawns on me, I gain a pit in my stomach. I haven't handled this well at all. I vow to show him how I appreciate and notice his efforts.

"I don't want you to be scared. We're good, Grant. Don't worry. What do you need from me?" I ask softly, taking a step toward him. I want him to tell me, to explain from the depths of his heart what my existence means for his, what I can bring to the table that is *his* life so that I can say it with confidence that he'll . . . That Grant will always stay.

Oftentimes I've wondered if this was an infatuation thing; that being with Grant is the first relationship I've had since Patrick, and therefore that makes me biased toward the way he makes me feel after having that shit experience. But when I look at him, really look at him, it comes easy, the realization that this is so much more.

I've been selfish—if Grant is going to make me feel so wanted and protected, then I need to do the same. Slowly walking toward Grant, I reach my hands out to rest them on his shoulders and lean my head back to look into his eyes. "What do you need from me, baby?"

"You. I swear. Just you." I follow my fingers as they toy with the buttons of his wrinkle-free dress shirt, processing the tranquility of what he said to me. I feel my shoulders relax, my head held higher. Grant *needs* me. *He* needs *me. How did I get so lucky? Who did I impress up there?*

Reaching on my tiptoes to be closer to him, I kiss his pretty mouth softly. "You have me. All of me," I whisper against his lips. Grant pushes his mouth deeper onto mine as he kisses me carnally, desperately until I'm out of breath.

"Do you mean that, Ava?" he asks, grabbing my face to scan my eyes. "No matter what?"

My eyes soften for this perfect, beautiful person, and he really is. Grant is kind and charitable, funny and exciting. He is everything I have ever wanted for myself. Being his girlfriend for the last six months has given me a glimpse into the serene life I could *actually* have, that he *wants* us to have. How many times has Grant mentioned marrying me? He knows what he wants and that's *me*. He's made it abundantly clear, so I shrug off the fear of saying those three words because who cares what they societally mean? I feel the love in my bones. I feel it everywhere.

"I love you." Grant's breath hitches, Adam's apple bobbing down his neck, staying perfectly still, watching me with terrified eyes. I say it again, this time with tears in my throat. "I love you."

"Ava."

"Say something," I plead urgently, panicking a little bit.

"I can't believe you just said that," he chokes, brushing his fingers through my hair. Grant takes my hand and puts it on his heart. It's rapidly beating. "Look at what that did to me."

"Don't have a heart attack if I say it again, okay?" I chuckle. "I love you." He nods slowly, taking my hand, and gently pulls me toward the bedroom. It's intense and different than ever before; slower, more intimate, scarier. It feels like my body shudders from even the lightest brush of his skin on mine, even though I've already had him plenty. The room is perfectly silent and still as we remove each other's clothing under his bedsheets. Grant climbs on top of me, naked, and puts his lips to my ear.

"I love you, Ava," he whispers. "I love you more than anything."

—⟋⟍—

"When?" Grant mumbles into my hair, his long, hairy arm wrapped around me, my naked body flush against his. My body is in desperate need of a hot shower, but I'm too comfortable in our mixture of sweat and moisture to move. I look up at him in wonder.

"When what?" I ask.

"When did you know?"

With my head on his chest, I trace the outline of his hard body and muscle with the tip of my finger, thinking about my answer. It was never a specific moment. It was gradual. I tell him exactly those words.

" . . . but I finally allowed myself to feel it after that big fight at my parents' house. When you found out," I sigh, stretching to kiss him. I remember my body feeling at ease when I let those feelings wash over me without denying them as I deliberately had until that day. It shouldn't be easy falling in love after being heartbroken, but Grant made it that way. I was the one trying to self-sabotage this relationship as a defense mechanism against something I feared would happen to me again but quickly realized that Grant is incapable of. I remember telling Bridget *I'm just gonna end things before they get too good.*

I am so glad she talked me out of it.

"What about you?" I ask Grant, wondering at what moment *he* looked at me and said to himself, *I love her.* "When did you know?"

He chuckles, kissing my head before speaking. "Unlike you, it *was* a specific moment for me."

I smile hugely, biting my lip, and give him the wettest kiss I can while in this position.

"Do I want to know? Did I say something ridiculous?" I roll my eyes and laugh, Grant following.

"Surprisingly, no," he says smirking, winking. "It was at that bar we met Devon at. You ran up to him and gave him the tightest hug and I'm like yup. I love her. That's the one. That's the girl I love."

That was so long ago. "You've loved me for the last two months?"

"So have you."

"Why didn't we just . . ."

"Because sometimes we both don't know what the hell we're doing," he rasps, laughing at our shared naivety. I climb over my male model boyfriend, straddling him, and flatten both my hands on his hard chest.

"Your eyes are scary," I say, looking into them.

"So I've been told." He chuckles.

"It feels good to finally say it. To tell you that I love you." He rolls our bodies over until he's on top of me.

"Liberating, right?" he mumbles into my ear, clasping his hands over mine and lifting my arms above my head, keeping them tightly there. I nod. That's exactly how it feels.

"If I knew how cathartic it was going to feel, I would've said it earlier. I was just scared. I've always been scared," I whisper, choking on my words.

Grant puts his hand on my cheek, glancing down at me with gentle eyes. His thumb brushes my cheek, my nose, my lips. I feel his hand shaking, his breath shaking, when he caresses my face.

"You're the light I thought I lost, Ava."

AVA

The next morning, two days before the deposition, Mr. Ellison and I review some of the questions Pat's lawyers might, and likely will, ask me at the upcoming deposition. He told me that I'm going to be under oath, that I have to tell the truth, the whole truth, and nothing but the truth. A court reporter will be there typing up a play-by-play of the deposition as it happens live, Mr. Ellison tells me, stressing that the legality of this situation is legitimate and I have to be my best, most honest self. He also took it upon himself to mention that I have to act unfazed by their questions no matter how invasive they may be; any emotional outburst can be used against me as if I had pre-existing mental health issues before what Pat did to me. They will try to claim that they aren't responsible for what I went through.

"They'll play the mental health card to their advantage. Don't let them."

It becomes all too real when Mom and Dad send me their flight information. They were able to find a fairly cheap hotel that isn't far from campus since it's off season in New York, so I can still stay at my apartment but also spend as much time with them as possible while they're here. I mean, it's not like we're celebrating anything, and this is definitely not a vacation of any sort, but having them close while I'm put in this situation is important to me. I know it isn't cheap between the flights and hotel, which is why I'm even more grateful for my

267

parents' support. I'm over eighteen—they don't need to be there—but I've been trying to find the silver lining in this entire situation so I don't retract into a sad hermit again. Bridget's been really good about getting me into that positive mindset, as she always has.

"Best-case scenario, you guys win the case and the bills are covered. Worst-case scenario is that you lose, but you still have me and the boys and your parents and Grant. You still have Grant, hon." It meant more to me than she could've known. Last time I had to face Pat, I did it alone. Now? Now I have an amazing boyfriend I can depend on, lean on, and that's a gamechanger for me.

—⁓—

Since it is now only two days before the deposition, I receive that dreadful email. I read the email's "invitation" in absolute confusion. " . . . *to be held at CGW Inc.*," followed by Grant's office address at the top of the page. I am beyond heated and enraged. Is this his way of "helping" me? You want to be a good boyfriend? I'm all for it. But *this*? This is overstepping. This is overdoing it. Take me to dinner the night of. Hug me, kiss me, make love to me. But *hosting* the deposition at your office? That's another level of hovering. That's out of line. I take the subway to CGW Inc. first thing after class, the elevator ride infinitely slow, as I panic and tell myself to calm down, to breathe. This could be a mistake.

However, I quickly learn that it is not a mistake. As I walk toward Grant's office, I'm suspended in place when I hear his secretary yell, "Patrick McCall on two!" and Grant reply with a gruff, "I got it! Thanks, Dina!" In the midst of my current processing, I see that Dina's noticed what I just overheard. Her wide eyes are an instant tell—a tell that this is *something*. Something very fucking wrong.

My instincts are hasty as I rush toward Grant's opened office door. I'm staring at his contoured back, his starched shirt as neatly creased as he is, when the words "What can I do for you, Mr. McCall?" are spoken. They bounce around in my head in Grant's deep voice, and if my hands weren't already trembling, they certainly are now as I stand at the office door, the printed email in my hand. And when Grant sees me, it's like he breaks me in two with the expression of fear in his eyes when it dawns on him that I'm here and I heard what he just said and I know who's on the other end of that phone call.

Watching him react, green eyes wide, knuckles white, his breath shallow, I feel dread and nausea engulf my entire body. I look at him with question and confusion, and it's making it hard to breathe, especially when I see that he's absolutely horrified. With a hard swallow, he says my name, but as soon as he speaks, I turn away. If I don't get the hell out of here, my legs will buckle and I'll break in front of every employee on this floor.

Dina stops me in my tracks when I shoot for the elevator. "It's not his fault," she says, pleading. "Please believe me."

I take a deep breath, but no air fills my lungs. "I don't know what you're talking about. I don't want to know," I strain to say. *My chest. It's hard to breathe.*

"He loves you more than anything," she says quietly, defeated. "Just know that he loves you."

I grit my teeth at every floor this elevator stops on, my fists tight at my sides, my heartbeat too loud in my head to function. When I finally make it out onto the street, gulping my first proper breath of fresh air in what feels like hours, the realization that I have nowhere to go twists in my belly. I can't go to my apartment like nothing happened, like my world wasn't torn apart minutes ago. I can't go back upstairs, and I have no solid friends to turn to because Grant consumes every minute of my life outside of school.

I aimlessly wander around Central Park in a delusional daze, dry heaving for a half hour, whispering "what the fuck" over and over under my breath, no doubt sounding like a crazy person. *What just happened? What did I witness?*

After hearing Pat's name, witnessing what I saw in Grant's frightened expression, I feel the need to do something more than just walk. I need to know why the fuck Grant Wilder was on the phone with Pat McCall earlier. When I told Dina that I didn't want to know, I lied. I want to know every single detail even if it will butcher my heart into pieces, so I head toward Grant's apartment. If I want answers, I'll find them there.

I'm not knocking, instead pulling out my key and unlocking the apartment door. He's the first thing I see when my foot crosses the threshold. I want to hug him and beg him to make me forget what I heard earlier, but he can't because he lied to me. With a scotch in one hand and his phone in another, Grant looks up from the couch. I pay no mind to his chiseled face, determinately walking toward his home office off the dining room. When he tries to come up behind me and follow me into the office, I lose it, mistakenly turning to face his beautiful eyes, his sculpted jaw. Immediately I notice the hollowness of his flat eyes, his pale face, chapped lips. All of this lying really took a toll on him.

"Don't you dare fucking stop me," I demand, shoving his chest before bolting into the office. I reach the file cabinet, luckily alphabetized, finding the "M" drawer to pull out Pat's file because I know there is one. If he called Dina's desk and not Grant's cell phone, they're somehow working together. I'm messily skimming through the folder, but Grant rips it out of my hand before I have a chance to read anything of importance. He shoves it back in the drawer and smashes it closed, the sound of metal on metal making me jump.

"Do not open that drawer until you let me explain," he begs. I don't look at him while he pleads with me, keeping my eyes trained to the anomalistic piece of lint on his pant cuff. I almost laugh at how uncharacteristic this is of him, but then again, I don't know him at all, do I?

"You know him," I say into his eyes. That was a mistake considering that a scared Grant is a stunning Grant, and he's terrified. He swallows hard.

"I do," he says, confirming what I already now know. His apathetic answer makes me want to scream. It makes me want to punch a wall. I ball my hands into fists at my side.

"Fuck you. I'm leaving," I say, walking past his pained face, my heart beating as fast as his did when I said *I love you* only yesterday. I might faint from this overdose of adrenaline running through me.

"I need to talk to you. Please," Grant whispers, straining his fearful, shaky voice. It hurts to hear but I'm so damn angry.

"I DON'T WANT AN EXPLANATION, GRANT!" I shout, turning to face him. He pulls me toward him, holding my head to his heart, nearly squeezing me close. I'm no match for his strength.

"Please don't go," he strains in a whisper. "I need you to know everything." This entire time he's been lying to me.

"I don't want to hear you explain shit because I don't trust you. You'll lie again."

He shakes his head hurriedly. "I won't."

Of course he won't. The worst is out. Grant has known Pat all along. I'm sick to my stomach, and as much as I want to leave, I need to know more. Curiosity is about to kill the cat.

"Show me the files and I'll stay," I negotiate with him, taking short, ragged breaths to somehow stop the rapid beating but knowing that I can't. Not while here, in front of him. I can't take even one deep breath because of the panic in my chest, the shaking.

"Deal," he mutters.

I'm already at the drawer, the folder in my sweaty hand, but I'm soon second-guessing whether or not I should even look. Before opening the file, I stop myself and look at Grant.

"Is this folder going to ruin me?"

He pauses for a long moment before replying to the ground. "Yes, Ava. It will."

My chest falls at his reply, but I don't care. This isn't about protecting myself anymore. This is about knowing the damn truth. Lowering myself to my knees, I lay the papers on the ground and skim through them, but these words—it's all gibberish to me.

"I don't know what any of this means. Just tell me. Explain to me how you know him." It's my turn to plead.

Grant squeezes his eyes tight before saying, "I don't just know him."

"Then what? What did you do?"

Nodding to the paper-covered rug, he says, "Read."

I skim through them again, deliberately focused on reading every word, and that's when something surreal catches my eye. I spot my name on one of the files in Pat's folder, and my stomach sinks.

Jumping from my position on the office floor, I reach for the file cabinet again; my gut is telling me that if I open the first drawer and sift through the C section, I'm going to find a folder with my own name on it. Grant doesn't stop me when he realizes what I'm looking for, and I don't stop myself in my search for the thing that will pain me even more. When he sees that I'm aiming for the drawer marked **A-D**, his breath hitches before he slowly whispers my name. And sure enough, there it is. I find the second folder that Grant knows is going to ruin me.

Campbell, Ava Ruth.

My heart drops to my groin, leaving a giant hollow space in its place. I feel physical heartbreak, my chest empty but tight all at once. Forget all the other files, this is the one that matters. This is the one that he held his breath for. This is the one that he whispered my name for. Before reading these pages from corner to corner, I grab Pat's file from the ground and fist both folders in my hand. I run past him, hoping to make it home and read in peace. I can't concentrate when he's watching me and as vulnerable as I am in this house. Before I can make it to the front door though, he's at my back, pulling my arm.

"You said you'd stay if I showed you. Don't lie to me."

I shove him with all my might, watching as he squeezes his eyes shut and takes the blow.

"*Lie?* I shouldn't *lie?*" I laugh dryly, in genuine awe of the nerve of this guy. "Is this some kind of joke?"

"That was the wrong word choice," he mutters, scratching the side of his unshaven jaw. I hadn't noticed the thick stubble until now, but it must be difficult to make time to shave your face when you're busy faking a six-month-long relationship with your "girlfriend." *Girlfriend.* I was his. He had me. I told him that I loved him for the first time only yesterday.

"My heart hurts." I weep silently, the most honest and raw that I've been with Grant tonight. Sometimes the tough act can only last so long "What have you done?"

He points at the folder in my hand. "Read. If you don't want it to come from me, then read your file, Ava, because I swear that you're holding the whole truth in the palm of your hand."

Taking a slow breath, I begin reading through the papers, document after document, each puzzle piece fitting into place. I'm on the verge of collapse and hyperventilation when I finally figure it out, despite all the legal terms on these files that I've maybe heard in passing but don't exactly know what they mean. It doesn't matter.

"You're . . ." I look down at the sheet to confirm, read it three times over, then look back up at him. "You're his . . .?"

Grant nods, focusing all his energy on the ground, not having the guts to look at me.

"Say it," I cry.

He shakes his head. "I can't," he says, voice cracking to betray him.

"FUCKING SAY IT!" My chest feels dense, weighing me down that I want to sit on the floor and stay here until tomorrow, but I stay strong and stand before him.

Finally, Grant glances up and knowingly looks into my eyes. "I'm Patrick McCall's attorney."

I lean my head back on the front door behind me and close my eyes to process what his words mean, the echo of his deep voice bouncing around in my confused mind. I force myself to replay it over and over. I don't think I'm breathing right now.

"Again," I croak.

"I'm Pat's lawyer."

Goose bumps. Vomit is trying to force its way out of my throat; with my eyes closed, I focus on inhaling and exhaling, swallowing the piercing scream, the wailing down, down, down. Time is moving incredibly slowly right now because that's how it feels when your life is falling apart around you. That's how it felt in the ICU and in my recovery room and at the mental hospital. And now, here. In Grant's apartment, what I was supposed to consider home. What I *did* consider home.

"My case?" I ask. But it's just semantics at this point. I open my eyes in time to see Grant nodding. There's this overall feeling coming over my body when he does. I'm encompassed in shudders, but my blood is boiling; I need to put my coat on, but I also need to jump into a freezing cold swimming pool. "How?" *How is this happening?* He doesn't answer. "This whole time?" The pain until now doesn't hit deep enough because I'm even more lost when he continues confirming what I wish he wouldn't. I want him to say no. I want him to say that he's Pat's lawyer but for a different reason. But he won't. "You've known who I was this whole time?"

"Yes," he whispers.

There it is. *Holy shit.*

"You knew about my abortion before I told you about it?" My voice is trembling. It doesn't sound like me. My hands, they're trembling. Everything is trembling.

"Yes," Grant replies.

"So, the deposition. The people questioning me. That's *you?*"

"Yes."

"No," I cry quietly. My soul feels rock hard; my throat stings. Tears pool in my eyes from the sharp awareness, too sharp, that the last six months of my life have been a lie. The man I fell in love with isn't that person at all. He's been playing the good guy and the bad guy all at once and I had no idea. He was backstage and center stage at the same time. Did anyone know? Did people know that Pat's lawyer was dating the plaintiff? I discussed the whole case with Grant. Is that even allowed?

"Our relationship is illegal, isn't it?" I ask, crying through my words.

"Very," he admits. His hands are in fists at his sides and I can tell he's dying to touch me, to do something. So help me God, if he doesn't stay put . . .

"So then why? Why'd you do this?" *How* did he do this? How did he hide this for *six months?*

"I couldn't let you go. I needed you. I had to make it right."

What does that mean? There's this sound in his voice that I can't quite put into words. It's not a cry, it's something so much more. It sounds like he can't breathe either.

Whatever Grant has told me tonight isn't enough. I need details. I need more. I force myself to spread out all the truths on the tiled foyer floor to dissect them one by one. I find more and more devastation, the pieces of papers damp from my uncontrollable tears.

My flight information from August. The address to my apartment, signed and paid for months before I got there. My class schedule at NYU. Rocco's.

Grant knew who I was; what happened to me; where I was from; why I'm here; how I got here. He knew everything. He orchestrated *everything*. Telling memories that I have with Grant are flashing through my mind as everything starts to make so much sense.

> *So, how are you liking New York?*
> *I love what they've done with the place.*
> *I'm proud of you.*
> And the kicker last night: *No matter what?*

"Are you the reason I'm here? You're the college sponsor, aren't you?" That's the only way he could have gotten all the information I'm currently staring at.

"I am," Grant confirms, his scared eyes boring into me as he continues to tear me apart.

"No," I breathe, curling my knees up to my chest, sobbing into my corduroys. He brought me to New York and stalked me and dated me. I am so terrified of this man.

"Please give me the chance to explain," he begs, the tears finally pooling in his stunning green orbs. Perhaps it's the realization for Grant that he's tainted my perception of him forever that allows the tears to finally fall because his Adam's apple has been bobbing nonstop for the last twenty minutes, like he's been gulping a lump down too. But he doesn't get to cry. He doesn't get to cry because *he's* the one who did this to *me*. *He's* the one who ruined *me*. This man is insane. He's a crazy fucking stalker, and I'm scared to be in the same room as him.

"No." My voice cracks; it's hoarse by now, from the time spent suppressing and finally releasing so many sobs. Grant walks toward me, kneels so we're face-to-face, but doesn't dare touch me.

"Ava, I am begging you to let me explain what happened," he cries solemnly, sniffling while pinching the corners of his eyes.

I look up, only for a moment, wanting to test myself. Will I give in? But all the good memories that rush to my heart when I look at this man have been permanently stained. The person he showed me was a phantom. There was nothing real about any of this.

I hurriedly stand and press my back to the front door as far away from him as possible. It's only about three feet.

"No way. I'm not giving you anything. You're a fucking stalker. Stay away from me." Breaking him with my words without feeling even an ounce of guilt speaks volumes, and there's only one word to describe all of it: I'm empty. My life is in total question right now, and it is way too much to process. It feels like I'm choking on my breath.

Grant's presence crowding me puts me in shock because it's not the comfort I used to feel. Instead I feel frigid and alone and terrified. I turn to face the door and Grant hovers above me, behind me, as I fist the doorknob. I talk to the painted wood instead of to him; his face makes this so much harder.

"You promised you wouldn't hurt me," I cry. "You broke my heart."

GRANT

M y sheets are bloody when I wake up the next morning, a pounding headache demanding aspirin, my phone ringing nonstop. Unless I hear her ringtone, it's going to stay that way, but I know that the feeling of joy from hearing that stupid fucking jingle is gone for good. Assessing what's around me, I recall the events of last night:

> *Ava found out that I'm Pat's lawyer.*
> *Ava knows that I've been sponsoring her life in New York.*
> *Ava and I are done.*

I knew this would eventually happen, I did, but God knows I never expected the chaos. The desperation of feeling numb because the alternative isn't anything I could handle. I've never felt pain like last night and I've never felt pain like this. This pressure in my chest, knowing that it'll likely stay that way as long as I live without Ava in my life. I watched her slowly break in front of me, and it tore me apart. I had a play-by-play, a front-row seat, to her heartbreak, and it hurt more than when she walked out my door. It hurt more because I love her so damn much.

Rubbing my knuckles to wash my bloodied fist, I notice Ava's toothbrush standing beside mine. I look at the mirror above my bathroom sink, and I hate what I see. I hate the person in my reflection because I did this to a girl who has already been through so much. I hate him so I punch him. Glass shatters into and around the sink, but I pay no mind to it.

Irritation flares when I enter my bedroom because this phone won't stop fucking ringing! Fisting it with all my might, blood spurting from the open wounds from the glass mirror, I hurl it as hard as I can until there's a dent in the wall. *Another* dent in the wall. When the echo subsides, I hear something in the distance. Banging. It's the door. When I squint to look through the peephole, I find Annie frantic.

"I know you're in there! Answer the fucking door!"

When I swing it open, she does a quick look down before finally seeing my broken face. There's only one thing that can warrant this reaction and she knows it.

"What did you do to her?" she assumes angrily, pushing past me, the clicking of her heels echoing in this giant room.

"Come in," I mutter, very much not wanting my big sister to see the evidence or rather know what I did to Ava Campbell. What I have been doing to her for the last six months.

"Did you fuck it up with the one good girl that's ever happened to you?" she asks, swiftly turning to face me.

I don't reply. I stay frigid, aloof, afraid that if one word about Ava exits my throat, I'll start wailing. "Why are you here, Annie?" I finally snap.

"The whole world has been trying to reach you all morning. Where have you been?" I wave an arm around me to bring attention to the mess that is my apartment. "Tell me what happened."

I can't face my sister so closely, her judgment clear as day in her eyes. Padding toward the kitchen to get myself a glass of water and aspirin, I take a drink and turn to look at Annie.

"She left me." I have to clench my jaw to keep from exploding or from squeezing this cup so hard that it'll shatter. Why is Annie making me talk about this? Will she just shut her prissy mouth up already?

"Why?" Annie probes.

I grit my teeth when I reply. "I don't want to talk about it."

She laughs frustratingly, like I'm pathetic. Annie sees right through me.

"You're such a fucking child, Grant. And here I thought she actually changed you."

I'm livid at her now because Ava *did* change me. I know it, I feel it. I'm not the same guy I was six months ago. Strutting across the room, I pull Annie by the arm and force her to face me.

"Don't you dare put this on her, Annie. *Ava did.* She changed me, but I was the one that fucked it up." It's like Annie is blaming Ava for not succeeding in changing me. That is a load of horseshit. I am changed. I am different.

"How!" she urges. "How did you fuck it up!"

"Ask Ansel," I snap.

"Ansel? I'm not asking Ansel. I'm asking *you*, Grant. Just be a man and tell me."

So, I do. I sit opposite Annie for a full hour and confess every single detail from the day the McCalls and Ansel called me until last night.

"Oh my God, Grant. This is a mess. They could sue you. They could take away your license. What the hell were you thinking?"

I say nothing. How could I? She's right. If and when the McCalls get wind of this, they'll set out to ruin me. I'm not questioning it, more preparing myself for the inevitable. At least I made a vow that this was the last case I'd ever represent. I'm done with the lawyer shit. It's too dirty.

"So that's it?" Annie asks, stunned. "It's over between you guys?"

Something tightens in my chest. I feel dizzy, hearing the words out loud of my new reality in someone else's voice and not the voice in my own head. I nod.

"Of course it is. Would *you* stay with someone who did that to you?"

"Never. And I want to say that I'm sorry but I'm not. You did this to yourself the second you hired Fisher, Grant. But I love you and you're my brother. I just wish you had made better choices. You could've come to me."

I watch as Annie swipes a tear from her under eye, and it makes me instantly emotional because of the disappointment in Annie's face. I reach to pull her into a hug.

"Why'd you screw it up? She was perfect for you," Annie cries.

Tears make their way into my eyes, and I kiss Annie's head. "*Because* she was perfect for me," I whisper. "I couldn't let her go, Annie. I mean . . ."

"I know what you mean. Ava is just so . . . *good.*" Annie gets it. She understands how I see Ava too.

I'm soon reminded of the first thing she said to me at the door, so I ask who's been trying to reach me.

"The McCalls got in this morning. So did Ava's parents. Dina called me when you and Ava weren't answering your phones."

Fuck. I forgot that McCall scheduled to meet with me today before tomorrow's deposition. I frantically rise from the couch to get ready but stop myself abruptly. These people fucked up my life. They fucked up Ava's life. Why am I rushing for them? Annie reads my train of thought and eyes me pointedly.

"*No.* I know what you're thinking. But if you don't show up, it'll make things worse. Dating Ava was illegal, Grant," she explains meticulously, hoping to convince me to get my ass out of the apartment and to the office right now. That word she just used. Dating Ava *was* illegal. It makes me sick to my core.

As I sit in the back of Lenny's limo, I replay every detail from start to finish, starting with the day I heard Ava's name for the first time to last night and the chaos of it all.

I was working as an in-house attorney at Dad's real estate office when his partner, Ansel, asked me to work a simple case on the side for a close friend. Pat McCall's father and Ansel were roommates in college. Ansel was no longer a practicing attorney, he hadn't reregistered in years, so the case was handed over to me, and I got straight to work. What I was told off the bat was that it was a child support thing. Easy as pie, right? But I quickly realized that it wasn't that at all.

Pat didn't stop mentioning abortion throughout the entire process.

"What if she just gets rid of the baby? We're off the hook then, right?"

I told him that technically he's right, but that decision was up to her, and our job was to prepare a case based on the assumption that she was keeping the baby. He strutted into his dad's office one morning with a giant grin on his face, and I'll never forget it until the day I die.

"You're fired, Wilder," Pat boasted, laughing maniacally.

My eyebrows pinched. "Excuse me?"

He winked at his dad, then turned to me. "No baby, no problem. Campbell is no longer pregnant, if you know what I mean."

Did I think that Pat had it in him to pressure a poor, young girl to abort her baby? No, I did not. I figured she didn't want to be a mom at eighteen and chose to terminate the pregnancy. Forgive me for flying home that night, because it never fucking occurred to me that Pat would ask everyone he knows to blow up her phone with slut shaming text messages and threats to abort the baby "or else." *I didn't know.*

In the weeks following my trip to LA, I felt unsettled when it came to that case. It seemed too easy. It didn't seem clean because of how cruel Pat acted about the whole thing, the fact that he got what he wanted, so that's when I hired Fisher to find out what he could about what happened to the girl Pat knocked up.

I read every inch of the documents listing what Ava endured at Saint Francis Memorial Hospital in San Francisco. I read about her NYU admission that she had to reject; why she traveled hours away from Arcata; why she spent weeks in the hospital. Fisher included a photo within his findings. It was her high school senior picture. I vowed to never work in law again after seeing her innocent face because it broke my fucking heart that I, along with the McCalls, did *this* to *her*.

When Ava's brother told me about the suicide attempt, I was more surprised that Fisher didn't catch it than about Ava not telling me. I hired Fisher a few weeks after I left LA. The suicide attempt, the mental hospital, the antidepressants—they all happened *after* Fisher's investigating. I knew about the physical pain she endured. I was never prepared to find out about the mental stuff.

As soon as I understood how badly Pat ruined this girl's life, that I felt responsible somehow, I took it upon myself to rectify it in any way that I could. An old college buddy of mine works at NYU and got me an in with the admissions office. I had them flag Ava's name; as soon as she called to register for classes, I was to be notified. She called them in March. The apartment was purchased in April. It was furnished in July, and cleaners were sent in two days before Ava's flight came in in August.

Fisher got to work again days after Ava landed in New York. I hired him to find out what she was up to, and Rocco's was the only other thing on the list of Ava's whereabouts besides the NYU campus and Target. I took her tea on purpose that morning. But when I tell you that nothing, *nothing*, could've prepared me for the feelings I'd experience when Ava turned and glanced up at me, a sour look on her face from taking that sip of coffee from my cup, it's the honest truth. It was love at first sight; I swear. She was pretty in pictures, yeah. But in person? She was perfect. Angelic and bright and exotic, and I knew I was fucked as soon as she opened her mouth and spoke the words, "I think I stole your coffee. That's tea."

I had to have her. It wasn't lust or curiosity, it was this intense desperation to repair what I felt I had broken. Ava's honey brown eyes looked so despondent, and I knew why. I wanted to make them happy again. When the Campbells served the McCalls and Pat called me days after meeting Ava at Rocco's, I wanted to die. I wanted to rip my hair out and murder Pat. I was starting to get to know this beautiful, strong, funny girl who he royally screwed over, and Pat was asking me to help ruin her even further. How dare he.

I tried refusing but I knew that I had to represent Pat because I was there for round one. It would've been too suspicious if I declined to represent him. This entire time, Ava was falling in love with me and I'd go to work every single day and take my regularly scheduled meetings, but I would also speak to Pat from my office phone, and fight against her and her family as a side hustle. And now she knows. She knows because Hilda, Dina's assistant, thought that yesterday was the twenty-first of February when it was the twentieth. The deposition letter was supposed to get sent out today, on Wednesday. Ava got the letter a day early. I was hoping to sit her down last night, before she got the email, and explain my involvement.

I don't know how that conversation would've played out. Probably the same either way, whether Ava found out from an email or from a conversation with me. Hilda isn't to blame here, even if she isn't the sharpest tool in the shed. It's all me. I led Ava on. I played her so bad. But every single part of what I gave Ava was real. My love, my emotions, my heart, my home—it was all real. And I would do anything to have it all back. I'd sell my soul to the devil if it meant that Ava would come back to me, but I know that's never going to happen.

Ava Campbell and I are done.

AVA

Mom and Dad flew into New York yesterday for the deposition at 10:00 on this frigid Thursday morning. The deposition at none other than CGW Inc. In complete humiliation, I had to sit my parents down in their small hotel room and admit that I had poor judgment about Grant. That for some fucking reason, I seem to attract guys who play me. Apparently, I give off a vibe that says, "Fuck me over! It's not that hard!" Right now, my anxiety is through the roof knowing that I have to see him and Pat and every other god-awful human being who has made my life a living hell. I'm about to be in the same room with two ex-boyfriends, one who doesn't know I dated the other one, both disgusting in their own way.

Mr. Ellison, my parents, and I step into the familiar elevator and enter the familiar foyer of Grant's office. I receive somber eyes from the receptionist because we've met, and pitiful glances from the staff because they've seen me here before. By now, they all must know that I was Grant's girlfriend. Was. Up until two days ago. From the gloominess of their glances, they probably also know what I'm about to go through. This is so dramatic.

Looking down to my shoes as we walk through the hallway and follow Dina toward the conference room, my heart stops when we pass his office. The door is closed and somehow, I wish it wasn't. Before she leaves the room, Dina holds my head against her mouth and kisses my temple hard. A single tear falls from my eye at this painful and wordless goodbye, even if I've only met her a handful of times.

"Ava, sweetheart," Mr. Ellison whispers from beside me when the opposing team struts in, sticks up their asses, heads held higher than weed. "Calm and collected, okay? They're going to be ruthless."

I pay no mind to what's happening around me, docking my focus on my hands in my lap. Pat's voice makes me nauseous, his dad's voice even more. *Eyes down. Don't move.* The room suddenly quiets, and I know it's because of him. Disgusted at myself, I know because I can smell his cologne, and now the scent that once brought wonderful memories fills me with dread and paranoia. The vacant seat across the table from me is now occupied. Of course he did. *Eyes down. Don't move.*

"Let's get started. State your name for the record please," Grant declares once he switches on the camera perched across from me on the long table. I have the hardest time looking at him, so I stare at the black glass circle that's recording me and say, "Ava Campbell."

"Your full name please."

I take a deep breath. "Ava Ruth Campbell."

"What is your date of birth? Where were you born?" Grant asks shrewdly.

I want to scream at him, at how fake he's being right now. *My birthday, Grant? The city I was born in? You were there! You drank with my family, slept in my bed, spoke to my parents. You were in every crevice of my life, Grant. How could you do this to me?*

My voice is shaky when I reply.

"May 22nd, 1997. I was born in Arcata, California."

Then, here's the kicker:

"Did you speak to anyone about this case other than your family and counsel?"

I stare at Grant across from me and freeze. I spoke to him about it, but I can't say that, right? He fucked me up, but I don't want to get him in trouble. I *cried* to him about it. I let him hug me and comfort me and make love to me to ease the heartache I felt about this eventuality: sitting with Pat and answering the questions his lawyers asked me, when all along, I was just afraid of him.

"No," I lie. He blinks hard and winces before looking down at his list of questions again. I took an oath and Grant knows good and well that I just lied. He asks me how I met Pat, how long I've known Pat, if my intention to pursue Pat was for money. The only semblance of comfort I feel is Grant's fist tightening when he asks me the questions that he knows will hurt me. The moment he says money, his knuckles turn white and his jaw flexes hard.

How dare he ask me that. He knows the answer, so why is he doing this on record? Did he not choose these questions? *He is their counsel!* I feel humiliated and Grant is the reason why the people at this table are judging me. It's the way Grant asks these questions that makes their concocted story so believable.

The questions don't stop for ten minutes, thirty minutes, and we're not even halfway done. The millionth file is pulled out of some central folder in the middle of the table and handed to Grant to recite aloud. He clears his throat and begins speaking directly to me, and I'm praying to God he doesn't say my name because of how beautiful it sounds in his voice to me, but then he does. The moment it slips from his mouth, I'm trembling. *Ava. Ruth. Campbell.* Four syllables and I'm begging for death. I lean into Dad's ear for an escape. "Dad. I need a minute. I can't breathe."

Dad looks at Grant and nods to the camera, motioning for him to turn it off so we're not recorded when he lifts me out of my seat and says, "We need a break." Mom, still sitting, glares at Grant, but I quickly grab her arm and walk us to the bathroom. With my body crouched down, I place my head between my knees and breathe. *Just breathe.*

"They're gonna use the fact that I needed a break to their advantage, aren't they?"

My mom stares down at me, shakes her head in disappointment. "Mija, how did you not know Grant was Patrick's lawyer? What were you thinking?"

Is she fucking serious right now? I've been asking myself that same damn question over and over for the last forty-eight hours. I've been dissecting every moment I spent with Grant for retrospective clues on how I should've seen this coming; he was just too good at his lie. That's the only explanation.

"Are you blaming me?"

She shakes her head, crouches down to take my hands in hers. "No, my love. It just hurts me that you're going through this. That he is your ex-boyfriend and asking all these nonsense questions. He needs to pay," she sneers angrily. Mom's Spanish shows in her passion for justice, her love for me, her rage. But saying Grant needs to pay worries me. I don't know how bad this can go if someone tells the McCalls that he dated me, and I don't want to find out. Was he cruel in his pursuit of me? Yeah, he was. But I'm not looking to ruin his life like he ruined mine.

"Mama, no. You cannot tell anyone about this. He can get in real trouble. Please."

My mother agrees to leave things as they are: quiet and cold and fake. She vows not to mention anything of the fact that Grant was sending me money monthly, paid for my apartment, tuition. *That he fucked me.*

For months. He fucked me for months. Grant got into bed with me and stripped me naked and told me that he loves me all with this knowledge in the back of his mind that I was clueless as to who he was when I gave him my entire life, my body, my soul, my heart. And he was doing it for what? Ridding himself of unmanageable guilt? To Grant, I wasn't Ava, the NYU student who he coincidentally met and fell for. Instead, I was Pat's ex, the girl he ruined and wanted to attempt to fix. I was a project to him. I was his fucking lab rat.

"I can't do this anymore, Mom. Please don't make me go back out there," I plead, crying into my elbow. I unscrewed the tube of mascara this morning as I somberly gazed at myself in the mirror and luckily thought twice before applying it to my eyelashes for this reason exactly. I knew I was going to be a teary-eyed disaster at some point today and walking into a deposition with mascara smeared under my eyes couldn't have been a good look for me or for my situation in proving that Pat is responsible for the downfall of my mental health. So, I saved myself a little extra embarrassment and went in bare-faced. The bags under my eyes are the only noticeable bit of color on my face. I haven't eaten in two days.

"Mi amor, I love you so much, but it is not over yet," Mom comforts me. Her eyes are so apologetic, and I know she would do anything to help me if she could, but she can't, and that's maddening.

I'm just so angry, so I snap at her loudly, hoping no one's right outside. "Well, make it over!"

Holding my head, she tilts my face to look at her, and I catch a hint of tears in her eyes. I can't imagine how hard it must be for her to see me like this, to watch me answer questions to Grant, someone who I loved so much. *Someone who I love so much.*

"Okay. We will go back out there, and I'll see what I can do."

I stand nervously at the glass door while Mom whispers to Mr. Ellison, who then announces that we will resume questioning tomorrow. I'm relieved, only slightly, because I see the way Pat rolls his eyes. Does he think this is a game? Does he think I'm acting? As soon as everyone leaves the conference room, namely the McCalls, and Mom and I walk over to our seats to get our bags, Grant throws himself at me, grabbing my elbow when I try inching away.

"Can I please talk to you?" he murmurs roughly so only I can hear. Goose bumps spread across the space he's touching.

I shake my head no, swallow thickly, hating and loving his skin on mine. "Ava, please."

When Mom sees that he's touching me, she loses it. "Leave her alone," she snaps. "Don't touch my daughter."

"Mom," I whisper loudly. "Stop. It's okay."

I hate that I do, but I give him what he wants and I stay behind. The farther I am from him, the easier this will be, which is why I'm thankful that this conference room is so huge. He waits in the corner, and we stand opposite each other in pure silence. I break my gaze when his stare becomes too much. Grant's eyes are the kind that are truly windows to his soul, and right now I can't witness how he's just as broken as I am. The difference is that he needs to act strong to carry this lawyer façade further. While I have the freedom to feel what I need to feel, Grant has to pretend that he is totally fine, and that stings a bit. I feel sorry for him.

"Why am I here?" I whisper, a hint of fear in my voice. Being alone with him is so terrifying. Two days ago, I would've had the most ginormous smile on my face, standing in a room with Grant. I would've run up to him and let him lift me, hug me, kiss me. Now? Now there's nothing. Now there's fear.

"You know what this all means, right?" he questions, his voice quiet and rough so no one outside this room can over-hear what he's about to say. "That we can be together when this is all over."

I want to slap him at the audacity to even inquire about such a thing. I breathe air through my nose in lieu of a chuckle because I really don't feel like laughing. *Is he for real? Why, because it's legal now?* Did he forget what he did? The legality of the situation isn't my concern. The *lying* is. The *dishonesty* is. His shoulders are hunched, palms flat on the table. The intensity of his gaze ruins me when he looks up, and I just want to get out of here.

"I don't want you to leave me because of this," Grant states plainly, his voice hoarse and strained.

"What do you mean? I already left you."

"Then I want a second chance," he rasps, pain flashing across his face at my passive reply.

"No," I retort adamantly, teeth clenched from anger.

He sucks his teeth and turns away from me. Grant stares out the window for a moment before facing me again. "Will you at least let me tell you everything? You owe me that, Ava." Grant's face fills me with fury when I look at him, but his child-like, pleading expression burns in my chest. God, I loved him like crazy. I still do.

"Do you think I care to hear what you have to say? I don't owe you a single thing." I actually laugh this time, truly dumbfounded at the nerve on this guy. I can't look at Grant any longer, so I glance lower at the table he's crouched over when I notice his giant hands, specifically the torn-up knuckles on his right one. How didn't I notice that earlier?

When he sees that I've noticed the fresh red scabs, he slides both hands into his gray suit pants pockets and straightens out. Part of me wants to ask what happened. Part of me wants to get out a tub of Neosporin and make it all better, but the other ninety percent doesn't give a shit. He did this to us.

"I don't even want to know," I mumble before rapidly walking out of the room. I'm waiting at the elevator when I hear his heavy breathing indicating that he's been power walking after me, right on my heel.

"Ava," he pants. He stands too close, the reception area feeling claustrophobic. "Wait."

"Please go away," I beg, my voice shaky and terrified.

He shakes his head, gulps heavily. "I can't. You know I can't." Grant places a warm palm on my shoulder, and I don't care that there are eyes on us right now, particularly Dina's, because today, I'm a mess, and if these people know the full truth of what transpired between this man and me within the last six months, they'd cut me some slack at my emotional outburst. Plus, it's not like I'm ever going to see them again. Or him after tomorrow, for that matter.

"I'm not yours anymore!" I shout, furiously shrugging his cupped hand from my body. "Don't touch me! Leave me alone!"

"Grant!" Dina snaps warningly. "Cut it out! Leave her be!"

I swipe under my eyes and avoid seeing his reaction to that explosion, stepping into the elevator that's just reached the floor, saving me. Literally saving me.

The next day I'm stronger when I sit down at the conference table, Ellison on one side of me, Dad on the other. Grant sits opposite me today too and wastes no time proceeding with the questions. This time, he has my medical files in hand. He grits his teeth as he begins to interrogate me.

"Have you been sexually active before Patrick McCall?"

What a start. If I'm going to be subjected to this ridiculous deposition, asked questions drafted by my ex-boyfriend, I'm going to do things my way. I feel cruel. I look up and stare into Grant's eyes.

"No. I lost my virginity to him."

He breathes heavily, his chest heaving slightly higher than it was before. It's awful of me but I find joy in the fact that he can't make it obvious that I'm hurting him and tries his best to appear indifferent. When he fires his next question, I notice the slight change in his voice, the way he's dying to punch something, punch Pat even.

"Were you aware that you were ovulating at the time of sexual intercourse with Patrick McCall?" Grant curls his lip, asks his question to the paper in his hands, then grimaces when he looks up at me.

"No. I was not aware that if I had sex with Patrick McCall on that particular day then I was going to get pregnant." I glance at Grant, his jaw tightening, teeth clenching, scabbed hands fisting. I'm breaking him a little bit with my specificity, and his eyes bore into mine *begging* me to stop, yearning for me to end this, but I don't want to. What does that say about me?

"Have you had a history of mental illness prior to meeting Patrick McCall?"

"No."

"Have you . . ." He has to pause for this one, clears his throat before continuing. "Excuse me. Have you experienced suicidal thoughts before the events that occurred at Saint Francis Memorial Hospital in San Francisco in August of 2015?"

"No," I state curtly.

"When did you start feeling suicidal?" he asks, his eyes looking up at me and apologizing over and over with just one look. Grant knows what this is doing to me. He's so sorry that I'm at the brunt end of this deposition, being asked questions about events that happened in my life that he knows I have a difficult time talking about. The apology in his eyes is quite frankly working. I can feel how sorry he is.

I take a deep breath before replying. "I started feeling suicidal when I succumbed to the peer pressure from Patrick and his friends to abort my pregnancy, which left me with an enormous amount of guilt and health complications."

Mr. Ellison asks for Grant to read a series of text messages that I received from Pat's friends on record.

"For the anonymity of the senders of these text messages, we are going to keep their names off the record. I will proceed with reading some messages that were sent to Ava Ruth Campbell's cell phone in August of 2015. These messages were acquired from Miss Campbell's cell phone." Grant clears his throat, his breath hitching when he has to look up and speak directly to me while reading the messages from my tormenters.

"This one says, 'abort the baby, whore.' Another one reads 'Pat isn't going to give you a dime so you better grab a hanger, you knocked-up slut.' 'If you don't abort it yourself, I'm going to come over there and punch—'

"Is this really necessary?" Grant abruptly stops to scold Mr. Ellison, smashing the table with his fist.

"Keep reading, Counsel," Ellison replies with a nod, assured that he knows what he's doing. It only helps our case to prove how pressured and threatened I was. That I may have never gone through what I did if those texts never came. I have a good feeling about this even if objectively it looks horrifying.

"'If you don't abort it yourself, I'm going to come over there and punch your stomach hard enough so you bleed it out.'" Grant turns green as soon as the words exit his mouth, and there's a barking sound that fills the room when he sprints from his chair and it smacks the wall behind him. I'm startled immediately, and my lungs turn into balls of fire, settling in my chest, confused and hurt and in love. If this isn't over soon, I'm afraid waterworks will storm out of me on record, on camera.

There are quiet murmurs amongst each team before Grant walks in a few minutes later, wiping his mouth with a white handkerchief and sitting back across from me.

"My apologies. Where were we?"

Mr. Ellison discusses any and all legal matters that I have no business commenting on after the last few questions are asked. Grant reads the list of medications I'm on, on camera in front of both teams, and I know I will never, ever forgive him for doing this to me. Until the day I die.

"We'll take the findings of this deposition to the judge and see you all at the court proceedings. Thank you."

GRANT

She was doing it on purpose to torment me. I have no doubt whatsoever that Ava was trying to be cruel, but as shitty as it made me feel, I understood it. I, the guy who was supposed to take care of and love her for the last six months, sat opposite Ava and asked her recorded questions about things that she had to mentally prepare herself to tell *me*, her boyfriend at the time. *At the time.*

That's the last time I'm going to see her. I watched as she lifted herself from the leather chair across from me, grabbed her phone and coat, and zipped before I could call out to her like I did yesterday.

She told me that she loves me three days ago. The last time I touched her, properly touched her, was Tuesday morning before she left my apartment. Ava woke up with the biggest smile on her face and immediately, before anything, said, "I love you."

It made me laugh at how excited she was to blurt it out so freely at the first moment she could. And then she said it about a hundred times while she was showering and getting ready for class, making herself a cup of tea to go, and packing up her computer and textbook that were still on the table from the night before.

"I looooooove youuuuuu," she sang, walking toward me, bundled up in a coat, gloves, and a gray beanie. On her back she wore her bag, and in her right hand she held the Styrofoam cup filled with jasmine tea, which I made sure to stock up on since it's her favorite.

"I love you more, baby. You are just . . . Mmm. What're you doing to me, miss?" I asked, holding her face, kissing her.

"Loving you." She winked. "Last night was perfect. I love you. See you later?" And she was right. The bliss we both felt that night was unprecedented. It was the first time we made love after both of us finally confessed to the big I.L.Y.

Ava meant every word. You can't fake a love like that, nor could I have faked the love I gave her the last six months like she might claim. I wish I could make her understand that it was all real. That I still feel every bit of that scorching love for Ava today like I did last week.

"Annie told me to call you, that you're going through some stuff. Is everything okay?" Mom calls to ask tonight.

"Yeah, Mom. Thanks for calling. Ava and I . . . well, Ava ended things with me."

She gasps. "Oh no, honey! Why? You were so good together!" she exclaims as eloquent as Mom is.

I figure I'll get it out of the way, so Saturday morning, the day after the final deposition, I make the hour-long drive to Scarsdale to sit my parents down and explain everything to them, front to back. I don't want Annie's big mouth to tell them what transpired between Ava and me. As much as I love my amazing older sister, she is quite the blabbermouth.

I lead my parents toward the living room, having to close the door in the back of my brain shut from all the memories I have with Ava in this room alone, and ask them to have a seat. I bend to sit in the armchair across from the sofa they're occupying and tell them the story of Ava and me with tears in my eyes, even though I'm a grown-ass adult. Dad interjects when I'm getting to the last part of the deposition.

"Holy mother of God, Grant. What in the hell were you thinking?" he barks, jumping from his seated position beside my mother.

My chest tightens at the sharp anger in his tone. "Dad, I—"

"Do not say one word, son. This is inexcusable! Not only did you break that poor girl's heart, but you could have gotten your license revoked!" he shouts, spit flying. "Your reputation is ruined if McCall finds out or tells anyone. You better find a way to win this case! Do you know how bad it'll look if you lose and they find out that Ava is your former girlfriend?"

Dad is right. Pat is one of those guys who enjoys drama. I'm sure he noticed some animosity between Ava and me yesterday, but as far as I'm concerned, he doesn't know about our history. But Pat has quite the temper, and if I lose this case against the Campbells, it'll only lead to something worse. I have never lost a case since I passed my bar exam, and I don't plan to make this the first one because I have to listen to my father and my gut, but I have a plan. I already know what I'm going to do when the judge declares McCall the winner of this case.

Because they will. The part of the story that Ellison is excusing is a key point to all of this: the *text messages* were what led to Ava's decision, not Pat himself. They don't have any proof that Pat pressured her because as Ava claims, it was via phone call and *through his friends*. But Ava isn't suing Pat's friends, she's suing Pat, and legally he isn't responsible. But like I said, I already have a plan.

The guilt in my chest is enormous not only because of the obvious situation, but seeing my parents' reaction to what I've done to Ava strikes a chord. It is unbearable to watch them with so much disappointment in their expressions. I know they raised me better than this. I pour out the heartache on the drive back home from their house, realizing that Ava will never sit beside me in this car again. Ava will never twirl in my office chair again or shower in my bathroom, and that's what does it. All the things that I'll never see Ava do anymore; that's what allows the release of the emotions from the last five days.

I lie in my bed and replay the night that Ava looked through those file cabinets and found concrete proof of her devastation and heartbreak. I wanted to tell her how much I truly love her; how bad I still want to be with her despite all of this, but I didn't have the guts in that moment as she held the documents in her shaking hands. The only thing I need is for Ava to know that it was real. She had me. She owns me. Ava is the love of my life, the only girl I've ever loved, and she hates my guts. I have one last thing left to do. Without knowing if she's going to respond, get mad, or ignore me, I shoot her a simple text. The moment the text message shows *delivered*, it is truly over.

I will never speak to Ava Ruth Campbell again.

EPILOGUE

November

AVA

Unknown Number: It was all real.

It's been nine months and a full summer since that god-awful February morning, and the number of times I have looked at that text message is mortifying. Even after everything he did to me, I still wish he would send another one, because staring at this lone message is getting old. Come to think of it, maybe he did, but I wouldn't know. I didn't change my number when things ended, but I did block his.

I can't say or think his name anymore because of the tightness in my chest I feel when I do, so I only refer to him as "he" or "him." It helps keep my mind sterile.

The memories don't stop no matter how much time has passed, and for some diabolical reason, my brain is sharper than it has ever been, remembering so vividly as if I'm still there with him. He was everything to me. He was truly my best friend. Not only because I told him absolutely everything but because of how much genuine fun we'd have, naked and clothed.

We'd be doubled over in laughter watching a movie on the couch or in his room, and it didn't feel at all romantic—it was simply a movie night—but those were the moments where I felt like he was my person. I remember one Friday night after a particularly hard school week, he made fancy cocktails, ordered Chinese takeout, and rented a movie. We were watching *Borat* together in bed, and at one point, he was laughing at my laugh because I was snorting uncontrollably at the accent. I'll probably never stomach watching that movie again. It would hurt too much.

Whenever I needed a second set of eyes when it came to my school work, I would call him over, and he would stand behind me with his hands on my shoulders while I sat at the kitchen island, squinting his eyes to glance at my computer screen and shout, "Oh! Okay, I get it. This is the formula for . . ." He was so smart. I could ask him a question about any subject, knowing that he'd have the answer to it, and I was taking four courses that semester.

I accompanied him while grocery shopping one night after school. He usually had them delivered but figured it'd be fun to go together and it was. Holy shit, it was some of the greatest fun we've ever had. He told me to get whatever I wanted so he could keep the things I like at his place for when I came over. Whole Foods doesn't sell Kraft mac and cheese. I stared down the junk food aisle, turned to look at him, and gave a wrinkled expression. He howled, had to throw a palm over his mouth because of his reaction to my reaction to the organic *everything*.

I remember needing water bottles, and it felt comforting when he lifted them up the stairwell to my apartment for me. When I saw the veins in his arms popping and heard the sounds of his grunting as he ascended three flights of stairs holding two cases of water bottles, I pulled him straight into my bed when they hit the floor.

When I had a free weekend, he'd take me to brunch on Sundays and, without fail, always ordered himself a plate of waffles no matter what restaurant we were seated at.

"I like to indulge on Sundays 'cause I'm an asshole about what I eat throughout the week," he said, laughing when I noticed that he ordered the same thing for the third week in a row. And he was a total asshole when it came to his diet. I would roll my eyes at him every time he would have some weird sprout in his fridge or pour hemp seeds in his smoothie. But he always made sure to have all the (non-organic) junk for me. While he ate egg whites and vegetables for breakfast, I'd pound Lucky Charms or Eggos right beside him. We could not have been more different.

Safe to say that statement is true. I remember one time right around Christmas, we went shopping and he needed a new coat. Well, he didn't *need* it, but he wanted to get a navy one since the one he got *for this year* was black. I shrugged, hopped in his car, and we made our way to Neiman Marcus. *The employees knew him.* I didn't know it was a thing to have a relationship with a salesperson at your most frequented department store, but hey, I didn't judge. Well, I may have judged a little when I saw that the $2,800 price tag didn't faze him one bit. I remember aimlessly sorting through the men's clothing section when they rang him up. I couldn't stomach seeing that much money on a receipt.

However, at the same time, he was incredibly generous. More generous than I've ever seen a person be. Every time we'd pass a homeless person on the street, he'd slip a $100 bill into their emptied plastic 7-Eleven cup. He told me that was the only reason he kept cash on him. When my jaw dropped and I asked, "Did you just give him a hundred dollars?" he shrugged like it was nothing. Like he did it all the time, and he did. He was the best tipper too. I've heard that you can tell the character of a person by the way they treat restaurant staff. It was a no-brainer for him to tip a hundred bucks on a $50 meal. When we went somewhere fancy, boom—$500 tip. It didn't matter if the service was excellent or poor. That wasn't it. He simply wanted to give to the less fortunate because he knew how fortunate *he* was.

"Hey," Chloe whisper-shouts across the table. We're sitting at the library studying for our last midterms before Thanksgiving break because we're ball and chained to each other. We have gotten incredibly close within the last nine months. Luckily, as the RA, she was able to pull some strings at the dorm and get me a room with a sweet foreign exchange student for the last few months of junior year. I had to take out a loan to cover housing, but it was worth it. I couldn't fathom the idea of living in that apartment again. But as junior year was coming to a close, Chloe and I became the best of friends, and now we live together in the dorms for our last year at NYU. It's been amazing.

"What're you thinking so intently about?" she asks.

I blankly glance at her. "I don't know, Chloe, what do *you* think I'm thinking about?" It's ongoing. It's a glue on my brain, a bruise that never healed. I still think about him and I can't stop.

"Babe." She speaks softly. "You gotta stop."

"I know but I can't!" I say with frustration. He won't leave my head. Why am I mad *at him* about that?

"SHHHHHHHHHHH!" a student from the table beside ours whispers.

Our eyes both widen, and we snicker in the palms of our hands. Chloe points to her phone and mouths, "Text me."

Chloe: What's up bitch.

I laugh and that same student gives me the eyes. "Sorry," I whisper.

Me: Just sitting across from this other bitch, you?

Chloe: Ha. You're hilarious. Now talk.

I take a deep breath, shake my head.

Me: Derek asked me out yesterday but I said no.

I joined Chloe's crowd of friends when things ended with him, which is how I met Derek. We hang out a lot as a group, and he pulled me aside after one of our shared classes last night to ask if I would let him take me out to grab a bite. For now, with the excuse of homework, I politely declined.

Chloe looks at me wide-eyed from across the table and mouths, "Why would you do that? He's so hot!"

I look at her plainly and mouth back, "You know why."

Chloe lifts up her phone, then texts me.

Chloe: It's been nine months babe

Me: I know

Chloe: What do you want? If it's not someone new then . . .

Me: Closure? Idk

Chloe: Let's talk outside

We collect our things from the long wooden table and skitter toward the library exit. While walking, Chloe turns to me and says, "What do you mean by closure?"

This is a tough one. Maybe I feel like we left things open-ended? I left his house and then I left the deposition and not once did I let him explain a thing to me, even when he asked to over and over. I was adamant about that.

"When I found out, I refused to let him explain, and I still stand by that refusal, but I've been so curious about what he had to say for the last nine months."

Chloe sighs and puts her arm around me. "You've been apart longer than you've been together at this point. Something's gotta give. I wouldn't encourage you to confront him, but if that's what you need—"

"I couldn't. Chloe, you only knew me after we broke up. I was completely at his mercy when we were together. I'm afraid that if I hear his voice, I'll want him back," I respond, my chest falling. "I know I will."

The longevity of my thoughts about him and what happened make me angry. But I beg myself for some sort of closure all the time. I have nothing left of him and maybe I want the opportunity to remember how bad he hurt me instead of how incredible those six months were. It's the good memories that stuck with me instead of the betrayal. That's not supposed to happen. Doesn't the bad outweigh the good when the bad is monstrous?

We ascend the dorm's stairwell toward our room and plop on my bed, laying our heads back in unison. Chloe has been the best part of my post-breakup sadness because she's the happiest, most uplifting friend I could ask for. And the advice she gives is always helpful.

"Let's think of other ways you can get closure without seeing or talking to him. What about looking at some old photos?" I shake my head, telling her that I sent them all to an old email that I never check, unwilling to delete them completely but also refusing to redownload any of them. And I don't. That, I can say with confidence. "Okay . . . what about reading some sweet texts from back then?"

"Deleted."

She groans and I laugh, squeezing her hand tightly. I'm not making this easy. "I don't know, Ava. What about Googling him? Maybe there's a picture of him in some random article or something?" she suggests, shrugging.

I look at her strangely, my brows pinched. "How would looking at a picture of my ex help me get over him?"

Chloe jumps up from the bed and faces me pointedly. "Okay. Hear me out. I think that the only way you'll feel better is if you forgive him. Not that you have to speak or let him know but for your own good. The anger is what's hurting you. If you choose forgiveness, it's easier to move on. I'm not saying that you'll forget what you guys had or what he did to you, because he was a huge part of your life, but he'll stay in the past once you tell yourself that you don't hate him anymore. You carrying this weight in your chest is keeping the relationship alive. Maybe if you search him up, look at a picture of him and tell yourself, 'He hurt me but I am forgiving him for *me*,' then you might feel a sense of relief."

How does Chloe always give the best advice? I relate to what she's telling me. The anger is what's fueling this desperate need for closure; if I'm being honest, it's not like I want to have a civil conversation with him. I just want to yell and beg him to tell me *why*. Just *why*.

"I love you; you know that?" I reply.

Chloe's advice is exactly what I need to hear. I pull out my phone and take a deep breath. She gives me a tight hug before sitting across from me, on her own bed. Typing in his name in the search bar makes me emotional, my fingers shaking as they type the G and the R and the A. But I'm not at all prepared for what I see. The first article at the top of the Google search butchers my heart. I gasp and abruptly stand from my bed.

"Chloe," I breathe.

"What? What happened?"

With lurid disbelief, I look up from my phone, my chest falling.

"He's engaged."

ACKNOWLEDGMENTS

First, I'd like to thank my readers for supporting the release of my debut novel. There is nothing I love doing more than writing and I feel beyond thankful that you've made it to this page. I'm excited for you guys to read the sequel.

To Dane, Adrian, Reba, John and the entire Ebook Launch team—thank you!! You have all made this self-publishing process seamless and organized. I couldn't have done it without every single one of you.

Rivky, it was a no brainer that you'd be the first person to ever read my book. You're my favorite. Love you forever.

To my three incredible sisters: I dedicated this book to you for a reason. You are all my best friends in the whole world. I love love love you, sista sistas.

Ema and Abba, thank you for teaching us the morals and values of what it means to be a good person. You have always guided us in the righteous direction and I wouldn't be who I am today if it wasn't for your unwavering devotion.

To my husband—thank you for pushing me to achieve my dreams, even if that sometimes meant I was spending more time with Grant and Ava than with you. I love you.

Lastly, to my son. Everything I do, I do for you. Mama loves you more than anything, ever.

Don't miss the continuation of Grant and Ava's story in the sequel: THE PATH OF A LOGICAL LOVER.

AVA

He's here. I know it. As ridiculous as it sounds, I can feel him in the room. I don't spot him until he claps along with my brothers, who are hollering and hooting as my name gets called and I walk across the stage at Radio City Music Hall for my graduation ceremony. My family is sitting on the right side of the room, and when they announce my name, I can hear a slightly louder clap on the left. My eyes glance to the side, my head turns a little, and I gasp when his green eyes look into mine. It's for only a split second, but it's there. The bomb-blasting, earthquake, vibrating, ground-shattering, emotional burst inside my chest and it's like whiplash that I have to turn away immediately, stumbling slightly when I walk off the stage and toward a seat in the audience.

What is he doing here? It's been . . . I haven't seen him in fifteen months. He looks different. But his eyes . . . Damn it. How did he even get an inv—

Holy shit. College sponsors get invites. He was invited because of *me*. I somehow spot Chloe in the sea of people and give her that wide-eyed, *oh my lord* look.

"What?" she mouths.

"He's here!" I mouth back.

"Who?" My expression says it all. Her jaw drops. "What the fuck?"

"I know!"

—⟋m⟍—

My parents, Cooper, and Connor came into New York for the graduation because it just so happens to be my birthday tomorrow. Devon lives here now, and I'm thankful that he and his girlfriend Sarah made it over here tonight from Brooklyn. When the ceremony is over, I dart toward my family first thing, hoping to mask them all from seeing him. We form a huddle and they hug me tight, kissing my head and saying how proud they are of me. I hand Mom my graduation cap and pull Devon aside. I don't want my parents to know.

"He's here, Devon."

My brother looks confused. "Who is?"

"You know who. He's here. I saw him when I walked."

Devon's eyes dart around the room, and he mutters a low "Motherfucker."

"Don't tell Mom," I beg. "She's gonna get all Spanish and embarrass everybody."

"Too late, Indiana," Devon says, nodding toward my parents, my brothers, and *him*.

I study their exchange, tighten my grasp on Devon's forearm, watching as he shakes Dad's hand, gives my mother a hug. *Get off them*, I want to say. *Don't touch my family.*

My heart is beating so fast, hands and feet perspiring madly at the shakiness I feel when seeing him after over a year of not. I hold my breath when he turns to glance at me, says goodbye to my parents, and proceeds to walk over here.

"I'm outta here," Devon mumbles. I watch as my brother politely nods his head toward this giant man on his way back to the rest of our family. I don't eye his path toward me because I'm so afraid to look at him. It's enough that a simple glance can knock me off kilter, but if I look into his eyes, I might pass out. He stops two feet in front of me and lifts his left hand up from out of his pocket to wave. I immediately fixate my eyes on his ring finger, his bare ring finger, and all I can do is stare at it. When he begins to notice what I'm looking at and why, he slips his left hand back into his pants pocket.

"Hi," he says gruffly.

"Why did you come?" I ask in a near whisper.

"I wanted to congratulate you."

Wow. You're a real Prince Charming, aren't you?

"You shouldn't be here."

"I know. I'll go."

I scoff. "Yeah, you do that."

He rocks back on his heels and stands up straighter, buttoning the top button of his suit jacket. "Happy birthday, Ava," he says before nodding and walking away.

My breath hitches. I'm a complete jumbled mess as I watch his tall body elegantly pass through the crowd and out onto the city streets. *Happy birthday, Ava.*

He came to my graduation. After everything he did to me, how he lied to me, he just showed up. How dare he.

"What did he want?" I ask my mother once I've reached their huddled group.

"He wanted to apologize. Said he never had a chance to."

I laugh bitterly. "What an ass," I mutter.

Dad puts a hand on my shoulder. "That mustn't have been easy, sweetheart. I'm sorry about that." I hug Dad tightly and relax my shoulders, not having realized how tense they've been the last thirty minutes. If I wasn't shaking so bad, I would have slapped him.

—⟐—

After a nice dinner with my family, I meet a few of my classmates and friends, namely Chloe, Derek, and the crew, to trash ourselves out at a nightclub in Chelsea. We have to celebrate our bachelor's degrees, bitches. About an hour into this wild clubbing, I realize how fucked up I am when I sit on the wobbly toilet to pee, leaning my head against the bathroom stall to balance myself. Maybe it isn't the toilet seat that's wobbly. *Why the hell did I drink so much?* I ask myself. But I know exactly why I drank so much. *How can he just show up?!* I feel enraged.

Strutting through the crowd toward the group, I stand flush against Derek and smile up at him. He's good. He's sweet and smart and relatable. I should take Chloe's advice and give him a chance. Derek grew up like me: normal. Derek didn't live on an estate his entire life. Derek isn't eight years my senior. Derek isn't Pat's lawyer.

"What's up!" Chloe yells over the loud music, slithering her way toward us. "Where'd you go?"

"To pee!" I shout.

"Come dance with me!"

Within minutes, I'm laughing and jumping and throwing my hands in the air because I graduated today and it's my fucking birthday soon. I check the clock on my phone.

"Guys, it's my birthday in exactly seventeen minutes!" I shout to the group.

"Hell yeah, it is!" Chloe informs us that she'll be right back, so Derek takes it as an opportunity to squeeze his way through the mob of our friends to be near me. He bends to speak in my ear. "Can I dance with you?" he asks.

I grin and laugh, kissing Derek's cheek. "What kind of question is that? Of course you can." I grab his hand because the adrenaline surges rapidly through me, and I pay no mind to the way I'm dancing because that's the best kind of dancing.

"Hey, hey, hey!" the DJ shouts into the mic, interrupting his well-played soundtrack, pointing to me in the crowd. "Shoutout to my girl Ava because it's her birthday! Boys and girls, you know what that means!" 50 Cent. That's what it means. Chloe is hyper and wild, singing at the top of her lungs, proud of herself that she likely coerced the DJ to play this song for me with her doe eyes and giant personality. I laugh at her when she tells Shawty that we're going to party like it's her birthday.

"You're crazy!" I laugh.

Chloe envelops me in the tightest hug imaginable and brings her lips to my ear. "I'm so happy we found each other. You're the strongest person I know, Ava. You deserve the motherfucking world, you hear me? *The world.* You're my favorite bitch. I love you so much."

I grab her face and kiss her sweaty cheek. "I love you more! You're my favorite bitch too!"

We keep dancing—why would we want to stop? And at one point, Derek slips his hand into mine, and it makes me smile. I squeeze his hand, and when he looks down at me, his eyes take on a serious note.

"I want to kiss you," he mouths, pointing to his lips. *Oh, what the hell!* I nod quickly, so he does it. He slips an arm around my waist, the other cupping my cheek, and leans in to kiss me deeply but I freeze. I freeze in place as if I've never done this before. As if the action of kissing is so foreign to me that I'm completely dumbfounded. I feel blindsided from the influx of feelings that overcome me when Derek puts his mouth to mine, and I quickly rip myself from his grasp, shaking my head.

"I'm so sorry!" I shout. "I can't kiss you, Derek! I'm so sorry!" I squeeze between the dancing clubgoers until I'm outside, heaving, my head bent and my hands gripping my knees. Chloe's right behind me; Chloe is always unconditionally there.

"You good?" I don't reply. "What happened? I saw Derek kissing you."

"That's what happened," I breathe.

"I don't understand."

"Me neither, Chloe. I don't understand. I gotta go."

She takes my hand, tugs a little, and makes me face her dead in the eye. "Promise me you won't go there." She knows what I'm thinking, what I'm always thinking. I shake my head. *Of course I won't.* "Promise me, Ava."

"I promise."

—⚋—

"Does he still live here?" I ask Bobby the doorman. He replies with a curt nod and motions for me to enter the building.

I drunkenly slipped into the back of my cab by the club, ready to recite the address to my dorm, but instead rattled off his address from memory. I hadn't said that street name in over a year, but it somehow, regardless of my drunken state, came easily to me like it was my own apartment.

I step onto the elevator still piss drunk, leaning my head against the glass walls and inserting the code into the keypad like it's second nature. It doesn't strike me as odd that it comes so easily to me until about ten seconds later. I reach his floor within a matter of seconds, and the familiarity of it—the wood and the paint color and his door—fills me with unexplainable fury. I ball my hand into a fist and bang loudly. No polite knocking. He barged into my life, my graduation, so this is my right. The face he gives me when the door opens is one of pure shock.

Made in United States
Orlando, FL
11 January 2022

13284697R00193